SMALL FAVORS

Small Favors

short stories
by
James Russell Mayes

Boston ◆ Alyson Publications, Inc.

Typeset and printed in the United States of America.

Published by Alyson Publications, Inc.,
40 Plympton St., Boston, Massachusetts 02118.
Distributed in England by GMP Publishers,
P.O. Box 247, London N6 4BW, England.

First edition: September 1994

5 4 3 2 1

ISBN 1-55583-258-X

The following stories have appeared in slightly different form in these publications:
• "Peggy Hagerman's Bikini," *Christopher Street*, Vol. 14, No. 19 (May 1992);
• "The Beer Tent," in *The PrePress Awards 1992–1993: A Sampler of Emerging Michigan Writers* (Kalamazoo: PrePress Publishing of Michigan, 1993);
• "The Hired Boy," in *PRISM International*, Vol. 28, No. 3 (Spring 1990);
• "Little Andy," in *Renegade* 9 (July 1994);
• "South Window," in *Short Story Magazine*, NS Vol.2, No. 2 (Fall 1994); and
• "Mayonnaise Sandwiches" (as "A White Meal"), *Passages North*, Vol. 14, No. 1 (Summer 1993).

Library of Congress Cataloging-in-Publication Data

Mayes, James Russell, 1959–
    Small favors : short stories / by James Russell Mayes. — 1st ed.
      p.   cm.
    ISBN 1-55583-258-X (cloth) : $19.95
    I. Title.
    PS3563.A9562S63   1994
    813'.54—dc20   94-19573
                                         CIP

Contents

Acknowledgments

Some of the stories in this collection have appeared elsewhere, sometimes under different titles and in different form: "Peggy Hagerman's Bikini," in *Christopher Street;* "The Beer Tent," in *The PrePress Awards 1992–1993: A Sampler of Emerging Michigan Writers;* "The Hired Boy," in *PRISM International;* "Little Andy," in *Renegade;* "South Window," in *Short Story;* and "Mayonnaise Sandwiches," in *Passages North.*

I would like to acknowledge the Tompkins Prize Committee and the Patricia Eldredge-Loughead Scholarship, both of Wayne State University, a fine and venerable school that gave me a great education; and the University of Michigan Summer Graduate Fellowship program; for their much-appreciated financial assistance and moral support.

Most grateful thanks to Sasha Alyson and editor Dick Lipez. And to special friends: Joseph David Hutting, Denise Brennan, Mary "Irv" Irvine, Lisa Zmich, Debbie Najor, Don Socha, Carol Munn, Bill Kueser, Jim Morrison, Joe Cullen, and my high school English teacher Robert Passi. Hi, guys!

How could I forget my own dear, sweet Edward? Thanks for the backbone. XXOOO.

To CHARLIE BAXTER: Teacher, writer, and friend

A thousand pieces of gold may hardly bring a moment's happiness,
but a small favor can cause a lifetime's gratitude...

—HUANCHU DAOREN

Oblivion

At three o'clock in the morning, Omar Nayland lay on top of his bed, and he fingered through the photographs that he had saved of his dead wife. In one of them, Eleanor marched for peace. All around her, the women in the crowd had raised their fists. They were chanting, Omar recalled. In the face of Eleanor, framed by the bare arms of the women around her, he was sure he saw an immense fatigue. He counted backward from the day of Eleanor's death to the date on the back of the picture. She had attended the rally only weeks before she had died.

Omar held the picture inches from his nose. He had forgotten this particular photograph. It was not a good one, he decided. Who had taken it? And why was Eleanor so exhausted? Months after her death, he was still obsessed with the details of her life. The moonlight of another morning split the curtains in his window. Omar tore the picture in half.

His mother appeared in the doorway. A light from the hall illuminated her body underneath her burnoose. Omar said, "Mother. What's wrong?"

"Om," she said, "there's a man downstairs. He came right into the house. He's walking around down there." Mrs. Nayland walked to the edge of Omar's bed. She touched him on the back of his wrist. She said with alarm, "He saw me in my pajamas."

Omar lay the pictures aside and rolled off his bed. He walked to the head of the stairs. At the foot, murky with shadows, an old man, white-bearded, began to climb the steps.

Omar said, "Can I help you?"

The man raised his head. He squinted into the light. "Where's the bar?" he said.

"There's no bar here." The man had to stretch his arm to pull himself upward. Omar stepped down.

"What kind of place is this with no bar?" He rested his leg on a step above himself. He leaned into the bannister. "Where is everybody?"

"You can't come up here." Omar turned. He waved his mother back to her room. Mrs. Nayland stopped in her doorway. She adjusted her turban, listening.

The man raised his voice. "I damn well can too come up there," he said. "I paid for my room. I intend to sleep in it."

"This isn't a hotel."

"Hell if it isn't." The man drew himself up, as if in challenge. He smiled at Omar. Or grimaced. "Where's the dancing girl?"

Omar leaned forward. "I'm telling you, you better not come up," he said. The man looked down at the carpet on the steps. Above him the light from the hall shone down on the white of his head.

Mrs. Nayland said, "He's out of his mind. Should I call the police?"

"Not yet." Omar looked at his mother. Her leg extended forward so that her big toe touched the floor. "Stand back," he warned. She disappeared behind him.

Omar brought his foot down. He entered the general gloom of the stairway. The man looked around himself. Omar said, "There's no room up here. We're all out of rooms."

The man took his hand from the bannister and stretched it out toward Omar. He smelled of gasoline. "The man at the desk said Room 3-B. He gave me the key." He held up a single key on a ring. A tag on the ring said, "Dodge."

"There must be a mistake," Omar said. The old man's mouth gaped. The two men stood on the stairs, gawking at one another.

Omar got an idea. "Do you have identification?" The man moved his hand back. Apparently he was reaching for his wallet. "I can help you. But I need a driver's license."

The man's body jerked. He reached for the bannister, but he slipped and fell forward. Omar squatted. He caught the man by his arms. He barely kept him from striking his head against one of the steps. The old fellow squeezed Omar's shoulders with his hands. For a moment, the men embraced on the steps.

"Let's get off the stairs," Omar breathed. He helped the man up. The old fellow felt incredibly light for his size.

He cleared his throat. "You're an angel," he said to Omar. He moved his hand down the bottom of his face, over his beard. "I suppose you want to wrestle?"

"Not in my pajamas," Omar said. He tried to emphasize the irony. "Let's go, before you fall again." The visitor had to hold onto the rail to turn himself around. Omar stood behind him. He held the man's elbow, and he helped him down the stairs.

"Where are you taking me?"

"Um, the front desk. I'll need to see your driver's license."

They reached the landing at the foot of the stairs. The man turned away from the open front door, apparently his entrance. Omar closed it. He directed the man back under the stairs to the kitchen. "Not much of a front desk," the man said.

Omar could see him more clearly in the brighter light of the kitchen. The man appeared about sixty years old. He reeked of gasoline, but he looked completely dry. He fumbled through his jacket. Omar suggested, "Try your back pocket."

"What am I looking for?"

"Your driver's license?"

The man reached into his back pocket and pulled out a wallet. He handed the whole thing over to Omar, and Omar opened it up. There was a driver's license. "Fred Charter," the license said. Mr. Charter looked less intimidating in a photograph. Evidently he was a few miles from home. The address on his driver's license was the Old Roman Road.

Omar pulled a chair out from under the table. "I need to make a call. Wait here."

"You'll see what you can do?" Mr. Charter frowned and sat down in the chair.

Omar walked upstairs and pulled on a pair of pants. He used the telephone in the foyer to call directory assistance. The operator gave him a number, and he dialed it. After several rings, a woman answered.

Omar guessed that she must have been asleep. "Hello," Omar said. "Is this the right number for Fred Charter?"

The woman said, "Yes it is. Do you know what time it is?"

"Yes, I'm sorry. I'm calling about Fred Charter."

"Just a minute." The woman put down the phone. Momentarily, at a distance, "Fred," the woman called. "It's for you."

Omar waited. He peered around the door into the kitchen. Mr. Charter had slumped in the chair. He rested both hands on the table. All the way from the foyer, Omar could smell the gasoline on him. The woman finally came back to the phone. "He's not here," she told him. She did not sound worried.

"That's what I'm calling about. He's over here, at my house."

"Who is this?"

"Omar Nayland."

"Oh, dear," Mrs. Charter said. "I don't know any Naylands."

"He seems a bit confused. Can you come into town and pick him up?"

"Pick him up?" Mrs. Charter sounded surprised.

"Well, I don't think he's in any condition to drive himself."

"Is he okay?"

"Well, he's mixed up. He thinks we're running a hotel here."

"My husband's getting along in years," Mrs. Charter said. "I'm sure he didn't drive. I would've heard the truck."

"That's quite a ways to walk."

"Could you bring him home?" The tone of her voice softened. "I really shouldn't be driving at night." She hesitated. "I'm a very old woman."

It was three-twenty. Omar hadn't had his coffee yet. Mr. Charter gave him a frightened smile from the kitchen. He was holding on tightly to the table. "I'll give him a ride, Mrs. Charter. You out on Old Roman Road?"

Omar wrote Mr. Charter's address on a slip of paper. When he returned the wallet to the man, he inhaled deeply. Evidently Mr. Charter had not been drinking, unless he'd been drinking a bucketful of gasoline. "I'll take you out to a place that has a room," Omar told him. He helped him up and guided him back through the foyer.

A woman's voice above them asked, "What's going on?" Omar's mother held the front of her bathrobe closed with two fists. "Where are you going now?"

In spite of the fact that she was standing on the stairs, Mr. Charter seemed to reduce her to half her actual size. He grinned at her. "We're going to the bar," he said. "Would you like to come along?" He winked at Omar's mother.

For a moment Mrs. Nayland looked terrified. Omar tried not to smile. "We're taking Mr. Charter to a place that has a room."

"Are you sure that's a good idea?"

"Yes, Mother, I'm sure."

"Of course he's sure. Why wouldn't he be sure?" The old man slapped Omar on the back. He opened the door for him. The two men walked out under the pillars onto the porch. Mr. Charter turned to Omar and said, "My God, you've got a round head."

✁

The moon was large and heavy and bright. Even in town, it left shadows on the ground. Driving out into the country under a moon as bright as that, it began to look like daylight before daylight began. The moonlight on the ground was a deeper yellow than butter, almost aromatic, the same rich color as corn bread.

Omar pulled onto Copernicus, and Mr. Charter said he was hungry.

"I'll bet you are," Omar said. "Did you walk all the way?"

"I told you that." Mr. Charter looked out his window and steamed up the glass. He had told Omar nothing of the kind, but he had an interesting memory, Omar thought. They passed from the suburbs to countryside in the space of a few minutes.

Mr. Charter said, "Do you know that house?" Omar slowed up. The man was pointing at a reconverted one-room schoolhouse. There still was a bell on the roof. Broken-down farm machinery filled the yard.

"No. Do you?"

"I think I do. There's a family of retards there." He looked at Omar and widened his eyes. "Can you imagine? A whole family of retards."

"You remember their name?"

The man brought a finger up to his beard. "Fishfry. Little Foxes. Fishlittle. That's it," he said.

"Fishlittle?"

"It's Littles. I was fishin' for that. The Littles live there now."

"You remember? That's a good sign." They passed a dark house on the other side of the road. "You know the people in that house?"

"Never seen it before in my life. I do remember the Littles, though. You know the mother just died?"

The silhouette of exhausted Eleanor pressed through the gum of Omar's three-o'clock mind. He pressed on the gas. "What's it like to live in the country?" he said.

"Think of a family of retards without a mother." Mr. Charter paused for effect. "My wife arranged a dinner at the church for them. What a sight! Some of the ladies at the church raised a fuss."

"How come?"

"No one in the family was a member of the church."

"You're kidding."

"It's a small church. We're Mennonites." To support his claim, the man pulled on the corners of his beard. "Much as we like to make fun of them, the Littles are poor. Not surprising, since they're a pack of retards. I wonder what will happen to those kids."

They drove into a woods. By this time, Omar had grown used to the moonlight. "It sure looks dark," he said.

"That's because it is dark," Mr. Charter said idiotically. "I know that house." He pointed to a barn, only feet from the side of the road.

"Good. But that's not a house, it's a barn. It's abandoned."

"That's where the first-grade teacher Miss Wonder used to live."

"In a barn?"

Mr. Charter gave Omar a skeptical look. "She was fixing it up," he said. Omar lifted his eyes. He watched the barn move backward in the rearview mirror. Mr. Charter said, with venom, "She was hit by that drunken Peasley woman." The car hit a bump in the road that Omar had not seen. For a moment he felt a weightlessness, then comfort from the gravity.

He saw an opportunity. "Do you live around here, Mr. Charter? It seems to me that you're familiar with an awful lot of the people."

Mr. Charter snickered. "Only the dead ones," he muttered. He cleared his throat. "People say they still see the ghost of Miss Wonder the First-Grade Teacher."

Omar glanced at the back of the old man's head. Mr. Charter was staring out the window again. "Up and down this road. You know how it is. Dust rises up. People think they see something when nothing is there." Omar pulled onto Ptolemy Road. Mr. Charter began to whistle.

The song he whistled was somewhat familiar to Omar, but he couldn't place it. He listened, searching his memory. Mr. Charter reached a phrase that came out a bit rough. He repeated the bars, until they were smooth. Then with practice he went lightly over the notes, completing the verse. "What was that?" Omar asked.

Mr. Charter said, with alarm, "What was what?" He sat up and looked out over the hood of the car. They had reached the intersection to the Old Roman Road.

"That song. I know that song."

"Sure you do," he said. It was clear that he meant the opposite.

"No, really. They used to play it on the radio."

"You're a god-damned liar. That came from a hymnal."

Omar looked at him sideways. "Will you tell me what the name of it is?"

"I forget. How did it go?" Omar paused.

Mr. Charter said, "Well?" The old man was going to make Omar hum it for him. Omar cleared his throat. "Louder," Mr. Charter said, as if he had already started. He held his hand up to his ear. "I can't hear it." Omar began to hum.

"Can't you whistle, son?"

In fact, Omar could not whistle. He stopped the car. He turned the engine off. The old man leaned toward him, and Omar hummed a few bars. Mr. Charter shook his head. He pushed a fuzzy ear into Omar's face, and Omar hummed the song as loudly as he could hum it.

Mr. Charter listened, and eventually he nodded. Suddenly, he threw his head back and whistled harmony. The two men sat in Omar's car at the corner of Roman Road. They went through two whole verses of the song they remembered.

"You got it?" Omar said.

"I got it. That was it."

"I know that song."

"I know it, too."

"What is the name of it?"

"I can't remember exactly."

"Do you know the words to it?"

"No," Mr. Charter shrugged. "But I'm sure that's what I was whistling. One hundred percent certain."

Omar started the engine. They drove a mile up the Old Roman Road. They came to a shed with a sign beside it that said "Farm Fresh Eggs." There was an address on the mailbox: 3003 Old Roman Road. "Here we are," Omar said. He pulled up onto a driveway humped with fresh gravel. At the end of the drive was a curious yellow light. The light brightened a tiny porch, and the porch was attached to a vintage Marlette mobile home.

Omar pulled up behind a Dodge pickup and braked. Mr. Charter opened his door. Before Omar could stop the engine, the old man had jumped out onto the gravel and slammed the door behind him. Omar got out. He sunk to his ankles in gravel. "This must be the place," he said.

Mr. Charter walked ahead of him, eagerly. "I know this place," he murmured. He sounded somewhat surprised. "I know I know this place." He walked up the steps to the small porch. He pounded on the door.

A woman in a longish dress answered. She was small and elderly. On the back of her head, she wore a black prayer cap. She pointed her finger at the carpet inside the door. "You get in here," she said.

Mr. Charter looked back at Omar, who was climbing up the steps. He said, "Who is this old woman? Where's my wife?"

🌣

The small woman stepped out onto the porch. She held out her finger. "Now, now," she said. The storm door slammed behind her.

Mr. Charter was angry. "She's not my wife." Omar pulled out the slip of paper on which he had written the address. "3003 Old Roman Road," the paper said.

"Are you Mrs. Charter?"

"I'm Ruth Charter." The woman showed him her aged teeth. "Sometimes my husband forgets," she said. "Could you help me get him inside?"

Omar recognized her voice from their conversation over the telephone. Clearly, she recognized her husband. He took hold of Mr. Charter's elbow. The man pulled away. "Liar," he said. "I want to talk to Ruth. Where's Ruth?" He pushed Omar into the porch light. Omar barely kept himself from breaking the lightbulb with his forehead. Mr. Charter ran down the steps and out across the humps in the driveway.

"Fred?" his elderly wife called. "You come right back here."

Mr. Charter turned around and shook a fist. "Witch," he said. "I'll find my wife if it's the last thing." He fell down into the grass.

"Fred, I will not come looking for you. Fred, I'll call the police."

A large girl in a sweatshirt and stretch pants pushed through the door. She was not actually a girl. She wore her hair in braids, but she was well over forty and overweight. Her mentality gave off the kind of optimism that undermined her maturity. Once the storm door closed behind her, she backed up against it.

Mr. Charter picked himself up. He scampered out of sight. The woman turned to Omar. She said, changing her tone, "Thank you for bringing him home."

"Do you think he'll come back?"

"Eventually." She reconsidered. "Maybe not on his own. Why does he smell like gasoline?"

"I have no idea."

The woman in the sweatshirt and stretch pants raised her hand. "I know," she said. "I know, I know, I know."

Mrs. Charter frowned. "Karmalita?"

"I saw him with the gas can," said Karmalita. "He said he was out of gas."

"Well, that's no surprise."

"He said he was going into town to get some gas."

"Oh, dear."

Omar looked out across the moonlight on the lawn. "Shouldn't we go find him before he runs off again?"

"Karmalita will get him. Won't you, Karmalita?"

Karmalita said, "I can get him. I know how." Without shyness, she smiled at Omar and held out her hand. He took it, and she pumped it with a great joy.

"Oh, I'm sorry," Mrs. Charter said. "Where are my manners? This is Karmalita."

Karmalita said, "I am very pleased to meet you." She giggled.

"My name is Omar Nayland."

"Karmalita is our adopted daughter. My husband and I found her when we were missionaries in Mexico." Mrs. Charter turned to her daughter. "Karmalita, your father's having a spell. You better change into a dress. Get your everyday slippers."

Karmalita opened the storm door and disappeared into the trailer. Mrs. Charter turned to Omar. "When we were in Mexico in 1963, they sold babies at five bucks a pop." Karmalita came back to them in another longish dress. It fit her quite well. She turned around in front of Mrs. Charter, who buttoned up the back. Karmalita sat down on the steps and threw her slippers onto the ground. "Beans, beans," she sang.

Mrs. Charter said mildly, "Karmalita."

Karmalita bowed her head and changed her tune. "Deep and wide," she sang nasally to herself. "Deep and wide. There's a fountain flowing deep and wide."

"That's better."

"Deep and wide. Deep and wide. There's a fountain flowing deep and wide." Karmalita dug her feet into her slippers. She lurched up onto her feet, and breathing heavily, she wandered out into the yard.

Omar asked Mrs. Charter, "Do you think she's going to be able to find him?"

The old woman shrugged. "Well, she's done it before. Karmalita's smarter than a lot of people give her credit for. She's slow, that's all."

Omar stepped into the grass. He watched Karmalita walking in her slippers. Still singing, she waded across the loose gravel in the driveway and on out of sight. Omar turned to Mrs. Charter, who had her hand on the door. It appeared that she was about to go back inside.

Wearily, she offered, "Would you like a cup of coffee?"

"Shouldn't somebody go with Karmalita?"

Mrs. Charter searched Omar's face. Once more, her voice changed. "Are you a married man, Mr. Nayland?"

James Russell Mayes

"What?"

"Are you a married man? I know it might seem like the five-dollar question. But if you were a married man, I could trust you alone in the dark with my daughter. Are you a married man, Mr. Nayland?"

"Oh, yes. I'm married." He remembered his wedding ring. He held up his hand to show it to her.

"How do you and your wife get along?"

"We get along just fine, Mrs. Charter. Don't you think I ought to be out there finding your husband?"

"I'm an old woman," she told him. She pulled open the door. "I can't be chasing my husband all over the countryside in the middle of the night."

"I understand, Mrs. Charter. I'll help find him."

"I thank you very much," she said. She closed the door behind her.

Because Karmalita was singing, it was not difficult for Omar to tell where she was. In spite of all the moonlight on the gravel, he edged over into the driveway. The humps of small stones made a great noise. He voyaged through them.

"Hey, what was that?" Karmalita shouted.

"What was what?"

She said, with disappointment, "Oh, it's you." Karmalita walked to the edge of the drive. She scratched at her bosom with both hands.

"It's me," Omar said, ankles deep in gravel.

"Well, keep it down."

"It sure looks dark out here."

"That's because it *is* dark," she said. She laughed uproariously.

Omar walked down the drive, past his Buick. It was much too dark for him to see anything. "Deep and wide," Karmalita sang. She turned and wandered down to the edge of the road. Omar followed her. She went a certain distance. She turned around and looked back at Omar, then back at the light off the back of the mobile home. The two of them picked their way along the ditch at the side of the road. At once Karmalita changed her tune: "Beans, beans," she sang in an exaggerated whisper. "Beans, beans, the musical fruit," she called into the ditch.

"I didn't know that was a song," Omar spoke out loud.

Karmalita said, "Shhh." She turned and put a soft hand on each of Omar's shoulders. She pressed her stomach into him. "It's my father's favorite song," she said. "Don't tell Mama." She turned and led him past the small shed near the road. "Beans, beans," she sang.

"Beans, beans," sang Omar. "The musical fruit. The more you eat, the more you .."

"Toot!" said a voice in front of him. Omar stood inches from Mr. Charter, who leaned in the shadows of the shed. The old man pulled Omar forward. He mashed his wizened face into Omar's and kissed him rough and hard on the lips. Omar tasted apples. Karmalita giggled at them.

Omar pulled himself free. He pushed Mr. Charter back into the side of the shed. The old man slid to the ground. He hugged himself, exhausted. "Toot?" he prompted.

Karmalita dug her fingernails into Omar's side. He stepped out of her way. "Beans, beans," she sang. "The more you eat, the more you toot!"

Mr. Charter's daughter held out her hand, and Mr. Charter took it. With his free fist, he rubbed an eye. "Will you help me find Ruth?" he whined. "Will you take me home?"

※

After an uncomfortable cup of coffee, Omar shook his head. "I really should be going," he told Mrs. Charter, looking at his watch. It was five o'clock. "I have to work this morning."

"Please," Karmalita said, smiling. "I'll give you some of our eggs."

Omar followed Karmalita down the steps of the trailer. She shuffled out across the humps of grass and up to the shed by the road. One side of the coop had been enclosed with wire fence. The other held a human-sized door. Karmalita turned at the door of the shed, and she said to Omar, proudly, "This is where we keep the chickens." She bent and settled her nose, nearly touching a padlock on the door. She turned the dial back and forth, slowly, carefully. "I'm the only one who knows this combination."

"But what if you forget it?" Omar said. Within the coop, a hen heard a strange voice and cackled. Karmalita ignored Omar's question. She pulled the bolt of the padlock free, and she dropped it into the hook on the sill. Pushing the door open a gap, she pressed her knee inside of it. Then using both hands to push, she opened the door all of the way. A rooster crowed. Startled, Omar felt his heart leap under his shirt. Karmalita turned and showed him her teeth. "They're a little bit shy, because they don't know you," she said, unaware of his fear.

She gestured for Omar to come near the door. He bent forward to oblige. A light snapped on. His eyes lowered to a patch of straw on the ground. There was a rooster, flapping its bright red crew cut. The light caught its feathers, which sparkled blue and green. Elegantly, the rooster held one claw forward, as if suggesting that someone might want to kiss it. Above the bird, all against the wall, in boxes that Omar guessed were nests, a dozen hens rested with their noses deep in spotless ivory breasts.

Karmalita said, "I don't like that rooster. That's Abraham Lincoln. He'll peck your eyes out if you look at him wrong." She spread her legs wide to block the door. She bent forward in a curtsey and spoke to them, "Chick, chick, chick." The rooster turned away. There were more nests, up the height of three of the walls. Omar stepped up behind Karmalita and smelled a warm sweetness of heat and animals and straw. Her hand slid gingerly under the hens. There was a steady low clucking among them. It sounded to Omar as if they were consoling one another.

He watched Karmalita pull out from under the hens eight or nine eggs, all brown. She handed one to him. The egg was warm. He nearly dropped it. Omar tucked it inside of his pocket.

Karmalita looked at him sharply. "Be careful," she said. Her voice was hoarse from the air, which was dry with feathers. With her free hand, she reached behind the door to the coop. She pulled out a cardboard egg carton. Karmalita filled the carton with her eggs.

"Here," Omar said. "I'll pay you." Gently he turned the egg from his right hand to his left. While he dug in his pocket with his right hand for change, he cradled it there. Some instinct told him that he wanted to keep it warm.

Karmalita held the carton open in front of him. "No, you don't," she said. "We have to pay you for your trouble." She looked at him sadly.

"Listen, one's enough. Eggs are high in cholesterol."

She shrugged. She closed the carton carefully, and she rested it on her stomach. "You want to raise chickens? You got a chicken coop? I could teach you."

Omar shook his head. Karmalita turned and snapped her padlock shut. Repeating the combination in a mumble to herself, she walked with Omar across the humps of gravel and back to his car.

Omar drove with one hand so that he could keep his egg warm with the other. He rolled it against his cheek. He could not get over how dark it had become so late in the morning. He passed down into a knoll, where scrubby trees grew up out of enormous ditches. Something gleamed whitely in front of the Buick. He slowed. On top of the gravel in the road, there were buds of white flowers arranged in a pattern.

The wheels of Omar's car rolled over them. Alongside the ditch, he saw the shapes of children. They stepped backward out of the light. They were playing in the road, he realized. The car passed between them. He looked out through his open window. A girl in a dingy dress stood inches from his arm. She froze. There were no adults in sight. Perhaps the children were waiting for a school bus. All of them were dirty. Obviously, they were poverty-stricken.

Omar stopped the car. He looked into the rearview mirror. The children rearranged themselves around the white blooms that blossomed in the light of his brakes. He shifted into park, and he opened his door. He only meant to warn the children about playing in the road. But once he stepped onto the gravel, the light from inside the car shone only upon his shoes. The door buzzed. He slammed it shut. He stood there, blinded, holding onto the egg. Lips still burning from the kiss of a crazy old man who had no idea what he had done, Omar listened to the footsteps of the children running away.

Peggy Hagerman's Bikini

Omar's dad gave him two dollars a week for raking the slime off of the beach every morning. It was an easy job because their beach was only three feet wide. Omar already knew what he was going to buy before he got paid on Saturday, so after he finished raking, he walked to the snack bar at the public beach. He waited around the new box of Nestle's Crunch bars like he was going to buy one until all of the old guys who were back from fishing had bought their beer. Omar walked up to the magazine rack and pulled down a copy of *Tiger Beat* magazine. "Donnie Osmond Shirtless!" it said. "Bobby Sherman, Jacke Wilde, David Cassidy, Mark Lester!" He didn't look inside of it. He rolled it up in his hand and walked over to the counter where Maureen Chinaberry was picking at one of the pimples between her eyes.

"That all you want?" she said. She scratched at her nose, like that was what she was up to the whole time.

"Yeah."

"For your sister?"

"Yeah."

She rang it up, and Omar gave her one of his dollars. He waited for the quarter, and then he ran around the back of the store to the boathouse. He sat on top of the tippy old aluminum boat that used to be Mr. Powell's before he died, and he looked through the magazine. There was a quiz on the back cover where they showed only a pair of eyes, and the reader was supposed to guess what famous guy they belonged to. He looked through the black-and-white photo story of the Osmonds at the beach, and he read a short interview with Bobby Sherman about how people thought he was stuck-up because he was quiet all of the time, but actually he was shy and didn't know what to say. "Someone for the younger girls," a title read, "Branden Cruz from *The Courtship of Eddie's Father.*" Omar realized that he had made a big mistake; this magazine he had been staring at from the checkout lane for the past week and a half was for girls.

When he looked up, the retarded girl who lived across the lake was walking up from the beach with one stiff leg. Her name was Ila Pitpath, and she didn't have any teeth on the bottom of her jaw so that her top teeth stuck out over her chin. Omar ran out from behind the boat-house.

"I have a present for you," he said. He held out the magazine, and her lips pulled up to show more of her teeth. Ila held back a minute, and then she pulled the *Tiger Beat* out of his hand. She frowned at the cover. Omar turned and ran before she could say anything. He walked home. He sat on the dock and kicked at the water. He waited for Bennie Ferguson.

※

In 1971, the summer that the girl across the lake drowned, and the same year Omar's sister Evelyn got her mouth washed out with soap for calling herself a flower child and dancing in her nightgown on the dock, their parents still lived sheltered lives. They believed in correct verb tenses and that sex education was best left out of the schools. They were big on how things should be said and by whom because, as far as they knew, Evelyn and Omar had never done anything seriously wrong and nothing seriously bad would ever happen to them. But Omar kept wanting things he wasn't supposed to want. For instance, his family never took a vacation unless it was to visit his aunt Florence in Toledo. His dad said they didn't need a real vacation because everything they needed for the summer was right there at home, and Omar had to suppose he was right. The tennis courts were opened up, and there was a small pool that somebody had pooped in once when Omar was a little kid. The snack bar sold frozen Milky Way bars on a stick. But the only good thing that happened to him that summer was that Bennie Ferguson came back to Mud Lake.

James Russell Mayes

Bennie Ferguson lived in two different houses because when he was in the second grade his father shot himself in the head because Bennie's mom was having an affair with their veterinarian. While he was in school, Bennie lived with his uncle Frederick, who was a self-employed electrician in Vickeryville, Michigan. But every time his mom got engaged, Bennie came to stay with his aunt Vi at the lake. Bennie was short and sturdy and dark, he said, because he had Indian blood in him. Whenever his aunt Vi took a picture of the two boys, Bennie would look as ugly as possible. And then, just before she pressed the button on the camera, his aunt Vi would say, "Bean farts," and Bennie would crack up. It was that easy.

The summer before, Bennie and Omar had rowed his aunt Vi's boat out to the log in the cattails on the other side of the lake and filled it up with about a hundred frogs. Then they rowed back across to the public beach where Evelyn and her girlfriends were oiling each other's shoulders on the diving raft, and they bombed the girls. Another time they told Ila Pitpath that Torie Campbell had a crush on her, and she was all over Torie in three seconds. Torie Campbell couldn't get away because he got a boner; if he stood up all of the older girls, the ones he was trying to impress with his muscles, would see it. Omar read a lot of books and he knew every episode of *Gilligan's Island* by heart; alone he was nothing. But with Bennie Ferguson he came up with all of these great ideas that only Bennie would be brave enough to carry off. The year before at the Labor Day softball game, Bennie Ferguson took Omar out behind the boathouse and pulled his pants down and showed him his butt. Omar laughed so hard that he felt the blood go out of his lungs. When Bennie said it was Omar's turn, he laughed and ran away from him.

Omar sat on the dock splashing the water up into the air, and pretty soon Lefty and her little baby ducks came paddling up. Lefty was one of the ducks that belonged to the high school biology teacher that lived across the lake. If anyone saw a white duck on Mud Lake, chances were it belonged to Mr. Townsend. Omar recognized this particular duck because she came with her five babies, and she had only the one working paddle; that's why he called her "Lefty." One would think that Lefty would only be able to paddle in circles, but somehow she managed. Omar didn't have any food for her, but he reached down into the water and pulled up some of the slime from the lake. He threw bits of it at her, until she figured out that it wasn't food.

Mud Lake was a small lake, and since the water carried every sound and enlarged it until one couldn't avoid whatever it was one heard, Omar looked up when Peggy Hagerman walked out to the end of her dock. Peggy Hagerman and her sister Jackie were new to the lake that summer, and so everyone was impressed with them; Peggy had large breasts and wore a bikini, and her sister Jackie had taught their poodle Cocoa to walk on its back feet with a fez on its head. Peggy Hagerman stood at the end of the dock in her bikini. She raised a can of beer to her lips, tasted it, and then tilted her head back for a guzzle. Omar was amazed. Nobody that he knew drank beer, and if any of his friends or any of Evelyn's friends had sucked down a beer right out in front of everyone like that, their mom and dad would probably have brought home a book from the public library on "Teen Drinking" and force Evelyn and Omar to read it. That's how Omar learned about sex; his dad came home from the library with a book called *A Doctor Talks to Twelve-Year-Olds*. Omar felt real mature, because he was nowhere near that old.

When he felt footsteps from the vibration of the dock, he felt them right up the bones in his butt. Lefty honked and turned in the water. Omar had started to turn around, but someone shoved him; he pitched forward into the slime. Mud Lake should have really been called "Muck Lake," because the bottom of it was more like a swamp than a lake. If one waded out from the shore until the water was up to his waist, then the muck would already be up to his knees. Omar knew because he tried it once. There was no way anyone could swim in it unless they rowed a boat out to the middle and dove in; that's why they kept a raft anchored out near the public access. So by the time Omar got himself unstuck from the bottom and could take the three steps back to the dock through knee-deep water, Bennie Ferguson was pelting him with more water and his shirt was all wet.

As soon as Omar pulled himself back up onto the dock, Bennie ran up the steps. By the time Omar ran all of the way up the steps from the dock, Bennie was behind their house. Omar ran barefoot through the evergreens that grew a few feet from the brick walls of their house, and he felt himself starting to swell up with a laugh. It was summer again, all of the sudden, because Bennie Ferguson was back. He felt the pulse of the summer light and all of the shades of green which had heaved up out of the earth since spring. As Bennie ran ahead of him up the sandy quarter mile of driveway through the woods, Omar shouted and his own voice came back to him as if the trees themselves were shouting back. Even the sand seemed to hold Bennie's footprints as if holding his feet for a moment in its hands; it shaped itself to him in the same way that Omar did. Now that Bennie and he were together, everything would cave in beneath the force of their bare hands and feet: the dead log where the turtles sunned, a muddy bank of crayfish holes, the stuck door to the boathouse.

Bennie shouted back at Omar because at once he had become invisible, and the sound chilled Omar as he ran under the cool shadows of the evergreens. Omar felt himself beneath his clothes sweating and breathing and bursting out of his skin into the air. Evelyn would say he stunk. Omar called again, and this time Bennie was suddenly behind and had risen above him. Omar looked up, and Bennie Ferguson pulled himself higher into a tree by way of a vine that hung to the ground. Twenty feet in the air. He called Omar up. Omar kicked at the bottom of the tree. He stepped from root to root around its base. The idea of height sometimes made him dizzy, but Omar trusted Bennie. Eventually he drew himself up next to him. They stood in the places where the branches pinched their feet into the trunk, and Omar heard Bennie's breath next to him. Bennie pulled himself around the tree and smiled. The tree branches pulsed around his head from the heartbeats behind Omar's eyeballs. They heard voices.

Evelyn and Darlene McCorkle, and this time they pulled Ila Pitpath with them, came through below them. The boys scrambled down the tree only seconds after the girls had passed it, so that the sound alone scared them and they screamed. Darlene and Evelyn ran, but they left Ila Pitpath behind them, and she stopped and began to cry until she saw who it was. Then she ran after the boys. Evelyn and Darlene ran back, too. They shouted that they would have Torie Campbell come beat them up, that Evelyn would tell Mom.

Bennie and Omar ran until they found a thick stand of pines to hide behind, and their feet were muffled by the soft pine floor. They had to bend over to breathe, and Omar leaned against a sticky trunk to scratch at a wounded foot.

"You okay?"

Omar wrapped his two hands around Bennie Ferguson's neck and shook his head until he punched Omar in the chest. Omar stepped backward until he fell in a bare spot on the ground on purpose.

"Hey," Omar said.

"Hey, yourself."

"I have something to show you."

They ran around the pines and, after checking to make sure the girls were gone, Omar walked ahead of Bennie, up the driveway to his own backyard. This was where he had put up the pup tent he had received for his birthday. Omar crawled inside, and looked out through the screened window. When Bennie came around the bend, he stopped and lifted his hands over his head.

"Cool," he said.

Omar showed him all of its features, including the floor and the flaps that tied over the windows. It was a two-man tent, so they both lay on their backs and watched the crowns of the maple trees move in the wind. Omar lay there, too happy even to say anything, and then someone pushed a face against the screen above Bennie's head. It was Jackie Hagerman, from across the lake. She laughed, and when Jackie Hagerman laughed, she snorted through her nose.

"So your boyfriend is back," she said. "Are you two making love, not war?"

Omar rolled over and sat up, and he told her to go to hell. Bennie sat up then, and he told her how terrifically ugly she was.

"What a sissy," Jackie Hagerman hissed. "You're both just like little girls."

Omar made an effort to lower his voice, to sound like his father did when he yelled at McCorkle's dog. "No we're not," Omar said.

"You are, too. Look how your little girlfriend is sitting."

Omar looked at Bennie. Bennie was nervous. He had folded his legs up around each other. He was leaning back, like he was getting a tan at the beach or something. Bennie and Omar ran out of the tent.

James Russell Mayes

They threw sand at Jackie Hagerman, and they chased her across Mrs. DeMarco's yard into McCorkle's driveway. Omar called her a bitch as loud as he dared, which wasn't very loud because his mom was sitting on Mrs. DeMarco's porch with Mrs. DeMarco, playing Ya-htzee. It was obvious how stupid Jackie Hagerman was and how ugly she was, and the boys affirmed that on the way back to Omar's pup tent. They sat down again. They kept an eye out for her in case she came back.

Bennie and Omar talked the whole afternoon, and they only went into the house to make a pitcher of red Kool-Aid. They brought the pitcher out to the tent, and they drank the whole thing before supper-time. After supper, they collected pop bottles at the public access, and when they turned them in they had enough money to buy a pop to share. They crossed the lake to the log where all of the frogs had been the summer before. They were hoping to find a nice fat one to stuff in Jackie Hagerman's mouth, but they turned out not so easy to find. Bennie poked a stick into the mud, and all of the sudden Omar had to pee.

"The nice thing about being outdoors," Omar said, turning toward the reeds and keeping an eye over his shoulder for girls, "is that you can pee whenever you need to."

"Amen," Bennie said. "I'm glad I'm not a girl."

"Me, too." Bennie peed, too, while Omar jumped up and down from one leg to the other. When Bennie had finished, the boys had to run. The bugs had starting to settle.

After it was just beginning to get dark, Omar heard his dad's accordion down at the public access. They followed the music down to the lake, and they started to meet others on the way too. Bennie's aunt Vi walked down the path ahead of them with her box of Cheez-its, and Irene DeMarco folded up her glasses and left them on top of her book about the Nez Perce Indians on the glider in front of her cabin. It took the boys only a couple verses to get down to the public beach, where the fire was going and everyone was sitting around the fire. Some of the older women had brought lawn chairs, and the men stood around with their arms folded. The kids mostly sat in the sand, or chased each other up and down the only sandy beach on the lake. Omar's dad only seemed to know enough songs to draw people there, and then once everyone had gathered around the fire, he threw a chunk of wood on it.

There was this ten or twenty minutes of coughing and slapping bugs until someone got Omar's dad to unwrap the accordion from around his waist and start up a group sing of campfire songs. The sparks rose up into the sky and seemed to get confused with the stars. The trees were lit up and looked twice as big as they were in the daytime. Omar looked out into the darkness of the lake, but he couldn't see it, except for where someone had left their porchlight on, and there were stars inside of the lake as well as above it.

After they all got through singing "Swing Low, Sweet Chariot" and "The Little Brown Church in the Vale" and "White Coral Bells," Evelyn and her girlfriends started up with the Leslie Gore song. They put their arms around each other and jumped up and down, and Peggy Hagerman started up the Rockette kick and Bennie punched Omar in the side, like he wasn't thinking about them already. The night was especially pretty, and everything smelled like the pine trees. There was a good mud smell blowing off of Mud Lake. Some of the mothers asked Omar's dad to sing a song, so he strapped his accordion back over his shoulders. He stepped into the firelight and played "Tenderly" with the whole Lawrence Welk treatment: the fancy notes, the drama swelling with each verse. Omar's dad had a beautiful voice, clear but at the same time mellow and full. He sang at a lot of funerals. The little kids began to fall asleep, and some of the older ladies, like Bennie's aunt Vi, who had forgotten her box of Cheez-its; McCorkle's dog stuck his head right into the box. But when the song was over, Bennie's aunt Vi hugged herself and wiped her eyes and cleared her throat.

"You have a beautiful voice, Leland."

A woman went "Aww," and everyone clapped. Omar wrapped his arm around Bennie Ferguson's shoulders and sang to him:

> *Your dirty knees*
> *Caress the trees,*
> *Tenderly*

James Russell Mayes

The boys next door
Fall on the floor,
Tenderly...

Bennie looked at Omar soulfully and blew him a kiss. Then he stiffened and fell over to the ground like a rock. His aunt Vi laughed.

"You boys really missed each other, didn't you?"

They had to beg her for Bennie to stay the night at Omar's place, and she finally gave in if Omar promised to bring him back for breakfast the next morning. Evelyn made a pitcher of green Kool-Aid for them, and they drank it all before it got cold. Bennie slept with Omar in his bed in the living room, which was really their couch folded out. The good thing about Omar's bed was that it folded out under the front window, and even though he could never see the lake while he was lying down, he could see the sky where the trees opened up.

Bennie told Omar about how his uncle Frederick almost got electrocuted when he wired a house in Vickeryville, and how his mom was always telling him his uncle wasn't suited for the job. They talked about Omar's tent and made a hundred plans, and they must have started to talk a little too loudly; Omar's mom shuffled out into the living room and told them to quiet down.

So they whispered. Bennie asked Omar where the Big Dipper was, and Omar couldn't see it, but he found Orion's belt. Bennie yawned, and he was still turned toward Omar so that Omar could feel the yawn against his ear. "That doesn't look like a belt," Bennie said. "That looks more like three stupid stars than a belt."

"What do the trees look like?"

"Like wolves."

"Good wolves or bad wolves?"

"Wolves are always bad," Bennie said. "Unless you raise it yourself, like a dog."

"They look sad to me."

Bennie rolled over and Omar could tell he was asleep because he accidentally pushed the bare back of his arm against Omar's shoulder. Omar looked out at the branches of the evergreen trees that spread out like shadows in front of the light coming up off the lake. They did look like wolves. The wind lifted them just a bit before he closed his eyes, so that they looked more as if they were howling.

The next morning, after Bennie's aunt Vi had asked a lot of questions about Omar's dad's short career as a gospel radio singer, they managed to keep a straight face through breakfast while she kept tucking her own darker hair under her new Eva Gabor wig. Soon enough, she started talking about her heart and then her liver; Bennie made faces at Omar from the other side of the table. Once they got away, the boys walked around to the other side of the lake to see if there were any frogs out at this earlier hour of the morning.

But they never got to the other side of the lake. To get to the other side of the lake, there was a bit of a steep hill to climb, and a stand of evergreens one had to walk through. Bennie's feet had not quite hardened to walking barefoot yet, so that held them up for a while, and he kept looking around on the ground to keep from stepping on pickers and stones. Finally, Bennie stopped walking, and looked into the giant ferns.

"Cool," he said.

"What?" Omar saw some polka dots in the bushes. "Hey, what is that?"

Bennie reached into the ferns and held up the top of a bikini so that Omar could see.

"Underwear!" Bennie said.

"It is not," Omar said. "It's Peggy Hagerman's bathing suit."

"Shh."

Omar jumped up, and they looked around in the bushes. But they couldn't find her bottoms.

"So where's Peggy Hagerman?"

They heard a funny noise. It wasn't someone talking, and it wasn't someone laughing. It was one of those in-between noises that sounds human, but not quite normal. Bennie and Omar looked at one another. And there it was again: a wet, snorty kind of sound. Bennie picked his way ahead of Omar through the trees.

Omar could tell that this was a big mistake. Generally, when Omar heard a strange noise in the woods, he liked to run the other way.

Bennie was going straight for it. He followed behind Bennie, but he kept his distance. Bennie didn't walk very far. He stopped short and pulled himself behind a tree. He turned around, and he waved at Omar to come closer.

Omar didn't want to, at first. But he figured Bennie must have known what he was doing. So Omar walked as quiet as he could, from behind one tree and then from behind the next one, until there was only one tree between the two boys. Bennie was pointing into the bushes and making faces like something was very funny, but Omar couldn't see anything. He could hear the wet snorting, as if it were very close, and that was about it.

Bennie scooted over to the next tree, the tree that stood between them, and he held his hand up to his mouth. "Did you see them?"

"Who?"

"They're down there. They're *in the nude.*"

Omar looked around the tree, and he thought he could see somebody's arm. Then he definitely saw the rest of Peggy Hagerman's bikini. Peggy Hagerman was lying on the ground. Torie Campbell had his head down between Peggy Hagerman's legs, and he was snuffling like a pig at the Ionia Free Fair. Omar knew what they were doing, but it looked as if Torie Campbell and Peggy Hagerman didn't know how to do it right. They obviously hadn't read any books, as Omar had. *A Doctor Talks to Twelve-Year-Olds* never showed anything like that.

It looked like Torie Campbell was eating Peggy Hagerman for dinner. Omar thought for a minute that she might be dead; she had her eyes closed, and she wasn't moving very much. But all of the sudden, she laughed out loud. She lifted her legs up into the air, and she wrapped them around Torie Campbell's head.

Omar looked at Bennie, and Bennie looked at Omar. This was something. Torie Campbell pulled his head out from between Peggy Hagerman's legs and he reached up and took off the rest of her bikini. "Wow," Bennie said. And then he reached over and grabbed Omar's wrist. Bennie Ferguson looked right into his face, so Omar knew this was going to be serious. Bennie said, "Cover me." He put his hand on either side of the trunk to his tree, and he swung himself around it. Bennie Ferguson ran right up to where Peggy Hagerman was kissing

Torie Campbell on the lips, and he grabbed her bikini off of the ground. He was already running away before they even looked up.

"Hey, you little shit." Torie Campbell and Peggy Hagerman jumped up off the ground. Omar saw them, because he was still standing behind the tree.

Bennie ran away: "Eat your lunch, Torie Campbell," he said. Omar probably should have run too, but he was looking at Peggy Hagerman without her bikini on. She was pretty; Omar had always thought she was pretty. But she looked a little strange without any clothes on. Omar had seen pictures of breasts before, but Peggy Hagerman's breasts weren't like the ones he had seen in any pictures; they were smaller and whiter, with the palest of nipples. She pulled herself behind Torie Campbell. She picked up his clothes and held them in front of herself.

Omar was afraid they saw him, but he was too afraid to run. He stayed behind the tree. He stood very still, until the ground started to shake. His legs knocked against the trunk of the tree. He felt shivers in his back and on his arms. He was sure there was going to be an earthquake until he started looking around. There weren't any cracks opening up. It was just himself; he was shaking like Ila Pitpath when she had one of her spells. The only difference was, Omar's eyes were open. Bennie called to him from the Indian trail, and Omar turned and ran as fast as he could. He heard Peggy Hagerman shout, and then he thought he heard someone running behind him. He ran back to the Indian trail, and Bennie was there with his half of the bikini. He tried to grab Omar's half, and Omar tried to grab his half. They ran back to Omar's house.

That afternoon Omar's mom had gone over to Irene DeMarco's cabin to play Yahtzee, and since Evelyn and her girlfriends had gone over to Dinah Fishburn's trailer, Bennie and Omar had Evelyn's bedroom all to themselves. Bennie said that Torie Campbell and Peggy Hagerman were both stark naked, and that Torie Campbell had "hair." "You know what I'm talking about?"

"I know what you're talking about. I saw it."

They both felt funny. They laughed very hard, and Evelyn's bed jiggled underneath them. Evelyn had left her Elvis Presley album on her record player, so Omar turned it over to the side that had "You Ain't Nothin' but a Hound Dog" on it and turned the volume up to number ten. Omar did "the Swim," real slow, and Bennie jumped up and down in front of Evelyn's mirror. He jerked around to the music, and stuck his butt out.

Omar snapped Bennie in the face with his half of Peggy Hagerman's bikini. Bennie pulled his t-shirt over his head, and wrapped it around Omar's neck like he was trying to strangle him. Omar pulled Bennie's shorts down around his ankles, and he fell forward onto the floor. Bennie wouldn't move, so Omar had to help him up. Bennie was laughing. He pulled Peggy Hagerman's bikini over his Fruit-of-the-Loom underpants.

"Dance, Bennie, dance." Omar clapped his hands, and Bennie walked like a girl up to Evelyn's vanity mirror. Bennie blew a kiss to the mirror. He rotated his hips.

"My name is Peggy Hagerman," he shouted above the music. Omar turned on the switch so that all of the little pink lightbulbs around the mirror lit up. Bennie stuck his butt out. Then he pulled his butt back in, and he stuck his hands up under Peggy Hagerman's bikini top and pushed the cups out into points with his fingers. "My name is Peggy Hagerman. I have boozies."

"Hey, hey." Omar turned the record player off, but Bennie kept dancing around the room. He jumped up on top of Evelyn's bed with his dirty bare feet and jumped up and down. "Hey," Omar said.

"What?"

"I have an idea. I have a *great* idea."

They opened up Evelyn's closet and looked through her clothes. There wasn't anything there that Omar saw that was particularly funny-looking, but Bennie seemed to like Evelyn's muumuu, and he pulled that on over his head. Evelyn had a straw hat, too, but Omar couldn't find it. Instead, he sprayed Bennie with some of Evelyn's perfume, and Bennie's eyes widened. He held up Evelyn's bright-colored muumuu at the knees, and he turned around so that he could see what he looked like in the mirror from the other way.

"I'm beautiful," he said. He put the palms of his hands on either side of his face and practiced a horror-movie scream. It was eerie; Omar laughed so hard that he had to scream, and he fell back onto

Evelyn's bed. When the boys heard the back door slam, they pulled Bennie out of Evelyn's muumuu and threw it back on the hook inside of her closet. Omar's mom pushed open the door just as he was hitching up his shorts.

"What are you boys doing in Evelyn's room?"

"Nothing," Bennie said, too innocently.

"Bennie had to change," Omar lied, brilliantly. "His clothes got wet." He held up Peggy Hagerman's bikini in both of his hands. It was still kind of wet; since he had wadded it up, it might as well have been Bennie's shirt or something. But Omar's mom didn't even look at Peggy Hagerman's bikini. She frowned and looked around the room.

"It smells like perfume in here."

"It sure does," Bennie said, walking past her through the bedroom door and out into the hallway. "That's strong stuff your daughter wears, Mrs. Nayland." She sniffed, but Omar didn't look up.

"You hang those clothes of his out on the dock to dry or they'll mildew."

Bennie and Omar walked out the back door. They ran as fast as they could up the driveway.

Peggy Hagerman's bikini provided for Bennie and Omar the game that they would play that summer. They stole an entire set of women's clothes: a sundress off from Mrs. McCorkle's clothesline, Evelyn's polka-dot scarf, a pair of panty hose that were too long from Bennie's aunt Vi. They ordered an Eva Gabor wig from an address in the back of one of Bennie's aunt Vi's catalogues, and they cut a bit of Bennie's hair so that the wig they received would match his own color. Since Omar didn't have a bedroom of his own, he kept the clothes in his pup tent in a brown paper bag. They waited until the afternoon, when Omar's dad was still away at work and his mom and Evelyn were out of the house. They brought the bag into Evelyn's room and took turns dressing up in front of her mirror.

They had to wait six weeks until the Eva Gabor wig came, and Bennie was so excited about it that he brought it over in the morning while Evelyn and Mom were still hanging around. They ran out to the pup tent, and Bennie pulled it out of the box and tried it on.

"It's beautiful," Omar said.

"Is it?" Bennie brushed his hand against the bright blonde curls. "It doesn't look anything like my natural color."

"It's kind of smashed from the mail, though, isn't it?"

Bennie took the wig off. He showed Omar how his aunt Vi fluffed her wigs each night when she took them off before bed.

It wasn't until the boys got the wig that they became a little more daring. Omar had told Bennie that yes, he did look like a girl and could probably fool his aunt Vi if he wanted to, but Bennie did not seem satisfied with that. Bennie wanted to know for sure that he could fool people. Omar agreed to walk with him in public somewhere, as long as he could tell everyone that Bennie was his cousin Mandy Elizabeth.

"Mandy Elizabeth?"

"What's wrong with that?"

"That's not a *real* name."

"What name do you want to have?"

"Jessica," Bennie said, raising his chin and watching his lips in the mirror. "My name is Jessica."

They waited for another afternoon, when the day grew long and tiresome and most of the kids were at the public beach while their mothers napped. They marched grimly up the quarter mile of drive-way to the road, and from the road to the highway that led to the party store. In the sunlight, Omar was not so sure that Bennie was as convincing as he was in the shadows of their pup tent or Evelyn's bedroom. At first it didn't seem to him as if Bennie knew how to walk correctly. Omar walked a few feet behind him and gave him instructions. Whenever Bennie tried to walk "like a girl," it seemed that he tried too hard and in this way gave himself away for what he was not.

However, Omar did discover that if Bennie walked in the way that he ordinarily did when he was not dressed up and wearing a bright blonde Eva Gabor wig, then he seemed to do fine. Omar adjusted his advice to him along these lines, and soon they were walking along the shoulder of the highway and discussing how best to order the soda pop at the corner party store.

Bennie started getting paranoid. "Did you see that car go by before?" he asked. He pointed at an old gray Beetle that pulled away around the corner in front of them.

"No."

"He just came back the other way," Bennie said. "Didn't you notice it?" Bennie sidled over to the other side of the shoulder, so that he wasn't the one closest to the road.

"You're a paranoid, Bennie Ferguson."

"No, I'm not."

A few other cars passed, and then the gray Beetle came by again. This time, Omar saw the driver. He didn't seem to Omar as if he were the kind of guy who would kidnap little boys. But the driver did slow down a bit; he speeded up only after he passed back behind them.

"Was that the same guy?"

"Yes, it was the same guy. I told you he was following us."

"He keeps going back and forth like that?"

"I'm sure that's the fourth time," Bennie said. It wouldn't have been so creepy, except that they were at a place along the highway where there were a lot of trees and not very many cottages. The next time the guy came up from behind them, Bennie squeaked and ran into the ditch. The wig hopped off of his head; he had forgotten to hold onto it while he was running. Omar ran after him, and picked up the wig. He followed Bennie back into the woods.

Bennie was scared to death. He had started crying. "Let's go back home," he said. "We'll just walk along through the woods here until we get back to your driveway."

They walked back home through the evergreen trees, and Omar held onto Bennie's hand just as much to keep himself from getting scared as to keep Bennie from crying again. The fellow in the gray Beetle passed back and forth a couple more times. It did seem as if he were looking for them. Omar wondered what a grown man would do with two little kids, and although he couldn't imagine it, the idea made him shiver. Each time the fellow drove by, the boys slouched down as low as they could, so that the higher brush in the ditch might hide them. After that, he didn't come back anymore. By the time they got back to Omar's driveway, having never made it to the party store, they were walking along the shoulder of the road again. Bennie had his wig back on, and Omar was still holding his hand. They were singing "You Ain't Nothing but a Hound Dog."

𝄇

The next morning, after Bennie and Omar finished their pancakes, and before Bennie's aunt Vi started talking about her liver again, Omar went down to the beach to look for Torie Campbell. Torie liked to think of himself as the lifeguard, even though Mud Lake never had a lifeguard, because the taxes were too expensive as it was and none of the families on Mud Lake had that much money to help pay for one. Torie was hanging around the door to the snack bar talking to Maureen Chinaberry, who looked real irritated when Omar came up.

They both ignored him at first. Torie kept talking about this dumb movie he saw at the drive-in with his best friend, even though Maureen and Omar knew that he didn't have a best friend and he probably went to the drive-in with Peggy Hagerman. And even though Maureen Chinaberry probably knew this, she kept on giggling and chewing her gum and saying, "Oh my Gawd" until it made Omar sick.

Then Torie turned to Omar, real cool, and he said, "So what are you hanging around here for so early in the morning?" He grinned. He looked kind of cool, like Montgomery Clift, except he had muscles. "Where's your little boyfriend, Bennie What's-His-Name?"

Maureen giggled and said, "Yeah, your little boyfriend," and Omar wrinkled his nose at her.

"I want to talk to you, Torie Campbell."

"Well, well," he said, "the little sucker wants to talk to me." He laughed his fake laugh because Maureen Chinaberry was there, and she laughed her fake laugh, and Omar thought to himself how worth it all of this was going to be if he could just get Torie Campbell to believe what he was about to say to him.

Omar jerked his head in the direction of the boathouse, and so Torie followed him. Maureen crackled her gum one more time before the screen door to the snack bar slammed behind her.

"Okay, kid. What do you have to say to me?"

Omar kicked his foot around in the dirty sand until he could harden his face to keep it from breaking into a smile, and then he turned around and looked Torie Campbell right in the eye.

"You know my cousin Mandy Elizabeth?"

Torie grinned. "No. She been here before?"

"No," Omar said. "She's just come to visit us for the first time. She's a nice girl, but she's kind of wild. She saw you today out on the lake, and she wanted to know if you'd like to come by our place for a soda or something."

"How old is she?"

"Oh," Omar said, trying to consider how old she should be, "she's about sixteen I think. She's almost old enough to be married. She's kind of homesick, and she likes boys better than she likes my sister Evelyn."

"Who wouldn't?" Torie said, and he spit. And then he laughed, as if spitting itself were something funny.

"She wants to know if you'd like to come sit on the back porch with her tonight and listen to Glen Campbell records."

"You're full of shit," he said.

"No I'm not," Omar said. "I promise, or you can beat me up. I swear." He decided he had to get out of there before Torie caught on. Omar ran away from him, and then he turned back once more to make sure. "This afternoon," he said. "Three o'clock. On the front porch. You know where it is. She really does like you." He couldn't keep from smiling.

"What does she look like? I didn't even know that you *had* a cousin Mandy."

Omar didn't bother to answer him. He figured that he got Torie Campbell curious enough so that he would have to stop by, whether or not he wanted to sit in their pup tent and make love to Bennie Ferguson or not.

✂

At three o'clock, Bennie was dressed up as usual, except for some Persian Melon lipstick that Omar had found in Evelyn's wastebasket that day; he stared at himself in the mirror for fifteen minutes, making his lips bigger and bigger until he looked like Bugs Bunny when he dresses up like a girl. Omar left him sitting in the pup tent and walked up to the front porch, to see if Torie Campbell was coming by. Jackie Hagerman was standing on their dock across the lake. She waved at him.

"Yoo-hoo," she called. "Little girl!"

She dove into the water, and Omar thought about revenge.

By the time Torie Campbell finally pulled up in his dad's old rowboat, Peggy Hagerman had come out on the dock with her can of beer. Jackie had pulled herself out of the water, that slimy water that no one in their right mind would ever have gone swimming in, and she was sitting by her big sister. They were passing the beer back and forth. Omar couldn't believe it; Jackie Hagerman was drinking beer. And she was only his age.

Torie walked up the steps from the dock, and smiled at Omar. It was the first time Omar had ever seen him smile without frowning at the same time. He wondered if Torie Campbell wasn't such a bad guy, after all. "So," Torie said. "I thought your cousin was going to be out on the porch waiting for me."

"You're late."

He looked at his wristwatch. Omar supposed he was trying to show off.

"It's only three-thirty. She still around?"

"Follow me." Omar walked between the evergreens and the north wall of the house. By this time there was a path where Bennie and he had been chasing chipmunks.

"Where is she?"

"She's reading," Omar said. "She's back here in my tent." He pointed at his pup tent, which suddenly looked small and an improbable place for a girl cousin to be sitting.

"Oh." That's all Torie Campbell said. As if it were the most perfectly natural place for Omar's cousin Mandy Elizabeth to be sitting. Torie Campbell walked up to the tent, and looked inside. Then he bent down and looked more carefully into the tent. "A blonde," Torie said. He laughed. "Why don't she say anything? Why's she all dressed up?"

"She's shy," Omar said.

"I'm shy," Bennie said. His voice cracked a little, out of nervousness.

"Go on in." Omar held the flap of the tent open for him. Torie Campbell bent over and crawled into the pup tent.

"What's your name?" Bennie said. Omar thought that was a nice touch.

"Torie Campbell. What's yours?"

"Jessica," Bennie said. "My name is Jessica."

"It is not," Omar said into the tent. "It's Mandy Elizabeth. I already told Torie Campbell that your name was Mandy Elizabeth."

"Those are my middle names," Bennie said. "My legal name is Jessica Mandy Elizabeth." His voice was starting to get hoarse on him.

Torie Campbell stuck his head out of the door of Omar's tent. He said, "I thought you said your cousin had tits."

"She does," Omar said. He couldn't remember saying that, though.

"I do," Bennie said. "They're little ones."

Torie Campbell smiled his familiar, mean smile. He pulled the flap of the door inside of the tent, and he zipped it up. Then Omar thought of something. Torie Campbell hadn't dressed up or anything. He wasn't wearing Brylcreem, and he hadn't even tucked his shirt in. Omar knew that something was wrong; Bennie wasn't going to pull this off. It was impossible. To Omar, Bennie Ferguson was a girl whenever he dressed up like a girl because they were goofing around, they were pretending. But Torie Campbell wasn't the kind of guy who liked to play pretend; anyone who had met him once could tell he didn't have the imagination for it. Torie Campbell knew it was Bennie Ferguson because Torie Campbell knew Bennie Ferguson. He knew it already, Omar could tell. He probably knew before he had come over in the boat.

"Mandy," Omar said into the tent. "Can you come out here for a minute?"

"Why no," Bennie said. "I'm having a little conversation with my friend Torie Campbell. Aren't we having a good time, Mr. Campbell?"

"We sure are."

Omar stuck his face right into the tent, and he saw that Torie Campbell had his arm around Bennie's shoulders. Bennie was looking up into Torie Campbell's face as if he were Elvis Presley. "I think you better come out here now, Mandy."

"I'm not going out there, Cousin. I'm fine right here."

Omar wanted to run away. He wanted to call for help, but he couldn't, not without everyone on the lake finding out what they had been up to. He paced alongside the tent and waited for what was going to happen. He heard some shuffling and an unbuckling noise. Omar heard Torie Campbell say, "You ever seen one of these before?" Omar heard Bennie say, "Yes," and he could tell something was wrong by the way he sounded. He sounded like Bennie Ferguson again.

"You know what it's for, then?"

And then, in his tiniest voice, Bennie said, "Help." Omar ran around the pup tent and looked down through the window into it. Torie Campbell had a knife. He held it under Bennie's nose like he was going to cut his throat.

"You get out of my tent," Omar said. Torie Campbell turned his head and looked at Omar through the screen. He spat, and the spit stuck onto the inside of the screen.

Omar decided it was about time he better run for help. His dad was at work, and his mom and Mrs. DeMarco had gone across the lake to visit Peggy Hagerman's mother. He didn't know where Evelyn was. He took off and ran as fast as he could to the snack bar, where Maureen Chinaberry was slouched over the counter. He told her that Torie Campbell had a knife and that he was going to kill Bennie Ferguson.

Surprisingly, Maureen Chinaberry believed him. She walked around the counter, and turned the inside lock to the door. She ran behind Omar, all of the way back up the driveway to his house. By the time they got to the pup tent, Torie and Bennie were gone. The Eva Gabor wig lay in the dirt in the backyard. It wasn't until they heard Bennie scream that they had enough sense to run around to the front of the house.

Torie Campbell and Bennie were on the dock. Bennie looked kind of eerie without the hair. Maureen Chinaberry and Omar were so surprised that they just stood there while Torie Campbell lifted Bennie up over the water in his dress. "Hey," Torie Campbell called out over the water. "Hey, Peg. Get a load of this." Omar looked up and saw that Peggy Hagerman was waving. Jackie put her hands over her mouth and hooted. "Yoo-hoo," they called.

Bennie kicked his legs, and Maureen screamed so that a few fishermen who had rowed their boat out into the middle of the lake looked up from their rods. "Hey, look what I caught," Torie Campbell shouted. The men looked back and forth. One of them pointed. Laughter floated back across the lake. Torie Campbell dropped Bennie into his dad's rowboat.

"What the hell are you doing, Torie Campbell?" Maureen and Omar ran down the steps to the dock, but Torie Campbell was too fast. He untied his dad's rowboat, and he began to row Bennie Ferguson out into the lake.

"Come on with me," Maureen said. She grabbed Omar's hand and they ran back up the driveway to the boathouse behind the snack bar. Omar helped her turn over the tippy old aluminum rowboat that used to be Mr. Powell's before he died. They shoved it over the sand on its bow and into the water. "Don't get in," she said. "You run up and get Bennie's aunt Vi. I'll take care of Torie Campbell."

Omar ran back up the driveway, and then over three lawns to Bennie's aunt Vi's place, and he knocked on the door. There wasn't any answer, so he ran around front. Bennie's aunt Vi was standing out on the end of her short dock. She already knew about it. When Omar came up from behind her, he held on to her arm, and she turned to look down at him. "What's going on out there?"

"Maureen Chinaberry's gonna get him," Omar told her. "Bennie'll be all right."

"Bennie's fine," Aunt Vi said. And then Omar saw her face. She was pointing out onto the lake, and he hadn't even bothered to look out there. Bennie was sitting in Torie Campbell's father's boat. And Torie Campbell was pulling off his shoes, was jumping into the water. Maureen had tipped over in her boat. She screamed.

✄

Afterward, when it was clear Maureen was still alive, and Bennie said she must've thrown herself into the water on purpose to get Torie Campbell to put his arms around her, everyone on the lake came out and stood on their docks as if someone had really drowned. The silence opened up to swallow the whole afternoon, until Bennie and Omar were nearly crazy with boredom. When Omar's dad came home he must have been able to tell right away that something was wrong, because he walked right out onto the dock and asked what happened. Omar told him, "Maureen Chinaberry almost drowned, Dad." And when his dad asked how, Bennie told him that she had fallen in love with Torie Campbell, and that she loved him so much that she almost killed herself with grief.

Bennie was looking out over the lake as if it were true. Omar looked at his dad, and he saw that his dad was looking at Bennie Ferguson as if something were wrong with him. And then Omar noticed that Bennie Ferguson was still wearing Mrs. McCorkle's old sundress. He still had all the lipstick on, and he was holding his Eva Gabor wig in his lap.

"What are you boys up to?" Omar's father said in a low voice.

"Come on, Bennie," Omar said. "Time to hit the pup tent." He pulled on his skirt a couple times, so he'd know what Omar was talking about. But Bennie didn't seem to want to come with him.

"You go ahead," he said. "I'll be up."

He was that way for the rest of the afternoon. When he finally came up to the tent, Bennie didn't want to see if they could fix his Eva Gabor wig. And he wouldn't even kill any ants. He changed out of his dress and threw it out onto the ground. Omar shouted, but Bennie didn't care. Omar had to go get it himself. He folded it up.

"Do you think we're bad people?" Bennie said. He rolled over on his back. He raised his hands up and rested his head on them, so that his two dirty elbows pointed up in the air. Omar was looking at Bennie's elbows, and then it occurred to him that what Jackie Hagerman had said was right: Bennie Ferguson did cross his legs like a girl. Even when he wasn't dressed up like a girl, and even though he wasn't a girl, Bennie Ferguson had something about him that was kind of like being a girl, but not quite exactly like being a girl. Omar wondered to himself if maybe he was that way, too.

Eventually the boys walked back out to the lake. They sat down on the dock. The sun had changed, so the light made the boards under their bottoms burn hotter. Torie Campbell had brought his dad's boat out again, and he rowed out into the middle of Mud Lake. Bennie watched him, and since Omar was with Bennie, he watched him, too. Torie Campbell rowed back and forth across the lake.

"I think he does it to exercise his arms," Bennie said. He turned, and Omar saw that he spoke with a deep respect about Torie. "Torie Campbell has excellent arms," he said.

The Arrogance of
Blond

Clay and Omar tested the water in their pool, to see if it was warm. "Like a bath," Omar said, flicking water drops at Clay. Clay spat an ice cube into the blue.

"That should cool it off," he said.

Someone called over the fence to them: "Yoo-hoo." It was Bob or Bill or whatever his name was. They had only ever seen his head, but that was enough for them to tell that the man who had rented the cottage next to theirs was as queer as Geraldo Rivera. "Having a tea dance the day after tomorrow," he called to them, waving. "Can you girls come?"

"What time?"

"Teatime, what do you think? Drop by." He raised a martini glass above his head. "Boysboysboys!"

"We'll be there," Omar shouted.

Clay muttered, "Not me."

Omar gave Clay a look, and he corrected himself. "I'll be there." He waved back at their neighbor with his own drink.

Clay opened the doorwall and walked into the air-conditioning. The house was close from the marinating veal. He wanted to read another novel, he thought. He looked through the books on the shelf over the fireplace. None of them looked remotely interesting.

Omar had a long-standing habit of following Clay around when they had been drinking. He walked into the living room, and he flopped into a chair. He took his shirt off. He threw it up into the air, and it dropped in the middle of the floor. He was bored, too.

Clay said, "I always forget there's no good bookstores in town." He shook the ice in his glass. "Why is it that for the first few days, I always feel as if I'm going crazy up here?"

Omar leaned forward to snatch the sleeve of his shirt. He lifted it off of the floor and wound it in the air above his head like a lasso. "We're slowing down. City life is too much of a rush."

"I guess we're settling in."

"Settling in, getting ready for summer." He let loose his shirt, and it flew through the air landing squarely on Clay's shoulder. It wrapped neatly around his neck.

Clay laughed. "Bull's-eye." He turned around to look at his lover. He smiled to himself. A pleasant thought: at his age, Omar still had a fine chest.

Omar walked up to the front window and looked out onto the lane. He raised his tumbler to his lips. He held it there, poised. "Oh, my," he sighed over the ice. "A sign. An omen." His empty glass frosted with steam.

Clay walked to the window. At the house across the street, a young man chained a bicycle to the porch railing. He was young, but not too young, Clay decided. He was brown and blond and thin and, most appealingly, half-naked. His nipples were as large as quarters, and flattened, stretched as they were by the muscles under his skin. And there was a lot of skin.

"I know what you need," Omar said. "You need to get laid." Another fellow was with the man across the street, hardly as striking, probably someone who was trying to look much younger than he was, Clay thought. He watched them chain their bikes to the railing in front of their small cottage. The blond one, the demigod, walked up the steps.

Clay inhaled. "Thanks for thinking of me, Omary." He watched as the man leaned forward to drop his shoes off onto the porch.

"Faggot shorts for sure," Omar said, poking a finger. It was true that one could see very much underneath them. Almost too much to be true, Clay thought.

"Come on," Omar said. He burst out the front door.

Clay leapt behind him. "Desperation," he warned.

Omar stopped and turned around to face him. "Mother's getting old. She needs a good hump." He touched Clay's wrist with the flat of his fingers. This was Omar's signal for complete sincerity. "So do you, dear."

Clay stopped on the sidewalk in front of their cottage. They called it a cottage, but it was a sizable second home. The lawn had just been mowed, and Omar had planted impatiens. Clay put his hands on his hips. "And which one do I get? The old one?"

Omar climbed the steps of the small porch. He looked at Clay from across the street. "So we'll have a contest," he called.

Clay jogged across the pavement and up the steps beside his lover. He had not been caught off guard, not exactly. "May the best man win," he said, irritably.

"I bet they're already stark naked and fucking like bunnies." Omar raised his fist to knock on the door, but at once they both could see the figure of someone who stood behind the screen. The someone must have heard quite clearly what Omar had said.

Next to him, and with pleasure, Clay sensed that Omar's ears were brightening with embarrassment. He recovered quickly, as usual. "We live in the house across the street." He turned and pointed to the house so that the shadowy man would know it was the big one. "Are you the fellow who's renting this place for the summer?"

The young man opened the screen door, and he turned out not to be the popular choice. Up close, it appeared that his hair had been lightened a few shades, and curled. He shook both of their hands. He looked at the two of them very carefully. "Yes," he said. "I'm Bruce. And this," he said, pointing into the screen at a pleasing shape that had formed in the half-light behind him, "is my fuck-buddy, Erik." They burst with nervous laughter. Clay strained to see Erik inside of the dark room.

"You weren't supposed to hear that," Omar said. He kicked a bare foot at the porch, charmingly. Bruce looked at each of them intently, into their eyes, and Clay could feel from it, just as Omar had been able to, judging from the glance that he had shot him sideways, that here was an opportunity, a frank and willing fellow, if not the youngest.

"You wanna come in for a drink?" Bruce asked.

"I already got one," said Omar. He laughed and scratched at his bare chest.

He's doing that on purpose, Clay thought to himself.

Then Bruce scratched his chest, too, and just under a nipple.

"Tell you what," Clay said to Omar. "Dinner's already started, and I can't leave it. Why don't you go on inside and visit with the boys? I'll cook up the veal."

"Oh," Bruce said, with sincere disappointment. "Maybe after dinner? We're not doing anything." He glanced through the screen door and squinted his eyes at the invisible, beautiful Erik.

A voice behind the screen said, "What about tomorrow?" A face pressed through, and the same screen that gave it light, distorted the young man's face with the blemishes of shadow. All the same, it was a shapely face, broad and smooth and open. In their admiration, the three men on the porch said nothing at all for a moment. A breeze picked up, and Clay, suddenly feeling the alcoholic mist, had the definite sensation of rising out of his espadrilles with the boughs of the shrubbery that surrounded the porch.

"Tomorrow be fine," Omar said, merrily. He was backing Clay down the steps. "How about dinner at our place?"

Erik, looking at Bruce, said, "Um."

"We've got a pool. We'd love to show you the house."

"Sounds good," said Bruce, leaning forward on the rail.

"Fine," Omar said. "Seven? Come on, Clay."

"Seven be fine," Erik said, finally. "Nice to meet you guys."

"Seven it is." Still feeling the billows, Clay followed Omar back across the street.

"You know, you used to be blond," Omar said.

"And you used to have hair."

He sighed. "That was decades ago."

Even from their own porch all the way across the street, they both heard Erik say, in disbelief, to Bruce: "The *big* house?"

Omar brightened. He looked up at Clay. "That's a good sign."

🕯

Omar praised Clay's cooking so much that it made the actual meal less wonderful, Clay thought. But he had tried a new soup, a cream soup of red peppers, served cold with a slice of radish and a sprinkle of thyme leaves floating on the top. He served an orange salad with radicchio in raspberry vinaigrette. They usually grilled in hot weather, anyway, and since he knew that Omar was trying to impress, Clay made a shallow pool of sorrel sauce on each of their plates into which he slid the salmon, aromatic from the grill. He garnished them with peppercorns and flecks of lemon.

Walking back and forth between the table and the grill and the kitchen, he watched Erik with interest. Their young man had worn linen shorts, but his shoes weren't right. The breeze caught the scent of someone's slightly oily smelling cologne, probably Bruce's, Clay hoped. The aroma was dark, he realized, not cheap, but a formal evening scent, much too heavy in broad summer daylight.

Erik admitted, after Bruce tried several times to prime his pump, that he had never eaten so well. He looked at his plate for most of the meal, but it was clear that he was pleased by the food, as he seemed to be by the appearance of the yard. Omar and Clay had adopted the habit of planting their backyard almost completely to annuals. It was usually the first thing they did together when they arrived on the island. All through the meal Erik raised his chin, and each time Clay tried to meet his eyes, he concentrated on the geraniums, or the ferny leaves of the cosmos, or the climbing roses called Golden Showers, looking and looking. Perhaps he was shy.

Bruce assured Clay, "Erik's having a good time."

Erik explained, "I love all the flowers." Then he complimented the dessert which was Omar's contribution: melon balls in lime glaze.

"I can read a cookbook as well as the rest of them." Omar raised his wineglass and his eyebrows at Erik.

Bruce's cologne trailed around the table and licked its oily tongue at Clay's nostrils until his nose was numb from the tingle and the back of his throat felt scratchy. Bruce squinted at the light off the pool. He brushed the crumbs from his lap. "That's a great pool," he said, admiringly.

This was the moment for which Omar had been planning. Each of the men at the table sensed this. Clay rolled his eyes and wiped his lips with his napkin, and Omar leaned over the table at Bruce. He lowered his voice and said, "Go for a swim?"

Bruce raised his eyes and smiled. Across from him, Erik stabbed at the last melon ball on his plate. "We didn't bring our trunks," he said, without looking up. There was a moment of cautious silence while the three others looked at one another. Bruce, in particular, seemed disappointed. He smirked at Clay, and then at Omar. He rolled his eyes and shook his head.

"Well," Omar said, tentatively, spinning the last of his wine around and around in the bottom of his glass. He spoke as if someone had written him a script and had shrunk it for him so he could read it through the Chardonnay. "I suppose you could swim without them." Bruce laughed. "Clay and I never swim with our trunks on. Not at home, anyway. Why do you think we had the brick fence put up?"

Erik raised his eyes. "Your landlord let you do that?"

"Landlord?"

Bruce slapped Erik's wrist. "They own the house," he said. "Not everybody rents."

Clay picked up the dessert plates. "Any more wine?" Omar and Bruce held up their glasses. He waved the back of his hand at Erik, as if to dismiss him, and the young man poured. The sound of the liquid of the alcohol poured through them. The breeze picked up.

Bruce cocked his head. "You sure it be all right if I go swimming?"

Clay, returning from the kitchen, giggled. "Not if you mind that Omar joins you." He sat down again, and he stretched his legs.

"There's no one shy here," Erik murmured into his glass.

"You're going too, aren't you, Erik?"

Bruce pushed his chair back from the table on the deck. He walked to the edge of the pool and pulled down his shorts. Then he pulled off the black bikini underwear that he had been wearing underneath.

"Very nice," Omar said. He whistled. "I think I shall join you."

Bruce turned around before diving in. Not so young, Clay thought, setting his glass back down. But so much younger than I am. If one has youth, he dreamed in his cups. He admired Bruce's complexion, and his arrogance, which shone icily through his almost youthful skin.

"Do it," Omar said. "Dive in."

Clay turned to Erik, who suddenly took an interest in his plate again. Emboldened by the sound of the water that leapt from the pool, he asked him, "How about you?"

"Oh, I don't think so," Erik said. He showed Clay his teeth, which froze him. The young man swallowed. "Maybe next time."

"Darn," Omar said. He pushed his chair back. "Come on in, Erik. You can wear your shorts."

"I can't. I just had them dry-cleaned."

"Clay will find something for you."

Clay smiled at Erik. "It might be a little big on you."

"Oh, dear," Omar said, and he slapped the sides of his face with his hands, "I hope it doesn't fall down."

"Leave him alone," Clay said. "He already told you he's shy." He felt like somebody's mother.

Erik said, "You were shy once, weren't you Omar?"

Omar wrinkled his face. "Oh, I get it," he said. "No."

Clay opened the glass doors for Erik and slipped inside behind him. He explained. "Omar doesn't know the meaning of shy. He was the one who brought me out years ago. Hell, he's fifteen years older than I am."

"And how old is that?"

"Now, now." He led Erik through the house, past the weight room and the Hockney to the guest room, decorated with Keith Haring prints. "My God," Erik said, mouth agape. "What a beautiful house."

Clay looked at him quizzically. "Thank you," he said. He opened a drawer that was a mass of bathing suits and posing briefs and swim goggles. He pulled out the longest pair of shorts that he could find, nearly pajamas, and he held it up in the air between them. "How about this one?" He meant it as a joke.

"That'll work," Erik said. He took them from Clay, and he waited until Clay had closed the door behind him before he changed out of his clothes. Clay took a deep breath and waited in the hall. Presently Erik appeared. He blushed attractively when Clay looked up and down. "Let's hit the water," he said.

Omar and Bruce were splashing one another in the shallow end of the pool. Occasionally Bruce leapt up and dove so that his bare bottom shone whitely. "Aren't you coming in?" Erik asked Clay, turning. Clay shrugged, and he shucked off his clothes. They slid into the water at the same time, while Omar and Bruce swam naked on their backs in the sunlight.

Clay walked through the water naked, out into the middle of the shallow side. With a shiver of pleasure, he felt someone's eyes on his

James Russell Mayes

backside. He turned around and discovered that Omar was smiling at him. "Not bad," he said.

"You never change," said Clay. He unwound a volleyball net, and the four batted a beach ball back and forth, hopping up and down in the water.

Once when Omar had to retrieve the ball, he caught Erik staring at him. He jumped obligingly, and his genitals swung up above the surface of the water. "The only way to swim," he leered good-naturedly. Bruce dove between Omar's legs like a porpoise, and he did not come up for air right away.

Clay tossed the volleyball onto the lawn. "There goes the game," he said. He turned to Erik, who squinted through the distorting waves. Clay tapped his elbow. "Let's get some sun," he suggested.

Omar and Bruce pulled an air mattress into the water. They began to wrestle over it. Clay spread lotion on Erik's back. "Turn over," Clay said. Delightfully, Erik did. As Clay brushed the lotion over the tender skin, it appeared that the young man became excited. There were goosebumps, an unmistakable pressure and heat against Clay's elbow. He ran the flat of his hand down into the front of Erik's trunks. Then he felt a grip around his wrist. Erik pulled his hand away.

"What's wrong?" Clay said.

Erik sat up. Glancing over at Bruce and Omar, who pawed at one another, "I don't feel so well," he said. He sat up on his towel. He hugged his knees. He stood up and adjusted his swimming trunks, which slackened on him. Erik walked over to the edge of the pool, and leaning forward with his hands on his knees, he vomited into the water.

Clay pulled his shorts on. He walked up behind Erik. He rubbed the young man's back. Once he had finished heaving, Clay gave him a towel. "Wipe your face," he said. "Go inside. Did you see where the bathroom off the kitchen is? Hop in the shower, and I'll clean this up." Erik walked inside.

Clay stood by the pool with his hands on his hips. He watched Omar with Bruce in the swimming pool. They used their hands and mouths on each other. He waited until they jammed the air mattress up against the side of the pool before he fished out the chunks of vomit. He flipped it into the compost bin, and he stirred things around with a pitchfork. He waited on the deck for the shower to stop, but it ran for quite a while. Eventually Omar and Bruce rolled over onto their backs. They splashed themselves clean and floated out into the middle of the pool. They fell asleep like spoons.

Clay knocked on the bathroom door, and when there was no answer, he poked his nose in. The shower was running, but Erik was not there. Clay walked across the street, and he knocked on their front door. Erik answered, shivering, still wrapped in a towel. He smiled, sheepishly. "I chickened out," he said. He frowned and pointed. "Are those two done yet?"

Clay laughed. "Let's take a walk," he said.

Erik looked into his face. "Where to?"

"Where would you like to go?"

"I don't care." Erik looked down at his feet. He leaned forward to pull a blade of grass out from between his toes, and this gave Clay more of a chance to lust after him. He looked at Erik's back and legs, which were really quite nice. He suggested that they walk to the gay beach.

He was hoping that the sight of other men his own age rutting in the bushes might inspire Erik to work up an appetite. But he said nothing as they walked along the sand, pretending not to look at the topless lesbians, sunny-side up on their towels. Someone on the beach had brought a CD player with them, and Connie Francis wrenched out a ballad. When the song was over, all the men on the beach clapped. "Sing it, Connie," someone cheered.

Clay asked Erik, "Are you all right?"

The young man shook his head.

They walked back to Omar and Clay's house, and Erik seemed relieved that the other men were toweling each other off, apparently having showered together. Erik and Bruce said little to one another. They walked back home.

Omar turned to Clay, and he chucked him under the chin. "Wasn't that great?" he said. "Didn't I tell you?" The older man caressed Clay, and he kissed him on the forehead. "You get laid, too?"

"Of course I got laid," Clay said. He pulled away, and he walked up to the front window. "I got a blow job in the bushes at the beach. What a man," he said. He tried to sound like Peggy Lee.

Across the street, Erik had just slammed the door. He walked down the front steps with his duffel bag. "I'm only speaking to Clay," he said when Omar answered the door. Omar turned around, and he blew a kiss at Clay.

We'll see how much sympathy pays, Clay thought to himself. He led Erik into the study and slid the doors closed behind them. But when he turned around, he saw that Erik was distraught in the dramatic way that young men often can be. "I can't take it anymore," he told Clay. His shoulders shook, and Clay reached an arm around him.

"What is it?"

Erik brought his face away from the front of Clay's shirt. "I'm leaving Bruce," he said, touching Clay's collar. "I told him to go to hell. Can I stay with you tonight?" Before Clay could answer him, he opened his mouth and cried like Lucille Ball.

Clay made the bed in the guest room while Erik watched. He threw each of the sheets out over his head and spread them out with his arms. The cool, laundered smell of them woke something up inside of him. To make the matter worse, once the bed had been made, Erik sat down on top of it. He looked squarely at Clay, and Clay walked directly to the door. "You all right, kid?"

Erik raised his head as if he was going to say something, but instead he began to cry again.

"Jesus," Clay said. What a noise, he thought.

"I'm fine. Really. I just get like this sometimes."

For a moment Clay thought of showing Erik his pornography collection that lined the walls of the closet. He decided against it. Instead he brought Erik a glass of water from the bathroom, and the young man took it thankfully. "That's better," he said, looking up. He smiled and rolled his moistened eyes at Clay. "Men," he sighed.

"Why don't you crawl into bed and get some sleep?" Clay said. "If you need anything, Omar and I are right down the hall."

"Thank you, Clay. I really appreciate this, I do."

Even before Clay had crawled into bed, he was chastised for not trying to have sex with Erik. "I can't believe you," Omar said. He took his glasses off and set them on the nightstand. "It's clear that he likes you. How can you sleep with that young thing all alone in the next room?"

"If I went to him," Clay said, leaning to kiss Omar good night, "then you'd be alone, silly."

"I don't mind," Omar said. He rolled over to face the window. Clay wrapped an arm around him, and they fell to sleep.

They both slept fine, until Clay felt Omar stiffen next to him. "Wake up," Omar said. "It's Erik." There were soft knockings on the other side of the bedroom door, and Clay pulled his robe on.

"What is it?"

"I'm sorry. You better come here."

"What is it?" Omar asked, sitting up in the dark.

"It's nothing," Erik said, changing his tone. "I'm just freaking out, that's all."

Clay stepped into the hallway and walked directly into him. "It's in the kitchen," Erik said. "I made kind of a mess." Clay turned toward the kitchen, and out of familiarity he walked easily through the dark. Erik followed close behind him, even bumping into him so that Clay felt his young male smell all around himself.

He turned on the light in the kitchen and saw a broken jar of pickles on the floor. Clay snickered. "I'm sorry," Erik said. "I'll pay you for them. I would have picked them up, but I couldn't find where anything is around here."

"The cleaning stuff's in here." Clay pointed to the pantry.

"Stay there," Erik said. "I'll clean it up." He pushed past Clay in his underwear.

"Stand back," Clay said. "Watch the glass." Erik lifted his foot, and there was a trace of blood on the bottom of it. "You okay?"

"Yeah, just a cut." Erik limped back around the broken glass and leaned against the countertop.

"Stay right there," Clay said. He found the light in the pantry, and he got the broom and dustpan. He raked up the rubble. Erik climbed up onto the counter and stuck his feet into the sink. It took him a few seconds to figure out how their postmodern faucet worked. He washed the blood off.

After the glass and pickles had been swept up, Clay mopped the floor. The kitchen smelled like gherkin juice, but the floor looked clean. He glanced at Erik, who rubbed his foot in the running water. "Did you find the glass?"

"Oh, I'm sure it fell out."

"Let me see."

Clay leaned forward and took Erik's foot in his hand. His elbow rested on Erik's leg, and he noticed that he was holding his breath. "Oh, that's not bad at all," Clay said. He looked up, and Erik's face was very close, broad and smooth. The young man finally exhaled, and both of them were kissing. Erik pulled Clay's robe open, and he touched his chest.

Clay struggled not to respond. "Please," he said.

Erik pulled his feet out of the sink, and Clay felt the water drops falling down his legs. Again the young man kissed him.

"Why not?"

"Why do you think?" For a moment Clay thought that Erik might begin to cry. But he stood next to him in the kitchen, looking into his eyes. They listened to the water, still dripping from the faucet.

Erik sighed. "You got a towel?"

"Under the sink."

Clay stepped back. He let Erik get it himself. He watched him drying his feet. When he started to put the towel back under the sink, Clay took it away from him. "We don't like to dry the dishes with toe jam." He tossed it into the hamper in the pantry.

"Sorry," Erik said.

"Oh. You mean the towel? Forget about it," Clay said.

Erik chuckled, embarrassed.

"All set?"

"I'm set. Thanks." Erik smiled his sheepish smile, which seemed to be the only smile he knew, Clay thought. He left him standing alone in the dark of the kitchen. He climbed back into bed, grateful that Omar had fallen to sleep and would not be bothering him with all of that naivete about sex.

In the morning, Erik let himself out without saying good-bye. But Clay heard him go, and he watched through the curtains in a window as Erik crossed the street and knocked on his lover's door. "You have a key," Clay said out loud in the empty bedroom. "Why don't you just open it yourself?" Bruce answered the door, and he stood folding his arms on the porch across the street. When Erik leapt into his lover's arms, Clay muttered to himself. "I thought so," he said. The young men stood in their doorway for several long seconds. He watched them kiss. Finally Bruce carried Erik inside, and the door closed behind them. "I'm glad I'm not young," Clay said, with wonder. He walked back to bed and fell asleep on top of the covers.

When he got back from the grocery store, Omar was as jovial as ever. He set the table on the deck. He clattered the dishes, served up muffins and fruit and toast. Instead of calling Clay to wake him up, he sang the official Girl Scout morning song.

"My," he said, smiling through the cracks of Clay's eyelids. "I told you that's what you needed. It's exactly what you needed. You look so relaxed, Davey. Honestly." He finished his breakfast in two minutes, while Clay sipped his coffee.

"Feel how dry my hands are!" Omar held his hands out in front of him. "It's all that damned chlorine," he said.

Clay looked down at Omar's hands. "They're reptiles," he agreed. Omar carried his dishes back into the house, and he returned a few minutes later dressed in slacks and a bright shirt. He wore a straw hat at what was once called "a rakish angle" and a pair of lemon-colored attitude glasses. He pulled them down on the bridge of his nose to appraise Clay in natural light. He rubbed his hands together, moistly.

Clay could smell the lotion at a distance of a few feet. "My. That makes an interesting noise."

"Very funny."

"You used too much again, didn't you?"

"No."

"You did, too. I can tell from over here."

Omar held out his fingers, which were thick with it.

"You always do! Oh, here." Clay lay the paper flat.

The older man giggled. "I love you so much," he said. He wiggled the toe of one of his shoes into Clay's instep. Clay stretched out his arms, and the two men rubbed each other's hands. "Well," Omar said. "I'm off."

"I'll say. Where are you headed?"

"Tea dance at Bob's, remember?" He kissed Clay on the forehead. "I thought his name was Bill.'"

Omar turned around in the doorwall. He pushed his ridiculous glasses up onto the bridge of his nose. "Whatever," he shrugged, and he left.

Their neighbor, Bill or Bob, or whatever his name was, turned the music up loud. Clay flapped through his newspaper. He left greasy fingerprints through it. When he looked up to admire the annuals, a bird called, "Brit, brit, brit Hume." The nervous laughter of men who had only just met swelled and rose and burst in the air above the house next door.

Cowgirl

Flora Lester never cared for cats. She never allowed pets of any kind into her house proper, as she felt for some reason that animals in general, and felines in particular, were connected to nature, itself primarily composed of filth. Although beer-drinking Mr. Lester loved cats all of his life, he yielded to his wife on this point, as with many other issues. So the Lester cats were stationed outside in the summer, and the Lester children would often find their father sitting on the back stoop, engaged in his peculiarly musical dialogue with them.

By moving the same hands that could make the strings of a piano ring like tiny bells, Mr. Lester created an oddity of music in his cats, often in groups of five or eight. The cats sang obscure low songs that would hypnotize his children with a deep sense of foreboding, but Mr. Lester swayed into ten-minute sessions of inspired praise for their beauty. A few feet away, he could cause a cat to stop and purr upon command. His voice would rise to a falsetto coax, and even the un-tamed and snaggletoothed barn monkeys, sinewy and spitting, would ogle and mew and fly in a leap of faith from an apple tree to his shoulder.

Among the dozens, there was a markedly prolific one named Chardonnay who ejected streams of kittens biannually into the general swarm. Chardonnay had arrived at the Lester farm pregnant to begin with, and nevertheless charming, despite her lopsided tabby dignity and vigorous orgies in the driveway. Although to a large degree and in some respects directly responsible for the great number of cats that stalked and hunted and played in the backyard, Chardonnay was actually a lovely and graceful cat that appeared most contented away from her means of production and lying alone somewhere in sunshine. With no one to clean or feed or to fight over her, she raised a loud purr grooming her luxurious fur.

As the population increased, the cats formed small groups for hunting and social purposes, and small battles broke out over territories and food resources. When Mr. Lester began to refer to the cats less in terms of hard numbers and more in terms of statistics and probability, the children kept by their mother's insistence a half bucket of water by the back door under the outdoor faucet with which to douse nighttime revelers. On summer nights when the noise was most exceptionally loud, she brought her white Bible to the dinner table. Mrs. Lester read to her children, a chapter at a time, the entire Book of Job. She used the word "plague" to describe the cats' negative influence on everyone's sleep. Mr. Lester called it a "Mardi Gras."

The children never tired of this continuous evidence of the life process revealed, and were just as excited when another new litter began to be born one early-summer evening after a rain had settled the dust in the road and the crickets had begun their vibratory rhythms. Olive and Betty showed Clayton how to make confetti out of the Sunday newspaper, and as rapidly as possible, he filled a cardboard box in order to house the litter. He was finished before any of the kittens were born. However, the cat refused the children's offering of a more-sterile delivery room. She lay on her side on a patch of straw that had remained from the previous winter's bales placed all around the foundation of the uninsulated house by Mr. Lester in an effort to keep his own family warm. Chardonnay lay unproductive for a good half hour under the Lesters' back porch, resting, apparently, from the bloody deliberation of her initial and unsuccessful attempts, before Olive realized that something was wrong.

After begging their mother through the voluminous billow of a stretch of white bedsheet half hung on the clothesline, Clayton raced to the rumbling Kelvinator and discovered under a plastic saucer a single wedge of Mrs. Lester's pickled bologna, so completely fermented that it had become to many of those more vulgar in conversation, legendary in its laxative effect. Ignorant of the complex biology of the female anatomy, Clayton reached through the ivory arms and shanks of his hovering sisters and fed the piece of meat to the cat.

Chardonnay devoured the pickled bologna and delivered her kittens in a rapid succession of nine abdominal clinches. Only after she had licked them dry with her bologna breath, Wallace removed the kittens as if they were fragile eggs and nestled them into Clayton's fresh nest. She accepted the manhandling of her babies begrudgingly, and pulled herself up over the flimsy wall of the box to nurse them. Olive and Betty stepped backward and folded their arms over their cardigans, while Wallace and Dortha and Clayton matched kitten mouths with nipples. The children shared for a moment, however briefly, that sentiment of warmth and relief and accomplishment associated with such primal stuff.

Then two women came tearing up the driveway on their English racers. One of them turned out to be a relative, a fifth cousin of Clayton's, and when he was told this and introduced to the stranger, a young woman with straight blonde hair and an infectious smile, his curiosity was piqued. So this was a fifth cousin, he thought: a woman with breasts. He had only just begun to include breasts in his drawings. However tapered and mealy he managed to gouge the bosoms in crayon onto the front of his figures, in houses, over landscapes, in the clouds when he was so inspired, this had been a risky departure in Clayton's style, particularly in the religious and fastidious Lester home. He took it as a sign of his budding artistic prowess that what he had drawn, which at times produced magical feelings in himself, could pronounce themselves in real life so amply.

Wynnona and her friend Paquitta needed a place to stay for a night after riding their bikes all the way from Pennsylvania, where they attended Bible college. They were visiting various of Wynnona's relatives, even the Lesters, who hardly remembered Wynnona from the last family reunion, and the two young women needed a place to recuperate before the next hundred miles they were to ride. All through dinner Clayton stared at Wynnona's Mexican friend with an unnameable intent. Paquitta had the darkest complexion of anyone he had ever seen in his life — face-to-face, of course. She wore a cowboy hat and enormous boots, with which she kicked the table legs from time to time throughout the meal. She looked like a genuine cowgirl.

James Russell Mayes

Before they went to bed in the downstairs guest bedroom, Wynnona and Paquitta sprawled themselves on the carpet in the living room, groaning from what Paquitta called their "saddle sores."

"How's life at the Bible college?" Mr. Lester asked them.

"I quit," Wynnona said. "I dropped out. I'm gone. History."

Mrs. Lester gave her cousin a concerned frown. "Whatever for?" she asked.

Wynnona pointed at Paquitta and said, "We both did. Right, Paquitta?" Paquitta nodded evenly. "I'd say we had a change of heart, Aunt Flora."

"Mother's not your aunt," Dortha interrupted, showing off a bit. "She's your first cousin once removed. That makes us fifth cousins." She smiled and tugged at her naturally curly hair.

Wynnona smiled. "That's right. I forgot."

Paquitta nodded. She went through a series of gestures and hesitations, but by this time everyone in the family knew that she intended to speak: "Was for the birds," she said, "Bible college," without too much difficulty. The Lester family nodded and laughed with polite encouragement at the foreigner who had mastered an American cliche.

"*How* for the birds?" Wallace asked.

The visitors exchanged looks. Wynnona rose from the floor and stretched herself, yawning. "I think it's time we got to bed, don't you think, Paquitta?" She winked at her friend, and Paquitta stretched out a weary arm. Wynnona pulled her up. They disappeared into the guest room, and no one heard a sound from them until the next day.

Reverend Bennett called the next morning. He had recently returned from missionary work in Africa and had brought with him a guest from the mission hospital, a doctor M'Butu who had "always wanted to see" the United States. The men had intended to surprise the Lesters with a visit, but at the last minute Reverend Bennett called, "Just in case you might be able to perform something musical for us," he said to Mrs. Lester. The Lesters had what might be loosely called a family band. It wasn't an especially good family band, but what the children lacked in virtuosity they made up for in volume. Mrs. Lester groaned silently to herself. The house had not yet been cleaned. The children had not practiced recently. Even so, she could not bring herself to say no to a minister of any persuasion. She hung up the phone and raised up a shout: "You have half an hour to finish your breakfast," she said severely. "After that, you'll help me clean the house."

There was a long session of shouts and giggles on the landing under the stairs, and eventually Wynnona and Paquitta joined the Lester family at the breakfast table. They were still in their bathrobes, although Paquitta's slid open to reveal an inch or so of cleavage, Clayton noticed, and Wynnona wore a brilliantly colored flowered one. "That's from Mexico, isn't it?" Mrs. Lester said, spilling her cereal. She scooped it into a pile on the tablecloth and walked back to the cupboard in silence. She returned with the box, and poured herself more with her enormous hands. She walked back to the cupboard and slammed the door.

Meanwhile Wynnona and Paquitta seated themselves next to one another at the end of the long table. Wynnona pinched her friend's bare leg, and Paquitta giggled in hysterical bursts that made Clayton jump each time in his chair. The children waited through fifteen long minutes, crunching and chewing quickly and otherwise silent, before they were done and, suddenly shy, excused themselves from the table.

Clayton's chore was to clean the stairs, which lowered into the living room. From the top step where he started, he saw Wynnona and Paquitta slip into the guest room at the foot of the stairs. Clayton always performed the best work that he could while sweeping the stairs, but he still took as long as possible. He knew that as soon as he was through, he was supposed to help his sisters, who were making the beds. He brushed with the whisk broom and scooped with the dustpan. He had reached a point about halfway down the stairs. He was singing a popular song he had often heard on the radio: "Chickaboom, chickaboom, don't you just love it?" and he heard a giggle from the guest bedroom.

"Stopstopstopstop," Paquitta screamed, and she burst into laughter.

Clayton paused for a moment on the stairs. Obliquely, he recalled that he was supposed to be working faster because of the impending visit of Reverend Bennett and his guest from Africa. With as much clatter as possible, he made his way down the stairs to the bottom step. It became necessary for his ear to be placed only inches from the closed

James Russell Mayes

door. He was bending over to sweep the last step, when he heard once more the giggling of his cousin's friend.

Wynnona herself laughed right out loud. Clayton distinctly heard her say, several times, "Get off me. Get off!"

He ignored the magical feelings that kindled in his ears, and he returned his brush and dustpan to its place in the closet off the dining room. Clayton reclimbed the newly cleaned steps to help his sisters make the beds. The sheets still wafted the comforting smell of the out-of-doors and fresh-mown lawn as they floated down through the air to cover Wally and Clayton's mattress.

"Look who came to help," Betty said.

Olive was less positive. "Your room is a mess. What is that smell?"

Clayton tucked in the corners of the fitted sheet and stood near enough to the bed as the flat sheet fell to feel the breeze of fresh air against his face. "Chickaboom, chickaboom," he sang quietly.

"You better not let Mother hear you sing that song," Olive said.

"What's wrong with that song? I like that song."

She said, "It's dirty."

"It is not."

"It is too. It's about sex." Clayton tried to remember the rest of the words. He wondered what the part about sex was. He managed while the song continued to reel through his head to keep it from his lips through the next three beds that were made, through the double bed and the single bed jammed into the girls' room, and the large one of his mother and father's. When he finally could not contain the song, and it burst forth again, Dortha called him a "pervert."

The final bed they had to make was the bed in the room at the bottom of the stairs, the room which Wynnona and Paquitta were using. Olive and Dortha made themselves busy gathering the great clumps of dirty sheets. Betty told Clayton that he should run downstairs and tell Wynnona and Paquitta that they were coming down to clean up their room.

"You do it."

"Don't be funny," Betty said, gathering a pillowcase out from behind the door. "They should be outta there, anyway. It's late!"

Olive said, "Remember what Mother said. You're supposed to do whatever we tell you to do when you're helping us."

"That's right," said Dortha.

So under their instruction Clayton walked down the stairs. The door to the only bedroom on the first story of the Lester home had never latched, and for this reason one always had to hold onto the doorknob while one knocked in order to keep the whole from swaying breezily inward. After the moment that it took to collect himself in the face of what had suddenly become an odd silence behind the door, Clayton held onto the doorknob with one hand and knocked with the other. He held his ear up to the door. He heard a rustling sound. There was still no answer. He knocked again. He returned his ear to the cool wooden surface of the door.

"Yes?" It was Paquitta. She sounded irritable.

His cousin asked: "Who is it?"

"It's me," Clayton said. "We have to come in and clean up your room."

"Now?"

"Mother said. You know the minister is bringing over that doctor from Africa."

"The minister?" Wynnona cursed. It was the first time Clayton had ever heard a relative, even a distant one, use such language. This was not technically a swear word, or at least not one of those specifically forbidden by God in the Ten Commandments, because it was not an example of His name in vain. However, there were other words one could use in order to allude to certain vulgar bodily necessities that in the Lester family were considered ill choice for conversation. Clayton was surprised. As a result he said nothing.

Into the living room Wallace dragged the old Eureka vacuum cleaner. Even above the noise, Clayton heard Paquitta, laughing uproariously. He considered if Paquitta might be the kind of demon sent straight from hell to make people do and think things evil. His cousin Wynnona said, "Shit," and Paquitta the cowgirl laughed about it. He couldn't believe it.

Olive and Betty and Dortha had been watching from the top of the stairs. The three sisters descended with their piles of wadded dirty sheets. Dropping these in separate chairs in the living room, Betty commanded Clayton to move away from the door. Betty and Olive walked up to it. They spoke loudly to each other above the sound of the vacuum.

"The living room doesn't look big enough when this door is closed," Olive said.

"It wouldn't matter so much," Betty added, "if it weren't the downstairs bedroom. It's right off the living room, so it has to be clean."

There followed a pause of a few beats, in which they heard more giggles and a curious smacking sound. Clayton's sisters turned around. "Go get Mother," they said to him, in unison.

Mrs. Lester was cleaning the kitchen linoleum and trying to wash the breakfast dishes at the same time. She did not wish to be interrupted. Clayton explained the problem to her as best as he could explain it, and because of her stern silence, he followed closely behind her through the house and into the living room, feeling vaguely that something interesting might happen. Mrs. Lester told Wallace to shut off the vacuum cleaner. As if ignorant of the loud laughter that carried into the living room, she walked up to the guest bedroom door, placed one hand on the doorknob, and pounded with her closed fist. She paused for a couple seconds. She pounded again.

"What do you want?" This time Wynnona was the first to speak, and she sounded irritated, too.

"You're going to have to get up and get out of bed and get ready because we have company coming over." Perhaps because she was in a hurry, Mrs. Lester shouted louder than was necessary. "Olive and Betty need to clean up that room and get new sheets for the bed." There was a moment or two of waiting, in which it sounded to Clayton that the women were holding a hasty counsel behind the door to the bedroom. He couldn't tell for sure, because his ear was not flattened against it. Then, "Okay," Wynnona called.

Olive and Betty sat back on the couch, and Clayton leaned back in his favorite chair in the corner of the living room to wait for them. The women did not take long to open the door, perhaps because they did not bother to dress themselves before bursting out into the living room. One moment they had resumed laughing and giggling, and just before the door opened, there was another loud "smack." Paquitta tore out of the bedroom with her bathrobe barely tied. Wynnona ran out right behind her, hair flying. They skipped over the vacuum cleaner and its cord. They ran through the dining room and into the kitchen and on into the bathroom off the kitchen.

The children rushed into the bedroom.

"Look at this bed," Olive said.

Betty agreed, "It's a mess!"

Clayton looked around the bed on the floor. He looked under the bed, too. He could not find anything unusual or out of place. "What are they doing?" he asked, ears throbbing.

"Clayton," Betty cautioned.

"What?"

"They're probably taking a shower," she said. Olive giggled. "You be quiet, Olive."

"Together?"

"Yeah," Betty said, throwing Clayton a pillow and then a pillowcase. "Why not? Paquitta's a Mexican. They don't have as much water in Mexico. That's why everybody drinks tequila all the time."

Olive said, "Mother and Father used to take showers together."

"Really?"

"Yes, but that was before we went to the Congregational Church."

"You two get to work."

Clayton was smelling one of the pillows. It must have been Paquitta's pillow, because it smelled like she did: dry and sweet and musky. It was a familiar smell, but he could not think of what it reminded him of. The open road, perhaps. The hair on his arm prickled up: magic, again. He pulled the pillowcase off the pillow, smelled it once more, and threw it into the basket of dirty sheets they took into the laundry room. The children were finally done with their chores.

They turned on the TV and tried to watch the *Andy Griffith Show* while Wallace vacuumed away under their feet. Once he turned it off and put it away, they could hear Aunt Bee telling Andy Griffith that he needed to treat his girlfriend "more special," that a girl needs "respect," to "feel pretty" now and then. Mrs. Lester came inside from hosing the duck poop off of the patio. She hollered for the girls to haul in the kitchen rug. Somebody said something about the kittens, which Clayton had forgotten in the race to clean the house. He clattered back outside. Chardonnay had licked the bloody film off her kittens. They had dried in the warmth of their box.

Fresh from the shower, hair still dripping, Wynnona and Paquitta walked outside in their bathrobes. They picked their way in their bare feet across the puddles on the patio. Paquitta raised up a great howl of "Kitties, kitties, oh, kitties." She had to be told by Wallace, as the girls stepped forward threateningly, that she couldn't pick them up because they were still too young. "If you touch them," Wynnona explained, pressing her arm into Paquitta's back as Dortha and Clayton watched with fascination, "the mother cat will smell you on their fur. She'll abandon them." This was a lie, of course. If the two had not been otherwise occupied, the women could have seen the children handling them gingerly only just before breakfast.

Reverend Bennett was vigorous and smiling, but Congregationalist to the bone. "Welcome," he would say at the church door. His smile would pull across his wide face and reveal not only the space between each tooth and a rather wide tongue, but also the flush of his tonsils, his uvula. When he was not inoculating the black children of Africa against the evils of their heathen lives, he volunteered as librarian for the area schools, including high school and elementary.

Reverend Bennett was the man who taught Clayton how to open a new book properly, how to carefully stretch the binding to keep it from breaking. As a result of the minister's guidance, Clayton learned how to appreciate the hypnotic smell of a fresh text, which like the poppies that Judy Garland lay among with Toto, would cause in him another form of magic, a dreamlike state of imagination and passion. Clayton would fall asleep with his face against the smooth pages and dream of black dancing stick people who played drums and rode in airplanes and danced a secret language with their arms and legs.

It was only ten o'clock when Reverend Bennett drove his yellow Volkswagen Beetle up the driveway and flipped open his door. He opened the door for the black man who held his face above the dash in the passenger seat. Doctor M'Butu unwrapped his arms from around his knees, leaned far back in his seat, and then unrolled a single leg onto the gravel driveway. Reverend Bennett negotiated the weight of his hips into a leverage device by lowering them, and by leaning back at the same time, he pulled Doctor M'Butu out of the car by his arm. "Reverend Bennett," Clayton had once heard a woman say in church, "was made like a race car. He's built low to the ground, for fast turns."

Dortha pulled Clayton away from the window and out the back door so that he could stand in a row with the rest of his sisters and brother, with their neatly parted heads of hair, their freshly scrubbed faces. Clayton had forgotten to wash his glasses, and so he stared at the doctor. Doctor M'Butu was black: not brown-black, but black-black. His skin was so shiny in the daylight that it looked polished. Reverend Bennett's pantcuffs flapped around him as he pulled his guest up to the end of the sidewalk where the Lester children waited to meet him in their clean shoes. Doctor M'Butu smiled and extended both large hands to Mr. Lester, who craned his neck back and looked up into his face while taking them both in his own small, delicately musical ones. He stepped on the tiptoes of his shoes in comedy of their difference in height, and Doctor M'Butu laughed. It was the first sound the children heard from him.

"Pleased to meet you," he said. He shook hands down the line of children, past Wynnona and Paquitta, who were ever so much more interesting, until he came to Clayton, who stared at the pointed toes of Doctor M'Butu's shoes. Clayton heard the man's laughter above him in the sky. He felt the breath of Doctor M'Butu in the moist part of his hair. "Such lovely babies. These two," he said, and he raised the stickshift of his index finger to third gear. "Are they twins?" Of course he was pointing at Dortha and Clayton, still the youngest and therefore the cutest. Clayton stiffened, and he felt his younger sister stiffen alongside of him.

"You are so cute," he said. "What is your name?" Doctor M'Butu squatted to look directly into the children's eyes. He looked most intently at Dortha. And Dortha was as frightened as Clayton.

"That's Dortha," Reverend Bennett said. He leaned so that the lower half of his body tipped forward and required the support of his hands on his pant creases. "She's adorable, isn't she?"

"That she is," Doctor M'Butu said. "That she is." He peered around at the Lester barnyard, strewn with various rusted farm implements and the chickens that used them as perches to escape the pervasive hunger of cats. Since it had rained the night before, most of the cats, with the exception of the few handicapped by disease or childbirth, had retreated to the barn for shelter. An old tom that the children called Deadbeat, with one eye and a fly-infested wound on his back, reclined in the mud by the patio, repeatedly scratching his head. Mother ducks and their young were twitching their rumps in the deep puddles that formed within the ruts of the driveway. Doctor M'Butu said, "What a lovely farm."

"Shall we go inside?" Reverend Bennett was eager.

But Doctor M'Butu seemed enthralled by whatever it was that he saw in the place. He looked out beyond the spilled chaff and the white down that had collected in gray heaps around the edges of the mud puddles. Clayton wondered if the man had ever seen a barnyard before. Doctor M'Butu looked back down into Mr. Lester's face. "Is there a place where we might go to walk?"

Mr. Lester pointed with his arm past the patio and out toward the fallow fields, the swamp, the woods. They walked up the steps to the patio, followed by Reverend Bennett, who held onto the front of his pantcuffs with both hands in order to keep them from dragging through the dirt. The children followed. Doctor M'Butu's hands were what caught Clayton's attention. Although the back of them was blacker than any black Clayton had seen on a man, the inner flesh was pink and as fair as his own.

Since Mrs. Lester had hosed and raked the duck poop off the patio, there was little for them to pick their way through except Deadbeat, who stretched himself and blinked one good eye at them. With a sympathetic sigh, Doctor M'Butu bent to pick him up, perhaps only to stroke him, perhaps to pry open his one glued eye. But Deadbeat had a peculiar bowel disease, so Olive distracted the doctor with the kittens under the porch door. Doctor M'Butu squealed delightedly as she placed an orange one like a bit of fuzzy fruit in his hands.

Paquitta glared at Wynnona, in protest, one would guess, of the handling of the helpless kitten by Olive and the doctor. But Wynnona cautioned her with a frown into a poutful silence. The group was walking peaceably up the driveway to the fallow fields, and if it had not been for a noise from the barn, a cross between a cough and a bray, they could have reached the swamp without incident.

"What is that peculiar noise?" Doctor M'Butu asked. Reverend Bennett, by now well familiar with the Lester family and the Lester family farm, looked nervously from side to side. A wisp, a curl of his hair popped out onto his forehead.

"Oh, that's our horse Cody," Clayton explained. "He's gotten a bad cough." As soon as he said it, he realized he should not have said anything or made something up, because he already had learned that most people think, when one says the word "horse," of an animal that is beautiful and friendly with a well-brushed coat and a star on its forehead: something called "Prince" that a boy could sleep with and feed apples. His thoughtless words brought the doctor's attention to the backside of the barn.

Cody had his head stuck out through one of the holes caused by a tractor accident. Although the children tried to convince him that Cody was all right, and that he only called attention to himself in order to be petted, Doctor M'Butu insisted on getting a good look inside his pen before he was convinced that what the Lesters had and called a horse was really a very old, very sick animal. Olive explained that a horse was never born with the scoop in its back like an inverted camel, and that hooves could grow longer than a rocking horse's struts if they were not properly trimmed. Doctor M'Butu agreed that, yes, it was only Christian charity that kept Mr. Lester from killing Cody mercifully and burying him well away from the rest of the stock, or the well.

Reverend Bennett, who had himself made a similar mistake in conceptualizing farm life and had brought upon himself a small series of disasters with a colony of rats, tried to sway him, but Doctor M'Butu insisted on taking a look at the rest of the stock. This meant that the children had to show him the bull inside of the pen where they were too afraid to go to haul out the manure so that his head nearly scraped the nails through the low ceiling above his head and he had to kneel in order to eat out of the manger; their seven pigs with their young collie Shep who had also come from a litter of that number and for this reason had become imprinted when his siblings were taken from him and now ate and slept with the pigs, even sharing ears of corn and lying in the mud with them.

All while they toured the Lester barn, there were darting motions around their heads, some of which were pigeons in flight and some of which, in less graceful bursts, were the barn cats pursuing them. As Reverend Bennett threw his glances here and there around the perimeter of the floor, the children led him even farther down the passage that led into the deepest recess of the barn. Clayton saw as he walked behind him, that Doctor M'Butu's back shivered. A pigeon in flight neatly missed a cat descending from the great darkness of wooden beams and ascending ladders above them, and Reverend Bennett jumped. Doctor M'Butu put out his hand into the air between them, as if about to steady him. Out from behind a smoldering bale of hay, a skinny old tomcat dragged a dead rat. There was a sudden silence, except for the cooing of the pigeons and the spat curse of the tomcat, as other cats climbed down from the lofts and ladders above. With narrow green eyes, the hunter bit through the broken neck of his prey. There was an audible crunching of bone.

Reverend Bennett exclaimed, "I think I am going to be sick." He turned and vomited onto his shoes. Paquitta moaned something in Spanish. Mrs. Lester found a handkerchief for him. Reverend Bennett wiped his mouth. The barn cats forgot the rat and gathered around his feet. The cats twitched their tails. Reverend Bennett leaned forward to wipe his shoes with straw. In a voice as smooth as a nighttime radio announcer, Doctor M'Butu turned around in the walkway and suggested that perhaps they might find the out-of-doors more suitable for the type of conversation that would allow them all to become better acquainted? The barn cats growled. They licked their kinky whiskers and sniffed at the puddle that the minister left behind.

They walked to the fallow fields and halfway down the fallow fields, and the sun came out from behind a cloud. Cabbage butterflies and imperial moths darted about in the tall grass of the fields. A breeze crashed up the hill from the swamp. The racket of red-winged blackbirds was like a great chorus. Without speaking, the group picked its way through the ruts and rocks of the hill they never cultivated because they used it for sledding, and down to the swamp where the cattails burled up their brown fingers on long green stalks, where the nests and colorful shoulders of the blackbirds bled through the drab green of the foliage.

Doctor M'Butu and Reverend Bennett stood for a long moment at the edge, on top of the brush pile the children had erected for just such a purpose summers before, by now decomposed to a dry pile of sticks and grass on which one could stand to survey the largely submerged lives of turtles. Clayton could hear the single bullfrog and took great breaths of that odor which was the smell of what was alive and the smell of what was most recently dead, mixing in the thick stew which was their swamp, the children's playground, the habitation of many of Clayton's dreams.

A single iris, "a flag," as Mrs. Lester called them, grew along the edge of where the deeper muck met the part where there was enough water to reflect the blue of the sky and its clouds. Doctor M'Butu put his hand on Clayton's shoulder in order to balance himself. Clayton felts his ears flush redly. Doctor M'Butu unlaced his black shoe, and then removed a sock. He rolled up the pant leg of his right leg, leaving his left leg and foot completely clothed. Clayton saw that, like the palm of his hands, the sole of the doctor's foot was fleshy and tenderly pink. How opposite his own feet and hands were, which blackened when they slapped against the earth. By the end of a given summer day, when his sisters stood ankle-deep in the water that they drew into the bathtub, and Clayton stepped in to join them in this summer nightly ritual of washing their feet, he would look down at his own feet under the water and the dirt would explode in dark clouds from the cracks between his toes, even up the backs of his legs.

They all drew in a breath as one, Reverend Bennett's quite audible, as Doctor M'Butu placed his enormous foot on top of the mud, and it disappeared with a sucking sound. The doctor squealed delightedly. He reached out far over the surface of the grime of the swamp and pulled out the stalk of the iris by its roots. Pulling himself back out of the water like a man on stilts at the circus walking up a flight of very steep steps, he turned and presented the iris, stalk and fan of leaves and all, not to Paquitta or Wynnona, not to Olive or Betty or Dortha, but to Reverend Bennett. Reverend Bennett looked surprised himself, and although he blushed with pleasure, evidently he did not know what to say. He raised both of his eyebrows in an expression the Lester family associated with his sermon on miracles, or his expression in prayer, if one had bothered to open his eyes. He smelled the iris, and he smelled it again, incapable of differentiating its delicate aroma from the volume of fertile smells which filled the air around them.

Dortha and Clayton exchanged looks, and then investigated the responses of the older children around them. No one had even noticed. Clayton and Dortha had observed the same curious phenomenon when Margaret Akin had whipped off her bra in the front room and stuck her baby Carmine's face right onto her exposed bosom and he snorkled away like a pig. A similar thing had occurred when after their maternal grandmother died, Reverend Brawn passed gas loudly for a solid thirty-five seconds in the elevator at the hospital. No one said a word. It was as if nothing had happened, and only the youngest of all of them knew: yet everybody had to know that something very important had happened.

"There is something about a swamp," Doctor M'Butu said. He turned and smiled at Reverend Bennett, who smiled back showing all of his teeth. "What a lovely place," the doctor said to the minister. The tone of his voice implied that he was speaking only to him, to no one else. "It is like the Garden of Eden."

"Well," Reverend Bennett recovered, perhaps in an effort to incorporate spiritual priority into the conversation at hand, "I would hardly say it is as beautiful as that, although it does bring forth that paradise from the Word of God." He pulled at another wisp of hair that had fallen onto the great width of his forehead. He tucked it under the rest of his dark curls. He looked around at the children, as if he had suddenly forgotten they were there, and he smiled. "Don't we have a concert to attend?"

The children watched as Doctor M'Butu balanced himself, once again using Clayton's shoulder for the purpose. He slipped on his long dark sock and laced up his shoes. The group turned around loosely and walked back up to the house, picking their way through the stones and ruts of the hill and back up through the Queen Anne's lace and timothy weed that bordered the fallow fields. "Chickaboom, chickaboom." This time Clayton heard the words to the song, but he was not singing them. He hadn't even been thinking of them. "Don't you just love it." Reverend Bennett was singing it, a popular song: a song that was played on the radio, a song about sex.

They reached the house, and Wynnona and Paquitta were conspicuously absent from their party. The children marched through the kitchen where their mother had been busy making preparations, and out into the front room where Doctor M'Butu and Reverend Bennett settled themselves into the two least uncomfortable chairs. They fussed over their guests. Reverend Bennett said yes, he'd love some tea, while Doctor M'Butu waved away the plate of Hostess Ding

Dongs. Clayton felt a slight wind from the doctor's hands. His ears were athrob once more.

✄

Before the concert, Wallace organized a formal search through the house for Wynnona and Paquitta. Clayton's job was to search the basement, so he turned on the light and looked down and saw that the basement had flooded from the rain. Now under normal circumstances, he would have listened and heard the noise of the Lester sump pump evacuating the rainwater, and he did recall that it had been humming away that morning when he had been sent to the basement to retrieve the cafeteria-sized can of Campbell's Tomato Soup that his mother would serve for lunch.

The appropriate action for Clayton to take would have been to pull the string to the lightbulb at the foot of the stairs in order to disengage the motor of the sump pump and to descend into the basement after putting on high rubber boots in order to investigate the specific nature of the problem. However, this sounded like a great deal of work to him, and he knew that a more immediate problem was to find Wynnona and Paquitta. They could not possibly have been wading around in a flooded basement, and because he also knew that the Lester family choral performance was immediately at hand, he decided that this complicated operation could be delayed until the guests left. Clayton did intend to notify his father or Wallace of the problem as soon as he turned off the light and closed the door behind himself.

Clayton returned to the living room. He heard Doctor M'Butu and Reverend Bennett speaking to one another in unusual tones. Perhaps what followed is the actual reason that he ultimately neglected to notify anyone of the dilemma of the sump pump. Since no one else had yet come back from their search, he stood outside the double doors to the living room and heard a key exchange:

"But I'm not a very good cook at all," Reverend Bennett said, as if severely displeased with himself. "I can't cook. I've never been able to cook. I can do anything else. I can sew. I can give enemas. But I am so disappointed that I can't cook for you, Bobo."

"Don't worry about that," Doctor M'Butu replied, consolingly. "Once you return to Africa with me, you will learn. And if not, we will hire a cook. All of that doesn't matter. What matters, my dear..."

The Reverend interrupted him in a whisper, sharply: "What matters is that we love the Lord."

Clayon heard Wallace's sturdy step on the stairs. The two men in the living room must have heard Wallace, too, for they were quiet instantly.

"Not upstairs," Wallace said. He punched Clayton in the shoulder, which was his usual form of punctuation.

Since they could not find Wynnona and Paquitta anywhere inside the house, including in the guest bedroom, to which the door hung open at the bottom of the stairs, the Lester children rearranged their parts in the medley slightly. Since Mrs. Lester continued the search alone, they eliminated the song which featured her saxophone solo.

Mr. Lester opened up their short medley of religious favorites as he always did, with the back of his hand clearing away all of the false notes out of the air with a glissando up the keyboard. Clayton and Dortha were pushed by the others toward the front where the scratches in their knees would show. Their father hit the note that Dortha should sing. She lined up her voice as keenly as she could: melody. Clayton also sang melody, because although his voice was strong, he couldn't keep track of all of the notes that would swim around his ears in the air. Although he did not yet play a musical instrument, Clayton sang with the best of them. However, he knew only two ways how to sing, and either he sang vaguely high or even more vaguely low, depending upon what effect was required.

His voice joined in below Dortha's, and after another "plink" of triple notes from Mr. Lester, the voices of Olive and Betty joined in. They sang alto, their father a masculinized alto, and Wallace a bass that he could not manage without a cough at the end of each phrase. Their individual notes became a chord which swelled in the air. They sang a Christianized version of "Bridge over Troubled Waters" in which the first-person-singular pronoun had been replaced by the third-person, with the obvious implication that "He" should refer, as it would in any old song out of a hymnal, to God Himself. Christian plagiarism feeds off of love songs on the pop chart. Perhaps one day there will be a Congregationalist version of "Chickaboom, Chickaboom," as well.

Having given up the search, Mrs. Lester clattered in with her dead mother's silver tea set. Reverend Bennett asked Doctor M'Butu if he wanted sugar. He said no, but he did want some cream, so Mrs. Lester had to walk back through to the kitchen in order to get the Borden's Half-and-Half. Meanwhile, Dortha had made her feet go pigeon-toed, so that Clayton had to remind her of it, and he meant to give her a slight kick with his shoe against her shoe, but he missed. Dortha stopped singing completely and kicked Clayton back, and since Wallace missed the sound of their two voices, which he used as a musical yardstick by which to measure his own tentative bass, his voice cracked. He broke into an eerie falsetto version of the high notes that Olive and Betty were singing. Dortha found her note and picked it up only a beat after they lost Wallace, but Clayton was holding his foot. He could not find the note inside of his head, no matter how he stabbed for it. In his nervousness, he felt himself about to wet his pants.

Sensing a problem, Mr. Lester cleared his throat. He stopped his own singing to listen, but continued to play with his back to the children. Mrs. Lester bustled back into the room. She gave Clayton a sharp look out of the corner of her eye before she set the cream cow onto the silver tea tray, a look that would shrivel a barn cat. Clayton found his note. Betty tugged at Wallace's ear, his adenoids shifted, and he too was back down with the rest of them. The next breath Clayton took felt sweeter than all of the rest that had come before it. They proceeded through their brief selections of "My Holy Valentine" and "The Lord from Ipanema" without further incident. Mr. Lester played beautiful, tricky little segues between each of the five verses of the songs they had selected.

Throughout the performance, Doctor M'Butu, who might be forgiven because he was unaware of what he was doing, had kept up a steady albeit low conversation with Reverend Bennett about the respective ages of the children and the order in which they had been born, the occupation of Mr. Lester, or the lack thereof, and even a general appraisal of their talent. Reverend Bennett raised his teacup to his lips, his broad shoulders to his ears, and giggled through the gaps in his teeth.

The penultimate song the Lester Family Choir was to sing was actually to be a duet that Olive and Betty sang, twitteringly high, while the rest of the children and their father hummed quietly. For this reason, Dortha and Clayton were to step aside and Olive and Betty were to step forward from out of the rest of the group. Somehow Clayton's feet got tangled up. Perhaps he wasn't paying attention or perhaps he wasn't used to wearing his clean shoes on the bumpy carpet in the living room, but he fell backward into Wallace, who, without much thought, shoved him forward into Doctor M'Butu. Without hesitation, the doctor's enormous knees opened up as if to receive him. Clayton felt his face against the tan linen crotch of the slacks, ears pounding.

It is to his credit that Doctor M'Butu was not angry, that he did not spill his tea or advise the young boy that he almost bit the weasel. Clayton was himself at pains to regain his fifth-grade composure while setting himself upright without placing his hand on any of the more prominent creases in the doctor's trousers. But he managed, with some assistance from his sister Betty, to raise himself from the soft lap to which he had involuntarily swooped. As soon as possible, he was back and singing with his sisters and brother.

But just as Olive and Betty resumed their duet, there was a great commotion at the back door. Mrs. Lester raised from her lap the tray of sugar cookies from which she had been eating with both hands. She dropped it gingerly into Reverend Bennett's lap and left the room. Olive and Betty were singing a lovely selection for two such beautiful and high voices. At one point Olive would sing the melody and then at the next she would pass it to Betty so that in his own Disneyfied imagination, Clayton thought of two birds, swallows perhaps, holding either end of a ribbon in their tiny beaks and working together to unwrap a package or to embroider a pillowcase. The commotion at the back door eventually subsided, except for a small shriek from Mrs. Lester. This was followed by the slam of the door to Wynnona and Paquitta's bedroom. A peculiar silence rose up behind the humming of the children like a great ominous cloud. Out of this silence, Deadbeat ran like a demon from the face of God with Mrs. Lester right behind him with a broom. The old tomcat looked around the room for a place to hide, and finding one, he raced for the trembling pantcuffs of Reverend Bennett, made his way upward, and dug into the man's lap.

Reverend Bennett rose to scream out the last note of Olive and Betty's duet. It was a perfect third above and in creepy harmony and closure to the performance, while Deadbeat, still suffering a gross intestinal problem brought on by the feasts of Mrs. Lester's pickled bologna that the children had been secretly feeding to him from their dinner plates, and a fear of brooms, ejected copious bursts of bright green fecal matter like a hose through the air, most of it all onto Doctor M'Butu.

Mr. Lester, having finished humming the last song without hearing the voices of his children behind him, must have felt himself to be in the familiar position of adlibbing a solo. He heightened the drama with which he performed the final number but paused at the end of each verse as if expecting someone, anyone, to join in. He turned his head, finally, and familiar with such scenes, he lifted his hands from the keyboard and twirled around on the spinning piano stool.

Reverend Bennett had placed his hands into his front pockets in order to prevent further damage. A long green curl of liquid extended under Deadbeat's tail and trailed down the man's leg. Mrs. Lester unhooked Deadbeat's claws from the minister's crotch. She accepted a towel from Betty and wrapped up Deadbeat, who degenerated into a mass of spit and claws. She handed this animated package to Clayton, and under her instruction he struggled with it through the dining room and the kitchen. Once more Clayton was called upon to think for himself, and upon brief consideration, since he knew that there were newborn kittens hidden in the space under the porch where he would soon release a trapped animal and that Reverend Bennett and Doctor M'Butu were probably not going to stay very much longer after this most recent event, he opened up the door to the cellar and rolled the towel out like a red carpet so that the end of it lifted Deadbeat just a bit into the air. He rolled down two steps before he reached out a stained paw and caught himself.

By the time Clayton re-entered the living room, his mother had momentarily disappeared with Reverend Bennett and Doctor M'Butu, obviously to provide assistance and comfort as they cleansed them- selves of personal and spiritual injury. Olive applied a wet soapy rag to the paintlike stain in the carpet. Everyone else was quietly seated, so Clayton also sat down, in his favorite chair in the corner of the front room. Once the music of the concert had been eliminated, however, other noises to which they were heretofore oblivious were now increasing in volume. This was the first thing that Clayton noticed. Behind the closed door of Wynnona and Paquitta's bedroom, Paquitta was screaming.

Anyone sitting in the living room would have come to her aid immediately, if she had not then laughed immediately afterward. She laughed outright. It sounded to Clayton as he pictured it, that she was laughing with her mouth widely open. She screamed again, a series of little screams, actually, followed by a loud guffaw. Each of these screams elongated itself into a curiously musical note and was punctuated by a smacking sound of equal duration. The effect was rhythmic and at the same time hypnotic, perhaps the reason that the Lester family and their guests all sat so quietly in the living room without providing comment on what it was that might be happening in the next room.

Doctor M'Butu and Reverend Bennett and Mrs. Lester had returned from the upstairs bathroom and stood at the bottom of the stairs, when Reverend Bennett lost all of his presence of mind, called out, "Are you all right in there?" and knocked on the bedroom door which, as he did not yet know, never latched, and swung open weightlessly so that all who were present in the living room, family and guests, instantly became unwilling witnesses to the activity within.

At first Clayton could not readily determine the nature of the scene. He did not see Paquitta, because he was looking at his cousin, who sat sprawled fully nude on top of the mess they had made of the bed that he and his sisters had tidied earlier that morning. Wynnona's head was thrown back so that her long blonde hair fell over her shoulders and down her back. Her legs were extended outward as if she had mounted a horse or were sitting on a rail. Most significantly, her breasts, large and trembling, were covered by two dark hands that were not her own.

The hands, of course, as Clayton quickly surmised, were those of Paquitta, whose head lay completely hidden behind a pillow. Only her nose extended beyond the hummock of embroidered pillow and goosedown and in this way revealed by its characteristic bump that yes, this was his Paquitta lying prone under the beautiful nude woman that his cousin had become. Paquitta removed her hand from one of Wynnona's breasts, and it hung as delicately as the blush of a pear from a limb. Paquitta then abruptly applied her hand to the side of Wynnona's hip and in this way provided for Clayton a source for the curious slapping noise he had heard several times that morning. In unison with this movement, she stiffened her muscular legs so that Wynnona raised slightly into the air.

"Yee-ha," she said.

Perhaps because Reverend Bennett was so surprised, he did not reach out to close the door right away and instead covered his mouth with both hands.

Clayton recalled an event which had taken place in Boston. While on vacation, after driving back and forth through the one-way streets that seemed to take the Lester family everywhere except where they had intended to go, Mr. Lester parked the station wagon and camper in a vacant lot under a wall spray-painted with the words in red: "LESBIANS UNITE." The entire family, Mr. and Mrs. Lester, Clayton, the girls, and even Wallace, crawled out of the car and stretched themselves and pretended to ignore the massive writing on the wall. Because nobody dared speak of it, to Clayton the words seemed more monstrous than ever.

He, above all, sympathized. However much magic might be hanging in the air around him, however he might feel it all up and down his spine, he knew that his family's reaction would eventually result in ill feelings toward his cousin, perhaps even a punishment of some kind. Clayton's family did not believe in such magic. Wynnona and Paquitta were so engrossed that they failed to recognize they had an audience. Mrs. Lester, whose jaw was tight and whose complexion had become unhealthily pale, reached forward and pulled back the door.

After a few seconds of clearing throats and looking out of windows, "Well," Reverend Bennett said. "I suppose we had better be going?"

His companion pulled himself out of Mr. Lester's favorite chair, and he straightened himself. With some relief, he affected polite banter: "Do you think so, Reverend Bennett?"

"Oh yes, we still need to visit the Grimewood family," he said with enthusiasm.

"Oh, yes. The Grimewoods." Doctor M'Butu bowed slightly to Mr. Lester. They shared an apologetic smile.

The air still held a degree of tension for which all were regretful. Little Dortha broke through it. Stepping forward from the safety of the group of children, which had huddled away from their parents toward the end of the living room farthest from Wynnona and Paquitta's room, she smiled redly. "Oh, but you must have some of Mother's pickled bologna," she said.

"Oh yes," the family agreed.

"But we don't have time," Reverend Bennett insisted, touching his hair. "We really must be going."

Mrs. Lester touched his arm and beamed instantly. "You can take a jar with you," she said. She had turned appropriately shy at this mention of her most renowned experiment in canning. As if to relieve her discomfort at so suddenly becoming the center of everyone's attention, rather than send one of her children to retrieve it for her, as was her habit, she herself walked through the dining room and kitchen in order to retrieve the pickled bologna. The others trailed a bit behind her, and formed a group in the dining room to exchange compliments for farewells. Good-byes always raise the volume in one's throat a bit. They talked a bit loudly, not only to cover further noise that might issue from the living room, but also because they were saying good-bye. They barely heard the last odd noise they were going to hear that day: not a scream, but three loud thumps. These were followed by a growling meow, and simply: a splash.

Since Clayton and Dortha were nearest the basement door, they fought over the knob and turned it and pulled it open. A dark wet shape scrambled past them and tore out into the kitchen. Although Mrs. Lester was quick, she hadn't been able to catch Deadbeat, and maybe it was just as well because she would have wrung his neck until his head popped off. Reverend Bennett fairly leapt into the arms of Doctor M'Butu.

The cat was soaking wet, and it got past everyone except Mr. Lester. He took Deadbeat up in his arms. Deadbeat was wet and shivering from the cold, and even so, he purred. Mr. Lester wiped the palm of his hand through the soaked fur as he peered into the darkness that widened out beneath them.

There was a small cry. It sounded like a meow. It came from the bottom of the steps in Mrs. Lester's voice. Clayton pressed past his father. He stepped out onto the landing at the top of the stairs and looked down the flight, past a skid mark of green cat poop to the flowered back of his mother's homemade dress. She sat on the last step of the stairs, up to her knees in water.

"Turn on the light," Mr. Lester commanded. "Are you okay, dear?"

Gestures

We always make love in a way that my high school biology teacher would deplore; "Sex is not an emergency," he counseled my class, several times, after a slide show. Our clothes are lying around us as if there had been some kind of explosion: a pair of his baggy slacks with one leg on the bed and one leg off, his boxer shorts on top of the telephone next to the bed, one of my socks hanging from a lampshade where I tossed it after I ripped it off. We're lying on the bed and I'm still panting, and then he starts up with his degraded act.

"Sex with you is so bizarre," Charlie says.

I sit up, in spite of my exhaustion — the older I get, the more this seems to take out of me — and I pull his boxer shorts off the nightstand and put them on my head.

"Do I look like the Sphinx?" I say. I roll my eyes as far as I can to the left and bend my neck from side to side. I try to imitate one of those Thai dancers with the three-pointed jewelry hats.

"You're nuts," he says.

I accuse him: "No hoochie koochie? You hate Egyptian art too?"

He rips his underpants off my head and tries to throw them out of my reach. But my hand is quicker than his; I catch them before they're over the side of the bed, a dramatization of some kind of desperate leap. I burrow my nose into the crotch of them, make moans and kissing noises. I pull the elastic of the waistband down around my neck.

"Stop it," he says.

Slowly I drag the undershorts off my head, my hair pulling straight back until the elastic snaps.

"Do you think I should have my nose pierced?"

"That's perfect," he says. "Because you're a cow."

"You mean a bull. You're having trouble with gender differentiation again."

"Moo," he says. Under the covers I am pinching the inch of flesh that has gathered around my waist over the past couple months.

"I'm in love with you. I want to have your baby." I try not to change the way my voice sounds. I try to say it as straight as if I were ordering a Shirley Temple in a biker bar. But I can't and I'll never be able to. What a wimp, I think to myself.

"Tell me something new," he says. But when I roll over and over back across the king-sized mattress so that my body lands perfectly lined up next to his: he kisses me on the forehead. Then he pulls on my ear, like he's thinking.

✄

"Okay," says Dr. Beard.

Thirty seconds are up, so it's time to move again. I kneel on one leg and face the window.

"Try and make your body more three-dimensional," he tells me. He is standing only inches away, but there is that visible boundary between us: the fully clothed and the nude.

"My body *is* three dimensional."

He ignores my joke. Or misses it.

"You want to give them gestures which will challenge them," he says. "You want to give them a chance to work on perspective, foreshortening. I want them to capture motion in each gesture."

I am standing in the middle of the drawing class on top of a short wooden platform with a blanket thrown down on it. There are easels, heads nodding briskly up and down, an occasional frown. Most of all, there are the eyes. The eyes do not see me; they look at my body.

"Okay," Dr. Beard says. I turn my trunk about 45 degrees and then my head another 45 degrees beyond my body. Directly in front of me is someone quite handsome, sketching away. It's a good-looking guy with a full head of curly, brown hair. I watch him draw, watch his shoulder moving up and down as he sketches. I try not to stare.

"Okay," he says again. This time I try a position I thought of before I came in today. I kneel down over the edge of the platform, careful to keep my balance. I reach down with my right hand beneath the level of my bare feet on the platform. I'm trying to position myself as God holding a compass in the illustration by Blake.

I notice I'm staring directly into the face of this guy, the good-looking one. He's frowning, tap-dancing with his pencil as fast as he can.

"Oh," says a girl. I wonder if she recognizes the pose. The eyes go up, the eyes go down. I listen to the general scratching of all of their pencils, the muffled voice of another professor in the next room.

A little while longer and then: "Okay."

I stand up, stretch both of my legs, and then lower myself to all fours, my ass raised a little higher than the rest of my back. To make the pose more interesting, I straighten out my right leg and balance on my toe. I bend the other leg and push my chin against my chest so I'm looking directly down the center of my trunk and out between my legs. The bright lights are shining on my back; I feel the heat there. But my balls must be freezing; they're tight, withdrawn. Right under them I see the same guy's legs, upside down between my legs. He's wearing hiking boots, a pair of green jeans.

I look down, away from his face, but of course I can only move my eyes. The rest of me has to freeze in this position for a few more seconds. For a moment I think that I can feel his eyes, first on and then off of me. I imagine I can feel the rough texture of his pencil, scratching out along the curves in my back and buttocks.

Now Charlie has a chainsaw out and he's ripping and snarling into the sculpture. The head of it looks alarming, as if his subject is wearing a helmet or something.

He has told me how his class meets every Thursday night, so I usually bundle up and leave the library around eight o'clock. Dragging in my winter coat and scarf and hat, I walk into the 3-D art building. I kick through the clay dust and the oak chips on the polished

Gestures   87 cement floor. Sometimes he gets me high in the elevator, because he has a key to stop it between floors. Other times he takes me to his locker in the hallway where he always has something strong to drink: whiskey or some fancy kind of brandy he stole from his dad.

We've had words about the chainsaw. Dr. Beard already talked to him about it and so did Dr. Bjornson. "It's fine," I told him, "if you're carving totem poles." Smoke jets out of the back of it.

"I think you need oil on the chain," I say. I try to stay out of the way of the flying chips of sawdust, which are all over Charlie and in his woolly brown hair. I say it again louder. Finally I have to touch his upper arm, the faded flannel plaid, to get his attention.

"What?" he says, startled. He pulls the blade of the chainsaw back up out of the wood. He sets it down on the floor to turn it off and the McCullough's gravelly growl rumbles off into an echo off the high ceiling. There are skylights up there. Sometimes a sparrow gets in.

He pulls the little triangle of a mask off his nose and mouth.

"Hi," he says, abruptly. "What?" Charlie gives me that look. It is the same look I noticed when I first met him in the drawing class: curious, penetrating. "Psychotic" was my first impression.

"That's not coming out of the tailpipe," I say. "Blue smoke, all that noise. Better check it."

He looks vaguely irritated.

"I promise I won't say anything about ruining a great work of art with a chainsaw," I say rapidly. "Have you checked the chain oil?" I start to bend over the machine.

"I know what I'm doing," he says, unimpressed. "Oil's fine." Jill said Charlie has that look because he's a double major: art and psychology. Obviously a dangerous mix.

I straighten up and give him my stern look.

"Hard day at the office?" I say. I'm only trying to help.

"No," he says. He takes off his fuzzy yellow gloves. He wants to talk.

"Leave them off," I say.

Charlie is sitting up in bed and in the dark I can see him reaching for his boxer shorts. They are so white they almost glow in the dark.

"Don't be an ass," he says.

I grab them and try to pull them away, but he pulls them back with a snap.

"That's not fair," I say. "You should at least wait five minutes after a guy comes..."

"You're full of shit." He lifts his feet through the legs of his undershorts, one after the other, and then slides them up his hairy legs. In one quick movement he stretches them out in front to slide them over his nuts and then slides his thumbs back along the inside of the waistband to pull them over his ass. He snaps the elastic one more time.

"I can't sleep with them off," he says. He sits on the bed and leans back slowly to lie down, bending his knees, pulling his legs under the covers.

"Right. Like it's too big or something..."

"Well." He's going to make a joke: it's in the tone of his voice. "It might get wrapped around me if I roll over in the night."

"Ha, ha," I say.

I roll over and over, away from him, to the other side of the bed. I'm on my stomach, so he can't see what I'm doing.

I hear his hair brush against the pillow when he turns his head in the dark.

"What's wrong?" he says.

"Nothing."

That's the trick, I think. He knows me just well enough to make things like this difficult. I'm sliding the scissors out from between the mattress and the box spring. Then it occurs to me that these are an old pair. They might not be sharp enough. They might make a noise he could recognize when I open them.

"If nothing's wrong, then why are you over on your side of the bed?" I love it when he gets like this. He sounds worried, as if his cocker spaniel were being put to sleep or something.

"I don't know." I roll back, over and over, until I am up against him. I've got the scissors closed in my right hand, pressed cold and flat against my chest.

"I don't like it when we argue," I tell him.

"Everybody argues," he says, automatically. "If we didn't fight, it wouldn't last."

"Okay. Take a break."

The class relaxes audibly. I get up off the blanket on the platform and hold my hand over my eyes to see past the lights. Then I step down onto the tile floor. I feel more naked without the heat and light.

Dr. Beard is holding out the blue bathrobe that he gave me when I came in.

"We usually take a ten- or fifteen-minute break in the middle of class," he says, "to give you a rest before your sixty-minute pose."

I take the robe.

"Great." This is my first time. I try to sound enthusiastic.

Dr. Beard steps onto the platform and turns off each of the four lights .

"How did I do, Dr. Beard?"

He gives me a smile and scratches his chin.

"Fine," he says. "You did very well for a first time. Try to remember with the gestures that we are trying to capture motion. Action."

"Oh. I get it. Okay." The robe is heavy and too large for me. I fumble with it, twist it around, try to find the belt.

"That's why they're only thirty seconds. That way you can afford to get more *dynamic* up there." He puts his hand on my shoulder and steps behind me, pulls up the limp end of the belt and extends it, drooping from the hole in his large fist.

"Thanks." I've never seen a hand so large; it's huge and chapped.

"Would you like a Coke?" he says.

"A Coke?"

He smiles again, automatically. I can see that he's used to this. They're so grateful to get models around here, especially men.

"Yeah, a Coke. On me."

"Sure. Thanks. I'm gonna walk around the room a little bit."

Dr. Beard walks out of the door. He's talking to a young woman with blonde hair falling to her hips. Somehow she looks familiar.

"His latest," a voice behind me confides. I turn around and it's the guy with the hiking boots. He's still sketching.

"You're kidding," I say. "And people know this?"

He's still working on his gestures, turning each page of his giant newsprint pad, filling in lines here and there with a sweeping arm.

"You think these guys come here to teach?" He looks up at me only to continue the conversation. Then he's back down into the pad, fumbling through the broad, thin pages.

"She's very pretty," I say. I walk around the easel to get a look at what he's doing. I want to see what I look like on paper.

"If you like the type."

I try to find something of me in there on the page, but it's just lines and limbs and ass. He flips the paper over to the next page.

"Name's Jill," he says.

"What?" I feel the air, a rush of it, pass through my bare legs as the door behind us opens and then closes.

"Her name's Jill." He looks at me with these eyes that make me look down, consider my toenails. "I hate people like that. She draws like a demigod and she's pretty too."

"It's not fair," I agree. One of his sketches catches my eye; he's caught me from the front and where my genitals should be, he's scribbled an ugly mess.

"No, it's not. Not fair at all."

"I heard the department here was pretty wild," and then, maybe because I'm nervous because I've just met him or maybe because it is my first day modeling, I feel the need to enunciate: "I have often wondered about that."

"You *have often wondered about that?*" he says, mimicking me. "Why do you pronounce everything so carefully? You talk like a grade school teacher."

"My mom was," I offer, embarrassed. Is this guy a jerk or what? I try to recover: "I refuse to deconstruct my grammatical formality with people whom I have never met." Feeling bold, I extend my hand.

"Clay," I say.

He looks up and then down again. He doesn't shake it.

"Sorry. I'm in the middle of this. Nice to meet you, Clay. My name's Charlie." For a second it looks like he might be turning red, but I really can't tell because he must get a lot of sun.

Most of the other students have left. I walk in my bare feet across the dusty floor. I want to see if anyone has done me justice.

"Do you suppose it's because I'm getting older?" I say.

"Shut up," Charlie says.

"I can talk," I say. "I think it's because of the feeling I get afterward. Like taking a bath or something. You feel fresh and healthy and clean and your body isn't dirty. It's beautiful the way they look at you..."

"Shut up," he says.

"How come?" I say. "Are you painting my mouth now?"

The top of his head appears over the corner of his canvas.

"No, I'm trying to paint your dick," he says. "It'll only take a second."

I lower my arms. I'm surprised how cold my skin feels when my hands touch my hips. My arms must have cooled off while the rest of my body stayed warm. I rub my arms with my hands.

"Hey," he says.

I jump: just a little. I can't help it. But I hold my ground.

"If you want me to model for you," I say, "I would suggest that you restrain your phallocentric insults."

"Oh," he says, brilliantly. He's standing to the side of the canvas now with his right hand on his hip, the same hand that holds the paintbrush. Then he raises his left hand in a flourish, some kind of blossom forming invisibly in the air under his chin.

"May we continue, Master Shakespeare?"

I return to my original position, or at least a close approximation. And he returns to painting. He pokes his head around the corner of the canvas, exposing the one sharply frowning eye.

" I know what you're thinking," I say.

"Shut up."

"You think feminism is a bunch of crap, don't you?"

"Please."

"And I'm not so big on Shakespeare."

"Would you stop talking?" he says. He clears his throat.

"If you're painting my dick, I ought to be able to move my mouth."

I hear the metal "click" when he drops the brush. He walks slowly around the easel and stands in front of me looking strange, fully clothed. His overalls are covered with spatters of paint, shades of green

James Russell Mayes

and blue and some other color that looks like dark wet spots on half of his chest.

"I need to concentrate." He brings both arms down and places a spattered hand on each of my bare shoulders in some restrained gesture of emphasis. "Let me *think*, will you?"

I will not look in his eyes. I dare to move an inch, to nod my head sharply in conceited apology.

"Sorry."

He spins on the rounded toe of his hiking boot and hides behind the canvas again. Maintaining my practiced expression of boredom, I check each shoulder for smudges. He's too quiet. I relax my mouth so there's a space between my lips: so the tension won't show. I'd feel more comfortable if he'd mutter to himself or something.

Now and then while modeling I allow myself a smile, a stretch. I relax every muscle in my back for a second and then snap back into shape before I see his eye again, The Curse of Ra. He glances over the edge of his canvas and sighs, a huge sigh. I imagine his breath blowing over the wet oils, over the blue shadows and the light of whatever the hell he's doing back there. I imagine that I can feel it, too: a light wind that blows across my exhausted, upraised arms.

I am surprised, unpleasantly, when Charlie finally shows me the first finished nude portrait. Nothing that I want to see is there; for instance, I'm very proud of the way my chest looks in the mirror lately. Everything I don't want to see is foregrounded, highlighted with shadows that lengthen in their distance from whatever the hell the source of light is. He's exaggerated the bony quality of my knees. And although he didn't paint in my face, the shape of the nose is more phallic than my dick is.

He tacks up the nude portrait over our bed and I'm impotent the first night. He laughs. For a week, I'm depressed. I refuse food and eat salad. I increase my workouts in the gym by one complete set of each exercise. Charlie pretends not to notice and acts like he always does. It occurs to me that he's probably painted all of his previous lovers and then presented their portraits as parting gifts when he broke up with them.

When faculty and students from the art department stop by the house, he opens the bedroom door and gives them a quick, outrageous assessment of our relationship, our "sexual inversion," as he calls it. I don't really mind that; what I do mind is his generosity with all of my faults: my skinny legs, my big nose, that bony witch's hand groping my thigh.

"Why did you paint me that way?" I ask him. "Why did you paint my fingernails so long?"

"That's my hand; that's not your hand," he says. "Go to sleep."

In the dark I try to picture his face. Three months now and I can picture parts of him, his big Irish ass, his lips working away at my fingers. I have feelings memorized: his arm is resting on top of my back and it curves under my arm. His hand cups my chest and his thumb brushes my nipple. Once I woke up in the middle of the night and he had his hand under the sheet, scratching my back: another feeling. But I cannot picture his face.

My feet are starting to get cold on the tile floor.

I walk past the other easels. These are only gestures so they aren't finished enough to look like me. But each of them is different. I move around the room and on each sheet of drawing paper the angle of my position changes a few degrees. Then I stop in front of Jill's easel.

At first I can't figure out what it is and it doesn't look anything like me. Just a lot of curving lines in different colors across the single page. But she's drawn several of my positions on top of each other, each in a different color. It looks sort of like stop-action film. Looking at it longer, I can tell the sequence of my positions, like movement. Some of them show me stiff and uncomfortable, a few others more relaxed.

"What do you think?" says a voice. I turn around and it's Jill.

"I'm impressed," I say. She smiles.

"Thank you. First time modeling?" She opens her hand and moves it back through the long drape of her hair. She makes me think of Guenivere or Joan of Arc before the war. If Jill rode, she'd ride better than a man. Even if she had to ride sidesaddle.

"Yes. Can you tell?"

"Well," and her eyes flash blue, "you're a *little* self-conscious. You'll get used to it..." She pauses to turn the page over and I can tell it's heavy, a better kind of paper than Charlie uses. I feel the little bit of wind the paper makes when it flops down over the back of her easel.

"Don't be so afraid to move. Especially for the gestures. We're supposed to be able to catch whatever you dish out up there." She laughs at her own cliche, and then leans forward with her elbow on the easel, holding her chin in her palm. "Action is what it's all about, darling." She bats her eyes cinematically.

"Hmm."

"Aren't you Barry's friend? Barry Winston?"

"Oh. Yeah."

"Did he talk you into this?" She looks at me closely. "It doesn't bother him, that you do this?"

"Oh no," I say. I smile in spite of myself, in spite of my color rising. "In fact, he doesn't even know that I'm here. I didn't tell him."

She laughs.

"Well I'm not gonna tell him."

"He thinks I'm taking the class."

"You're evil. I like that."

"And you're sarcastic. Is that a wig?"

"Okay," says Dr. Beard. He rushes into the room, the corners of his long smock trailing behind him. He smiles at Jill. "Ready, Clay?"

"Yo," I say. She laughs. I walk up to the platform and Dr. Beard clicks on each of the four bright lights. Then he steps down off the platform, leaving it to me.

"Okay," he says again, this time to the class. "We'll do a couple of thirty-minute studies today. That way the new model can get used to holding still so long." He smiles. "Ready, Clay? Try reclining or a sitting position: something you can hold for a little while."

I try to act casual, the way I might undress in front of a new lover, anyone who has never seen me naked. By now of course they've seen me once. But I turn away from them anyway and undo the belt. I try to think of others who've done this: Rock Hudson, Quentin Crisp, Ronald Reagan. I open the front of the robe and feel it dropping off my shoulder. Then I hand it to Dr. Beard and turn around.

Already they've forgotten me, are drawing what they see. It's the eyes again, their concentration.

I lower myself to my knees and then lie flat on my back with my buttocks pressed against my ankles. I stretch my arms out over my head. And then I turn my head to the side, toward the class, toward Charlie's easel, and just behind his shoulder, toward Jill's.

✂

"You mean," I say, trying to sound drowsy, resting my chin on Charlie's shoulder and pressing my nose against his warm neck and at the same time switching the scissors from my right hand to my left, "you mean you want this to last?"

"Don't be an ass." He's talking tough because he's about to say something nice. "Of course I want it to last," he says.

I realize too late that I should have turned the scissors around; as it is, they are traveling unseen and blade-first down into my crotch. I lower my left hand slowly, pressing the cold scissors against my skin so he won't feel them between us.

"Don't you want it to last?" He sounds tired.

"What?" I push the scissors carefully into the narrow space between my legs and hold them there, between my thighs so that I can put my fingers into the two holes. This will be difficult because I'm lying on my right side. I will have to do it with my left hand, the hand I don't favor.

"Don't you want it to last? Narcissus. What's wrong?"

"Nothing." I pull my arm up from under the pillow and lean my head against his shoulder. "Of course. I want it to last forever," I say.

At the last minute, I change my strategy. I'm up on top of him, sitting on the tops of his thighs and pulling the scissors out in the darkness, switching them clumsily from my left hand.

"What?" he says. It's all he has time for. By then I've slid the left leg of his boxers up to the elastic and for one difficult moment I've got this rickety pair of scissors against his skin, struggling to cut through the thick band of elastic, the flimsy material.

He's bucking up and down with his hips, holding onto my hands. He doesn't know what I'm doing, but he's holding me back just the same.

Someone is pounding with a hammer at the other end of the sculpture room.

Charlie focuses in on me and squints his eyes through the noise.

"You know Barry Winston, right?"

I freeze. I feel him watching me. I can feel my color rise, too: up to the bottom of my ears before I control it. I swallow.

"Oh yeah," I say, nonchalantly. I'll never know why this is so hard for me. I try to ignore the hammering, to talk through it. "I know Barry. Do you?"

He kind of laughs.

"What's so funny?" I've done this over and over and it never gets easy. It's always best to wait for them to call the first shot.

"Let's get a drink," he says.

I try to avoid walking in time with the beat of the hammer. We move through the other students who are working on their projects, mostly in wood. A few stand around smoking. A woman stands in front of a couple of full-length mirrors, shaping a massive self-portrait in wax with a metal spatula. Another man is building a kind of shelter around a ceramic vase out of scrap wood. I smile and nod at Dr. Bjornson as we pass by. Dr. Bjornson is okay; Charlie already introduced us and since I fall into that pretentious "artistic" category as a model, I'm accepted by the "artsies" around here. It doesn't take long to learn that Rembrandt is in and Rubens is out. Nobody seems to mind that I crash their sculpture class.

We get to his locker and Charlie pulls out the hooch and turns around to face me. He hands me the flask, nodding his head politely.

"Whiskey," he says. Finally the pounding stops.

"God, I hate the noise," I say. In one motion I'm screwing off the cap, feeling the sticky lips of the flask within my own and gulping down.

He looks around, making sure the coast is clear.

"I know Barry," he says.

"Really?"

"Yeah. I do. How do you know Barry?"

"I just know him," I say. "That's all."

He looks at me for a second. He raises an eyebrow. "You sure? That's not what I heard."

My throat grips the liquid pouring in. I bend over like a sick cat, try to keep my mouth on the lips of the bottle at the same time I'm trying not to choke.

Charlie starts laughing again. I knew this would happen. I should've gone to a bigger school, a bigger town. Everybody around here knows each other.

"You okay?" He thumps me on the back, through my wool coat.

"What did you hear?" My voice is hoarse with liquor.

He stops to consider for a minute. He nods his head politely again and lowers his voice.

"I hear you were lovers. I heard you and Barry were lovers."

The burn goes out of my throat and something hard and dry drops into it. But I'm not a wimp. I might be a faggot, but I'm not a wimp. I wait a minute and catch my breath so I can look him in the eye when I say it.

"So," I say. "Who told you that?"

"Barry did," he says with satisfaction.

The skin on my forehead feels hot against my palm. "Okay. That's true. We were lovers for a while. So?" My fingers tingle with sweat, even with the cool bottle in my hand.

Charlie doesn't blink. His face changes. But he's acting too cool; I hate it when people start acting smooth on me. I hand him the bottle.

"So what," he says, pressing it to his lips. "You still with him?"

"No. We went to a lot of parties and broke off after two or three months. So what's the difference?"

He pulls the bottle away from his mouth, brings it down, and I hear the little fizz coming up through the opening. He smiles.

"You got me beat. He wouldn't even go out with me."

"Oh my God," I say.

Charlie laughs.

"Oh my God. I could kill you for that." I put my hand on his shoulder and he knocks it off.

"Not so fast." Like I was jumping him.

"I'm sorry. It's just that I thought you were straight. I thought we could be friends."

"I thought we already were." He blushes; this time it's unmistakable. There is a slight coloring that wavers on his face and makes him swallow. It forces him to consider his hiking boot, which is kicking against the metal door of his locker.

This is stupid, I say to myself.

"I hate this. I hate sincerity. And now we have to talk about Barry, right?"

"Not if we don't want to," he says. He stops kicking the locker. Then he slides his left foot across the floor so that he is the same height as I am with his legs spread, his hands on his hips. He looks at me evenly. "We don't have to talk about anything if you don't want to."

"I liked Barry," I say. "But he didn't understand me. He didn't trust me. I don't want to talk about him."

"I know. It's not like you. You'll end up getting sincere or something."

He follows me back down the hall to the sculpture room. We walk past the Ugliest Sculpture in the World and he pulls the ski cap out of my coat pocket and throws it into the tuba-shaped opening at the top.

"You did that like basketball," I say.

"A body like that and you're not an athlete?" he says.

"That's good," Dr. Beard says. He guides the class in starting the exercise, pointing out the major lines, the direction of light. Most of the students are sitting on stools now; they become serious and silent in their work. I listen to the lights buzzing above me. Dr. Beard walks from easel to easel, giving quiet advice.

"Anybody bring music?" he says.

A girl in the back offers: "I brought my tape deck."

"Great."

"Joni Mitchell okay?"

Some guy in the back groans.

"Fine," says Dr. Beard. "What one you got?"

"*Blue.*" She putters around with her tape deck and I watch her bending over in the corner of my eye. I'm beginning to wonder if my knees can handle this.

I look at Charlie and he's shifting around on his stool. He looks up at me and then down at his pad. I look past Charlie at Jill, who's chewing on the end of one of her pencils. She looks up and sees me looking back at her; she smiles. The music plays. And Joni sings. My chest rises up and down as I breathe under the heat of the lights.

Then I notice that Charlie keeps shifting around. The way he's sitting on his stool, I have to avoid looking at his crotch. His jeans are a little too tight, a little too worn. I wonder if he wears colored underwear. He keeps shifting his weight from side to side, then pulling on his crotch. He draws for a bit. Then he looks up at me, right into my eyes with that expression of his. Then he looks away, ducks his head down, draws some more.

Modeling takes concentration, I tell myself: especially nude modeling. I try to regulate my breathing. I count to 48. I think about my aunt Beatrice and how she looked at her funeral. But the feeling does not go away. It is the same feeling I had when I was fourteen years old and discovered Thomas Eakins's "The Swimming Hole." It starts with an odd tickling feeling inside my stomach. Then it shifts down into a pressure within my lower abdomen, something wanting out. Each time I take a breath, the pressure increases.

I take in a lot of air. I suppose I wouldn't be the first one to get aroused in front of a classroom of art students. Even Gerald Ford did this, right? I try to think of other things; the way a dog arches its back to take a shit, the dead calf I had to bury behind the barn when I was eleven. I try to think of the way vomit smells on the morning after an alcoholic binge. But nothing seems to help. I feel the familiar weight, my crotch gets heavy.

This guy Charlie doesn't help either. He acts like he can tell, like he's guilty or embarrassed about something. I look past him at Jill. She seems to be concentrating on my arm. Her hair flows over a shoulder, makes a waterfall over one arm. Charlie clears his throat and erases. He looks around the room, then at me. He looks down, then at me. He draws a little. Then he shifts in his chair again.

I begin to think about the position I've chosen for the exercise. In about two minutes I'll be lying flat on my back like this, with a big bonus in the air. I try to think about repercussions. What if Dr. Beard has to break up the class? What if they just keep on drawing? I picture all of them laughing. I imagine Dr. Beard making a joke with a colleague. And then I wonder what the sketches are going to look like. Sometimes I wish I'd been raised Catholic; then I'd have all of those

James Russell Mayes

prayers memorized and I could just whip them out when I felt the need. I wouldn't have to rely on the Holy Spirit.

"Hail, Mary," I say to myself. Joni sings away about Christmas and some river she wants to skate away on.

Charlie scoots his stool back and it makes a squawk. He stands up and in two seconds he's out the door. I don't bother to check out his ass. There's a little bit of wind on me and I exhale gratefully. Maggots, I'm thinking. Dead birds. Bambi's mother. Joni sings about being selfish and sad: "I've gone and lost the best lover that I ever had," she sings.

And then the feeling goes away: just like that.

I relax my breathing a little, with relief. I trace my thoughts backward to whatever prevented the crisis. Would the Virgin intercede in a situation like this? It was probably fear, I suppose. Maybe the music. Once I read on the back of a piece of sheet music that "Music soothes the savage beast." I lie on my back and wait and wonder what Charlie is doing in the bathroom. I wonder if he smokes.

My nose is starting to itch, so I wiggle it, which doesn't help. I take a chance and scratch it real quick with my right hand. Then the door opens. Out of the corner of my eye I can see two people in the doorway. Charlie must have brought someone in with him. The two of them make a big deal out of looking as if they're trying to be quiet; both of them bow their heads politely as they make their way through the other students. They get safely behind Charlie's easel and then they look up.

By then I've already recognized the penny loafers, the yellow argyle socks. It's Barry. For a moment it's even more quiet in here than it was before; the tape is between songs. I hear Barry clear his throat, his tightened, angry throat. And I can't help it; I close my eyes, I shiver as I listen to his shoes clicking out the door. And then that breeze again. I keep waiting for the music to start. I have the whole album memorized and I can't remember what the next song is.

"What the hell are you doing?" Charlie says.

"You're gonna get cut," I say. I order him to hold still; and in one second I've spread the material out with my left hand so that the scissors can close down and cut through the leg of his shorts.

"There," I say.

I throw the scissors over the edge of the bed.

"What the hell did you do?" But he can feel they've been cut; he's got his hand down there.

"Dammit." He sounds less angry than disappointed. Resigned, I suppose, in the way all men are when their undershorts have been ruined.

"Ha hah." I try to sound triumphant. I start pulling the sliced shorts off of him.

"You're paying for these." He slides out of the other leg and tries to kick them off the bed, but I've got them now.

I sit up on my knees and wave his shorts around.

"Thank you, thank you," I say to the invisible and roaring crowd. I throw them kisses.

Charlie kicks me, a little too hard, in the back of the leg.

"Oww."

"Do you know how much I paid for those?" In the dark I can see the outline of his face. I don't really know if I am looking at his face or if I am just imagining what it must look like in the dark.

"Worth it," I say.

I'm holding on to the elastic waistband. I snap them at his head, try to make the sound that a whip makes when it cracks at the rump of a dark horse.

"Ass," he says. He is totally disgusted, so I collapse, as dramatically as possible, onto my back with his colors spread out neatly over my face.

"You're sick."

"You shouldn't wear underwear to bed," I say, the material tickling my lips as I talk through it. "No one should wear underwear. We should all go naked..."

"I can't believe you did that." But even though he's interrupting my inspired effusion, he says it as an afterthought. This means he is tired enough to give in and he will sleep naked tonight; I've made it too difficult for him to sleep otherwise.

I breathe in loudly, take in all of the perfume his undershorts can provide.

"You're sick."

"Art stinks," I tell him. "Quite literally. That's why."

"Did you work out today?" Charlie says. He's standing up on top of a wooden fruit crate. He's trying to turn the sculpture around by tipping it on one end of its base and then onto the other end.

"What are you talking about?" I look up from my scented magazine. I love scented magazines. This one's *GQ*.

He's having a hard time turning the sculpture; there isn't much space in his new cubicle to move around in. I don't know how the department could call this studio space.

"I thought you were going to start working out every day?" He gets down off the crate. He kicks it around another 45 degrees in relation to that figure he's been working on. Then he steps back up.

"Sometimes I work out every day."

"And sometimes you work out every week?" He gives me that look again, only this time without the frown.

"Yes," I say. "That sounds more like it. Once a week. Very good."

He wrestles with the giant hunk of wood one more time before I offer to help him.

"Oh no," he says. "I can't decide what part of this I want to work on. I'm just eyeballing it."

I try to eyeball it, too. I try to act like I know what I'm looking for.

And then I ask him: "Who's that going to be, anyway?"

The Beer Tent

Wally Lester was sitting in the American Legion Beer Tent at the Cousin City Frontier Days. Glenda Johnson had given him a Stroh's, and Wally was halfway through it before Doug Hogan came in and sat down beside him at the picnic table.

"How you doin'?" Doug said.

"Fine," said Wally. "Good."

Doug raised his eyebrows. "Where you been? I haven't seen you for a few days."

Wally set his beer down. "I been out of town," he said.

"Out of town. You hear the news? You hear about that cousin of yours named Travis?" Doug was smiling whitely with the news.

"Now you know I don't have a cousin named Travis. There's lots of Lesters and Peasleys around here, Doug. But I don't know one of them that's related to me that's name is Travis."

"You Angus Lester's first cousin?"

Wally had to think for a minute. "Yeah," he said. "In-*law*. So."

"So you got a second cousin named Travis. He's your father's cousin's son, and that makes you second cousins, see?"

"Yeah," Wally said. "Sounds like a second cousin to me. So? What happened to my second cousin Travis Peasley?"

"He's in jail," Doug said. He ordered a Stroh's for himself from Glenda. He waited for Wally to look at him sideways.

"So what he do?" Wally said. He drained his first beer fast, before Glenda came back, so he could order another one.

James Russell Mayes

"You know Ray Wilder?"

"I know Ray Wilder."

"Well, he was there. He saw the whole thing. And now he's going to testify in court about it."

"What whole thing you talking about, Doug?" Glenda set the beer in front of Doug. She leaned her hip against the picnic table and took off her glasses.

"Well, see Travis knew Ray because they rented rooms in the same hotel in Birch Corners. It was one of those hotels for poor people, the kind of place that takes the welfare."

"So, you talking about that again?" Glenda said. "You're telling that to everyone who comes in here. You havin' another beer, Wally?" Wally nodded. Glenda walked away.

"Don't you listen to her," Doug said. "This is news. You listen to me. Ray asked his mom to take them over here to look for jobs."

"What was his mom's name?"

"His mom's name?"

"Yeah," Wally said. "I might not know any Travis Peasley, but I might know his mom. What was her name?"

Doug stared straight ahead. "I don't know," he said. "I don't know." His face lit up. "I know she was a Stevens before she got married. And her sister married one of those Pitpath boys and had that retarded baby over on Mud Lake."

"But you don't recall her name?"

"No, I'm sorry, Wally, I don't recall her name. But now that doesn't matter, does it, because it's not her that's in jail. It's her son, that Travis Peasley."

Glenda set down Wally's beer and wiped her hands on her apron. "Why don't you just cut a long story short and tell him what he's in for, will you?"

"Why don't you just hush?" Doug said. He smiled at her and tugged on his shirt collar. "You just wait on your customers, will you? This is *relatives* we're talking to."

"So, what happened?" Wally said.

"She agreed. How could she know? She drove them into town in her old Chevy Malibu. I must've seen that car a hundred times. The three of them stopped at the Bamboo Room for coffee. Ray's mom was going shopping, I guess."

"Yeah."

"As soon as she left, Ray and Travis went across the street to the beer tent. This here beer tent," he said, pressing his thumb on the white paper tablecloth. "Travis had a couple beers. They were sitting in here, just like you and I are sitting in here now."

"Yeah. So."

"Now, see Travis had a cousin, Harvey Powell. He lived in one of those mobile homes by the Protestant cemetery. Harvey was a lot older than Travis. He was almost sixty. You know him? Harvey Powell? He used to have a hardware or something."

"I know him," Wally said. "I know him."

"Yeah, so did I. Travis called him 'uncle,' on account of him being so much older than him. Anyway, they walked over to his trailer, and the whole time they were planning on buying his truck."

"Are you going anywhere with this?"

"Huh?"

"I said, 'Are you going anywhere with this?'" Wally had pulled the brim of his baseball hat down over his head. He looked squarely at Doug.

"They sat around the kitchen table," Doug said, slowly. "They were talking, drinking beer."

"A lot of that going around."

Glenda laughed. When Doug looked up at her, she ducked behind the counter.

"They talked about Reverend Bennett," Doug said.

"What about Reverend Bennett?" Wally pulled his beer away from his mouth. He narrowed his eyes.

"Now I'm not saying anything about the old minister, myself," Doug said, "but I guess they were talking about Reverend Bennett."

"What were they talking about Reverend Bennett for?"

"Hell if I know, Wally." Doug's voice rose. "All I know is that there was talking, and they did it about *Reverend Bennett.*"

"How do you know about all this?"

"I don't know *anything* about *anything*, Wally. I talked to Deputy DeLeau, and he says there was a confession and arrest. And he says there was a lot of talk about that queer old minister."

"If anyone has anything to say about Reverend Bennett..."

"I know, Wally. I know. Anyways, your cousin Travis Peasley..."

"He's not my cousin, Doug. He's my *second* cousin."

"...your second cousin, Travis Peasley, went into the kitchen. He pulled a couple drawers open. He came back with a knife."

"What he do?"

"Your *second* cousin, Travis Peasley, pulled old Harvey Powell out of his chair and stabbed him in the neck. The old man fell on the floor. And *then* Travis stabbed him in the stomach."

"What?"

"He must've stabbed him twelve times, deputy said. Twelve, thirteen times."

"You gotta be kidding me."

"Ask around about it. He probably would've stabbed him some more, except the knife got stuck in the floor."

"No way."

Doug held up both of his hands and showed Wally his palms. "Honest," he said. "Honest."

"How come I didn't read it in the paper?"

"Happened three days ago. Those boys went right out to Harvey's truck and tried to start it." Doug put his beer down. He put his hands on the table to brace himself. He began to laugh. "The truck wouldn't start. They flagged old Lumpy McCorkle down, that old fellow that mows the lawns. They got *him* to try and give 'em a jump." Doug pulled a big red handkerchief out of his pocket. He blew his nose. He wiped his eyes. "Those boys walked all over town with blood all over both of themselves. Nobody even asked what happened."

"Why not?"

Doug was folding his handkerchief. He held the two halves of it in front of himself and looked down into it as if he were reading a book. "I suppose nobody was paying attention. I swear, Wally. You sound surprised. It's not like Detroit around here. I swear. A person could die." He widened his eyes. "A person *did* die."

"Who finally got them?"

"Nobody did. Their mother took 'em all the way back to Birch Corners. They were sitting in the hotel for a night before Ray, that's the other one, the innocent one, the witness, he said he *had* to tell somebody." Doug Hogan drained his beer.

"They find the body?" Wally said.

"Oh, yeah."

"He dead?"

"Well, of course he was dead, Wally. Don't anybody live very long if they been stabbed two dozen times in the chest."

"I thought you said 'a dozen.' "

"I don't know what I said, but that Harvey Powell was dead."

The two men drank their beer in silence. A man in a green suit stopped into the beer tent. He gave each of the men a pamphlet on self-installed satellite dishes.

"I can't believe it. Harvey Powell."

Doug said, "You see the balloons today?"

"The balloons?"

"The big balloons, those hot-air balloons." Doug was cheerful again. "They went right up into the air, about six or seven of them. You didn't see them?"

Wally picked at the label on his beer bottle. "You read the Detroit paper?" he said. "You want stabbing, you read a Detroit paper."

Glenda brought them a couple Dixie cups of mixed peanuts. "Don't you start in about Detroit," she said.

"Why don't you just wait on the customers?" Doug said. "Why can't a man have a conversation without you flapping in?"

"I'm tired of all this talk about Detroit, Wally Lester." Glenda held her fists on her hips. "It makes me sick just hearing about it." She walked over to the next table. A few men from the Catholic church ordered beer and popcorn.

"Them hot-air balloons," Doug said to Wally, "they had more than a dozen. They went right up into the air."

High Street

Al goes on about how nice it is to be hanging out with such cool people, and someday when his ass is rich, he's going to throw a huge party for the three of us. And did we bring the pot? Dana says, "Sure," and she reaches down between her boobs and grabs out the bag of pot. She hands it right over to him, like they're both forgetting who paid for it. I had to pick up pop cans for about a month to get the money. "Oh wow, man," he says, sniffing all over the bag of pot, "I think I can smell some of you in this, Dana. Let's smoke some." So she pulls out her little pipe, and he goes, "No way, man, I hate pipes. They burn your lungs. You know what, you got papers?" No, she didn't have papers, and I didn't have papers.

"Well, I do." He runs back into the house, only he takes the bag with him. But I don't catch on right away. I figure, he's just going in to roll us some doobs. Dana and I are standing outside Al's house, listening to the bugs and stepping back away from the curb whenever a car goes by because we don't want all the light on us. She's going on about how glad she is that Al got a job at the Sweet Onion, and how if everything works out and he does good, then maybe he can get me in too.

I just kind of shrug, because I don't really know Dana that well yet, we only met about a week ago at the Bird and she was a stoner, too, so she got us high. But then I'm thinking how she's already sounding like Ma now: "Get out and do something with yourself." Maybe I don't want a job. My dad had a job. He worked at the bowling alley right up until he died. It didn't do us much good. We still had to use food stamps. Then Dana goes, "How long have you known Al?" And I say, "Oh, a while," but I don't tell her that Al and I went to high school together and we're like pretty good friends. So she goes, "I know why you don't have a girlfriend. I mean, Al already told me that. But why doesn't Al have a girlfriend?"

I know why she's asking, because Al is kind of cute and he has this long blond hair that goes down to his shoulders and he is *so* cool. So I go, "You got a crush on him, Dana?" It's really a joke, because who does she think she is? Dana weighs about three hundred pounds, I am not exaggerating. And the first time I saw her, I thought she was retarded or something. She has those big puffy eyes like retarded people do. She wears tennis shoes and gym socks under her dress. She's got real curly red hair, but it's so thin I'm looking at the shine of her scalp off the streetlight.

Al comes up to the screen door, and he holds up a joint in each hand. "So come on inside," he says. We get up to the door, and Dana says, "Oh, I don't know about this. Didn't you say your mom was sick?" And like both of us at the same time say, "She's always sick," and then Al laughs, but he says, "She's asleep." So we still can't make any noise because his mom would have a fit if she knew he had us over in his room. "My mom doesn't like me to have girls in my bedroom," he says. He pokes Dana where her fat sticks out, and she acts like it's all she can do to keep herself from laughing.

"Come on," he says. We follow him through the house. It's kind of hard once we get past the kitchen, because it's only half lit up, and it's hard to walk through a dark house if it's not yours. But we get past the living room, and his mom is sleeping on the couch. But Al's mom is always sleeping on the couch. We go into Al's room, which is dark because he has the lights off and this giant candle lit. His bed is a mess and there's underwear and shit lying all over the floor, and Dana is looking around like she's real interested in all of this stuff, just because it's a guy. Probably the Christians are a lot neater than Al is. Dana lives with a bunch of Christians.

To me, the room smells like it's giving off vibrations, but I've been getting high off and on all day with Dana, so I'm thinking that probably it's just what I *want* to smell and not what's really there. It smells

James Russell Mayes

like a locker room, like he's been working out or something. "Can't we turn the light on?" Dana says.

Al goes, "No way, I'm supposed to be in bed right now."

"What do you mean you're supposed to be in bed?"

"Lights-out at ten o'clock," he goes. "My mom's real weird about stuff." And I'm like, it is kind of weird that Al has a bedtime and everything.

So we're sitting in the dark with just the one candle lit, and Al pulls up the two joints. He gives one to me and one to Dana, and he goes, "Well, one of you oughta light up." I look at Dana and say, "Ladies first, man," and so she lights it off his candle and then she passes it to Al. He takes two or three good puffs off it, and so I have to reach over and take it right out of his fingers before it's all gone. So while we're sitting there on Al's bed, passing the joint back and forth, I should be wondering about my pot and instead I'm wondering to myself if that really is the smell of something Al's been doing in his bedroom. I'm kind of patting the sheets around me in the dark, just curious.

Al is talking about Jim Morrison and what an artist he was and how after the crowd left a Doors concert there would be all of these women's underpants lying on the ground. He keeps passing the joint back to Dana when it's my turn, and so I have to grab it from him each time, like I'm invisible or something. I'm wondering how high Al must be, because he's sitting between us and getting a toke twice as often as either one of us are. Dana is going, "Oh my, oh my," like it wouldn't take a kick-start dildo. And then my head starts swelling up on me.

I'm dizzy, and when I reach for the joint, there's a slope to the bed. I have to fight gravity just to keep my head from falling on top of Al's knee. I reach over to give the joint to Al, and there's not much of it left. We have to do this tricky thing with our fingers. I drop the joint and it falls into Al's lap, and it's still lit. Dana says right out loud, "Oh," and then she slaps her hand over her mouth, and Al is like brushing it off his pants and then brushing it off the bed and stomping on it with his beat-up shoe. And all the time he's pissing at me, what am I doing, and then I'm kind of leaning forward and my forehead is on Dana's leg and I can't pick it up.

"Are you feeling all right, Bennie?" she says.

I go, "I think I smoked too much."

Al goes, "Hey how much of this stuff you been smoking?"

"We been smoking all day," Dana says. "Bennie and I are getting acquainted."

"You shouldn't smoke so much, man. This stuff is good."

"I feel like I can't breathe," I say.

"He needs some air."

"Let's take him outside."

So Al picks up my head and pushes me over onto my feet, and Dana feels all soft under me while I'm leaning my way out of his bedroom onto her. At the same time Al has his hands on my back. I'm thinking, This is what friends are for. I don't deserve a friend as nice as Al. They haul me out into the backyard, and he says, "You just breathe deep now and you'll be okay," and they lie me flat out onto the grass. It's wet and cold, kind of. I can feel that much through the back of my shirt, but I'm really thinking about, all I can think about is: breathe, breathe, breathe.

Al goes on talking about how I shouldn't smoke so much, and I have to pace myself, and be careful man, because he worries about me and stuff like that. Dana says, "You think he's gonna be all right? Let's get him some water." And Al says, "No, he'll be all right, I had the same thing happen to me once. All he needs is some good air." But Dana says she's going in to get some water out of the kitchen, and is that okay? And Al says no, like he's all pissed off, and he'll get it.

So while we're out there in the yard, I can hear Al open the back door, and Dana kind of bends over me. I can smell her breath because it smells like peanut butter. She's not saying anything. She's just bending over me like she's about ready to bite my lips off, and I see her almost right on top of me and I say, "I can't breathe, I can't breathe." But I'm getting the creeps. Now I know Dana's smart because she goes to college, but I'm thinking: Touch me once, you're a dead woman. I put my one hand up, and then I put my other hand up so both of them are on either one of her shoulders. She's smiling big like she's gonna kiss me. But I push her away, not too hard.

I have to look at something, because if I close my eyes I'm going to disappear. That's what it feels like. I'm looking up at the sky, and everything is too far away. So I look over at the pile of old tires Al has in his backyard. I'm staring at these tires, not looking at Dana, until I hear Al. He lifts up my head, and Dana is taking the cup out of his hand. She's trying to pour water into me.

"Swallow," she goes, and I'm going way back now: all the way back to Mama and the high chair. I'm banging my foot on that high chair. I take the cup myself and drink some of the water. That helps. Al takes the cup away from me, and he puts his fingers right into the cup. He wipes his hand over my face. I'm feeling good enough to get up already. I like how they're all worried about me.

Al says, "You okay, man?" And I say, "Yeah, I'm just way stoned." And then I say, "I better get home." Dana says, "You sure you can make it?"

I'm waiting for Al to offer to let me stay at his place. We did that a lot when we were in school. But Al doesn't say anything, so I walk on out of there before Dana can screw me into walking her all the way home.

✄

It only takes me about half an hour to walk there. I live in a trailer park south of town off Old Mission Road. If I had a job, I'd have a car, and then I could probably get my own place, too. But the trailer park isn't so bad. It's an okay place, mostly because it's a family park. College kids aren't allowed. But there are a lot of little kids around, and last year two men and their wives tried to kill off their own four kids by burning down one of their trailers with all of the kids inside. Some retarded kid overheard them talking about it beforehand, and they're all in jail now. The trailer park can be a pretty weird place, especially when you're high. But tonight I'm walking on past Lennie Mathewson's trailer, and it looks like Lennie left a little beer on his porch. That's cool. I find three bottles that aren't even opened all mixed in with the other empty ones, so I stick them under my jacket and carry them home.

My brothers are still up watching television, and I should probably tell them they should be in bed. Ma's working at the hospital cafeteria. Harlen and Dean watch too much TV, but I figure twelve and fifteen ought to be old enough to decide for themselves. I'm not too worried about them. I'm thinking I better get my ass in bed before they smell the pot. But they don't even notice. Everything smells like Camels to Harlen and Dean. They're sitting in a cloud of smoke, and Harlen says, "Hey," but I duck down the hall and lay the beer out onto my bed. I'm into the second one before I start feeling okay again, and then I reach into my pocket and feel for my bag. It's not there. Al took it into the house and once we got inside, he never gave it back to me. I'm thinking, He's probably smoking it with Dana while I'm sitting on my bed drinking beer all by myself. I have an idea to walk all the way back into town, but I'm tired. I figure I'll get him early in the morning.

But I'm still high in the morning, and it takes me a little while to get going. It's almost noon before I get into town, and by the time I get a coffee and a bag of Fritos at the 7-ll, I know it's way too late to catch Al at home. He has to be to work at nine because he does the prep. I walk over to Dana's, because I figure maybe he gave the bag to her to give to me, and I'm hoping she's home. She showed me which window was hers, and so I throw a stone up against the glass to see if she's in there. It's just a little stone, and it doesn't make much noise, so I have to pick up a bigger stone. Finally I get one big enough to hear, and she sticks her big mug out through the curtains. I wave at her.

She acts like she's all pissed off, but she comes to the door in her bathrobe, and waves me on inside. I like to go inside people's houses and see what everything looks like, so I figure it would be neat to see how a college kid lives. Dana takes me upstairs, and she's being real nice, but the place looks like a dump to me. Dana lives in this room in the upstairs of a house with about a half dozen other students. They each have their own room, and they share an upstairs kitchen, but it's kind of cramped and small. The downstairs is where the landlady lives.

The only thing they have to lock their room when they're out is this padlock on the outside of their doors. The rooms are clean, but they're real small, and when we go past her roommates up the stairway, they do look like born-again Christians: three guys who wear glasses and a girl with pimples all over her neck. I say hello when we go past, but Dana has to introduce me, even though we all have to speak real low because we don't want to wake up the 500-year-old lady downstairs. I'm thinking, Big deal. I walk around her up the stairs in front of her and she's walking up right behind me, and we don't say a word until we get to her room. She closes the door behind me.

She turns around, and it's like she's trying to be mad at me. She has that look. But she has trouble being mad because she likes me so much, I can tell. It's like, when I smile, she can't help but smile right back. I'm trying to be nice, but all I want to do is get my stuff back. She says, "I know what you're here for. You want your bag, don't you?" And I say, "That's right. Al give you my stuff?" She says, "No," but she smiles, like she's playing with me, so to tell you the truth I don't know whether she has my bag or not. I say, "Why not?" And she says, "Because Al has it."

"I was afraid of that."

"He said you could get it from him tonight."

"After he smokes the whole bag, maybe."

There's really no place to sit except the bed, but Dana sits down on that, and she scoots her butt back against the wall because there's a window right next to her bed. "Oh, Al wouldn't do that, would he?" She looks out of the window while we're sitting there, like she's trying to wake up. I bet she's still buzzed. I bet Dana isn't used to getting as high as Al and I do all the time.

I'm poking through her stuff, like you do when you're at somebody's place for the first time. She has all of these Joni Mitchell records lined up, like she takes good care of them. "You got a stereo?" I say. She says, "No, but Evinrude has a record player in his room, and he lets me play my records over there all the time."

"Who's Evinrude?"

"Just some guy," she says, all mysterious like I'm not supposed to know. She reaches down the front of her bathrobe, and straightens her underwear or something. "I think I'm still stoned. God, we smoked a lot yesterday. What time is it?"

"Can't you see the clock? It's twelve-thirty."

"Twelve-thirty? I missed my design class. Shit." She rubs her eyes and gives me this look like it's the end of the world to miss her dumb class. But she doesn't get up or anything. I'm betting she skips class a lot.

I look through the records. There's this picture of Joni Mitchell and she's kind of sitting cross-legged on the ground with her head sticking out, sort of like an ape. So I say, not really thinking that Dana probably likes the way that Joni Mitchell looks, since she likes her music so much, I say, "God, she's ugly."

Dana says, "No, she is not."

"She is too. She looks like the wife of the head ape on *Planet of the Apes*."

She's wrapping her robe all tight around her boobs. "You don't know what you're talking about. I saw *Planet of the Apes* and there was no head ape," she says.

"There was too."

"Well, if there was a head ape," she says, rubbing her eyes with her fists, "then he didn't have a wife, because the only ape wife was Zera, and Joni Mitchell doesn't look *anything* like Zera." So we're laughing about that, and then Dana goes, "You're jealous."

"She's a baboon," I go, and I'm holding up another album cover. On this one, she really does look like the kind of monkey that would swing down from a tree and drop a coconut on your head. I am not exaggerating. "Mon-key. Go-rill-a."

"Hell, do you know anything about music?" Dana says. "Have you ever studied music? I have. Ask me what good music is. You don't know anything about it. You are ignorant." Which is true, but I'm thinking that's kind of mean of her to say so. I scratch under my arms and make monkey noises until she puts her hands over her ears. She closes her eyes, so I tickle her feet. "Yah," she says, and she pulls her feet away. But she likes that. I can tell she likes that.

"So what do you wanna do?" I say.

"I've got classes, Bennie."

"'I've got classes, Bennie.' Don't go to class, Dana." I reach out and poke her where her fat sticks out, like Al did. She giggles, and I say, "You know anybody else who's got some pot?"

"Is that all you want to do is smoke?"

"I know how to have fun," I say. "You may be smart and you may be rich, Dana. But I know how to have fun."

"I'm not rich, Bennie."

"You are too. Come on. Let's do something."

"You're kidding, right? You're just saying that to get me to go with you. And then I'll skip class, and then what?"

"Come on, Dana." I hate to be bored. I would rather do anything than be bored.

She slides off the bed and walks over to the closet door. When she opens it, I'm looking inside and I can't believe how big her closet is. "That's a huge closet," I say.

"It sure is. I can change my clothes in there when I have company." She leaves the door open a crack, and I wait on the bed for her. She says, "I can't believe I'm doing this. I never skipped class before. Not here, anyway."

"You already have. You already missed the first one."

"But I still have speech class." She opens the door and she's wearing the biggest pair of army surplus pants I've ever seen in my life. She goes, "You like my new tennis shoes?"

I go, "Yeah. Let's go to the dams."

✄

I take Dana down to the dams, and I know this real good place there where all the little Indian kids go swimming. There's this place in the bulrushes, and it's perfect if you're Marlin Perkins, because nobody can see you, but you're still close enough to the water to hear the fish jump. So we're looking at the water, and I'm thinking about sometime last summer when there was this guy down at the dams who was real friendly to me. He wanted me to wrestle with him, so we wrestled. But then he wanted me to go swimming with him under the dams. He said it was real cool under there. But I can't swim, and to tell you the truth, I was afraid of the water. I never saw him again, either.

Dana and I sit down and bum about the pot for a while. Dana has this bowl she made in art class, and she pulls it out in front of me and we stare at it for about a minute. I'm thinking about how when you're high, everything feels different. It's like the time I got my glasses: Each little leaf sticks out all by itself. All the birds sing louder. Being outside when you're stoned is the greatest. Dana lies back onto the grass, and I'm thinking how I can see the beach if I sit up on my legs. I'm scoping out the kids from the reservation who come down to swim off the dams.

"We oughta go skinny-dipping," Dana says, and she sits up again like it's a real good idea. I'm thinking: Good idea, but not with you, woman. "You wanna go skinny-dipping?" And I'm thinking right then that I see something good, real good, and it's up under the trees off the beach. "Hey," she says, and she kicks my foot with her foot. I say, "Yeah, right. With all these people around." She keeps kicking her leg. She says she's bored: "What do you wanna do?" So I say we ought to go out to the beach.

We go out to the sandy place under the dams, which is about as much of a beach as you'll ever get so close to town, and since I don't have any trunks, I take my shirt off and use it for something to lie on top of. Dana just sits there, looking at me without my shirt on, and then she goes: "You don't have hardly any hair on you, do you?"

I roll over onto my back. I say, "No. Sorry, but my legs are real hairy." She sits there looking at me, and then I see her arm reach out and she pinches me on the butt.

"Hey."

"You have a hole in the back of your pants, Bennie." Now I don't know about that, but I'm not liking her squeezing on my ass like that. She's like some big pile of something on top of the beach until I roll over on my stomach, and then it's like she can't resist herself. I'm ignoring her, and I'm scoping out this one Indian guy who's sitting in the shade behind me. He's dark. He's sitting next to another guy on this old uprooted tree that's lying on the ground. Right when I look up at him, directly at him, he grabs his crotch like he's got an itch. So I check out everybody else, and Dana is just sitting there watching the water. Even the guy beside this guy is talking to somebody else, and I can see they got a cooler of beer. I look back at the guy, he grabs his crotch again, so I smile at him, not right at him, but sort of in his general direction. I start chewing on my thumbnail. The Indian guy pulls his fingertips up to his nose, like he smells something.

I look at Dana again, and I kind of check her out by saying something like, "This is great, isn't it?" And she says, "Good stuff," and then I tell her I gotta take a piss. "Can I go with you?" she says, ha, ha. I say, "As bad as I gotta go I'm afraid I'd get some on you," and then it's my turn to laugh. "That's gross," she says.

But by then I'm back on the path, ready for Mr. Scratch-'n'-Sniff. I'm kind of standing there, looking around, and the guy does come through the bushes with a beer in his hand. He holds it up like "to the

James Russell Mayes

Queen," and then he puts it on the log. He smiles. It's always nice when they smile. It takes a lot of guts when you think about what could happen. He unzips his pants and I unzip my pants. We piss like we're just taking a piss.

"They say when it comes out clear like that, it means you're drunk," I say. I notice that he's kind of checking out behind him. "Oh yeah," he says, and I'm surprised that his voice sounds so much like a little kid's. He looks kind of old. "I'm drunk," he says. And then he shakes his dick, like to prove it. I look at him from the side, so I can get a good look at it. But then I see this pregnant Indian girl standing just off the path with her arms folded. She's watching us. So I shake off myself and reel it in and zip up, and by then the guy sees her too, so he does the same thing. I don't know what else to do, so I sort of look around on the ground like I lost something. I'm kind of wandering nowhere in particular, but sort of away from the pregnant Indian girl with her arms folded.

The guy follows me down the path. But the girl follows him. She's not even looking at me now, it's like she's trying to get his attention. He ignores her. And the whole time he's giving me these looks like: Forget about her, let's do it right here, right now, hit the dirt, boy. He's got this big grin on his face. But I'm freaking out. It's not like I know who this guy is. And what's the lady doing with him, are they married or what? I walk out to the edge of the water and follow the dingy sand back to the beach.

When I get back to the beach, Dana is sitting out there just like I left her. It's like everything: the water, the kids and all the noise, everything is moving but her, and she's so still that I'm thinking she's in a different dimension or something. I knock her on the shoulder, and she looks up and smiles. Her eyes get real big and she says, "Do I look as ragged-out as you do?" I say, "I hope not."

I'm watching the Indian guy. He's standing in the bushes, and he's got both of his hands in his pockets. He's looking at me, still smiling big time. I don't see the pregnant Indian girl anywhere. I'm thinking about Al and what a pig he is sometimes. "Al gets out of work around four, four-thirty, right?"

She rolls her eyes. "Come on, Bennie. Forget about Al. You said we were going to do something."

"There's a lot of stuff we could do. What do you wanna do?"

"You said you had something fun we could do."

I'm looking around, and I can't really think of anything. It's not really like I want to be with Dana, anyway. It's just that I'd rather not be by myself. "We could go swimming," I say.

"Oh, right," she goes. "With all these people around."

"No," I go. "Not skinny-dipping. Swimming. You never went swimming with your clothes on?"

"With my clothes on?" Like she doesn't believe me, I'm this crazy guy who goes swimming with his clothes on and everything. She likes me, I can tell she likes me. So I get up and I pull her like we're going into the water, and Dana screams like any woman does when she's about to be pulled into the water. I push her down onto the sand, and she rolls over, and I pull her brand-new tennis shoes off. I make like I'm gonna throw them into the dams.

"Bennie, you stop that right now. You put those shoes back."

"'You put those shoes back.'" So I throw the shoes down, but I grab ahold of Dana and pull her into the water. I'm walking right out into the water, waist-deep, and I'm pulling her with me. Damn, that water's cold. Dana's screaming her head off, but I'm thinking she must kind of like it, and then I see my Indian friend. He's real drunk, and he raises his beer up in the air like "to the Queen" again.

"Bennie, I'm soaking wet," and then she comes after me, and she pushes me backward into the water. And I'm like trying to tell her that I don't know how to swim or anything. We're getting real close to the dams. So Dana pushes me backward, and I go back but I'm not feeling the ground under my feet anymore. I start kicking my legs. I'm moving my hands like you're supposed to when you know how to swim, and I give her this look.

She goes, "What's wrong, Bennie?"

"Dana, I can't swim." And she goes, like it's real funny, "Oh, right." And then I say, "No, Dana. Really." And it's true. So she believes me. I'm up to my neck, and the current is pulling me backward, and I'm just breaking even, keeping my head above water. I'm going, "Dana. Help me, man. I'm going under."

So Dana jumps under the water like some lifeguard or something. I'm just kind of losing speed and moving backward even faster, and

James Russell Mayes

I'm hearing the water real loud in my ears. Then she's underneath me. Dana comes up out from underneath me and she drags me back out of the current and up onto the other side of the water. She's soaking wet, and we're both dripping all over the place, and I feel like I almost died. I go, "You saved my life." I say it over and over, like I can't believe I'm alive. "You saved my life," I say.

Dana starts laughing at me, and I go, "What's so funny? What's wrong? You think it's funny? I was almost dead!" And she goes, "No, Bennie. Your hair isn't even wet. I saved your life and you didn't even go under."

✄

We walk back to her place, and we're both so wet that we go "squish, squish" all the way home. I put my arm around Dana, and I'm going like, "You saved my life. You saved my life, woman." And then I push her away, but she grabs my hand. We're holding hands, like we're both going steady or something. It makes me feel good and mean but happy at the same time, holding hands with this big fat girl down the street. It doesn't bother me if some of the college people on her street are looking at us funny. I think to myself, The funny thing is that they think my girlfriend is fat, and that we're both soaking wet, not that I'm a faggot. So I pinch Dana right in her big fat butt at the stoplight on Bellows where there's a truck and two cars waiting. Two guys in the truck put their heads back. They're laughing at us. It doesn't bother me, because I made them laugh.

We go on past the City-County Building, and I'm not really paying attention, I'm looking at that strange-looking rusty building on Main. When I was in high school, I knew the janitor that worked in there. He gave me some whiskey to warm me up. It was Christmastime. He must've seen me poking around outside. So he let me in. He stopped the elevator between floors, and after I did what he wanted me to, he got me high in the elevator. He tried to give me his winter coat, but I took the bottle of whiskey.

So I'm getting kind of quiet, and I push Dana away, but by then we're almost to her place, and I'm getting tired of my jeans squishing on me, even if my shirt's dry. She pushes the door open. "Get in there," she says. I walk in and she closes both doors behind us. I know

I didn't do anything, but I'm still glad the 500-year-old lady isn't around.

"I can't believe you, woman," I say. "You're a mess."

Dana laughs. "Let's go upstairs and get some dry clothes on." And I'm thinking, Oh boy. I wonder what color dress she's gonna put me in. We're walking up the stairs, and then she says, "Why don't you come on up and have dinner with me?"

I go, "Let me see," like I have to think about it. "We got up around noon. It's almost four o'clock, right? I guess it's about lunchtime." She puts her head back and laughs right out loud, like she does.

"You be a good boy and I'll get you high," she says.

"I thought you didn't have any dope on you?"

"I don't, Bennie. You'll see," all mysterious-like.

No one else is upstairs, so I guess it's late enough in the afternoon so the Christians already ate. Or maybe it's too early. I follow Dana into her bedroom, and she gives me this giant bathrobe. I go into her closet, and I take my clothes off. I put Dana's bathrobe on, and when I come out of the closet, she's still taking her clothes off.

I go, "Sorry." I go back into the closet, no big deal, and Dana says, "That's okay. I'm not shy, Bennie." That's when I should've figured out what was just about to happen. I wait for Dana to get done, and when she goes, "All clear," I come out of there, and she's got a dress on. A big dress. We go into the kitchen. Dana pulls out the hamburger. She starts making these hamburgers, and she makes more than I think we'll ever be able to eat. The whole time she's sticking them into the pan, she's saying stuff like, "I love to cook. You know what I mean? I like everything about it: the smells and the color of the food and the way it feels in your hands." And then she reaches under the plastic and whips off a hunk of hamburger and puts it into her mouth raw.

"That's gross," I say.

She says, "It is not." I'm just trying to keep out of her way while she's opening these cupboard doors and pulling things out of drawers. All I can think about is how good a hamburger tastes when you're high.

"You never ate raw hamburger before?" I tell her I never did. "You wanna try some?"

James Russell Mayes

"That's sick. That's gross." I'm thinking to myself, I had no idea how low class Dana was, eating hamburger raw and stuff. But she's being nice to me the whole time because I'm probably the only company she ever had. So we eat and the hamburgers are real good because she put Lawry's Seasoned Salt on them. We eat them on plates with a lot of ketchup, which is how I like mine.

After we're done, she turns on the burner under a big pot with grease in it. "What's that?" I say, and she says it's her frying grease. The pot has about two or three quarts of grease in it and it smells like fish. "What's it for?"

"It's to fry the hush puppies in," she says, and she drags out a bag of flour and a bag of sugar. She puts some dough together and then drops it with a big spoon into the grease. She lets them boil in the grease for a little while, and then she fishes them out with another spoon and rolls them in the sugar.

I'm kind of grossed out, because I'm thinking that even though I usually do the cooking for my brothers if there's cooking to be done, the only frying I ever do is with a couple eggs in Blue Bonnet margarine. Ma never fries either. But I'm trying to learn something because I get tired of eating the same kind of thing all the time. We wait until they're cool, after she's made about two or three dozen of them, and then she starts into them before I do. I can't even pick them up, they're so hot and my teeth always hurt if something's too hot, so I wait while she's eating away on them. When I do take one, I burn my tongue. But they have a good taste to them, kind of burnt on the outside but like doughnuts in the middle.

"Good meal," I say, and I mean it, and it was better than I'd thought. I'm so full, I'm thinking how full I'd be if I had my pants on. So we go back into her room. I'm thinking how pot always makes the food taste better and how I wish I didn't have to ask. "I was kind of hoping you were gonna get me high," I say, real smooth-like.

"Yeah, I know," she says. "I could tell. Sorry." And then she's laughing, like it's some kind of joke.

"Listen," I say. "That's my pot. If Al rolled you a joint out of my stuff, you oughta share it with me."

She's shaking her head like she can't believe it. "I don't have any of your pot, Bennie."

"Then where'd you get the pot?"

"I don't have any pot."

"So how come you said you'd get me high?"

She's pulling on her ear, but this time she's smiling at me. "You ever smoke resin?"

"What's resin?"

"Resin?" She's sticking the end of her thumb into the bowl of her pipe and she's rubbing it. She pulls her thumb out and sticks it in my face. "See this black stuff? That's resin. I can't believe you didn't already know this." But I only smoke joints. How would I know? Dana tells me how the black stuff inside of your pipe can get you really high if you scrape it out into a pile and smoke it. And I'm thinking, Wow, this sounds real sick. She says it doesn't make you sick. It turns your shit green, but it doesn't make you sick.

So I'm like, let's try it. It's worth a buzz. We sit on her bed while she straightens out a giant paperclip and scrapes around inside of her pipe. She goes on about how this resin inside of her pipe is the good kind because it's like gooey tar and that means it'll kind of melt while it's burning and get us twice as high. So she cleans out the inside of her pipe, and it takes about twenty minutes.

I'm just kind of lying back on her bed in her bathrobe. And I'm getting kind of depressed because I've got this bag of pot I spent a month collecting pop cans for, and I can't even get high with it because it's over at someone else's house. I'm thinking stuff like why should I bother sharing weed with people, if I never get it back? Which is true, but if you can't get high with somebody else, then why even bother? I used to smoke by myself all the time, but all I got was paranoid. I was sitting around in the trailer, and Ma was at work and my brothers in school. I was staring out the window and hearing all the women who were screaming at their kids. That's how low I'm feeling, while Dana's cleaning out her pipe.

She finally rolls the resin all together into a little ball, and she pops the ball back on top of the screen to her pipe. She lights it, and it sits there under my nose and kind of glows like a coal. It isn't harsh or anything, it doesn't hurt my throat, but after only two tokes, I can feel the spirals going off inside my head. Before I pass it back to her, I'm feeling good again, right away. We're having a great time, passing it back and forth, looking out of her window alongside the bed.

Then Dana says, "Getting high always makes me horny."

I'm looking at her, and she's grinning big. And so I kind of change the subject. All I can think of to talk about is Al, how I'm so pissed off at him. But I don't stop there, I go on and on, it must be because of the weed, I don't stop and I tell Dana all about Al and me, and how I always kind of liked him in a different way than he likes me. I tell her even though I'm so pissed off at him, how much I really like him. I do. And shit, the only reason I bought the pot in the first place was because I like to get him high, and even though I know he's not like I am, I keep getting him high just hoping that maybe one day he'll be horny enough to give me some of what he's been giving all these girls he's been with since high school.

Dana goes, "How many girls has Al been with since high school?" I have to think a minute, and then I make up some number, because really, there's too many to count. I tell her a dozen or so. Dana just shakes her head. She goes, "You're lonely, aren't you? You don't like being by yourself all the time, do you?" And of course, stupid me, I don't let it go there, I go on and on and on. I start in about how sometimes when I'm with him, I feel like I love him. Not just friend love, but real love, how he makes me feel like things aren't so screwed up as they could be.

"Oh, I know, I know," she goes. Her eyes are so big, and they're getting real watery while I'm talking about this stuff. "I'm lonely, too," she says, and I'm thinking she's gonna cry right there. I'm sitting there in her bathrobe. I'm feeling sorry for both of us. Dana leans back onto her pillows, and she lets out the air. She tells me how she's been watching me all along, and I've been sitting there for a good long time, and did I know that she felt the same way about me as I did about Al?

"No," I say. She's looking at me with that look on her face, and then she starts in about how she saved my life. "I saved your life, Bennie," she says. "I'm so glad I saved your life, you know?" And I go, "No." She says, "If I hadn't been there to pull you out of the water, you'd be dead. Do you understand that, Bennie? You'd be dead. You wouldn't be here right now." And I'm thinking about standing up and leaving, but she makes a joke out of it all the sudden, she goes, "You'd be in hell right now, where you belong." She laughs. I'm looking at her like I can't believe this, all that stuff about her being in love with me, and then I see how her nightgown kind of lifts up so I can see more of her fat legs. I'm starting to get a little scared, too.

All of the sudden somebody's banging on her door. We both jump off the bed. I'm about to shit right there in her bathrobe, but Dana grabs ahold of my arm and says, real normal, like we were smoking cigars, "Who is it?"

"It's j-just me, Dana." It's some guy. "It's Evinrude. C-could you hold it d-d-down in there?" And the voice sounds real femmy, like the guy behind that door was giving blow jobs in kindergarten. Dana opens the door, just a crack, so hopefully he won't smell the dope. She says she's sorry, real nice to him, but I can see this one Christian eye kind of sticking up over Dana's big fur ball of a head. And the eye isn't looking particularly nice to me. I'm wondering how much the guy heard of what we were saying.

"Hey," I say. That's what I say when somebody's looking at me. I sit back down on the bed, like it's no big deal going on in there. "Hey," he says, and it sounds like he's from the South. Either that, or he's making fun of me. The guy tries to get his face around Dana's head, because she's kind of blocking the doorway to keep him out, but then his face sticks out next to her ear. I'm thinking: Not bad.

"W-w-well, I have st-st-studying to do," Evinrude says, like he's bragging. "What's your name?"

"Bennie," I say. "Nice to meet you," and that's all I can get in because Dana closes the door on him. She does it so fast, I have to laugh. Through the door, I hear the guy say, "S-see you around." We don't say anything until his footsteps go away. Dana sits down on the edge of the bed, and I kind of fall toward her because the bed is too soft. "God damn it that bummed me out," she says. "Him coming in here like that. I'm tired of living with Christians."

"Are we gonna be all right? I mean, do you think he heard what I said?" She's looking at me like she's real stoned, like she's thinking something. She acts like she doesn't even care about it. She says, "I think I'm real horny," and she puts her hand on my leg. "Knock it off,

Dana," and I pick up her hand and put it down onto the bed. She makes a pouty face. She says she wonders what I got underneath the bathrobe for her to suck on.

I go, "No, let's smoke some more." Dana says no at first. I pinch her leg, and I pinch it hard until she screeches a little bit, and then she says, "Okay." We smoke another little ball of the resin. All the while we're passing it back and forth, she's looking sad with those big eyes of hers. I go, "You okay? You getting too high?" But she's saying, "No. Nothing." We do that back and forth a couple times until I see how stupid I must be starting to sound.

Dana gets up and she's stretching with her arms over her head. She says she really does have to get out of her dress. I go, "Why? You just put it on." She makes up some lame excuse about how it's too tight or something, which is probably true. She gets up and goes over to the closet. I'm thinking how stoned that resin got me. I'm feeling good, and I'm thinking how great pot is. It really is, it's great. I can see why Al loves the stuff. And I don't wonder he does just about anything to get high.

Well, Dana's standing by the closet at the foot of the bed. I'm just looking straight ahead at the door because I don't want to see anything that I don't want to see. And the next second she's on top of me. I'm on my side, and Dana's on top of me. She's reaching around with her arm and grabbing into the bathrobe at my chest. She's kissing my ear and sticking her tongue in it.

Dana's going, "Oh, Bennie, oh, Bennie," her hands are squeezing my chest, and I can feel her legs on either side of me like she's riding a horse. Up and down she goes. I'm lying there underneath her. She's not really as heavy as I'd think she'd be, but I'm wondering what the hell I should do. To tell you the truth, I start praying. I pray to Jesus himself, and I ask him to save me from my sins. I say to him, "Jesus, if there's anything about me you don't like, I'm sorry. But please get this woman offa me."

And lo and behold, when I open my eyes, right in front of me on the bedspread, a miracle, I believe in Jesus: there's the ashtray with her pipe and lighter in it. I reach out and I grab ahold of the lighter. I say, "Get off me, Dana." Dana stops for a second, just a second. She says, "No." And then she starts up again, with the kissing in my ear and the hands moving down to my belt. "Oh, Bennie," she goes. "Oh, Bennie, I love you, I really do love you."

So I say to her, "Are you gonna get off me, Dana?" She's going, "Come on, Bennie. I got you high, didn't I?" And she must not've seen the lighter because she starts pulling on the belt to the robe, like she's going for the goodies. "Oh, Bennie," she says. "Oh, Bennie, you're not really gay, are you? I don't think you are, not really. Let's be lovers, Bennie. Let's be secret lovers." I don't even wait for the rest, I just go. I light it right under her arm, which is right in front of my eye. She screams, too, like a monster movie, and she's off of me. She's standing at the edge of the bed and she's grabbing onto her arm. "What did you do? What did you do?"

"I told you to get offa me. Knock that shit off, will you?" I get up and walk right to the door. And then I remember I'm wearing a bathrobe, so I got to go back into her room to pull my pants on. And it's hard putting them on, because I have to pull them on while I still got the bathrobe on to keep her from looking at my ass. All the time, Dana's standing behind me with her dress half off, she's going, "Don't leave, Bennie. Don't go," and she starts crying. She won't dare touch me, because she knows I have the lighter and I'll burn her hair off if she tries it again. "Please don't go. You're not mad at me are you?"

What the hell. I lie to her. What are you supposed to say? "No, I'm not mad at you." And when I turn around to walk out the door, Evinrude is standing there, like he knows what's going on. He takes one look at Dana with her dress opened up in front, and he takes one look at me trying to get out of there. He grabs ahold of my arm, and he goes, "Wh-wh-where are you going? Wh-wh-wh-what's going on here?"

I push him back against the wall, and he's turning red and squawking like a chicken. He goes, "F-f-f-fuck you!" I'm grabbing him by the collar, and I say, "You're welcome to, if you got the balls, chickenshit." I move my face close, and I go, "Once you got your dick inside, I'd cut it off with my ass." I'm thinking about maybe kissing him, too. Dana starts up with, "Please don't go, Bennie. Please stay." Like now we're gonna sit around and eat hush puppies and hamburgers or something. "Bennie. I didn't mean it. I was just being foolish."

I can't believe that woman. I can't stand looking at her. I let the Christian go, and I have to stomp around in my shoes for two minutes to get them on. I'm not about to be standing around in wet clothes. I walk down the stairs and out onto the porch. I'm walking down the steps, and I'm thinking I'm tired of people taking advantage of me. I'm tired of walking all over town just to spend some time with people I don't even like. And I'm tired of them smoking my pot up.

I'm all the way out the door and almost down the steps before I get my bright idea. I walk around back of Bertha's place. I walk up the grass where the driveway used to be, and I walk into the little old garage. Dana's bike is leaned up against the wall, just inside. So I take it. I ride out onto the sidewalk and over the bumps up to High Street. High Street's not a joke. It really is the name of the one street that cuts through town and separates the town kids from the college kids. I take High Street all the way over to Al's place. It's a real smooth ride.

It's all quiet at Al's place, because his mom won't let him play the stereo before dinner. When I come up to the door I can't hear anything, not even a TV. So I knock. I hear Al's mom and she calls in that voice of hers, "Al? Al!" And when Al's mom screams, she screams like she's in real good shape. I keep banging on the front door, and I'm getting pissed off because I know Al must be in there. He gets off at four-thirty or something, and why else would she be calling him? So I keep on banging on the door. And pretty soon, it turns out it is his mom answering the door. She's real short when she's standing up, and she doesn't even smile at me. She's looking old in the daylight.

"Oh," she goes, "it's you."

"That's right, Mrs. Roethlisberger. Is Al home?"

"He's in the shower, Bennie. You know, he hasn't been feeling well today."

"He hasn't?"

"Oh, no," she says. "You know, he didn't even go in to work today?"

"He didn't?"

"Why don't you come in. I know he'd be cheered up to see you, Bennie."

"That'd be nice." I follow her back through the hall and into the living room. She sits down on the couch, and she's pointing to an old La-Z-Boy so I'll sit there and not anywhere else.

"I hope you don't mind if I lie down," she says. "My heart is easily strained."

"You go right ahead," I say. She has the shades all pulled, or I'd look out the window. There's not much else to look at except her. So I'm looking at her, and she's looking at me. And I feel like I should be saying something, but I don't quite know what to say. And since she's not saying anything, I'm not saying anything, so we're both not saying anything. She smiles, so I smile. She's lying on the couch with this nice look on her face, her eyes wide open, and she snorts. I'm sitting up, I can't believe this, I'm waiting to see if she's just breathing hard, but then she does it again. She's snoring. Fell right to sleep like she was getting high on all that medicine the doctor gives her. Al's mom is fast asleep with her eyes open wide.

"Hey," Al says. I look up, and he's standing in the doorway with a towel wrapped around him. His mom kind of snuffles like she's going to wake up, but she doesn't . Al smiles. He sure looks healthy to me.

"Hey," I say. I sit up, and I'm about to give him hell because, knowing Al, he probably smoked half my bag away. But he puts his finger on his lips and points to the old lady. He goes on down the hall into his bedroom, and I have to follow him. You can't wake up a sick old lady. Finally we get inside his room. He's going to close the door behind us, but before he does, his mom starts calling to us. So Al has to call down the hall to her: "Do you need something, Mother?" I'm looking at him like I'm about ready to kill him, and his mom calls in to us: "You boys be good, now."

I sit down on the bed. I'm smelling Al, and he smells like soap and shampoo. He closes the door. He walks over to his chest of drawers and pulls out one of the drawers. "How's it goin', man?" I'm looking at him, and he's smiling, like he thinks it's real funny to smoke my weed when he's the one who has the job. Then he unwraps his towel. He throws it on the floor; he's standing there, smiling at me: bare naked.

I look at him, and then I look at my shoes. My face burns. I swallow hard and think about something else, anything else: Raw hamburger.

James Russell Mayes

High Street. Pregnant Indian girls. He'll never guess I got jumped on by Dana. He'll never guess I stole her bike. I look up again, and he's just standing there, with his hand on his hip. It's like he's waiting for me to say something, but I can't talk. I'm waiting for him to pull on his undershorts.

But I think that's why he doesn't pull them on. Instead, Al laughs. He holds my bag up to his nose like it's the greatest stuff he ever smoked. It's like he's got me there in his hand when he squeezes it. I don't even notice if the bag's that much smaller. Al's bare naked. When he laughs, his dick jiggles.

"Wanna get high?" he says.

The Hired Boy

The dream is like this: it's a flying dream. Melanie first, off the roof in her nightshirt like in *Peter Pan*, her arms held out to control the wind. Clay is behind her, gliding through the waterfall of willow leaves and into the dark space that is the sky at night. They fly around and around the house and then around the three maple trees in the front yard, higher and higher until the house is small enough to fly away from. When they can't see the barnyard anymore they fly low over the dark fields, close enough so that Clay can see the glimmer of stones under the moonlight, in the fresh furrows of the plowed field. He holds his arms out like Melanie and flies as low as he can up the gentle rise of a hill, daringly close, so that he won't be pulled away from the earth by the stars or the temptation of other planets.

By the time they see the fire they've been flying for hours. Clay's arms are tired. The black air is cold. Melanie flies down, and he is right behind her. They drop down among the cowboys who sit around the fire. But Clay lands in an odd way; he straddles the man he lands on. He wraps his arms around the man's neck as if the man were a pony at the free fair. The man's hat falls off, and both of them fall backward in surprise. Clay feels a weight against his chest, his heart beating under the pressure of what he holds.

When he wakes up he has that feeling that something awful has happened. There is something curious that he doesn't understand, and he doesn't know what it has to do with cowboys. He's had cowboy dreams before, riding horseback through the sage, tracking mountain

James Russell Mayes

lion. Other dreams were not like this one; he can't sleep the rest of the night, counting out memory verses from the Bible on his fingers.

Melanie squats in the driveway, dirty hands on her dirty knees. She is writing how many years old he is with her finger in the earth, and from where he is kneeling in the dirt on his knees, the eight is sideways. He's that many years old, and now Mama will let him have his own garden. The hired boy will bring in rocks from the fence row and put them in a circle around the little birch tree in the front yard. He'll dig up the ground and spread a layer of fresh manure in the bottom. Clay will watch from the front porch while the hired boy fills in the rest of the earth.

Now when he looks at a photograph, there is always some tree that he forgot or an expression on someone's face that he failed to memorize. It seems that Clay remembers more clearly when he has no visual cues: Melanie's hand under the piano lid, a slice of turkey sticking out of the side of her mouth. Later there would be the way she looked at him through her glasses or how careful she would be when she wore a dress. If he crossed the furrowed field today, her arms would reach up through the grass and her hands would pull him back for a moment. Her dead body would push him up the hill to the house: forever.

When Clay looks down at his own hands, he's holding a clump of red radishes, wet under the tap water. It's the red of the radishes in his soiled fingers, the round weight of them and then the memory of pea blossom from too long ago. It is as if he just woke up. He is bending over the kitchen sink, washing them off, the last from the garden. He tries to remember; it's summer now, this year, but he's been thinking about that other summer.

When the guys at work ask him, Clay tells them that he lives alone because he likes it that way. He talks to himself a lot, and he likes to read for hours in the bathtub. If he needs something, he brings it in or he grows it himself: like the radishes.

Clay remembers that he has to walk Sal, who is sitting near the front door. His mind falls onto the shape of the clip on her leash, an association: the shape of the numeral eight. He's standing in front of the sink one moment. And the next moment he's out in the barn with his cousin Melanie. He knows that he's a lot younger, because she's young: this is the summer when he was eight, and she stayed with his family. He remembers, because his shoes are too tight; when he takes them off tonight, his mother will pull them away. She'll cover him up with the summer sheet. But she'll leave his feet sticking out. He's too old for this, but she'll rub them, first one foot and then the other in her large, dry hands. She'll tell him about Saul on the road to Damascus.

Clay follows Melanie in her daisy-printed overalls. They're trying not to step into the manure on the floor of the barn. He wants to ask Melanie a question. But when he pulls on the strap of her overalls, she spins around with a finger pressed into her lips. She frowns, as if he's done something wrong. Then she turns and steps over a pile of scours, the sweet manure from a calf that's taken too much milk. Clay looks down at the puddle, a brilliant yellow porridge. It smells like the powder they use to wean the runt calf.

He hears water splash and someone laughing. There's the hired boy, standing up, bare naked, in the water trough: he's got hair down there, between his legs. His body is red with sunburn; sunlight comes in through the cracks in the barn wall, presses the bright stripes into his skin. The hired boy stands up to his shins in the water. Melanie is laughing. She must have crept up on him while he was taking a bath, and Clay has followed her. The hired boy wades across the width of the water trough in three long strides. The ragged towel goes around the white line of his waist, the tight skin around the hired boy's navel. They don't run until he leaps over the side and starts after them.

When the hired boy rushes forward, the cold water splashes outward. Clay looks down, and there's water on the front of his Levi's; the cold water from the sink is splashing up, almost overflowing. He turns off the faucet and catches his breath. That summer ... it is as if he has trouble breathing ... before they cut back on the livestock, before he was old enough to do the rest of the chores himself, even before they rented land out to Mr. Jorgenson: Mama had a hired boy. His name was Garth.

Clay decides to take a bath himself, to sit in the tub with a stack of comic books and the paper. He has the day off, because it's Saturday and the local paper doesn't stuff inserts on Saturday. He sits down on the toilet. He opens a double album in his lap and dumps the weed out on top of it. He rolls one more joint. Then he squirts Palmolive

James Russell Mayes

dishwashing liquid into the tub. The hot water's running before he remembers to let Sal out.

When Molly comes up the walk, he's standing in his bathrobe inside the front doorway. Molly gives Sal a dog-hug and steps up onto the porch in her sensible black shoes. Molly wears neat clothes. She always kind of dresses up when she comes to see him. Clay lives in a small house; he has to step back from the door to let her in.

"Do you know what time it is?" she says.

"Yeah." He looks down at his wrist where his watch usually is, but it isn't there.

"It's two o'clock," she says. "And you're not even dressed yet."

"I know," he says. "I've been up since eleven."

Molly walks over to the bathroom door and looks in.

"You taking a bath?" she says.

"About to," he says. He wraps his bathrobe tightly around himself, ties the cord.

"Well don't let me stop you," she says. She smiles at him. Clay looks away.

Molly walks into the living room and sits down in his rocker recliner.

"I'm bored," she says. "I'm bored as hell." She holds her head with both hands and sways back and forth.

"You wanna do something?" he says.

"What you got in mind?"

"You wanna smoke some?" He pulls a joint from the pocket of his robe and holds it up.

"Take your bath first," she says. "You look like shit."

Clay walks to the front door and lets Sal in. Then he goes into the bathroom and closes the vinyl accordion door. He pulls off his robe and scratches his balls. Then he lowers himself into the hot water and the bubbles. He hears Molly walking around in the other room, the jingle of Sal's collar as she follows her.

"Whadda you got in the sink?" she says.

"Radishes. I'm not through cutting them up."

"What a mess," she says. Again, she laughs.

"I like my privacy," he says, "when I'm taking a bath. You mind?" He hears the TV; she must be back in the living room, changing channels. The rocker recliner makes a noise; he can hear the sound from the bathroom when she sits down. When he lies back in the water, he remembers that he didn't eat his breakfast this morning. He turns his head and sees the white terry robe, hung over the seat of the toilet.

Friday night was popcorn night. Sometimes Mama would make fudge and hide warm dabs of it in the bottom of the bowl. They put the metal bowl of popcorn on the chair beside Melanie's bed. He remembers the pajamas, too. They both had white nightshirts that Mama sewed up for them. That night was hot, because as he remembers it, sinking into the bubbles, their nightgowns were off and thrown over the back of the ladder-back chair. The window was open.

Clay looks around the room and Melanie isn't there. There's a chill from the dark. He feels awkward standing in his underpants in front of the window. Now there's a voice.

"Clay," she says. A hand is waving from the window. "Come out, Clay." He steps out onto the shingles, and then he can see her: Melanie with her stringy hair and her skinny back. She turns around and even though the night air is as blue as creek water and just as deep, he can see her toothy smile, the freckles on her nose. She's not wearing anything except her underpants. She's only ten, but Clay feels a height in his legs, even in the dark. There's a sticky hand around his wrist, and she pulls him out.

"Come on, retard," she says. He steps carefully across the roof, still hot from the sun under his bare feet. Now he can see better . The wind blows through the willows above the roof, and the leaves rustle like a wall of water. They duck under the waterfall. Furiously breaking off branches, Melanie steps all the way over to the edge of the roof.

"What are you doing?" he says. She giggles, and then she turns around.

"Make a window," she says. She's talking low, in confidence. "Garth's got the barn lights on." He helps her, breaking away sticks and then pulling off leaves from the hanging branches until they can see the barn better. Melanie leans back against the biggest branch of the tree, a limb that comes straight up from the ground only an inch from the edge of the roof. From there she stares out through the newly fashioned window in their hideout of willow. Clay looks out the window too; the light shines out through the cracks in the barn wall, casting shadows of giant boards down the hill.

"I don't see a thing," he says. "What's he doing in there, anyway?"

"Playing with himself," she says. He turns around to look at her, and she laughs uproariously. She has to slap herself on the lips, because her hand remembers to be quiet before her mouth does.

"Melonhead." He remembers his name for her. "He is not."

Melanie slaps his arm.

"You're in love with him," he says. "Aren't you?"

"Aren't you?" she says. She presses herself against him, and he can smell the popcorn on her breath. She's wrapping her bare arms around him so that he can't get away. She's blowing words into his ear: "We saw Garth naked, we saw Garth naked, we saw Garth naked." His ear feels fuzzy inside and warm. Vowels pour out over the sticky feet of consonants; words roll over the back of his neck and down his spine. A train howls through town miles away, and when a strong wind picks up, the leaves rush against him, brushing his face. It sounds more like water than wind.

His arms make a splash when they come down on either side of him. Clay sits up in the tub.

"You all right in there?" Molly says. She's shouting from the living room, above the noise of the TV. "Are you stoned already?" she says.

"Yeah." He sinks back down, relaxing his back. He makes a quick wash of himself. Then he steps from the tub. He feels the ring of suds around his shins and wipes it off.

"I wish I had a place with a shower," he hollers, sociably, through the vinyl door.

"I wish I had a place with a tub," she hollers back.

He slaps open the door and locks it there with the flimsy tie-thing.

"You wanna take a bath here?" he says.

"No," she says. Molly looks embarrassed. She rocks forward in the chair. Molly is kind of pretty. She has big, brown eyes. A nice, lean shape in the body. "I mean, I don't take my bath until I go to bed. Shower, I mean."

Clay and Molly sit on his back step. He pulls the joint out of his pocket, and Sal crouches down beside him, watching the movement of his hands attentively.

"Garden looks good," Molly says. She coaxes Sal over to her side of the step with one empty hand. She pats her on the head, and with her other hand she passes the joint back to Clay. He takes it, and Molly brushes her hair back with her fingers.

"Thanks." He draws in on the joint and feels a head rush, the backyard turn. He's walking around the radishes and the peas in his vegetable garden. He's wearing his stiff new play shoes and stepping from stone to stone to stone, around in a circle. He's falling and falling, and it's not actually that he really is falling; it's just that there is a falling inside of him.

He gives Molly the roach. She sucks on the end of it until all the smoke is drawn out. She licks it to make sure it is cool enough and then sticks it in her mouth.

Clay is restless. He walks over to the garden: a half dozen tomato plants, the peppers, leaf lettuce, and the row of carrot where the radishes used to be. He remembers the sweetness in immature peas; he should have planted peas this year. Lacy carrot leaves shiver, the pepper leaves and then the young tomato plants tremble. Clay feels a breeze cross his bare arm; the hair there puckers into goose pimples.

"Why don't we go skinny-dipping?" Molly says. A cloud has passed; she pulls her arm down from her forehead where it was blocking the sun.

Clay has already thought about that. He was afraid she might suggest this.

"I don't think so," he says. He bends over to pick a stone out of the dirt. "You bring a pair of cutoffs?"

"No." She stands up and wipes off her bottom. She really is kind of pretty. The way she moves, or something. So why doesn't he want to go skinny-dipping with her? Clay watches her.

When Molly looks up at him, she blushes.

"I don't need to go swimming," she says.

Clay drops the white pebble into his pocket. He opens the back door to let Sal in. Then he and Molly walk around the little house through the front yard, and they walk down the street. They walk as far as the newspaper office, where they both work. He directs her through the parking lot behind the building.

"Follow me," he says.

"Where are you going now?" she says.

"We don't want them to see us stoned, do we?"

Behind the newspaper office, there's a railroad track. She catches up with him, and they walk along the track.

"You're silly," she says.

"I am not," he says. "Everything I do is logical." She steps from one railroad tie to the other.

"Everything you do has its own logic."

He balances one foot before the other, toe to heel, along one of the iron rails. The train comes through at 9:15, and they know this because Melanie got a watch for her birthday. He counts thirteen summers since he saw her in her underpants, since he felt the tar shingles bite into his back while they lay against the slope of the roof and counted how many dogs they heard bark at the train.

Out of boredom they dig the moss out from between the shingles and throw it over the side of the roof. Melanie can whistle, and she makes missile sounds as the clumps of moss drop over the edge. Some nights the train is late. He lies in bed holding the pillow for fifteen minutes before he hears the whistle, and he knows that she is in her room too, grinning in the dark. Some nights they listen to the cats yowling out behind the apple orchard, and Clay wonders if Tabitha or Saluki or Deadbeat will come back the next morning with ripped ears or a torn claw: bloody prints across the boards on the porch.

They collect dreams. That is what they talk about. Dreams hang heavily in the hickory limbs above them; they come knocking down onto the roof until they land with a splash in the water trapped in the eaves trough. It is the sound that carries him, with Melonhead. The train plows through the middle of a dream and whistles right out into breakfast under the ladder rungs of sunlight through the overgrown lattice outside the breakfast room window. She had the same dream again, and she tells him that over jam. The gray wicker crackles. Her silverware flashes in the sunlight, the ham and eggs. When Mama walks out to the road for the mail, they sneak sherbet from the groaning refrigerator and run out to the barn. A morning wind blows across their knees through the cracks in the wall. Pulling the spoon clean from under her milk mustache, she tells him that she has dreamt about the beagles rolling on their backs in the dirt, about wheat grown tall outside the window of the hideout. She warns him about the legs of the approacher, the boots and the overalls. It's the hired boy, stepping over barbed wire.

They walk through vacant pasture, radiating with dandelions and the quality of sunlight which is the same color. It heaves up into his face, up from the earth: that ridiculous yellow. Not only the light makes him breathless, looming down over the patchwork of the fields in the afternoon: clover and beans and corn and alfalfa. The farmhouse is on a hill; they can see all that from the roof in daylight. Clay and Melanie stand up on the roof in the middle of the day, and Clay feels the height as if it were just another feeling, like being sad or mean or mad. Melanie says it's because you can see everything. When they aren't on the roof or in the barnyard, they sit in Mama's rocking chair on the wooden floor of the screened porch. They wait with the cats in their laps and watch the place where Garth threw down salt for the stock.

Three deer approach through the silence at the edge of the woods. Melanie says they smell the salt. Clay is telling her about his own dream. And then the wind changes; he and Melanie are still flying through the air when the deer are frightened, gliding over the reeds. In Clay's telling, they never land. And when they are gone, it is as if they had never been there. Maybe the deer heard him speaking. Maybe they smelled something that didn't belong in the marsh along the edge of the pasture.

"As if they could tell," Molly says.

It is full summer; Clay hasn't noticed until now, but the chickweed is overgrown, blue and leggy along the track. There's the sound of a lawn mower, the squeak of some kid on a swing. Clay hops off the rail of the train track. He has to push a branch out of their way as they walk along a sandy path that runs up an incline above the track.

"Watch it," he says, holding the branch so Molly can walk past.

"You high?" she says. He has to catch up. She turns around, and he watches her wipe the sweat off her forehead.

"Oh yeah." They walk down into the woods along the trail that leads to the dam. He kicks stones along ahead of them, and Molly plays too. She chases one of his stones in her sensible shoes and then kicks it back to him. Then each of them chooses their own stone; they kick these ahead of each other as they walk. It's an old game he used to play with Melanie.

Molly spreads the blanket out, and the two of them sit on the beach at the foot of the dam. A hundred years ago, it was a mill pond. It gave the city power when the city wasn't much of a city, or at least as much as it is now. There is talk at the paper about turning the area around the dam into a park. The university has already bought the land. It's still a place where westside kids go swimming without a fee. A lot of them come from the reservation after curfew; they smoke dope and drink beer and sometimes, when the cops come through to check it out, they hide under the water. They hold their breath until they're left alone.

"Wanna go swimming?" Clay says. He doesn't look at her when he asks; he's watching the guys on top of the dam.

"No. I didn't bring anything to wear in the water."

"Just go skinny-dipping," he says. He looks at her, and Molly looks away. She digs her shoe in the sand.

"No." She gives him a sharp look, and he laughs. "Not with all these guys around." Molly sounds irritated. A large group of young men crowds around a keg at the top of the dam, talking loudly. There's a stand of cottonwoods over the dam; when the wind picks up, a million white puffs of cotton float out through the air above the water. They pour through the air like dandelion seed.

Clay watches a few of the men build a fire. Some of them gather wood. Someone crumples up newspaper, lights a match under a stack of tinder. Smoke curls out between the photographs and fine print. A guy in a black hat kneels before the flames, blowing into them to help them spread.

"A fire," Molly says.

Outside the barn, the hired boy chops off the heads of chickens.

Clay stands up.

"Let's go wading," he says. He helps her up by giving her both of his hands and pulling her up. His hands feel wet in her hands, which are smooth and dry. Clay and Molly walk slowly into the water, up to their knees by the time the current is strong; the ground underfoot is packed and pebbled by it.

Then Melonhead throws her white Bible onto his lap.

"You have to win," she says. "You have it easier than I do, because you're in the third grade. If you learn twelve verses, they give you an *Illustrated Children's Bible.*"

"'Though I speak with the tongues of men and of angels, and have not charity, I am become as sounding brass or a tinkling cymbal.'" It has rained, and he is following Melanie across the boards laid down through the mud between the house and the barn. "'And though I have the gift of prophecy and understand all mysteries, and all knowledge; and though I have all faith, so that I could remove mountains, and have not charity, I am nothing.'" They are reciting his memory verses; it is Melonhead's favorite chapter from the Bible.

With one hand, Garth holds the hen by her two feet. He rests her on her full breast on the block.

"Reverend Brawn says that even though it says 'charity' in the Bible that it means love," she tells him. She picks up a white stone from the driveway and throws it into the reflection of a tree in a mud puddle. "So when you say it Sunday, use the word 'love' in place of the word 'charity.'" The thorns and branches of the tree become a ring and then more rings within the puddle. *And though I bestow all my goods to feed the poor, and though I give my body to be burned and have not ... love ..., it profiteth me nothing.*

The hen won't resist; she lies on the block with her neck up, the wings spread out as if she were ready to fly up at the sky as soon as her soul is free from the dark space under her spine.

"Love is all it takes to fly," she tells him, matter-of-factly. She points through the daytime darkness of the barn, up the wooden rungs of the ladder into the height above the haymow. "If you can love everything in the world, everything you can think of, then you can fly."

Love suffereth long, and is kind; love envieth not; love vaunteth not itself, is not puffed up. While in bed each night, long before taking each rung of the ladder under the stiff brown leather of his new play shoes: Clay has tried it.

Doth not behave itself unseemly, seeketh not her own, is not easily provoked, thinketh no evil. Every thought that comes to him, he will learn to love.

Rejoiceth not in iniquity but in the truth. Every word, every object, every person he knows. *Beareth all things, believeth all things.* Even if it kills him. *Hopeth all things.* He hears the chop of the hired boy's axe. *Endureth all things.*

The higher Clay goes, the slower he goes. His hands prickle with sweat, and when he looks down through the rungs of the ladder that frame his face, he sees the haymow, the great pile of straw below him. Melanie stands beside the pile of straw, shouting up the verses from her memory.

"'Love never faileth,'" she says. And Clay says the words with her. *But whether there be prophecies.* A prayer. He steps up one more time, holding himself close to the rungs. *They shall fail.* He hears the squawk of another hen through the barn wall. He is holding on as tightly as he can. Another chop. He feels it all along his arm: dust falling down from the top of the barn. *Whether there be tongues, they shall cease.* His nose tickles. Another chop. It's a round rung, smooth and polished from a hundred years of age; he stares at it, holds on as tightly as he can. *Whether there be knowledge it shall vanish away.* Clay sneezes. For a moment the rest of him disappears. The snot blows out of his mouth and nose, and he comes back feeling dizzy. *For we know in part and we prophesy in part.* Both hands are still gripping the solid rung. It is as if everything, the whole world, has turned around.

But when that which is perfect is come, then that which is in part shall be done away. He looks down to find his center of gravity. The distance opens up beneath him like the dark mouth of a giant. Light falls through the wide gap between the barn doors. He is several feet in the air, above the pile of straw.

"'When I was a child,'" Melanie accuses, raising her arm and pointing up with her finger, her neck craned back: "'I spoke as a child, I understood as a child, I thought as a child.'" Then she smiles. Her arms are straight out on either side of her. She whirls around once, a complete circle, from her position on the ground. She falls back into the straw so that she looks at him from upside down.

"'And when I became a man,'" he whispers. He cannot say it loudly enough; she does not hear him because his body is held so still. She cannot see that his lips are forming the words, because the rest of him is so quiet. He moves his eyes to look down, and the four walls of the barn revolve around his vision, as if he were looking through binoculars: as if he were actually very small and round in a square world, a box. He's holding on tightly, so high up in the air that the roof of the barn curves around him like a globe. *I put away childish things.*

"Fly," Melanie says. Clay looks down his nose over the bird shit on the rung. He looks into her eyes, and she trusts him. He breathes in; the air is dust.

Another chop, Garth laughing: a curse in the barnyard.

"Goddammit," Molly says. She's got her arm out in front of her face to protect it from the water; her makeup is running down. "Stop it," she says. She's standing up to her ankles in the Chippewa River. Clay has gone all the way in, is splashing, trying to get her wet. He laughs.

"Come on," he says. "Come on, Mol Old Girl." Her clothes and her magazine are all wet, and she's pissed. He wants her to tell him to fuck off. He wants her to splash him back. He wants both of them to dive in with all of their clothes on and to come out laughing, a big scene for the guys on top of the dam. But Molly is honestly angry. She rolls up her blanket, packs everything together. She walks up the steep beach, into the trees.

Clay knows that she wants him to follow her, to apologize. He sits down on the wet sand with his ankles in the water. He doesn't want to think about Molly or what Molly wants or what he doesn't want from Molly. He watches the guys from the frat, who are standing by the fire. He'd like to forget about Molly. He'd like for Molly to tell him to fuck off and then leave him alone. The guys at the top of the dam are waving at him. They wave for him to come over.

When he does join them, somebody offers him a plastic cup of beer.

"You a townie?" the guy says.

"I guess so," he says. "I used to go to school here." This guy wears a Stetson, one of those "bad guy" black ones. It hangs from his neck over the back of his bare shoulders, like in those old cowboy movies when the men ride into town with a pistol in each hand.

"Name's Duane," he says. "This is Fred and Tony and that's Mike with the beer." Mike wears a beret. He offers Clay a beer, and Clay takes it. When they go looking for firewood in the bushes, Clay follows Duane. He slaps his back for mosquitoes as they bend over, looking for dead limbs.

"Fly," Melanie says. Above him, the pigeons flatter the air with their wings, out of the rafters, down over the haymow in a jumble of

James Russell Mayes

body and dust in the yellow air. He clings to the highest rung of the ladder in the barn, inches from the pigeon nest, the sound of wings around his head. Outside of the barn, a mourning dove shudders.

"Baby," she says. She cups her mouth in her hands and rages at him from below. "Faggot. You faggot." He can't fly. Clay is not like Melanie; he knows that now. Melanie is brave. Melanie loves the hired boy, the dirty red-haired kid from down the road who does the chores and smells like a horse and takes a bath in the cow trough. The pigeons reel in the air below him. They climb through the air to the nests; they grow used to his body at the top of the ladder. Melanie is gone.

When the rest of the stock is sold, when the hired boy leaves: even when Mama has the weeping willow cut because it interferes with the plumbing, Clay won't see that these are gone. He sees Melanie, laughing at him from the floor of the barn. He sees the willow tree, the ladder: even the hired boy, chopping off the heads of chickens.

There is one last time to see Garth, walking with his pregnant wife Sandra through the tombstones, up to the edge of the grave. After the funeral, the three of them drive out to the intersection. Sandra waits in the car while he follows Garth, kicking through the beanfield and then the ditch. They are looking for something: not a plastic sandwich bag, not the case for a pair of missing sunglasses. For about a second, Clay wonders if Melanie really could fly. But he can't ask her at this distance from the body: this height.

Soon after the sun goes behind the trees, it is dark. Duane has to keep splashing him with water, getting him wet, urging him in; Clay is not so easily convinced. There's no moon when they climb the rocks to the top of the dam. There's no moon, but Clay can still see almost everything around them in the dark. White seed from the cottonwoods are snowing over the water. They stand at the top. Both of them are supposed to jump. But when Duane goes over, Clay does not. He watches the legs of his new friend, the curve of the lean body as he dives into the suds.

He is still at the top of the ladder when Garth walks into the barn and looks around. Clay makes a sound in the bottom of his throat. That's how Garth discovers him. When he climbs up, the rungs tremble in Clay's hands from the heavy boots. He hoists himself up, so that his body covers Clay. He straddles him with his legs. The big hands rest on the rung above his own. The plow boots stick out large and long on either side of his play shoes.

With long, freckled arms around his arms, the rough dungarees against the backs of his bare legs, and the feel of the hired boy's body leaning into his back, Clay stops shaking: he solidifies. A breath moves through his hair, a tickle in one ear; the wide chest swells into his back, then pulls away. They step down a rung. One rung and then the next one under it, the left feet and then the right. They step down together, a step at a time with both feet resting on the next rung for one second. They go down backward, as if they were one person with eight limbs: an insect lowering its body backward into its hole.

"Let's race," Garth says. Clay looks down, and they are low enough. He jumps down the last few steps, tries to escape by dropping down between Garth's legs into the haymow.

He picks Clay up, and holds him in his arms like a baby. He wades through the loose straw of the mow to the window of the barn. He holds Clay out over the edge of the open window, and for a moment Clay knows he's going to die. He sees the blood sprawled over the grass below him, the entrails and the feathers. His mouth falls open, and he screams. When Garth lets go, the ground rushes up until he crashes into the loose pile of straw. The straw gives way underneath him, and he's still screaming. He chokes on the dust.

Duane comes up out of the water. The flow carries him away from where the water churns, where the whiteness lights up the dark. Clay's new friend stands up and looks around.

"Clay?" he says.

"Up here."

"What the hell," says Duane. "You jump?"

Clay feels motion; Garth is beside him on the straw. Then he is on top of him. Fingers pull his shirt out of his pants. The fingers scratch his stomach. Clay throws a fist out. And Garth pulls back. Clay is up, pushing his head forward. He pushes Garth backward, and then he's on top of him, sitting on his chest. His hands are slamming into him; the body bucks up and down underneath him. Then there is the solid grip of the hands on his wrists, pulling him down. The face is inches away. Clay kisses him.

James Russell Mayes

"I'm coming," he says. He tries to sound like he isn't a chickenshit, but his voice cracks open anyway, over the sound of the water. "Where do I jump?"

"There's no ledge," Duane calls up. "Just jump out as far as you can, and the current will carry you out." Clay sees an arm moving in the dark, hears a splash. As if this were natural, the easiest thing in the world.

"Come on," says Duane. "The water's great." He goes under again with a snap. Then two feet stick out above the surface; he's standing on his hands.

Clay decides to go down fancy, with his arms held out on either side. The air is clean and fast, and it smells like bruised leaves in the dark. He comes down hard on the water; but underneath, he curls up into a ball and holds his breath. He hugs his knees to his chest and rolls over and over himself. He hits something, and then he feels a hand. An arm pulls him up.

He breaks up out of the surface, and he's laughing and choking at the same time. He puts a hand on each of Duane's skinny shoulders and pushes him back until they're both under the water. He holds him there for a couple seconds. He feels the lean muscle. Then Duane has his legs and pulls him under. Clay escapes; he swims away a few feet. He swims up to the surface, casually cleans the water out of his ear with a finger.

"Let's do that again," Duane says. But Clay walks up on the beach. The rest of the guys have gone home. There are still coals around the bonfire. Clay sits down in the sand, and Duane walks out of the river.

"Still a beer left." He pumps away at the last stale beer in the keg.

"You can have it," Clay says. He's feeling shy again, but he's also feeling tired: a good tired.

"Let's share it." Duane sits down beside him. He hands the beer to Clay. He fiddles with the front of his swimming trunks, as if the string is too tight. They pass the plastic cup back and forth.

"We gotta take the keg back?"

"Yeah. Better keep an eye on it."

The face changes. Garth spits at him, and Clay feels the spray across his face. At least his arms are free. He runs down the pile of straw. He bends over in the grass, and he picks something up. It's warm and bloody, and it flies through the air. Then there are feathers. Clay looks down. There's blood on his shirt, the heads of chickens around his feet in the grass. The hired boy stands up. He throws another one. And then another one.

When Clay knocks over the bucket of water, and when the water pours onto the ground, steam rises out. A few plucked chickens roll onto the grass. Garth is shouting. Clay decides it's time to leave. He walks unevenly around the wide horseshoe of the gravel driveway. He tries to hum, but his throat is too tight. There are things inside of his pockets that he forgot: a useless key, the pebble he recalls is a white one, a buffalo nickel that Melanie gave him.

The back door reaches him too soon. He doesn't want to go in. He runs to the front of the house and crawls under the porch. He waits there, holding his breath until his shoulders start shaking, until the air comes out in gulps. He covers his face with his hands. His fingers are hot and wet. He looks out through the broken lattice and the burdock leaves growing around the front step. And there's dust hanging in the road; he knows, without seeing or hearing it, that a car has passed. One of the neighbors must be driving into town.

"Why don't you just take those off?" he says.

"What?" says Duane. He snaps the elastic in his trunks. Then he laughs a little.

"It's giving you that much trouble. You ever go skinny-dipping?" Clay stands up and slips his cutoffs down over his butt, down the wet fuzz on his skinny legs. He lifts one foot and then the other one, stepping out of his shorts.

"All the time," says Duane. "Sure." He walks into the bushes, and Clay has to wait for him while he takes off his trunks. When he comes out into the open, Duane is white and shivering, and his hair is all matted down from the water. He walks with his hands over his crotch, but the beach is steep and he has to hold his arms out in order to balance himself. He laughs.

"Don't mind me," he says. "I'm just as dirty-minded as you are. I'm just..." He sits down abruptly in the sand next to Clay.

"Bashful," says Clay. "I know what that's like."

"Good. Then you'll appreciate my situation." Even though he's sitting down, Duane has to keep moving, first by combing his hair with his hands and then by jiggling his leg: as if he were nervous. Clay looks into his face, and he looks away shyly.

Finally, he runs into the water, and Clay is right behind him. They dive in and come up waist-deep in cold river water. They splash each other. They struggle for a moment. Clay wraps his arms around Duane and picks him up like a baby. He swings him around and around, and then he drops him under.

Clay knows that as soon as he comes up for air, Duane will be after him. He takes off out of the water. He runs up the side of the dam in his bare feet, careful not to scrape his toes against the stones. White seed from the cottonwoods is stuck to the water on his legs. He runs out over the top of the dam and this time, without hesitation: he jumps over the edge and into the water.

Lola Gets

W hen I discovered the Kid, he was frightened and surrounded by ugly cartoon types. A girl with my history didn't have to ask, because I could smell it all over him, even through my Lorna Luft lorgnette from yards away: virgin. First time in a gay bar, and he must have peed Jovan Musk Oil all over himself. I waited for Louie Bologna and Carmen Cheese to run to the little girls' room to powder their noses, and then I made my first rescue. I scared all the boogeymen away. I whisked him over to my table. I bought him an Uncola. For about ten seconds, you know how it is when you don't know somebody, I thought I could fall in love with the child. It took me a minute to figure out the difference between what I was there for and what he was there for.

I must say he looked a little Hispanic, the darling, with a tad of impetigo on his lip. His eyes were the most startling green so that I wanted to reach out over the table and pull them out with my fingernails. I could've stirred them around in my Blue Hawaiian like ice cubes. The kid wasn't taking the fish bait. He was cruising like a cowboy in a jail full of sailors, but I could tell he wasn't going for it. It takes a special kind of person, if you know what I mean. I may look like Joyce Carol Oates, but under all of this fluff and feathers, I'm not much more than a man who's mighty uncomfortable crossing his legs on the bus. Most people clock me, right away. They clock me faster than a sister.

I waited until he was looking away, at some beef on the dance floor. I whipped up my lorgnette, and I stole another peek: a beauty! I knew right then that he was worth all that trouble I was about to go through with the Hard-on Boys. I asked him what his name was, and his ears turned red. "What's *your* name?" he said, and his eyes narrowed in the smoke. I gave him my show name, because it's about all I ever get to show. "Do you mind if I ask you a personal question?" I said, not if he didn't mind getting a personal answer, and he said, "What's your *real* name?" The kid talked in italics. I batted my eyes real good. "My name is Bennie Ferguson, if you want to see my driver's license. Friends call me Lola."

I never found out what his name was. Louie and Carmen came back. They took over the table, *my* table. And it is my table, they save it for me every Wednesday night! They were all so coked up we could barely make indecent conversation. Louie kept bending over and sticking his tongue into the Kid's ear, and the Kid seemed pretty disgusted, or maybe he was a little drunk. I started asking questions. "How did you meet these boys?"

Louie Bologna snorted, and Carmen Cheese showed his teeth. What a couple they made, drugging up these poor boys and taking them home to ravish them in their Royal Oak condo. "We met at the movies," the Kid said, and Louie said, "Yeah, the movies, right?" The three of them laughed, and the Kid's ears turned red again. I forgave them. Lord, the Kid didn't know what he did, picking up those two. And the Ugly Brothers were so far gone, they resolved me.

"I love the movies," I said. "What film? What cinema?"

They interpreted my question rhetorically. They stared at the dance floor, where a man dressed in a turban was unfurling it behind himself. Eventually, of course, a stripper had to come out, and this was preceded, as usual, by a brief message over the loudspeaker by the lisper in the sound booth: "Put your hands together for Giovanni," and no one even bothered to clap. In the Rolled Roast bar, no one claps unless there's meat on the table. They want a man's biggest secret, and it better be big.

Evidently the Kid was not used to such display. Giovanni whipped off his rip-away running shorts, and, having sniffed them, cast them over the Kid's beer. I guess Giovanni liked that particular song, because he hadn't even been tipped once. He worked on his corkscrew like a kitten under his jockstrap, and Carmen and Louie began to hoot.

I pulled down my lorgnette and eyed them both with disdain. Such a show! The Kid stirred uncomfortably, although a bit pleased, I believe, by all that manhood stirring up the breeze, and I must admit, it does prickle up one's hide to see the G man so involved in self-display. Those other two elbowed each other like real men at a horse race. I ordered another Blue Hawaiian, and then I came up with my idea.

I downed my drink and followed Giovanni backstage, just in time to keep him from getting dressed. "I have a twenty-dollar favor to ask, G.G." The boychild grinned. I told him my plan, and lest the guests at my table move their feast, I returned as quickly as I could to them.

"I have something special for you," I said to the Kid, pinching his arm. He curled his lip and rolled his eyes, clear indication that the combination of drugs and alcohol were having the effect on him that Louie and Carmen desired.

"What is it?" he asked.

Carmen and Louie leaned forward. "Yeah, what is it?" Perhaps the rat boys suspected something.

There are two male strip bars in the Detroit area. The more famous, and perhaps the one with the better reputation, is actually in Windsor, a sort of Canadian suburb of Detroit, where, under Canadian obscenity laws, a person is not fully nude as long as he wears anything at all: a tie, a hat, a tasteful (or *dis*tasteful, if you prefer...) scarf, whether the totem pole is out for wampum or not. In the United States, of course, God Save the Queen, our laws are much more specific: a man may not show his genitals, although he may wiggle his ass free to the breeze. Many folks from Michigan make the drive to Windsor's club because they may fully view the horselike manhood of the French-Canadian race. In Canada, *they're* the meat. But for those with a racier bent, they can break the laws right here in God Bless America at the Rolled Roast. It has its charms.

There's a one-way mirror at the entrance, closely watched by an employee or two of the bar, through which each entry is closely monitored. Sensitive to these approaches, of tourist women and straight men, of police, are the dancers themselves, who, for the right tip, will break the law, any law at all, in a second. Late at night at the Rolled Roast bar, dicks are flopping around in the air. But the Rolled Roast has another advantage. A patron at the Windsor Club would not be allowed to touch the flesh. If he were to do so, he would be immediately expelled by the mouth-breathing, brutelike management. Only if one pays for a table dancer, $20, and they stand on a crate and not your table, and only if the dancer wishes to slap the side of your face with his slab of Canadian bacon, then and only then can contact occur between patron and *danseur*. Not so while one is Rolled Roasting: touching, in fact, is encouraged by the dancers, who, in turn, love to get carried away, particularly if the part of your body that is touching them is safely sheathed in money. I have seen with my own eyes dancers who have become so inspired with the amount of their tips from individual consumers that they leapt from the runway and whipped down their G-strings to rub their gleaming manhoods, all slippery with sweat and oil, against the somewhat aged and usually hideous, and therefore lonely, bodies of their patrons.

At once Giovanni leapt into our midst. He pulled the front of his jockstrap down and whopped James Bond out onto the table. The three sat up straight and widened their eyes as if they were hallucinating. "I'm afraid it's all too real," Giovanni said, tipping over a drink. I had to catch the glass before it hit the floor. "I'm sorry I couldn't get it hard for you, but...," and he bent as if to whisper what he shouted near the Kid's ear: "...I had to take that cock ring off before my dick fell on the floor."

Carmen drooled through his rodentia, "It almost reaches that far now." I, however, was pleased to see that the Kid was too embarrassed to respond. I turned to Giovanni and winked at him when he walked behind Carmen and Louie. At once he sat down on Louie's jutting lap and lifted his legs to use Carmen as his footstool. With his arm around Louie's neck, and his feet working on Carmen's lap like a baker works bread dough, my dancer pal whispered something into Louie's ear, and the three men, two fully clothed and our hero nobly naked, collapsed as a group into one another, just to keep Giovanni from falling flat on his ass.

The Kid by now had collapsed upon the table, with his head supported by his drinkipoo. I pulled him back and helped him up. "Hey, where you going?" Louie said, and I told him the child and I were making a trip to the little girls' room. "Just make sure it's not the little *boys'* room," Carmen said, which is understandable. The men's room at the Rolled Roast is the place for quickie sex. Believe me, I know. I promised Carmen not to, dragged the Kid outside, and pushed him into the passenger seat of my car.

"Where are you taking me?" he moaned.

"Where do you live?" He wouldn't tell me at first, obviously confusing me with the vultures that had just been circling, or perhaps afraid of what someone might see when the dome light went on. I told him my dome light didn't work. I was only going to drop him off. But he still wouldn't believe me, he wouldn't give me his address. What was I to do? I couldn't leave him on the street. We drove around a bit. I found the local Big Boy and we went inside and I told Billie Kaye to give him one of those lovely massive desserts off the place mat. Big Boy does have the most wonderful hot fudge brownie sundaes, and Billie Kaye's a sweetheart waiter. He's from Kansas. I've had a secret wish he'd ride me like a bronc and spank me with my hoopskirt afterward. The Kid said very little, nothing really, except "Thank you" after he'd finished. I spent most of my time up at the salad bar, ogling Billie Kaye's ass.

I left a tip for him, and we walked back out to the old bomb. As soon as we got in, he gave me some posh address in Huntington Woods. I picked up his hand and patted it. "Very good, sweetie," I said. "Now you better learn who you can trust or you'll never get anywheres in this world." I didn't even turn into the drive, that's how nice I was being, because I knew how much that would hurt him. I drove up onto the curb with a lurch, and he got out. He was just turning around to say "Thanks," I imagine, either that or "Fuck you," when an enormous man, a planet, really, came hurling down the drive.

"You fucking little faggot," the planet said. He bent over and looked into the car. I crouched, and I was about to shift into drive, full speed ahead, when what I thought was a jealous husband started flailing his arms at the Kid. He was calling him fag names. He was going to hit him. If it talks like a husband, if it smells like husband, it's a husband, right?

I rolled down the window, thank Goddess I've got electric, and I shouted to the Kid, "Get in the car. He's drunk." The poor child put his hand on the door handle. The planet reached out and gave him a socko in the side of his face. The Kid opened the door, and I pulled him in. I drove ahead before he closed the door, and we circled the block a few times before we figured out that the best thing was for him to come to my place. I had to get home fast, because I was driving drunk.

We made up a bed for him on the Famous Couch in the living room, and my pit bull Precious lay right down with him. I trust who Precious trusts, so I knew the Kid was good, just a little confused. I asked him if he wanted to talk, and he said no. He lay right down with all his clothes on. I left the bedroom door open, just in case. Sure enough, it was a good thing I did, because after a little while I heard him crying away in there, so worked up he was.

"You quit your crying and go to sleep," I called to him. "Whoever that fat man was, he's an ass. He don't know what he's got in you."

"It's my dad," he said, and he started crying all over again.

"You hush, child," I said, and even though he couldn't see it, I raised my finger at him in the dark. "Lola's here. She'll take care of you, child."

He said, "I'll bet." That's what he said, after all I did for him that first night. I should've known what that would mean, but I said nothing. I closed my eyes, and I swear I saw Mel Gibson on the inside of my eyelids. He was naked, and he was on a surfboard, and he was grinning like the devil. The world is full of handsome assholes, I said to myself.

✂

The only reason there is for a girl like me to go to a bar like the Rolled Roast, and what I mean by a bar like the Rolled Roast, I mean the kind of place where you can always tell the married man because he's making out with another one in the john, just like I used to do when I was married, the only reason for putting up with any of it is, they play the tango on Valentine's Day for all the men in dresses to dance to. I love to tango! It means "touch" in one of those Hispanic languages.

The Kid was gone by the time I got out of bed in the morning. It's hard to believe I met him at the Rolled Roast, but let me tell you, it's not what you think. I never saw so much as his underwear, he's as good as straight to me, that's how much of a Mama's little sweetie he is. The Kid wasn't my type, anyway. The kind of man I love died a few years back, Gary Cooper is the kind of man I'm talking about. And I wouldn't throw out John Wayne, either, so long as he wouldn't shoot me once he found out what I got slapping back and forth between my legs. I doubt either one of them could handle a second pistol under the sheets, if you call that a fair fight. I love Gary Cooper! Let me hear you say, "High Noon," in forty different languages. All my friends at the Silver Dollar Show Bar used to say I looked like Grace Kelly with glasses. Back when I was blonde, "Princess Grace," they'd call me.

She's dead, too. Oh, don't get me wrong, I know who I am and all that, I'm not living in the past, and I've got my service pension, which I consider payment for the limp, but I'm not living on welfare. I may not be beautiful, not anymore, but I am mysterious, I can say that much. I knew what I was giving up when I left my wife and the job at Sears. I am an entertainer! The sacrifice I made, I made for art, and it's not really a sacrifice at all, because I'm always entertaining. I hop out to the store to get my groceries, I'm entertaining. When I walk Precious through the neighborhood, I'm entertaining. It's my life! Who cares if all the show bars closed? Let's hit the streets, that's what I say.

I bet it was only a couple weeks before I saw the Kid again. AIDS was one of the greatest hits among my friends, they played it in all the bars and baths, it was just catching on to be the Top of the Charts Killer that it is now. When I performed with the girls at the Silver Dollar, for a while there every week we'd lose another one in the lineup. Esther the Snake Lady, Wanda the Whip, even the man who looked like a bulldog who did the Carol Channing numbers. It wasn't like New York or San Francisco. We knew what it was before it ever got to Detroit, but that sure as hell didn't help us any. We didn't know what to do. The audience dwindled. Straights didn't come, because they were afraid they'd catch something off of the sticky stuff on the chairs. For a while I wore a simple black and did a Judy Garland set, so I could get off of work and go to the wakes already dressed and in the mood.

One night I was sitting on my stool singing, "The Man That Got Away," and bored as hell, even while I'm emoting up the ass. I started getting goose pimples, I swear, and I was feeling naked up there onstage with the spotlight on my tits. They were fake back then, of

James Russell Mayes

course. I stood up and I belted out the last verse, the part where I do the Judy with my bangs. I tried to get myself all wet. You never know when a man who's kind to strangers is going to show up, and whoever he was I wanted to show him my shit, so I did it and better than usual. I got off the stage, and I walked back to the cow stall, that's the dressing room there, and there was the Kid in a leather jacket with some slicked-back homo preppie type. "So," I said, unsurprised, I'm never surprised by anything. "So. It *was* you."

He laughed and said, "We're sorry. We came in on the middle of your act. But you were great. You really were." Evidently he was surprised that I was a showgirl. He shook my hand and introduced me to his friend, whom I already didn't like because of all of the "we" stuff in the conversation. "We" is a hell of a pronoun when it doesn't include "you." "Do you remember us?" he said.

"Half of you," I said. "Of course I remember you." And he said to Little Miss Argyle Socks, "He saved me from some pretty grimy dudes," and I said, "I know that's right," and Little Miss Argyle Socks looked down her nose. "Let's hope I won't have to do the same thing tonight," I said. Nobody got it. Nobody ever gets my jokes. I'm a singer, not a comedian.

I asked him, "Buy you a drink?" But the Kid said, "No. Because I want to buy you a drink. I owe you one." We all three sat down at my table, and after I was sucking on my Blue Hawaiian, I looked over at him, and I said to the Kid, "What's your name, Kid?" I started to cry, because here we were, and all my girlfriends were dead, and I was feeling closer to him than to anyone else in the whole world, and I didn't even know what his name was. I was blubbering like Karen Lindley in *The Poseidon Adventure*, and he pulled out his handkerchief and told me my makeup was running.

"You're a fine one," I said. "You don't even wear makeup. I can't stand it, I just can't stand it." His preppie friend said they better go, and all of the sudden the two of them were about to leave me, all alone and crying in my cups, no place to go, and no one to meet once I got there.

"I gotta show, too," the Kid told me. Right then I should have known, but what can I say? I was crying like Mickey Rooney. I said, "Fine, just fine." The Kid asked me, did I want to come along with them? I said, "Oh, yes. Could I?" I blew my nose and said, "Are you sure? Get me outta here, Kid, just give me a minute." I grabbed my purse, and took one minute to fix my eyes, and when I got back they were gone. The Kid left a phone number on a napkin on the table. I stuffed it away, and I drove home weaving back and forth between the lanes of traffic. It was Thursday night, so I made my popcorn and a batch of cocoa fudge. I soaked my tired dogs, and Precious, cuddly Precious and I watched an old movie together.

You've probably already guessed, but the Kid was dancing at the Rolled Roast, where else? I found out months later, when I didn't have anything better to do because my last best girlfriend had just checked into the hospital forever, and I needed a drinkipoo bad. I drove over to the bar, and as soon as I walked in the door, who should I see up there on the runway but the Kid himself, his shirt off and wearing leather pants, and a body I really hadn't thought he was man enough yet to have.

Actually the only ones that were interested in him were vultures and the Ugly Brothers. Everyone else was too drunk to notice him. Pearls before swine, as usual. I couldn't take him. I tipped him fast, before he could get hardly anything off. I went to the ladies' room, or I tried to. More and more it seems as if it's hard to get into the ladies' room at the Rolled Roast. It's not the sex, of course, which doesn't bother me at all, it's the D-R-U-G-S. Worse and worse, I swear, all over town, as if they think it'll replace sex. The problem is, even if you don't want to go in the head and do the drugs, you can't get in there because someone else is, and they lock the door on you. So I waited and waited, and I knocked and knocked, all the time checking back over my shoulder to see the Kid take one more G-string off. I had to admire his modesty, sticking all of those things on himself like that, but he kept whipping them off himself, one after the other.

Finally, I just couldn't hold it anymore, I had to dash into the men's room, whatever might be going on, and lucky me, one of the three urinals was free, and I whipped my dress up and yanked out the Old Philosopher, and let the drinks loose. Why is it they always put ice in the urinals at these places? I'm standing there pissing my guts out, and

James Russell Mayes

the steam is rising, I'm smelling Chaps by Ralph Lauren, and I notice the guy next to me whose elbow I'm rubbing against, he's rubbing his elbow up and down like an oil derrick. Now that's not unusual, not in that kind of place, but I didn't dare look. I stood up against the wall like any other guy, and looked at the ceiling. I spit, I whistle, just like anyone else.

Then I got nudged. It wasn't a jerking-up-and-down kind of thing anymore, it was *definitely* a nudge. I turned, and looked, and I thought I recognized him from somewhere, some preppie kid in an argyle sweater vest. He had his pants dropped around his ankles so you could see his pimply ass, and he was playing the fiddle to beat the devil. I took a look at that girl, and I yawned in his face. But you know how it is when you're young like that, and horny, and you think you've got the lizard under control, but instead it takes you over like chocolate ice cream in the fridge? He didn't stop as soon as he should have, or pull back. He turned sideways and spit, and a slimy dab of Miracle Whip dropped onto the merchandise, I mean my Halston that I sewed my goddamned self.

"My dress!" I cried. I slugged him hard, the trash. He fell back against the door to one of the stalls, and the doors at the Rolled Roast don't have locks, I suppose to make it more interesting during a tiresome shit, so he went through the door and landed in somebody's lap. I jiggled Old One Eye, so he wouldn't be leaking into the dress, I'd taken on enough bilge for one night, and I turned around at the door. The dear boy's head was still in the man's lap, but by then he'd rolled over so his butt-crack was up, and he was munching down on whoever the hell that fuzzy-knuckled man was sitting on the poop chute. The kind stranger had onto him by the ears, sizable as they were.

I walked out, in a huff, I admit, and I waited at the end of the bar for the Kid to be done with his own negligible business. I was tapping my nails on top of the runway, and he got the wrong idea. He sauntered down to the end, just above where I was standing, and he hunkered down, whipped down the front of his G-string, and began to unwind his average-sized but beautifully shaped cock. He grabbed me by the back of the neck, and he pushed my face into his slinging prop, all the while I was thinking of that Indiana Jones movie, the one where the ugly bald guy lost his head in the blade of the helicopter.

I would have tipped him, but I already did, I was afraid that he'd ruin the makeup, so I pulled his wrist off me and told him he had the wrong idea. He laughed. *He laughed.* He reeled in Mr. Peckerwood and tied it back up, and he slinked back down to the hooters and the jeerers at the other end of the runway. I would have left, and I was getting my purse, when I turned around and saw that the man cruising the bathroom had finished with his business. He was standing by the door, slicking back his hair, spraying with Binaca. I knew *right then* who this chick was. It was Mr. Argyle Socks who was dating the Kid. He was cheating on the jockstrap dancer I loved! I returned to my table immediately. I sat down and ordered three beers to sober me up.

I drank as much as I could, and I got uglier and uglier, until I wasn't thinking straight. They had to tell me it was closing time. I said good-bye to the boys, and the girls, and I shuffled out into the moonlit parking lot. The moons of Detroit are beautiful, in spite of what you might think, and I wanked out my ebony cigarette holder and tootled on a ciggie until the boys came out. I took off my heels and I followed them to their car. Crouching behind the bumpers, feeling like Columbo, I heard Preppie making his Evil Plan. The Kid wanted to go home, tired, poor dear, from so much artful dancing, and probably hungry for some genuine affection.

Preppie said he wasn't tired, and he wanted to drop the Kid off. "Don't go out again," the Kid was saying. "Can't you stay home tonight? Let's get drunk and watch a video." But Preppie wasn't after what the Kid had to offer. They started to argue. I ducked back to the old bomb, and I followed them. What happened was what I knew would happen. Preppie dropped the Kid off at their apartment in the Cultural Center, and he proceeded up Woodward Avenue at approximately fifty miles per hour.

Except for undercover cops, Woodward Ave can be fun at night, especially when you're lonely. I was much too drunk, and every time I stopped at a light, I looked over to my right and saw someone else who was drunker. Where are the cops on a night like that? I could barely keep the wreck on the road, and I have a blurry memory of people at a bus stop leaping away from the curb, but otherwise I managed to keep up with the Kid's sleazy lover. He went to the Wood Six Theatre, which is about the sleaziest All-Male Adult Theatre XXX

James Russell Mayes

I have ever been to. I waited for him to park in the street. Finally he went inside. I pulled up into the lot, which Preppie probably didn't know is free for patrons of the Wood Six, because, frankly, who would pay for parking in that area, and who would use the theater if they did, in that kind of neighborhood? It's no wonder they can't hire somebody to clean the place up inside, and the toilet never works. I pulled my panties off, out of habit I guess, and I pulled my knee-highs off of my legs, which were starting to get the five-o'clock shadow.

I assumed that Preppie was already inside. I paid my seven dollars, which is expensive, I know, if you consider the quality of the films you see, but I guess you're not paying for that anyway, and when they wouldn't let me in because someone new was working there, at least since I'd last been there, I stepped back and hiked up the dress and showed him the credentials. "Take the wig off," the guy said, and I said, "What?" He said, "Take the wig off, fella," and I said, "Why?" He said, "New rules. You can leave the dress on, but you gotta take off the wig. We can't have you scaring away the customers." So I whipped off my two-for-one deal that I bought at Wig Town in Highland Park for $35, and I banged my hips through the turnstile.

It was the usual crowd, I'd say. Half of them had their pants down, and the other half were leaning over them with their heads bobbing up and down, and some hungry-looking forty-year-old with a tired-looking cock ring was making his way down the line, stuffing his sausage into whosever mouth was open. His dick was like a washrag you'd use to wipe the floor with, that's how used it was. You could see the carbuncles on it from yards away in the dark, it was that big, and slippery-slimy. I lined up against the wall next to a little Rumpelstiltskin, one of those short fellows so red in the face you know he's got blood pressure and would heart-attack on you if he ever had the luck to get nookie from another living, breathing human being. I turned around and I felt like Snow White, surrounded by dwarves, so many were on their knees. Was the circus in town? I couldn't see Little Missy anywhere. He wasn't in the tea room, I thought, I hoped. He wouldn't use the tea room here, would he? Forcefully, I strode back to the theater john.

Rumpelstiltskin followed me in. I looked up when the door closed behind us, and he waggled his eyebrows. "Did you come from the state home, too?" he asked, reddening further. Now that's a field trip the state of Michigan would pay for, I chuckled to myself. Ever since Engler cut back on the welfare, I suppose he's made retards pedal their asses to pay the room and board. This one reached out with his little hands. I pushed him back. "Don't touch the Charmin," I said. But he was a quick one. He reached around me anyway and pinched me on the ass. I stepped on his foot and held on to his ears until he looked real sorry. It didn't take long. Nevertheless, when I let go, he pulled down his pants and showed me the most lovely little lacy underthings. He wore garters and frilly socks. He pulled up the bottom of his camisole, and I saw that underneath it, one of his caseworkers must have tied a blue ribbon around the tiniest piece of meat I ever saw in my life. It looked like bait on the end of a hook. The bathroom was empty, except for him, so I closed the door behind me, and held it closed, until the fellow started knocking from inside.

I'd have to hide in the tea room, that groping sea of thrashing male lust, I knew. Although it had been at least six years since I'd had sex with groups of more than three, I knew that the room with the least light would be my only escape. I let go the door and leapt into my shady past. The nostalgic smell of it hit me first: sweating male groins. There were arms and legs, and I think I stepped on someone. Someone else pulled me back against the wall. He pulled up my dress, which didn't seem to surprise him, and just before he sucked on Old Uncle Joe, I smelled a familiar and very specific smell. He perched something wiry on the stem of my crotch. It was metal. Was it handcuffs? I reached down and touched it, felt something flat and made of glass. I recognized them immediately.

I pushed the fellow's forehead back away. I rushed from the tea room with evidence, Thank Goddess. "Hey," his voice called after me. "Come back!" I avoided Rumpelstiltskin by running up the aisle, and I leapt over the turnstile. The only thing bad that happened was that somebody had smashed the passenger window out of my old bomb. My eight-track tapes were gone. I brushed the shards of glass off the seat. I gunned out of the parking lot and out onto Woodward. I was thinking to myself that the poor jerk in the tea room was going to have to give a blow job to get a ride home.

I don't know why I was so happy. Thank Goddess, I'd saved that cocktail napkin. I called up the Kid. "Who is this?" he said, on the other end of the line.

"Lola," I said. "Remember me?"

"Oh," he said, sleepily. "You don't sound like you at all."

"Well, who *do* I sound like?"

"Tom Bosley."

"That wasn't nice, Kid. I oughta hang right up."

He didn't hear. He pulled the phone away from his mouth, and I heard him say to his friend, "It's the loon." Now, I'm not actually *sure* that's what he said, I know I'm not birdlike, but I am sure that whatever he did say, it ended in "-oon," so I suppose he could have said, "It's the tune," which is more musical, or "It's the buffoon," which is a possibility considering the circumstances, or even "It's the goon," which is downright mean. I would like to think the Kid was better than that.

"What is it?" he asked. I must've woke him up. He sounded very sleepy.

"I won't keep you," I said, "but I've got something I think you oughta see."

"What is it?" he said.

"I want you to meet me at the zoo. It's very important."

"The Zoo. I don't think I know that place."

"It's not a place, you fool, it's the zoo. Woodward and Ten Mile."

He laughed. *He laughed.* "I'm supposed to meet you at the Detroit Zoo?"

"Look for me at the Island of the Spider Monkeys. I'll be wearing a yellow hat you won't be able to miss."

"I believe you," he said.

"Come alone," I whispered, "or I'll make a scene you'll never forget." I hung up on him before he could argue.

The hat was a bit dramatic, I decided afterward, but that's what I had told him, and I only had one yellow one. Actually it was lemon, and immense, so large it could keep me and a friend dry in the rain, and I'm no Skinny Winnie. Thank God it wasn't windy that day.

But it was hot. I was sweating at the bars around the Island of the Spider Monkeys, trying not to notice that every single one of them was playing with himself. There are no trees around the Island of the Spider Monkeys. Their rosy little dinks were stretched out on the rocks in the sun, and I was nearly fainting under the weight of that hat. I walked around and around the Island, trying to stir up some air. I picked up a brochure on condoms off the ground. Why were they distributing those at the zoo? I used it as a fan. I was beginning to worry seriously about how long I'd last in the heat, when at last I saw the Kid behind a cloud of cotton candy. "Here," he smiled, gamely. "One of these is for you." It was so nice of him, I felt a bit guilty throwing the love of his life away.

I took the cotton candy, and I suggested we find some shade to sit down in.

"Oh," he said, concernedly. "You must be hot in all of those clothes."

It's true. I had worn a lot of clothes. A girl like me can't have fun in a tank top and shorts. In my case, it's the clothes that make the woman. We wandered out under a row of elms that someone had bothered to save from that treacherous disease from Amsterdam, and we walked up to a fence where llamas were eating straw. Or hay, whatever.

I suppose I should have told him right away where his Tony had been and what his Tony had been doing there. I should have whipped out those glasses right away, and waited for the Kid to ask me where I'd found them. But he was having so much fun. He started spitting at the llamas. "Watch this," he said, and he spit through the bars. Two of the llamas lifted their heads.

"What are you doing?"

"I'm spitting at the llamas," he said, taking a wad of cotton candy in his mouth and spitting it through the bars. One of them walked over. It looked quite tall.

I told him to stop it, again, and I knew that something terrible would happen to punish him for what he was doing. I stared straight ahead holding on to my purse, which was a matching lemon yellow, and I pitied the poor animals that were kept in cages. At any moment, I was sure the guards would rush over and carry the Kid away, for common

　　　　　　　　　　　　　　　　　　　　James Russell Mayes

rudeness, if nothing else. Meanwhile, he kept spitting through that fence. A little boy walked up on the other side of me, and with bad aim, spat popcorn. His father dragged him away, crying and choking.

Out of interest, I suppose, other llamas drew close to the barrier. "Do you see what you've done?" I said to the Kid. "Do you see the trouble you've caused?"

He spat once more, and he said, "Look out." I turned my head, and I looked up into the face of an animal which was filled with contempt for me. It was personal. The llama spat. My face was drenched. It stung my eyes. I reeled. "Are you all right?" the Kid asked. I felt his sticky hand on my arm, guiding me.

We walked a distance away from there. I still couldn't open my eyes, but I no longer smelled the llamas. He guided me backward until my legs touched a bench. He told me to sit down on it, and I did. I asked him, "Did anyone *see* that?"

"Um, of course not," he lied, kindly. He put something cloth in my hand. What a gentleman. "It's a handkerchief," he said. "It's clean. Wipe your eyes."

"Oh, dear," I said, and that's all I could say. "Oh, dear." We were at the Detroit Zoo, for God's sake, and surrounded by children. I couldn't even see far enough around me to tell if I could curse. We sat there for several long seconds, while I tried to regain my eyesight. I wiped and wiped my eyes with the handkerchief, but when I tried to open them, even through the sting, all I saw was blur.

"What is it you wanted to show me?" he asked.

"Just a minute. Let me recover here." It wasn't the time, not yet.

"No problem," he said. "Take as long as you need." He seemed so pleasant, I thought. He was probably in love, poor thing, as if there is such a thing. I wondered if maybe, just perhaps, I *shouldn't* expose his boyfriend.

I wandered blindly out away from the bench. I could make out patches of light and shadow, even that there was a person a few yards away on my left, and another little person next to him, a child or some kind of large-headed ape. "Lola," the Kid called to me. "Lola, wait up. What's wrong?" I ran up off the paved path and onto a hummock of grass. I nearly fell over. There was something large in front of me. I could see that much. At first I thought it was a small building, a bathroom maybe, where I could escape from the Kid and blow my nose. It rose slowly into the air. "Be careful down there," someone called to me from above.

I rubbed my eyes. I still couldn't see a thing. The Kid called from behind, "Lola, can you see? Get back here."

"What is it?" I asked him.

"An elephant." So it was an elephant. The attendants must have a crane, I decided. They had strapped a belt around his stomach, and they were lifting it up in the air. But why?

The voice above me called down again, "Look out down there, folks. This animal's sick." I rubbed my eyes. I forced myself to open them again, in spite of the sting. Yes, it was an elephant. It's trunk was all tied up in a bandage. The Kid was there beside me.

"Stand back," he said. "That elephant's not sick. It's *dead*."

The animal continued to rise, inches at a time. "Are you sure? They might've put it to sleep."

"Well, look at its eyes," the Kid said. I tried to see its eyes. I pressed my face upward and strained to see, but by then the animal had begun to swing. "Stand back," someone called to us.

Another workman called from inside the enclosure, "Get those people away from there. He's going, he's going."

"He's gone," I said. I suppose it was a natural effect of being strapped around tight by the belly and the fact that he swung in circles around my head like one of those spools they use to determine whether you're giving birth to a boy or a girl. Fate let a great big fart that day. The elephant let loose with a turd the size of a cabbage.

One of the workmen called down to us, "Watch it." We did. The Kid and I saw it coming. We stepped out of its way. God knows how much the thing weighed. We separated, it fell right between us. A meaty chunk of it stuck to my dress. We watched it roll down the path like a bowling ball. Someone's child was knocked over.

"We're not safe here," I said to the Kid. "This place is totally unsafe."

"I told you to stand back."

"That's not what I mean. I mean, *the zoo* is unsafe."

"There's just one more place I gotta see. They had it in the paper."

"I don't think so," I said. "It's a sign. Don't you believe in signs? I think we better get out of here."

"Don't be superstitious, let's go. Nothing's going to happen."

"You can't promise that. The whole place is going up in flames, I tell you."

"No it's not. I just want to see one more thing. Please!"

"What is it?"

"You didn't read about it? They had a big picture," he said, kindly. "It'll be a surprise, then." I followed him as well as I could, limping through the debris. He took me to the Cat House. "The Only White Bengal Tiger in Captivity," the sign at the entrance said. And as soon as I walked into that building, I felt watched. I'm a showgirl, I sense these things.

"What is it?"

"I'm being watched," I said. I could feel it all over me like Giorgio perfume. A man in front of us turned around and looked at me. He nudged his wife, and she turned around and looked at me, too. They walked around to the other side of the cage. This meant that I was right up next to the bars. An immense white tiger stared through them, I mean right at me. It stood up. It looked much bigger when it stood up.

I said, "So that's what it is." I looked over at the Kid, who suddenly looked frightened. "It was him all along," I said.

The Kid stepped back. He muttered, "Lola?"

"I suppose he smells the turd mash on my dress," I sighed. "Nice tiger."

He stretched himself lazily, he was a male, I could see that much, and a randy one. He turned to face the other direction. "Hoo-ah." That was the noise he made, I swear. I was covered in a spray of tiger urine.

"Oh, dear," I said. What could I say? The hat, my dress, my purse, even my matching lemon pumps were in shambles. A crowd gathered instantly.

"Are you okay?" a man asked. "Is she okay?"

"She's fine," the Kid said. An attendant walked up with a stack of white towels. He handed one to me, as if this was nothing out of the ordinary. "That means the tiger likes you," he said in the accent of someone who is missing two front teeth. He smiled and showed us the gap. "He is marking you with his scent," he said. Someone in the crowd laughed. I turned my head and glared at him.

It was a retarded boy, developmentally disabled, whatever. I suppose he wasn't laughing at me, necessarily. Perhaps he didn't have enough sense not to. I suppose I was a sight. But he clocked me. I saw it in his face. He pulled away from his mother, and he walked right up to me. He said, "Hi, John!" like he thought he recognized me. He looked right into my face, right in front of everybody, like they do. His voice went up three octaves: "You're not John! I thought you were John!" I pulled the sopping brim of the hat down over my face, and someone dragged him away.

For a moment I got more attention than the very rare tiger in the cage. The Kid and I rushed around the tiger cage to the exit, which had crowded with more onlookers. I suppose the smell helped us make our way through them. The crowd parted, and we walked barrier-free, out through the in door. I told the Kid to forget about the whole thing as we scurried for the parking structure. It wasn't that the animals were so dangerous or disgusting, which is true, come to think of it: it was because I was already starting to *relate* to them. I had to get out of there before it was feeding time. I'd either set some loose or throw myself over the bars into the alligators. I would have.

"What is it you wanted to show me?" he asked.

I couldn't tell him after all that. Would you? "Do you believe in signs from God?" I asked him.

"No," he said. "I don't believe in God. I guess I can't believe in signs from him."

"Well, here," I said. I pulled one of my cards out of my damaged purse. "I want you to have this," I said.

"What is it?"

"It's my number." He groaned. "It's not what you think, child." I bent forward to stick the key into my car door. My sight had returned completely. "I just want you to have it," I said, "in case you're ever in trouble. Don't be afraid to ask for something if you need it, okay?" I managed a smile, dripping with spit and shit and piss as I was. "I worry about you."

He smiled, with gratitude, I like to think. "Sure," he said. "Thanks." I told the Kid good-bye, and he waved at me before walking away.

I went home, and Precious nearly tore me apart because of the smell. I threw them all away. I didn't even try to save the dress, because I knew, as strong as that smell was, it would always come out of the Woolite smelling like tiger piss. What a day! Defeated, I knew what I needed. Nothing like spirits to raise the spirits. I drove out to the Rolled Roast. I ordered three Blue Hawaiians, and I drank until my face felt as red and swollen as a beet. It sure beats pinching the cheekbones.

✄

I drank until Christmas, 1991. I pulled out onto the street, and an enormous German shepherd dog ran into the headlights. Of course I couldn't stop in time. I braked, and I softened the impact, but I could feel the weight of that dog through my foot on the pedal. The poor thing spun around in the middle of the street. Ghostly, it looked in the headlights, the dog from outer space. It turned exactly 180 degrees, and it walked right back across the street where it had started from. Amazing, I thought, a miracle. That dog does just fine.

I held on tight to the steering wheel, until the jerk behind me honked. I pulled ahead. I must have been very drunk. I remember swerving up into someone's yard, right over a spirea bush I think, but it was hard to tell because it was dark, and all I could see were the ruts in the snow I'd made across the lawn. I stopped the car only just in time to keep from driving through a window. I got out and limped around the car. The tires were fine, but I'd killed the bush. I pulled off my wig and scratched my head.

My lights shone into a dining room, and what looked like a happy family sat around a table. They were drinking coffee and eating carrot cake, I think, although I can't be sure. There was a baby grand piano in the larger room behind them. Some old fossil of a granny, someone my age, played at it. Beside her on the bench was a little girl. She was wrapped in a red-and-green afghan, the Christmas colors, and she sang. I did not recognize the tune, but it was a beautiful song, the kind of song that only a child can sing. A birthday, I thought, another birthday. I backed out over the lawn before the music stopped, and I headed out onto Woodward in the wrong direction.

I didn't notice at first. I was thinking about the house back there with the family in it. I was thinking about Christmas, and how I honestly had nobody on earth to give a present to. Was it really almost 1992? It was late, I was drunk, and there were lights ahead of me. I didn't know they were headlights until they were all around, on both sides of the car. There was a great deal of honking. As soon as I knew what was going on, I pulled up over the strip of lawn on the boulevard and sideways into traffic on the other side, and I hit a man on a motorcycle. I wasn't going fast. I watched the bike drop over. The man on top of it curled into a ball and skittered out over three lanes of traffic. I stopped the car long enough to see he was okay. At least he had the good sense to wear a helmet, I thought. He stood up, eventually. I pulled up onto the curb. I was just going to turn around. He took one look at me, he ran flat into the bricks in the side of that building, and he slid right to the ground. No witnesses, thank God. I took right off.

From the shock of the accident or the booze, or both, I forgot where I was going. I stopped at a red light, and I closed my eyes for a second just to keep from getting sick. I must've been there for a long time. I never saw the cops pull up. What did the trick was, they turned the flashing lights on. I saw them in the rearview, and then I caught a glimpse of myself. "My God," I thought, "I've got blow job written all over my face. They'll beat the shit out of me." I pulled off the hair again and set it in my lap, so they'd know I wasn't trying to get away with something. Our Friend the Policeman can be funny that way. One of them walked up and asked me for my driver's license and registration.

I saw it coming. I'd seen it a hundred times on *The Andy Griffith Show,* and I struggled not to say, "Yes, Ossifer," but I must have been trying too hard because I slipped, and that's *exactly* what I said: "Yes, Ossifer." He asked me to get out of the car, and for the life of me I couldn't remember how the door worked. Mr. Policeman, a kind one this time, really, he opened it for me, and I fell out flat on my ass.

The dress was ruined. My two-for-one $35 Special from Wig Town rolled into the next lane. A bus from the suburbs ran right over it and squashed it flat. The policeman said, "That could have been your head. *Sir.*" Of course, I spent the night in jail. And all through that nasty body cavity search? They never even asked why I had a lorgnette *and* a pair of glasses.

For the next several weeks, I spent so much time in the twelve-step group I barely had a social life. It seemed like everyone at the UU Church was trying to impress: someone would start out, "I puked green vomit, and I passed out on the floor for two whole days," and the next one in line would say, "I puked black vomit, and I passed out for *three* days." The idea was, "I'm more of a drunk than you are, nyah, nyah." I got tired of that fast. What a bore, I thought, let's get on with our lives. One night I hoisted out from under my dress a bottle of booze, for effect, you know, to shut them up. Plus, I was curious what they would do. Would they pass out paper cups? That never happened, of course. A man screamed. The women were all on top of me. I let them have it, they could do what they wanted with it, I walked out.

I went for a long walk. Hell, I couldn't drive anymore. At least they hadn't pinned that hit-and-run on me. Luckily, the cyclist had such a case of shock that he thought I was a woman, you know, a real one. He didn't even get the color of my car right. Thank Goddess for tinted visors. What was it I really needed? Why was I so lonely? I reached down into my purse, and I came up with those preppie glasses that I'd stolen from the Kid's boyfriend. I needed friends, I decided, I needed to see my friends. I needed to go someplace where everyone knew my name. I remembered that it was going to be Valentine's Day, and I knew it wouldn't be the same if I wasn't sitting at my table with the other drag queens, waiting for one of those men in chaps with their buns sticking out to ask us to dance. I took the bus to the Rolled Roast. I ignored the fifteen-year-old juvenile delinquent who sat in front of me with girlie porn. He kept pushing it in my face like it would change my religion. That night started out much worse than it ended, thank the Goddess.

All of the old girls were gone, except for Delilah, who owns a pet shop downtown and looks like Buddy Hackett with a Lilt perm. She sat with me and drank bottle after bottle of beer, but I was good. I wouldn't budge from my Diet Cokes. I nearly drank the bar dry of it. Eventually the waiter, a punk who spiked his hair so the zits on his scalp shone through, tried to ignore me. "Why don't you order a *pitcher* of this stuff? We sell it by the pitcher," he said. I refuse to sit at a table behind a pitcher of anything. After a while I had to start tipping.

The old lineup at the Silver Dollar Show Bar had been creamed, I mean *creamed* by the plague. They closed it down. "We're the only ones left," Delilah told me, like she ever had the looks to be in show business. No, even though she'd been *everyone's* Friday night, even though she charged only five dollars a pop for blow jobs in the parking lot when anyone else would have charged at least a twenty, Delilah had been spared. Thinking of all that talent, thinking of all those looks, it was hard not to bust open crying with her.

Of course the Kid walked in. He came in to the old joint where he used to dance, wanted to say "hi" to the girls he used to work with on Valentine's Day. He looked good, still clean-cut and baby-faced, just looking at him was good for the heart. I watched him order a beer at the bar. He looked around, and I waited for him to spot us. He did. He didn't pretend *not* to. He said something to the bartender, Tillie, I think it was, that old bouncer bodybuilder queen, and he must have asked her what it was I was drinking, because *she* brought over a Diet Coke. "From the Kid," Tillie said, putting it down. I stuck my tongue out at the waiter.

I looked up at the Kid from across the room. He wasn't wearing a leather jacket or an aviator's scarf, not even smoking a Tiparillo. He wore a nice pair of new jeans, I love that deep denim color, and he must have been to the March on Washington one time or other, because he wore a Pride sweatshirt, with a tie on underneath, the idealist! The Kid was just *himself,* only just a bit better, and I loved him for that. I gave him the Queen Elizabeth wave, and he touched his forehead. He was writing something down. He finished his drink, I don't know what it was, and he walked over to the old table, where, rather suggestively, Delilah was swilling Old Mil out of a longneck bottle, it's hard not to advertise once you're in the habit. The Kid leaned over, and he picked up my old biddy's hand off the table, age spots and all. He kissed it, tenderly, Maurice Chevalier–style.

He said, "Do you want to tango?"

I said, "It takes two."

I fell into his arms. We soared back and forth across the floor through the older, wearier birds. I don't mind leading when I have to.

The tango makes it worth it. "I can't handle all this back and forth," he said to me. He turned me in a circle, around and around and around. My hairspray stuck to his temple. I was dizzy. We were out of control. I felt a bit sick, too, from so much Diet Coke. I was determined not to trip, but parts of me flailed loose and outward. I fell right over.

The Kid caught me. He picked me up from my graceless swoon, and he carried me in his arms like I was Vivien Leigh, if I do look more like Phil Silvers now than Joyce Carol Oates does. He carried me out from under that damned tacky spinning light. "Oh, dear," I said. "I'm afraid I've had too much diet pop." He lowered me into my chair, and while propping me onto my elbows, he ordered me a Blue Hawaiian. He remembered.

I leaned sideways and held myself up with the back of my chair. I sucked on my Blue Hawaiian like it was Elvis Presley. "That's so much better," I told him. It did settle my stomach. He sat down across from me, and he leaned forward over the table to wipe at something out of place on my face with his clean white handkerchief. When he put it back into his breast pocket, he pulled out a valentine. A *valentine*. I ripped it open faster than shit. It was one of those *ugly* valentines with a drag queen on the front that was supposed to be funny. Why do I always get those kinds of valentines? I'm a drag queen, and I'm supposed to find them funny? It said, "Valentine My Ass," or something not funny like that. But in his own hand, he'd written, what did he write? "I want to move in with you. Can I move in with you?" Something like *that*.

I didn't know what to say. I wanted to run into the little girls' room and straighten my eyebrows and improve the line of my lipstick. Too late. I turned to nudge Delilah with the elbow, but she was gone. I looked across the dance floor at the men's room, just in time to see her backside disappear through the door. Poor dear, I thought. She'll always look like someone's navy buddy in a dress. In twenty minutes she'll walk out here, and she'll be wiping the piss off her knees with toilet paper.

I made a sincerity check. I hoisted out my Lorna Luft lorgnette, which was steaming with the heat off my bosom, and I frowned right through it into the Kid's eyeholes. I said, "Let's get something straight here. I'm old and I'm set in my ways, Kid, but I'm not stupid."

"Preppie threw me out," he said.

"He threw you out?"

He smiled. I think I saw a faint blush. "I need to find a place to stay."

"You fooled around on him," I said, realizing. It was all over his face. "Didn't you?"

"Yeah. So."

I laughed out loud.

He smiled at me so sadly, like he was giving up so easily. "Whatever Lola wants," he said. The child had been through so much.

"Don't get me wrong," I said. "I care for you deeply, Kid. It's just that I've been your adopted mother since before you started dancing here. It's been years since I had the buzz in my britches for anyone. Mark Spitz in the 1970 Olympics, I believe. I can't change, Kiddo. You don't want to sleep with me just to have a home sweet home."

He laughed at me. *He laughed*. "Oh, that's not what I meant at all," he said. "That's not what I was talking about. Lola, you're not my type."

I recovered quickly. I always do. It's one of the things I like about myself. I reached across the table, and I grabbed him by the necktie. It was all so crooked. I took a big breath. I straightened his tie for him. "You don't get what I'm saying, do you, Kid? You can live with me," I told him, avoiding his eyes. "But let's be honest. We're roomies, not honeymooners. *Sisters.*"

He almost leapt on top of me from across the table. He lay his rosy little cherub cheek against my boobs, which were real by that time, I think. I knew that everything was going to be all right between us. I can be the Virgin Mary, if you nix the Virgin part, speaking words of wisdom. "You move in with Precious and me," I said. "But I won't have you out all hours. No making a mess. If you got a boyfriend, you have him over for dinner, just like everyone else does. And Thursday night is popcorn night. Do you have a car now?"

International Male

Bryan's stepfather Leonard stood on the front stoop with the door open. He grinned at Bryan, lifting his ear to the air, as if to get a better hearing of the racket off the overpass. "I definitely got the wanderlust, kid. Hear those trucks?" He closed the front door. He walked in to the kitchen table where he had stacked his gear, next to a bottle of beer. With a shrug he seemed to decide that he ought to sit down and finish his drink. He looked at the kitten Bryan held out in his hands. "What's that there?" he asked.

"Morocco," the boy said.

Leonard took his hat off. "I killed another one?"

"With your big feet you did."

"Aww, shit. You had a name for this one, didn't ya?"

"Morocco, Dad."

Leonard threw his hat down on the table. "I'm not your dad. Stop calling me 'Dad.' If you woulda kept these cats inside the box, I wouldn't be stepping on 'em all the time. You know how I am in the morning."

"Don't worry. You won't be doing it anymore," Bryan said. "This was the last one." He held the little corpse up to his chest and leaned against the sink.

"You still got Persia here. She'll be popping out another batch. Won't you, Persia?" The old mother cat wound herself around Leonard's knees under the table. He reached under and tugged at the kink in her tail.

"Leonard, I want to go with you. You said I could."

"That was before your mother ran off."

"Why can't I go with you?"

"You got school, Bryan."

"You know how many times I played hooky when we lived in Butternut?"

Leonard was pleased with the fact, as Bryan knew he would be. The beer snorted out through the man's nose, and he pinched his nostrils to squeeze out the sting. "Well," he said, wiping his eyes, clearing his throat, "maybe you won't end up like your uncle Randy, after all."

"Maybe I will." He raised his eyebrows, challengingly. "Maybe I already have."

Leonard squinted at him. He picked his hat off the table and slapped Bryan's arm, gently. "Probably you will," he said. He shrugged. "I don't wanna hear about it. You're not going, Bryan. I got you that gobbler to raise for a good turkey dinner." He finished his beer, and he handed the empty bottle over to Bryan. He waited while the boy, hugging the dead kitten to his stomach, rinsed the bottle out in the sink with one hand. Bryan stacked it neatly in its carton next to the wastebasket. Leonard tossed his sleeping bag at him. "Come on," he said. "Show you how this is done."

"Carry it yourself," Bryan said. He let the sleeping bag roll down his arm.

Under the weight of his sleeping bag and duffel bag and the brown bag of peanut butter sandwiches that Bryan had made for him, Leonard gasped. "I told you I got to see my brother Clark. He might end up in jail or something."

"Or something," Bryan mumbled. He stared into the braid that wound down Leonard's back. He followed him out the trailer and into the yard. They walked up to the pen of the young white gobbler.

"You call up Uncle Randy on Thanksgiving," he said. "He'll come out and do something with ya." As he was walking across the yard, littered with broken jars and oil cans and tires, Leonard slipped on a beach thong and landed squarely on Persia. "Shit," he said, kicking at the cat. Bryan bent to pick her up, but she scratched him. She could not use her back feet anymore. The old cat writhed and lunged behind a pile of rusted auto parts.

"I'm not doing the turkey," Bryan said. He raised his voice above the sound of the trucks on the highway. "I won't do shit for Thanksgiving. I won't go to school, either. Come on, Leonard." The turkey crowed a tentative, shivery gobble.

"I'll call you when I get to Texas," Leonard told him. He walked up the grassy embankment to the highway. Alongside the shoulder of the road, Leonard dropped his things in the dust. He turned away to face the oncoming morning traffic. He stuck out his thumb. In spite of himself, Bryan liked the fact that someone was going to have an adventure. Even though his stepfather was leaving him behind, Leonard was the only one Bryan knew who could make it all the way to Texas.

A truck stopped and let off a wheeze of steam. In big navy letters along the side, it said, "Gordon Foods." Inside of it, a bodiless head with a cap talked to Leonard through the passenger window. The door opened up without Leonard touching it, like magic, from the inside. He tossed his bags up. He climbed into the truck. Leonard rolled away. He didn't even look back.

Bryan dumped the gobbler's dirty water pan. He told the bird, "You're gonna die, too, you idiot." He held onto dead little Morocco while he sprinkled out a handful of chopped-up corn on the ground. "Why do you think we call you Gobbler?" He kicked at the enclosure. The bird flapped backward.

He got a spade out of the shed. He dug another hole behind the trailer where they buried the animals. He tossed Morocco into the hole and covered it with dirt. He walked around the trailer to the front. He looked through the auto parts in the backyard for the old mother cat. Persia seemed to have crawled away somewhere.

When his mother left for the upper peninsula with a truckload of men from the Vlasic plant, Bryan had stayed with Leonard. He thought that if he did, eventually his mother would come back for him. He was hoping that she might work things out with Leonard. Leonard had similar hopes. They were a family, after all. He was generous with Bryan and let him stay, "as long as need be," he said. For weeks, Bryan went to school and told nobody. Then Leonard started getting calls from his relatives. His brother Clark, who had been in and out of various Texas mental institutions, had disappeared. For some reason, Leonard felt responsible for him. He had always wanted to check out Texas. He had talked about it with Bryan and promised him that one day they would go there together.

Only hours after Leonard left without him, Bryan woke up in the middle of the night. The trailer was cold. He dressed himself and walked over the kitty burial ground to the fuel tank. He checked the gauge with his flashlight. It was on E. He knocked his fist against the tank and heard a melancholy ring. "Damn," he said. He kicked the tank. Then he heard a growl. Bryan fell backward onto the ground. Underneath the tank, a cat's eyes glared into the beam of his flashlight.

Bryan tried to reach underneath the tank, but Persia screamed and scratched his hand. He moved around the back of it, thinking that he might be able to pull her out from behind. He shone the flashlight onto her bottom. Something had been chewing on her. She was leaking a half a foot of guts out of her backside. Bryan picked his way through the yard to the shed. He found Leonard's axe leaning inside the door. With the head of the axe, he dragged the old cat out from under the tank. He raised it up in the air, missed her head twice, sliced her belly and two legs before he got it right. "Damn," he said, shivering, feeling weak. He left her unburied and went inside and sat in the dark at the kitchen table with his coat on. He figured. Leonard had left him eighty bucks to take care of groceries. That wasn't nearly enough to fill the tank.

Once the sun was up and before the bus came, he called the gas company. He asked, "Do you sell half tanks?" "Half tanks?" the lady said. "Just a minute." She did not cover the receiver, so he could hear her talking to somebody else. They were laughing. "No," she said, back on the line. "Sorry." Bryan hung up. He could not think what to do. He called his uncle Randy. He left a message on his machine, thankful for an excuse to talk to him. Bryan liked his mother's brother. After the beep, he said, "Uncle Randy. This is Bryan. I got a problem. Dad, I mean Leonard, left to go find Clark in Texas, and the fuel tank's empty. It's getting kind of cold. You help me out?" He left the number on the machine, in case Uncle Randy had forgotten it.

When he got out of school the next afternoon, Uncle Randy was waiting out by the buses. "Hey," Uncle Randy said. He waved and smiled and showed his dimples.

"Hey, yourself."

"Come on, I'll give you a ride home." He patted Bryan's back, and they walked across the street to his truck. "I have to stop at the post office, first," Uncle Randy said. He reached across the seat and poked Bryan in the ribs. Bryan flinched.

He was going to wait until Uncle Randy had got his mail before he told him the whole story. But when he got back into the truck, Uncle Randy was preoccupied. He had quite a pile of mail. He sorted through it until he found a letter, and he slapped Bryan's cheek lightly with the envelope. "True love," he said.

"You got a boyfriend?" Bryan asked him.

"I got more boyfriends than you got dead puppies buried behind your trailer." He cocked his head.

Bryan asked, looking out at the bowling alley across the street, "How about kittens?"

"Oh, no," Uncle Randy said. He looked aghast. "Kittens, too?" Bryan gave him a look, and Uncle Randy visibly swallowed a giggle. "Your mom ever tell you about her big-headed cat? This cat had a head that was as big as a cabbage. It was this big, really." He held up his hands.

Bryan changed the subject. He only intended to borrow money from his uncle, the amount for a tank of fuel oil until Leonard was back from Texas. He explained the situation. Uncle Randy did not say much for the rest of the drive. At least he was not mad at him, Bryan thought. They drove past the water tower and the industrial refinery. Uncle Randy was thinking to himself. "So let me see," he said, pulling up in front of the trailer. "Your mom ran off a couple months ago..."

"You knew that."

"...and now Leonard decides he's got to go to Texas, and you don't know when he's gonna be back?"

Bryan shrugged. "Couple more weeks, at the most. Clark's a nut, Uncle Randy. He might be in a lot of trouble."

"You ran out of fuel oil, and you don't have any money."

"I got eighty bucks. That's enough for groceries."

"It doesn't matter, Bryan. You know what I think about Leonard. He'll probably come back with a pound of dope from Miami. Anyway, you shouldn't be here by yourself."

"I think I can manage," Bryan said, doubtfully.

Uncle Randy smiled his smile. "You wanna come stay with me?"

Of course Bryan wanted to stay with him. "You wouldn't mind?"

"You're sleeping on the couch," Uncle Randy said. "You got a sleeping bag? Get your stuff." Bryan flung himself up the steps and into the low-ceilinged trailer. He emptied his underwear drawer into his mother's old suitcase. He packed his favorite book, *The Boys on the Rock* by John Fox, which he had filched from the public library. Out from underneath his mattress, he pulled three issues of the *International Male* catalogue. He tossed them in, as well, and some clothes.

He slipped the suitcase into the back of Uncle Randy's truck. He had opened the passenger door and was about to climb into it, when he heard Gobbler chortling from his pen. "Aww, shit," he said.

Uncle Randy looked up from a letter he was reading. "What?"

"The turkey," Bryan said. "What're we gonna do about Gobbler?"

"The turkey? Hell, put her in the back."

"What are we gonna do with her?"

"I got a double garage," Uncle Randy said. "How much does that bird shit?"

✂

Uncle Randy had a very nice, very small house in a neighborhood only blocks from Bryan's school. He liked to work out. He had set up his weights in one of the bays of the garage, so before they could set up Gobbler's wire cage, they had to move the weight bench. Bryan asked, "Where do you want this thing?"

"Let's move it into the driveway. That way, after we get the turkey inside, we can sort of hide it behind all this stuff."

"Is this legal? I mean, for you to keep him in town like this?"

Uncle Randy shrugged. "I don't know. If it isn't, we'll find out soon enough." They set up Gobbler's pen. Bryan softened the concrete floor with a bale of straw that had been sitting out in the weather.

James Russell Mayes

"That's ripe," Uncle Randy told him, holding his nose.

"It's mildew. It's all we had." Bryan set out some chopped corn, and Uncle Randy filled the turkey's water pan. They leaned against Uncle Randy's truck and watched Gobbler gawk over his water. "Thirsty," Bryan said. He smiled at Uncle Randy, just so he could see him smiling back.

Uncle Randy showed Bryan his refrigerator. There wasn't much more than some vegetables and a kind of Jell-O thing with nuts on top that Uncle Randy called a "dump cake." "I think probably all of this stuff in here is about two weeks old," he apologized. "I'd take you out for a bite, Bryan, but I've got a date." He opened up the freezer. "Here's some TV dinners. It's not much, I know. I suppose I could cancel my date."

"Don't do that, Uncle Randy. I'll manage. The milk good?"

"I get a gallon every week, whether I need it or not."

"Good. I'll make some soup, then."

"Soup?"

"Sure. It's not hard. You got this whole bag of potatoes. This onion's all right. And, hey, celery, too." He held up a limp stalk.

"That's not good."

"It's okay to cook with. I love potato soup. You do much cooking?"

"Not really." Uncle Randy stripped his shirt off and wiped it under his armpits. "Well," he said. "I gotta shower. Just pretend I'm gone already." Bryan found an apron hung in the broom closet behind the refrigerator. He put it on and peeled the potatoes. He listened while Uncle Randy whistled to himself, laying out his clothes. He waited until the shower stopped before he cut up the vegetables and rinsed them under the faucet. Uncle Randy appeared, looking sophisticated and dreamier than ever.

"Have fun," Bryan said. Uncle Randy winked at him and left. Bryan enjoyed cooking. It relaxed him and made him feel homey. He let the soup bubble for an hour before he took it off the burner and added the milk. He found an immense bowl in Uncle Randy's cupboard. He filled it with soup, and he garnished it with a tablespoon of a delicacy: real butter that he found next to a block of fuzzy cheese in the door of the refrigerator. He was just sitting down in front of Uncle Randy's television, when somebody rang the doorbell.

Bryan wiped his hands on his apron and opened the door. A short man with longish hair stood on Uncle Randy's doorstep. He wore a plaid suit coat. He carried a brightly wrapped package. His face looked like Don Knotts, all bug-eyes and fish-lips. Looking terrified, the man asked, "My God, how old are you?"

"How old are *you?*"

"Okay, you got me. Here. This is for you." He handed Bryan the gift. His hands were shaking.

"Really?"

"Can I come in?"

"Umm, sure." Bryan stepped back to let the man in. The fellow looked around him at Randy's front room. Bryan sat down on the couch and ripped open the present.

The man looked down at his hands. "You look much younger than I thought you were. I hope you like it. I did exactly what you said to." Bryan lifted a pair of underpants out of the box. They were moist. They smelled. "I didn't have a jockstrap," the man said.

"Gross!" Bryan shouted. He dropped them into the box.

"I tried to find one at MC Sporting Goods, but you said all-cotton. I did exactly what you told me to, Randy."

"Randy?" Bryan closed the box. He stood up and shoved it into the man's stomach. "I'm not Randy. You made a mistake."

"Are you sure? I'm very sorry."

"Randy's not home. He's out. I'm his nephew."

"His nephew. Right." The man walked dazedly to the door, clutching his unwrapped package. "I know that was your voice on the phone."

Bryan forced a smile. "We sound a lot alike. Hey, don't worry about it. It's all right, really."

Looking around Bryan into Randy's living room, the man wiped his nose with the edge of his index finger. He held out the package to him. "I don't suppose? No." A tatter of wrapping paper fell onto the floor.

Bryan picked it up and gave it to him. "I'll tell him you stopped by," he said.

The man said, "I can't believe." He walked out the door and ran down the steps to his car.

Bryan called after him, "Hey, wait a minute! What's your name?" The car door slammed, the engine revved. Bryan watched him pull out into the street. He headed east, anyway. Bryan closed the door. He went to the bathroom and washed his hands. He walked into Uncle Randy's room, which was mounted on all four walls with half-naked males: dancers, arms and legs wide, poised in colorful photographs midflight.

On Randy's bureau there was an assortment of old Barbie dolls: Barbie, her best friend Midge, their little sisters Skipper and Skooter. Bryan knew their names. There were two Kens, a white one in his swimming trunks and a black one in a tuxedo. Bryan picked up the white Ken and bent his legs so that he could sit on top of the black Ken's lap. It was impossible for them to bend their faces for a kiss, though. "I know how you feel, man," he said.

He finished his soup and cleaned up the kitchen. He turned on the television and zapped through Uncle Randy's cable stations for a couple hours. He wandered out to the garage and checked on Gobbler. The straw did smell pretty bad. Gobbler seemed to like it, though. He was eating it. "All the more to fatten you up," Bryan said.

※

When Uncle Randy came home, he was much too early to have had a good time. Bryan told him about his visitor. "I answered the door, and I told him you were out. He wouldn't tell me what his name was." He stretched himself and yawned.

"What's today?"

"I don't know. The sixth, I think."

Uncle Randy slapped himself on the forehead. He leapt into the bedroom. "No, it's the seventh. Shit! I made a date with the guy, and I forgot to write it down!" He walked into the living room, untucking his shirt. "Did he say anything?"

Bryan smiled, not too widely. "He did have a present, a package for you."

"Where is it?"

"He took it with him."

Uncle Randy sagged into a chair. "What he look like?"

"Don't you know?"

"It was a blind date."

"He looked like Don Knotts, only uglier."

"God, I'm glad I missed him. I hope he doesn't call back." He sighed. "All the men in this town look like has-been television stars," he said. "I'm serious. I've dated Tom Bosley and Gavin McLeod. In a moment of painful weakness, even Charles Nelson Reilly. Buddy Ebsen had gingivitis so bad that he filled my front hallway with a stink. The best I ever did was Henry Winkler, not even as the Fonz, but as himself. With the receding hairline and that probing beagle nose?"

"You have to give yourself credit for trying," Bryan said. He pulled off his shirt. "I'm about ready for that couch." He stripped and fell back on top of his sleeping bag. He closed his eyes. He listened to his bachelor uncle moving through the house, shutting off the lights and checking the doors.

"Still awake, Bryan?" Bryan opened his eyes and saw the man's silhouette in front of the drapes. "Forget the 'uncle' part. It's making me old too fast. Call me Randy, okay?"

"Really? Hey, cool."

"Get some sleep. I'll try to get ahold of your mommy in the morning."

"Can't you just call her 'Mom'?"

Randy pulled in his chin. He laughed. "You'll get used to me, child. I'm just like your mommy myself." He pressed the tips of three of his fingers into his chin. "More of a bitch, maybe. More of a slut."

"I doubt that."

The next morning, a Saturday, Bryan woke up to find Randy picking through his suitcase. He smiled at Bryan, sadly. "I better take you shopping, child."

"Why? My clothes are fine."

Randy held up a pink jockstrap. "Your underwear's in order. It's your outerwear needs work."

They spent the afternoon in the stores. Randy bought Bryan some basic quality items: two wool sweaters and a pair of Rockports, socks

James Russell Mayes

and a couple pairs of corduroys. Randy asked him, in front of the service counter at TJ Maxx, "You sure you don't want any socks?" The two men at the counter looked slyly at each other. Bryan merely raised his eyebrows and tried to feel superior.

Once outside in the parking lot, "Is there anything else you want?" Randy asked him.

Bryan was trying to look directly into the sun. "How about a fur coat? I've always wanted a fur coat."

"Fur coat up your ass," Randy said, nudging him. "Is there anything you need?"

"Let's get some groceries."

"What do we need groceries for?"

"I'll buy them."

"Save your eighty bucks," Randy told him.

"Are you sure?"

"I'm sure."

"Thanks." Bryan smiled hopefully. "What do you want me to make you for dinner tonight?"

He made beef stew with beer in it and biscuits for his uncle. Randy made some calls to the Vlasic plant to track down Bryan's mother. When he walked into the kitchen, "Any luck?" Bryan asked him.

"I made a few calls. Somebody's getting back to me on it."

For the hell of it they went through Randy's basement and found what Randy called "incriminating evidence" of his age. Bryan pulled an old guitar out of its case, and Randy played a Buffy Sainte-Marie song, surprised that he could remember all of the words. He put the guitar away. He blew off the dust on a board-game box. "Hey," he said. "Look. Mystery Date." The game still had all of its pieces. They played. Randy thought that the nerd was cuter than the jock.

"I don't think so," Bryan said. "I like the Dream Date, myself. He looks like a Ken doll."

"My God," Randy said. "Are you into Ken? I have two Kens in my bedroom."

"I know. Hey, when I was a kid, one of Mom's boyfriends took me into the toy department and told me that I could have anything I wanted. You know what I picked?"

"Ken."

"Right. And the whole time I was pointing up at the Ken doll, the woman behind the counter kept saying, 'Oh, no. That's for *girls*. You don't want that. You want a GI Joe.' Guess what I got for Christmas?"

"GI Joe," Randy said, rolling his eyes. "Adam West, or whatever that cowboy doll's name was back in my day. We all did. That's why I bought my *own* Ken dolls. And Barbie and Midge and Skipper."

"And Skooter, right?"

"Right, very good." Randy lifted his chin and mocked a look of superiority. "That's why a fag needs money. The child that's got her own, right?"

"Right." Bryan raised the bottle of beer that his uncle had allowed him. "To Barbie and Ken," he said.

"No. To Ken and Ken."

Bryan developed a sweet, sentimental affair with Randy's VCR. Each night through the week, once he had pretended to do all of his homework and then had lied to his uncle about getting it done, he watched a different musical that Randy picked up for him from Blockbuster Videos. He saw *Gigi* and *Gay Purree*. He saw *How to Marry a Millionaire*. He saw *Some Like It Hot*, of course, and all the Judy Garland he could withstand. When it came on the CBC he watched *Anne of Green Gables* with Randy, and when Gilbert Blythe came down with the scarlet fever, they both began to weep. Bryan could not help himself. He snuffled out loud, and Randy laughed. "What a couple of sissies," he moaned, wiping at his tears. He ran to the bathroom and came back with a box of Kleenex.

On Friday they had a Rupert Graves film festival and stayed up very late discussing the actor's mysterious hold over Randy. "Let's take a look at that butt again in slow mo. I wish I were chasing him around that Sacred Lake!" Bryan was giddy from his one-beer limit.

"I'd eat *his* handful of dust."

"I'd be *his* Scudder."

"Your grammar improves with alcohol."

Inanely, Bryan said, "My grandpa does, too."

"Tell me, if someone were going to make a movie of your life," Randy asked him, trying to sound British, "whom would it be?"

"Ron Howard."

"Ron Howard! Surely not the way he looks these days."

"No, not even in *Happy Days*, but I'm an Opie, you gotta admit." He smiled so that his bulging cheeks made his freckles more conspicuous.

Randy pulled the throw blanket over his head and pinched Bryan on the cheek. "Such a baby face," he sighed. "An all-American face. Apple pie and hot dogs."

"Hot dogs?" Bryan fought back. He jabbed Randy in the stomach. "Who would you choose?"

"Me? I don't know. I hadn't thought about it."

It was true. He had not thought about it, Bryan realized. He had only been asking for Bryan's sake, not his own. "You have to think of somebody. Who's your ideal?"

"Oh, that guy on *The Rockford Files*. What's his name?"

"James Garner? You gotta be kidding! Now he's old."

"He wasn't always that way," Randy said, defensively. "He was kind of sexy, once. He doesn't have to act, he's just himself."

"No way," Bryan said, touching his knee. "No way. Roger Moore."

"Yeah, he's old, too." Randy sighed and patted his stomach.

"Well, if I could pick Opie when Ron Howard's gone bald, you can pick Roger Moore when he was James Bond. He was young once. Roger Moore, really. I've been thinking about it all along, ever since you took Mom and I swimming at the lake."

"Mud Lake? That was years ago." He looked at Bryan closely. "I can't believe you. I didn't even have a stomach back then."

"You looked great, really. I remember. James Bond, I swear." Their faces were inches apart.

Randy stuck a piece of popcorn up each of his nostrils. "Let's go check on the bird," he said.

"You mean Gobbler?"

Randy wrinkled his nose. "How can you name something that you're gonna be eating in two weeks?"

Bryan shrugged. They sneaked out to the garage and turned on the lights. Spooked, but pleased with his visitors, Gobbler obliged them with a throaty chuckle.

"That's such an eerie sound," Randy said.

Bryan nodded. "He's getting fatter."

They sat on the box of Randy's pickup, tossing leftover popcorn into the pen. Bryan started to fall backward into the box, but Randy grabbed his elbow. They were poised on the gate of his pickup. They both fell backward. "Ouch," Bryan said.

"You hurt your head?"

"Naw."

"Let me see." Bryan bowed his head, and his uncle brushed through his hair. Bryan felt tingles in his neck and his shoulders. "Nothing but a bunch of goosebumps on your neck. No, you're fine," Randy said. He flapped his fingers through Bryan's hair to mess it up. He wiped his hands on his knees. "Bedtime."

"I guess that means couch-time, for me."

"Sure does."

Randy had more clothes in his closet than Bryan had ever seen, which was probably why he took an hour whenever he had a date, just to decide what he would wear. "What's this guy like?"

Long silk sleeves flashed up into the air. "I don't know," Bryan said, punching outward with his fists. He held in his stomach to tuck the shirt in, and his navel became an eyelid.

"Another blind date?"

He shrugged. "Considering the pickin's in this town, I'm sure you can't blame me for sending my high school graduation picture to the *Advocate Classifieds*." Bryan gave him a shocked look, but Randy did not notice that he was kidding. "I'm sure he's not as cute as you are, Bryan. Not as young, anyway."

His date arrived early. Randy was primping with his hair, so Bryan got to answer the door. The man's name was Jeff, and he was not "not young," but short and extremely good-looking. He almost looked like Rupert Graves, a short Rupert Graves. However, he did not have an English accent. He shook Bryan's hand. He said, "Nice to meet you. My, you look young."

"Oh," Bryan said, showing him in. "I'm not Randy. I'm Randy's nephew."

James Russell Mayes

"How wonderful."

Bryan giggled. He tried to think of something to say.

Jeff asked him, "Are you coming with us?"

Randy said with his fists on his hips, "I don't think so." He stood in the doorway to the bathroom, his hair newly perfect and shining with the light coming at him from behind. He pulled his coat out of the closet and pulled Jeff out the door. Bryan watched the Acura carry them off. "Beats Don Knotts," he said to himself, steaming up the window. Randy did not come home until quite late.

✄

Bryan switched to horror. He did a whole run of Alfred Hitchcock: *Spellbound, The Birds, The Man Who Knew Too Much*. There was a certain scene which he considered genius: a couple in an old kitchen spent what seemed like hours committing a drawn-out and difficult murder. The scene was gruesome and long, but Bryan was fascinated. He played it over and over. He showed it to Randy.

"Oh, that tired old thing," Randy said.

"No, it's great. I think I'm getting a buzz from the violence." Bryan rewound the tape.

"It's not the violence, it's the violins." Randy snatched the remote from him, and he turned off the sound. "I'm serious. Play it again with the sound off. You'll see."

They watched the scene together in dull silence. Amazed, "You're right," Bryan said. "It's nothing without the sound."

"The power of music. I'm always right, child. Except about men. Guess what?" He was smiling at Bryan, eyebrows raised.

"What?"

"I have another date. I hope you don't mind, child."

"Why should I mind?"

"Jeff wants to take me out again. He called me at work today."

"A date with the same guy twice?"

He looked at Bryan, grimly. "It doesn't happen that often, does it?"

Bryan followed him into the bedroom. Randy threw two pairs of shoes on the floor. He shoved them in a line with their toes against the mirror and stepped back and forth between them, trying out the different looks. "Are these too Granny Grunt?"

"Can I go out with you, sometime? I mean, not like on one of your dates, or anything. Just out with the girls, you know? To a movie or something."

Randy looked up. "I don't know why you'd want to. Sure, child." He touched Bryan's face with his hand. "You must be getting lonesome, huh? We'll see how I get along with this one, okay? He could turn into Fozzy Bear when we get out in public."

As before, Jeff showed up early. Randy was ready for him. "Don't wait up," he said, pecking Bryan on the cheek.

Jeff opened his arms. "Don't I get a kiss?"

"Stop," Randy said, slapping his wrist. They left with an eagerness that was tangible to Bryan. He waited up late, watching Judge Wopner, and then *Divorce Court*. He woke up at four o'clock with the TV still on. Randy had not come home.

Bryan hit the remote and rolled over. He fell back to sleep. Late the next morning, his uncle came home. He was whistling. He sang in the shower, too.

In the afternoon, Jeff came back. He did not seem to mind it when Randy suggested that Bryan join them for brunch. He brightened. "What you want to eat?"

"Pizza."

"I knew it." They took Bryan to Shield's. This was a noisy place, lively with large families and rushed waiters and sports talk. They got a booth near the fire, and Bryan looked over the menu while Randy and Jeff pretended to watch the football game on one of the dozens of televisions in the place. The waiter walked up, and when Randy turned to order, he said, "Oh my God. Opus."

"Randy," the waiter said, looking like he had swallowed a cube of ice. He wore a tuxedo that only went down as far as his waist. Underneath it, he wore brightly colored boxer shorts. He glanced at Jeff and Bryan.

"Cute outfit," Randy said. "I didn't know you worked here."

"I don't," said Opus. "I mean, I know you didn't know." He reached out and pinched one of Randy's triceps with two fingers. "Working out?"

James Russell Mayes

Randy pulled his arm away. "A little."

Opus cleared his throat, flipping his stack of orders up in front of himself, as if he could hide behind something so small. They ordered the vegetarian pizza, because it came with sliced almonds on top. Opus took their orders, and he was gone.

"So," Jeff said, cool, amused. "Opus."

"That's Opus," Randy agreed. He tugged at his collar, pretending that he couldn't breathe.

Bryan and Jeff laughed with glee.

When Opus returned with their drinks, he eyed Bryan up and down. "Dare I ask for ID?"

Bryan looked at Randy.

Randy said, "For a Coke? I don't think so."

The waiter leaned forward and winked at Bryan. "You don't look a day over eighteen, child." Bryan blushed.

"Oh, leave him alone," Randy said, gently. "He's fifteen. He can have a Coke, can't he?"

Opus raised his eyebrows. He clutched the round tray to his chest. He placed his nose inches from Bryan's and said to him: "Anytime you get tired of these old queens, you're always welcome with me." He slid a card out of his breast pocket. Bryan read, "A hard man is good to find. Opus McClintock. (517) 584-5555."

When he looked up, Randy was white with anger. "You're disgusting. You ought to be ashamed of yourself."

Jeff stood. "Could I speak to the manager, please?"

"What for?" Opus put a hand on his hip. "You afraid I'm gonna get some of the same stuff you been keeping all to yourself?"

"Are you going to get him? Or should I get him myself?"

The waiter with the tails held up his nose. "I'll get her for you." Bryan waited until he had turned his back. Then, loud enough for Randy's ex-lover to hear, he said, "Chicken-chaser." The conversation at the tables around them stalled.

Bryan's uncle raised his glass at him. "I'm proud of you. There's a lot better places to be sticking your thing than up that tired old girl. Believe me, I been there, child, and Opus, for me, ain't been no crystal stair." Bryan giggled.

"Not so loud," Jeff pleaded. "If these guys found out they had three faggots in here, they'd beat the shit out of us." Randy winked at Bryan. Bryan liked that he was one of three faggots.

The manager assigned a new waiter to their table, and the rest of the meal passed wittily. Randy and Jeff had their own plans for after dinner. They asked Bryan if he might want to rent another video?

"No," he said. "Not really. I was thinking I might check out the movie down the street."

"In the afternoon?"

"It's cheap that way."

"What time does it start?" Randy asked. "We'll give you a ride, if you want." They finished the pizza. It was really quite good, in spite of the fact that it had no meat on it.

Randy and Jeff dropped Bryan off at the theater. A long line had already formed. He waited in the cold for twenty minutes, and when he finally reached the usher at the door, he realized that he should have bought his ticket first. He raced back to the ticket window. "Sold out," the sign said. The boy behind the window shrugged, chewing his gum. "Cheap shows go fast," he shouted through the glass. His gum popped out and stuck on the window in a polygon of steam.

In the bitter sunlight, Bryan walked home. It was cold, and the wind blew, but the house was not too far. "It's just as well," he told himself. "Even if you do get to see his butt, who wants to see a girl end up with the guy?"

Bryan was not thinking when he saw that Jeff's car was parked in front. He let himself in with Randy's extra key. Randy's coat and Jeff's coat lay on the couch. The rest of their clothes trailed through the living room. Bryan found a pair of boxer shorts. He knew for a fact that Randy did not wear boxer shorts. He lifted them to see: no, they were quite clean. They smelled heavily of cologne. He heard a giggle from Randy's bedroom. At least they closed the door, Bryan thought.

He walked as quietly as he could to the kitchen. He made himself a sandwich, and he ate it over the sink to keep the crumbs off the floor. When the telephone rang, he picked it up quick. "Hello," he said, with his mouth full.

A woman's voice said, "Randy?"

"Um," he began.

James Russell Mayes

"It's Tennille. Listen, you little faggot. Stop tracking me down, will ya?" The woman on the other end of the phone had a rattling laugh. Bryan's food froze in his throat. "Can't take a joke, eh? How you doing, little brother?"

"Fine."

"What's wrong? I'm doing just fine up here without that asshole Leonard. I got a job and everything."

"Where?"

"At a bar in Marquette. I'm calling from work. What's up?"

"Mom."

"Bryan? Is that you? What are you doing at Randy's, you little shit?" She laughed and laughed. "Uh-oh. Something's wrong, isn't it? What happened?"

"Leonard went to Texas, Mom. I been here with Uncle Randy."

"I'll bet you are." She covered the receiver, but Bryan heard her coughing on the other end of the line.

"How you doing, Mom?"

"Fine, just fine. Listen, kid. You want to come up here and live? I'm serious. I got a nice place to stay, and you can go to school up here as well as anywhere else." She waited, and then she said, "Meet yourself a little Indian friend. Or whatever. Come on up, Bryan. I want you up here with me. You'd like it."

"Why don't you come back down here?"

"I got a job now, I told you. You gotta come up here. You can't stay with Randy all your life." She paused. "He didn't offer to let you stay with him, did he?"

"No, Mom. He didn't."

"I see, well, good. I wouldn't let you stay with him, anyway. Now listen, it might take me a few days to get down there. I should be able to sometime after Thanksgiving."

"After Thanksgiving?"

"That's what I said. You know I don't have wheels, and your mama's new boyfriend is out working on a job. We'll get down there as soon as we can, okay, honey?"

"Okay, Mom."

"Now say good-bye, cause I gotta get back to my tables, babe."

"Good-bye, Mom."

"See you real soon, honey."

Bryan was not hungry anymore, but he made another sandwich. He wandered into the garage. He pushed the button that opened the door. He sat on the edge of Randy's pickup truck and threw pieces of his sandwich into Gobbler's pen. He fed the bird and watched while he worked away at the food. Leonard had once told him that the oil from the peanut butter would keep a bird warm in the cold. Bryan listened to the mothers in the neighborhood, calling their children to come in. "It's time to eat," one called.

"What are we having?"

Small children from the neighborhood walked by. A little girl in a white winter coat that was spotlessly clean saw Gobbler. She called to the others, "Look! A chicken! That man has a chicken in his garage!" The troupe of them stopped at the foot of the driveway, craning their heads and bending their knees at Bryan.

He jumped to the ground, still holding his sandwich. "You wanna see him?"

They ran up the driveway and into the garage. They asked if they could pet the chicken.

"It's not a chicken," Bryan said. "It's a turkey."

The little girl in white touched Gobbler's tail, and the turkey swung his head around. The children giggled. They were a group of lovely children, Bryan thought, with lovely new winter coats and matching mittens. Much too lovely. "His name's Gobbler," he announced with his mouth full of sandwich. "We're going to chop his head off and eat him for Thanksgiving."

As if this was the first he had heard of that, Gobbler lifted his head. The little girl in white said, "We have to go now." One of the little boys began to cry. Bryan followed them out onto the driveway. He opened his mouth to show them his half-chewed sandwich. The children screamed. They ran out into the street.

"Not a truck in sight when you need one," Bryan muttered. He took a nice, long walk.

When Bryan got back from his walk, Randy and Jeff had gone. He waited up for his uncle, lying on the couch on top of his sleeping bag in his Palermo mesh bikini briefs that he had ordered through the mail. *Baywatch* was on. When Uncle Randy finally came in, he turned on a light. "Oh," he said, clearing his throat. "If you're going to sleep, you should turn this off." He walked up to the TV and turned it off.

"It's okay," Bryan said. He hit the button on the remote to turn it back on. "I was watching it. I'll turn it down." He lay back to adjust the volume, and he pressed his crotch outward. "Mom called."

"You're kidding. What did she have to say for herself?"

Bryan looked up at him. "She said she's got a job in Marquette."

"Great." Randy slumped exhausted into his chair.

"They're coming down to pick me up as soon as they can. She said it would be after Thanksgiving, though."

"You stay here as long as you need to." Randy scratched himself under his armpits. He cleared his throat. "Where did you get that?" he said.

Rolling onto his stomach so that his buttocks would press through the mesh, Bryan said, "What?"

"That dink basket."

"I ordered it out of a catalogue. It's comfortable."

"It is not. It's obscene." Randy snickered. A sexy commercial came on the TV. The two of them were silent, watching soap bubbles crawl down the muscles on a man's back.

Bryan said, "Randy? I want to give you something."

"Give me something?"

"A present. For letting me stay here."

Randy frowned. "Don't give me anything, okay?"

"I didn't buy it," Bryan explained. "I still have all the eighty bucks that Leonard gave me. I didn't even spend it on the movie. It was sold out." He stood up in his briefs. "I want to give you something."

Randy covered his eyes. "Will you put something on?"

Bryan did not. He walked to the closet in the front hall and pulled out from his mother's suitcase his gift for his uncle. He had to give him something. He knew what Randy liked. He lay it down in Randy's lap, and he stood nearly naked in front of him.

Randy opened his eyes. He unwrapped the package, which Bryan had so carefully camouflaged in the colored newspaper print of the Sunday comics. He pulled out Bryan's Buns brief, the Sock, the

Cruiser brief, and the Lava bikini. "I can't wear these," Randy said. "My ass is too fat."

"They're not to wear," Bryan said.

"Then what are they for?"

"They're dirty," Bryan said. "I wore them each for a day, and the jock I wore in gym class." He picked the Sock out of Randy's fingers. "I wore this one lifting weights in the garage. I didn't wash them. I thought you might like that."

Randy pulled the Sock up to his face. He inhaled audibly.

"Look," Bryan said. He slid his fingers under the elastic in the briefs that he was wearing. "This is the Palermo mesh bikini. Do you like it?" He turned around and paced the length of the couch and back. "You can have this, too, if you like it." He widened his eyes. He tried to assume a particular expression that he had seen on his favorite model in the *International Male* catalogue.

Randy cleared his throat. "Gross," he said.

"Don't say that."

"Listen. Bryan, please." Randy was looking down at the heap of dirty underwear in his hands. "I don't know how you would know about what I like or what I don't like," he said, "but I don't like this." He pushed them at Bryan. "You trying to get us into trouble? You can't be giving shit like this to your uncle. Look at you, man."

Bryan bent forward to pick up the black French thong, which did seem small and wrinkled without a man inside of it to stretch it out. "I wanted to give you something that would make you feel handsome, I don't know." He felt himself give way. He ducked into the only room in the house that had a door to slam.

It happened to be Randy's bedroom. Bryan slammed the door, and he lay down on his stomach on Randy's bed. It was still messed up and smelling of Jeff's Aramis and Randy's sweat. He sniffed at the pillow and got a whiff of Randy's hair, which, unlike the sheets, smelled human, like a body: like Randy's hair, just hair without the scent and animal-like.

He didn't cry, of course. He was too humiliated to cry. "Let me live with you," he wanted to say. "I can move in, and I can walk to school from your house. We can go shopping together, and I'll show you how to make beef stew with beer in it. We can drink coffee together every morning, and I'll rub your back when you knock it out of whack. I promise I won't fall in love with you again." He waited in Randy's bed, wondering if perhaps he might come in to him and they could do it in the stripes of moonlight that shot across the bed. He closed his eyes and waited.

The tea kettle whistled. Shortly afterward, Randy knocked on the door. He carried in a cup of tea. He set it on the nightstand. He turned on the lamp. He sat down on the edge of the bed, and he ran his hand up Bryan's back. "There," he said. "There, there."

"Don't touch me," Bryan said. "Unless you mean it."

The hand withdrew. Randy said, eventually, "I mean it. I just don't mean it like *you* mean it, child."

"I'm not a child."

Randy sighed. "I brought you some peppermint tea. You want some?"

Bryan said nothing.

"When I was in tenth grade I had a huge crush on a friend of mine," his uncle said. He breathed through his nose abruptly, to stifle a laugh. "He was a friend of mine, but he didn't like me in the same way, you know? I had him overnight once, and I was so excited. He was bored. It was awful." He paused. "It wasn't the worst night of my life."

Bryan rolled onto his back. He wiped his eyes. "What *was* the worst night of your life?"

"Oh my gosh, there were so many." Randy rolled his eyes up into his eyelids, thinking. "There was this one party I went to. I met this dairy farmer. I fell in love with him right away. I wanted to move in with him. I wanted to milk those cows. And then, not an hour later, in the line to use the john, somebody made a joke, and Mr. Man-of-My-Dreams tilted his head back and laughed. He only had four teeth in his head: two on top and two on the bottom, right in front. These were the four teeth I was looking at all night, assuming that they continued around in rows on either side. What could I say? I was ready to haul cow shit before I saw those teeth. Know what I'm getting at, child? I mean, Bryan?"

Bryan sniffed. "Only go out with a dentist?"

"Bryan, honey, it doesn't matter to me so much that we're related, you know, it's not like we ever saw each other that much or anything, but you're so young. You don't even know if you're gay for sure or not."

"I'm gay," Bryan said into the pillow. "I'm gay. I know I'm gay. I've always been gay."

"Have you ever slept with someone? Have you had a boyfriend or fallen in love or anything like that?"

"I don't have to," Bryan said. "I know."

Randy stood up and walked over to his bureau. "Well, maybe you do," he said. "But you got to know for sure before you go making plans." He giggled, and Bryan looked at him. His uncle had picked up Barbie herself and was holding her by the hair. One hand on his hip, he spun Barbie above his head like a lariat. "You need to rope someone your own age, pardner, not nellie old Uncle Randy," he said. He let Barbie go. She hit the wall with a thud. She slid down the wall to the floor. Randy stepped on Barbie's face. He pressed down with his toe and twisted it as if he were stepping on a bug.

"Poor Barbie," Randy murmured. He dropped to his knees on the floor. He reached under the bed and pulled out a gift, neatly wrapped in paper that had written all over it, "Bitch," "Cunt," "Asswipe," and "Prick."

"I was gonna give this to you when your mommy showed up. You want it now, or later?"

Bryan ran his fingers up and down the package. "You got me a dildo!"

"Not quite. Similar, though."

Bryan unwrapped it. Framed by a cellophane window in the box, dressed in his classic white dinner jacket, was Ken. "Oh, I love it," Bryan cried. "Is this the original box? Is he mine? Can I keep him?"

Randy kissed Bryan, oh-so-chastely, on the forehead. "I'm gonna miss you, child. Now get to bed."

"You're not nellie, Randy. You're not old."

"Child," Randy said, holding up his fingers, measuring an inch: "Flattery will get you just this far."

Unexpectedly early, Bryan's mother showed up at Randy's house on the day before Thanksgiving with a bottle of Jagermeister and a new

James Russell Mayes

leather jacket. "You've grown," she exclaimed. She squeezed Bryan's shoulder, and she patted his stomach. "You're filling out real nice." In comparison, Tennille had lost a lot of weight. Bryan and Randy exchanged worried looks. She had brought with her a new boyfriend, a tall man with glasses in a snowmobile suit, and something from the U.P. for Bryan: a half-grown German shepherd pup named Arrow. The dog was shy, but Bryan got her to smell his hands. She licked his face.

It took Bryan a lot of conversation to get his mother to stay for Thanksgiving dinner. "It's the least you can do," Randy said. "I mean the kid fattened the turkey up and everything. You can sleep in my bed."

"Well," Bryan's mom said doubtfully. She looked at her new boyfriend.

He shrugged. "Sure," he said. "Why not? I love turkey meat."

Gobbler had grown quite heavy, but not nearly as fat as the colorful ones that Bryan remembered from the bulletin boards in elementary school. After Randy and Bryan loaded him into the back of the pickup, Arrow hopped right up into the cab next to Bryan. "I think that dog likes you," Randy said. They drove out past the water tower and the industrial refinery. It snowed big flakes, a pretty, Charlie Brown snow. The door of the trailer hung open. There was a foot-sized hole in the siding. "Wanna check it out?" Randy asked him.

"Naw," Bryan said. He walked out to the shed. Randy followed close behind him. When Bryan turned around with the axe in his hand, Randy stopped him short. He lifted Bryan's chin with his fingers. He looked him in the eyes. "You don't have to go with her, you know. You can stay with me. I'll talk to her." He laughed, a kind, but a self-conscious laugh, and he pulled his hand away. He punched Bryan's shoulder. "I'll put you up until you graduate, okay? And then you're on your own."

Bryan looked at the dark hole in the side of the trailer. "She's my mom, man. I don't even know this guy she brought with her."

The bird flapped so much, it took both of them to slide Gobbler out of the back of the truck and over to the chopping stump. Bryan lifted Gobbler up onto the block. His voice two screws tighter, "Hold on to his legs, like this," he said.

"I don't know if I can do this."

"You can. Here." Bryan showed him how to hold on to Gobbler's thick legs.

Evidently Randy had never seen anything's head chopped off before. He held on just fine while Bryan worked away at the last stubborn tendon. But when the head of the bird slid off of the top of the stump, and Bryan lowered the axe, and Arrow rushed forward, Randy let go of the turkey. Headless, the body jumped, solid, onto its feet. It shuddered. It lifted one leg, then the other, as if trying to account for the loss in weight.

Arrow licked at the blood in the grass. Near the dog's foot, the gawking turkey head watched its unconnected body march away. It did a complete flip and chugged up the embankment. Too small for how fat he was, Gobbler's wings stiffened, as if he might fly straight up into the falling snow. A truck came rolling by, and the headless bird at the side of the road broad-jumped. Bryan and Randy watched a good turkey dinner turn under the wheels.

Only in French

Sometimes I think if someone stopped me on the street and gave me a reality check, I wouldn't be able to pass it. Usually I don't know what day it is, for example. I know the president of the United States is Jimmy Carter. I know that the hostages from the American embassy in Iran are still not free. Everybody's talking about that.

But any given person never knows what's going on. It could be all-American imperialism, for all we know. Again. Or a mistake of some kind that nobody wants to admit, like why did we support the Shah in the first place? I still think: All this news is going on, and how does it help me to know it, except to make me want to stay in my room and not go out at night? I think about Kami, the student on our floor that I knew from Iran. We were going to be roommates. He was a premedical student, friendly. I didn't see much of him after the crisis. He moved out to Brooklyn with relatives.

There is other news, too. Local news. Like the rumor that the Beatles are getting back together for a concert in Manhattan. My new roommate Nikos skipped his classes for the day just in case the rumor was true. That way he could run up to Madison Square Garden and buy tickets right away if it ever happened.

But it didn't.

"Just another goddamn media hoax," Nikos says.

I am trying to cross the street on the way back to my room, and suddenly I see yellow. A taxicab flashes by about three inches from my nose. My arm automatically swings up with the middle finger in the air. "You drive like a fuck," I am yelling.

Some people do not care, I tell myself. Some people do not care if you dive in front of their car and let them kill you, except that it would make them late for their hair appointment. I love New York. I step back onto the curb to get my breath. The first time I did that Linda and Peggy said I was a real New Yorker. Omar the King of Manhattan. I heart New York.

Linda puts her lips close to my ear and I lean toward her.

"He's gay," she says.

She's talking about Randy, of course. He just walked into the cafeteria. By this time even I have heard how Randy got into trouble the morning after he moved into the dorm because he took a shower with one of his roommates. The third guy woke up and walked in on the two of them. I could picture the whole thing. It sounded like something that would happen to me. I felt sorry for the other guy. He freaked out and moved the same day.

"So how can Peggy be in love with somebody gay?"

She leans toward me again and I cock my ear toward her. At the same time I lower my head I look at Randy who is waiting in line. But here they say "waiting *on* line."

"She's a fag hag," she says. She says it like it's supposed to mean more than what I think it does.

I'm busy filling my face, so I give her a look that is really more of a question.

I take another drink of my soda. Randy is obviously bored because he's looking all around the cafeteria. He spots me.

I look down, back at Linda.

"I mean, I like her just as much as anybody else does," Linda says. "She's a *very talented actress.*"

I'm thinking: Here it comes.

She takes a piece of lemon and squeezes it into her Coke.

"But let's face it. She's ugly."

"You're terrible," I say. I look up and see that Randy is bending over the counter to talk to the sandwich man.

James Russell Mayes

"It's true. She'll never get anything more than bit parts for fat women. Funny parts. She'll never be anything more than a character actress. But *that's* not my point."

She drops the piece of mauled lemon into her Coke and jabs it around with her straw.

"What is the point?" I notice that Randy's wearing tight green corduroys and a bright checkered shirt. It's not that he wears nice clothes so much as that he always looks *good* in them.

Sauve, I think. Nobody uses the word "sauve" around here. Not out loud, anyway.

"That's why she falls in love with gay men."

"She does that a lot? Or is this the first time?"

Randy is looking around the room, probably for somebody else to sit with.

"The first time," Linda says. "As far as I know. But I've seen it before. She can't deal with straight men, nobody would date her anyway, so she falls in love with *him*. If he *were* straight, he wouldn't fall in love with *her* anyway."

"I thought they were just friends."

"Well, they are. That's what *he* wants."

"So what's the problem?"

"*She's* the problem. You just don't get it, do you?"

She looks down at her macaroni and cheese and sighs with frustration.

"They got drunk one night, and they slept together, and now she wants to make more out of it than it is."

"They slept together?"

"That's what I said."

"You mean they had sex?"

"How would I know?"

"Well, if he had sex with her, how can he be gay?"

She says, *"He's gay."*

Randy has just noticed us, like we were here all the time and he hadn't seen us before. Linda waves him over. I look down at my food.

"How can you know for sure?" I ask the rest of my sandwich. "How can you really know for sure unless you were gay yourself and you slept with him?"

When I look up again I'm looking at him, and he's smiling, a winning smile above an open shirt collar, making his way through the tables toward us.

I look back at Linda. Her voice is low: "Trust me. I know." She looks up at our guest and takes on that comedic posture she learned at the Strassberg studio. He sits down, and "Randy, *darling,* " she says. "Have we survived our diction class?"

I keep thinking, She needs a cigarette to pull that off.

✁

Nikos shows me his photo album. He is very proud of his photography. He has several pictures pinned up on the wall. Now he's taking a course at NYU.

First there is a picture of a house.

"This is a picture of my house," he says. The sun is shining down, brightly, on the house. There are piles of bricks in the foreground and the lawn has no grass; it is an unfinished house.

"My father is building a new house," he says.

He and his brothers? He and his brothers are sitting on the concrete porch, eating sandwiches.

"It looks like your father is making you and your brothers build a new house," I say.

Nikos laughs.

But I have an important question.

"Did your mother slice your sandwiches straight or diagonally?"

Nikos looks mystified.

"You know, most people's mothers, when they make sandwiches for them, they slice them straight across the middle. My mom sliced them diagonally."

He doesn't seem to get what I'm saying.

"Diagonally," I repeat. "From corner to corner. You know what a sandwich is, right?"

"My father makes me a sandwich," Nikos says. He seems to be struggling with the language, but he likes to play dumb sometimes. I've noticed that his accent gets a little heavy when he's around women. I'm not sure if this is another little show of his or not.

"Okay." I am impatient with him. "So your father makes a sandwich. Does he cut the bread across the middle or from corner to corner?"

"Our bread doesn't have corners. It is round."

"Oh."

I give up, point to a dark green photograph on the facing page. "Who is this?"

"My grandmother." His grandmother is small, but she appears to be happy: good teeth, anyway. She wears a black scarf over her fleecy white hair. A babushka? No, that's *Polish*. And a black dress.

"Still alive?" I wonder. I bet she wears black shoes, too.

"Oh yes. That was last summer."

In the picture, Nikos sits at a table with her, you can tell that they sit under the trees because everything is muted with a green darkness and then there is also the way the light shines, crosshatching over the dark hair on his bare arm. Posing with the fork in his mouth, Nikos leans down, his arm around his little grandmother, two pairs of eyes open wide in the shadows.

"You have blue eyes?"

"No," he says. "Green. Green eyes. Look, look, look."

He is craning his long neck toward me over the photo album. Even his neck is hairy. He always leaves the first three buttons on the front of his shirt unbuttoned. I notice that the hair on his neck makes a trail down into the front of his shirt.

When I look up, he is smiling at me and making his eyes so wide that I cannot fail to see that yes, they are, after all, green eyes.

"What is it?" Nikos says. "Green eyes, no?"

Our noses almost touch.

"You're right."

I try not to think about his penis-shaped bottle of Pierre Cardin, standing attentively on the table next to his bed.

❧

"You dance like your body is falling apart," Nikos tells me.

"Thank you." My back is tingling. A single drop of sweat runs down my spine under my Hawaiian shirt.

Linda is holding tightly to my hand with both of her hands. I shake mine out of hers and back up against the wall next to Nikos.

"You like to dance," he says. "Don't you?" He talks evenly through the loud beach music. He is smiling with those brilliant white teeth of his. I notice that his two front teeth overlap a little. I turn to Linda, who is standing behind me, also leaning against the wall.

"I love to dance," I say. I have to talk loud, because my voice doesn't carry.

I feel his breath against the back of my neck. "You like to move your butt," he tells me, while I'm smiling at my girlfriend. I laugh before I can stop myself.

But then I stifle the laugh and raise my eyebrows, as if I'm actually offended by this. I turn to Linda to see if she heard this, but she's talking to Peggy, the fag hag, who's standing on the other side of her.

Peggy is a big woman, quite round in fact, and she always over-dresses. For everything, even a dorm beach party. She's wearing heart-shaped sunglasses, a huge straw hat, and a bright flowered skirt that flimsily reaches below her knees. Otherwise, her breasts would probably hang off to either side, I think to myself. Peggy brightens when I look at her. Linda is talking to her about a mile a minute, but Peggy interrupts.

"Do you dance with fat girls, too?" she asks, cutely, across Linda.

"I love to dance with fat girls."

Peggy takes my hand and leads me out to the crowded dance floor while hoards of onlookers in bathing suits and cutoff jeans move out of our wake. There is that initial moment of self-consciousness when we move a little carefully to accommodate the narrow space. I catch Linda's face through the bobbing heads and smile. She smiles back for a moment, and then she turns to Nikos. She's talking away as furiously to him as she was to Peggy. We both have taken diet pills before we came. I can see the effect in my dancing and in her talking.

I turn back around to grin at Peg, who smiles broadly while she bumps and grinds those massive hips of hers. She moves her arms gracefully, in a sort of Hawaiian way, and her legs and hips move in a circular, sexy motion. Her feet barely move at all, but that skirt of hers is flipping around and alternately exposing and hiding the rounded wideness of her legs.

James Russell Mayes

Then I *really* start dancing. It always takes me a little while to warm up. But something inside is splitting up and breaking out of me, and I want to shake it loose. I start shaking all over. My arms shoot out. My legs rock back and forth so I can keep my balance.

Peggy gives me an appreciative raise of the eyebrows. That only gets me going. Must be that caffeine pill. I reverberate. By now the crowd on the dance floor has thinned out. They've noticed that I'm dancing with the fat lady. They let us get it on.

"We're so good," Peggy says. I laugh and move my hips.

We dance and dance and dance through three songs in a row: the Beach Boys, the Supremes, Elvis. The smell of Peggy's Chantilly Lace perfume begins to clog my lungs.

I stop.

"I'm exhausted." Now it's her turn to laugh. She grabs my hand and pulls me off the dance floor.

"It's no wonder you're tired. You dance like your body is about to explode." We lean up against the wall next to Linda and Nikos, I'm catching my breath. Peggy is smiling at me with those huge, beautiful lips of hers, those fascinating lips that look like something you could fall into with your whole body. "Like a seizure," she says. "You have this ... epileptic style of body movement."

"Watch it. That disease of jester and genius runs in my family."

"Really?" She snaps into a pout of sympathy, sincere, as if she knows I am joking about something true.

Linda catches my eye.

She whispers, "Your roommate's an asshole."

"What he do?"

"Did you know he has *three* girlfriends?"

"No, you're kidding!" I reach around her toward Nikos, and I slap him on the arm. "All right," I shout, "go for it, Nikos!" He reaches around Linda to slap me back, and she pushes our arms apart to walk between us. She comes around on the other side of me, holding onto my shoulder.

"It's the way the American girls walk," he says. Like that's his explanation.

Linda shouts at him from the other side of me. "The way we walk?"

Nikos is keeping an eye out for the girls coming in and out. Looking at every other woman but the one he's talking to. "Some of them." He bends down so that both of us can hear him. But he won't look at either one of us. "They come to our country, they walk like they want to be raped," he says. "You shoulda seen them, these American women."

"I've seen them," I say.

He gives me this look.

"I look at American women every day," I say. I'm talking loud, but now he turns his face away, acts like he doesn't want to hear it.

"I would never think of raping a woman because of the way she walks down the street." He's listening. I know he can hear me. But he smiles and nods at this blonde woman with long legs.

"Well, it is true," he says. "You do not understand," he says to Linda. "Our women never walk like that."

"Our women," she says.

✄

Out of the blue, Nikos tells me that a car needs some work and that he needs me to help him on it. He has a job working weekends for his uncle, who owns a garage in Queens.

Even though I insist that I don't know anything about cars, which I honestly don't, Nikos insists. I put on my ripped-out jeans that have holes in the knees and this dumb old t-shirt that somebody gave me once.

We take the train out to Queens. Even though it's the middle of the day and a weekend, the train is crowded. Nikos and I keep bumping up against one another.

He shows me his uncle's shop, a narrow brick building with more height than I have imagined. "Where is everybody?" I ask him.

"Everybody who? It's just you and me, my friend."

He shows me the car. The car is pretty old. The car looks hopeless to me. I have to read the metal letters on the hood to tell what it is: a Buick.

Nikos rolls out a blanket onto the pavement. He sets his toolbox on the blanket. He tells me to sit down there, and he slides under the car. I'm sitting by the toolbox. I'm looking at his legs in baggy coveralls, trying to remember all the names to each of the different kinds of tools.

I hand them down as he asks for them: first the WD-40, then the ½-inch ... no, the ⅝-inch socket wrench. I listen to him working away down there. Each time I give him something, he says, politely, "Thanks."

I am thinking he does this because he's a foreigner. The only people in New York City who are polite are the people from other countries. Unless they're from the Midwest, like me.

I don't say much. I let him do all the talking because I don't want to sound as stupid as I probably am about this stuff. He's making jokes, about nuts, ha, ha, and bolts. They're stupid jokes, but I laugh. Foreigners are so cute, I am thinking. Anything he says could get me going.

His hand comes out from under the car. He touches my knee. His dirty hand turns over, palm upward. He says, "Give me the chisel."

As efficiently as if I were right beside Chad Everett in the operating room, I whip it down to him. He asks for the hammer, and I give it to him, just as fast.

Nikos is banging away under there. The next time his hand comes out, he touches my leg. More than that, he *squeezes* my leg. His fingers feel around for the holes in my jeans, and he tickles my knee.

He says, from under the car, "Is this *you?*"

"Yeah." I try to laugh.

He laughs.

He reaches out. He squeezes it again. I move my knee. "What do you want?"

"Nothing. All done."

"All done?"

Twenty minutes under the car, and Nikos climbs out. He brushes himself off. "Om," he says, "this is worse than I thought. I call my uncle later."

He is looking greasy and rough.

He asks me, "Will you get my back?"

I'm thinking, even though I've been looking at this guy every night and morning for the past few weeks, we're roommates after all, I'm thinking: Look at that face. Even under the dirt, he is so cool. He gives me his big dirty hand to help me up off the blanket.

I hold onto his cuff, and he pulls me up.

He asks me again, "Get my back, will you?"

So I brush off his back. I avoid the big pockets on his rump.

Nikos smiles. He picks up all of the tools from off the blanket. I grab the blanket. I am trying to be helpful, because I haven't done any work at all, really. Nikos misses a tool. It rings on the concrete floor.

I say, "You missed one." I pick it up.

"Want to clean up now?"

I stop. I turn around. Nikos is looking right at me. It's like he's looking for something. Again he smiles. He can see too much, I think. I turn away, like I'm checking out his uncle's stupid garage. I turn around, and he's still holding that smile like a picture up to the light in the garage.

"Good," he says. My knees are shaky. I know this is supposed to mean something. It's a signal, right? But I don't want to think about that. I just want to run around and yell or hit him or something.

Nikos unlocks the back door to the building. He holds it open with his back so I can walk in first. I'm walking up the stairwell to the apartment he uses on the weekends for his job, the place where he claims he takes all of his millions of girlfriends.

He is behind me on the stairs with all of the tools.

He pokes me in the butt with a corner of the toolbox.

I yip. I speed it up. I hop up those steps two at a time.

Nikos speeds up, too. He keeps poking me in the butt, first with the corner of his toolbox. And then with his fingers.

I'm running up the stairs. I'm thinking he's getting a little carried away.

He's laughing. He even laughs in Greek.

He's got me laughing, too. I go up each flight of stairs, around and around. Nikos is right behind me. He's gaining. I get to the top, all out of breath, and he's so close to me that I can't open the door. It opens *out*.

I turn around to push him.

He pushes back. The toolbox slides down his leg. He's got his hands on my face. He's got his face up to mine. He's kissing me. The inside of his lips is wet and warm. The outside is dry and rough. He kisses me hard and soft at the same time. His tongue goes in and out: hard and soft. Mostly wet.

James Russell Mayes

I hold on tight to the blanket between us. The wrench in my hand that was cold when I picked it up rings hot down the steps. Nikos licks the hair on top of my head. I feel his tongue moving all around on my head and in my ears. "Om," he says. "Om."

I never liked the sound of my name before he said it.

We kick through the door into the apartment, which is nothing special, a mattress on the floor. Nikos turns the shower on.

We really do melt out of our clothes, like Erica Jong says.

"Who are you?" says the teacher.

Suddenly I'm not sure. I look at my notebook for the room number because this isn't my French class. Am I in the right building?

No, I am not in the right building. I have the right room number. But I'm not in the right building.

I feel myself turn colors. I walk out of the classroom and out into the hall. Are they still laughing at me in there?

"Main floor," I tell the elevator man. The elevator is very quiet: no pushing back between the other bodies, no anonymous someone crackling their gum in my ear. Everyone else is in class.

This old building is falling apart, I think to myself.

I sit down on a bench in Washington Square Park and try to straighten the wire rims of my glasses. I hate my glasses. But it is a nice day, and I have a letter in my notebook to read from someone that I used to go to high school with: Allen Hart. Allen Hart is writing me a letter all the way from Michigan State University, and he is writing to tell me how he is in love: with a woman.

I think how nice to be there, back in Michigan. And how Allen Hart put his arms around me once when we were goofing around after the school play. Of course we were only joking, pretending to be fags. We enjoyed that a lot. What a hoot. We both went to Boys' State in the eleventh grade. There were so many of us high school juniors all packed into the one dorm, we had to wait on line to use the showers.

It dawns on me, finally. It is Tuesday, and this is why French class is in the other building. It will be too late for me to get anything out of the lesson. I don't want to feel another room of eyes on me. I don't want to feel my chest squeezing all the air out of my lungs or to feel my hands prickling sweat while I wait for the French teacher from Seattle, Washington, to call on me.

Once again I would become another person: a stupid, bashful person who does not know what to say or how to say it in French. This is an active class, some new teaching method, and there are a lot of questions and answers and the repetition of all those words in French. We are not allowed to speak in English. Only in the language that we don't even know yet, only in French.

✄

"What are you doing?"

I pull my hands away.

"I thought you liked this." I stand up next to Nikos, next to where he is sitting at his desk. And then I move around behind him and start rubbing his shoulders.

"Om," he says.

"What?"

"Stop that."

"Why? I thought you liked this."

"I do not like it." He keeps trying to write, but he can't seem to. He keeps picking up his pencil and then putting it back down again.

"You seemed to like it enough when I was doing it last weekend."

"Yeah. Well, that was last weekend. What if somebody comes in here?"

"Like one of your three girlfriends?"

"Yeah, what if my girlfriend comes in here?"

"Maybe we should tell them," I say. "I think we should tell them all. I think we should go to France together. We can learn the language, and then we can live happily ever after."

I laugh at my own joke.

It is a joke, I tell myself.

Nikos is very quiet.

"I was joking," I say to him. The muscles in his shoulders are all tensed up now. "It was just a joke. Relax. You're all tensed up now."

"Om."

"Yes?" I'm trying to sound real casual. I swing around beside him so that I can see his face, but he's looking down into his lap.

James Russell Mayes

"Don't you say that." He raises his head so that he can look me directly in the eyes. "Don't ever say that. You tell anyone, I'm gonna kill you."

He looks bad. His eyes are all red and full of water.

"Are you *crying?*" I can't believe this. I start rubbing his arms with both hands.

"No. I am not crying."

"Why are you crying? Is it that bad, is what we did so bad..." I want to laugh out loud.

"Om."

I stop. He takes my hands off of his arms and then he pushes me, ever so gently. Away.

"You were not raised the same way I was," he says. "My father, my mother. This is a very bad thing."

"Great. Nikos? Whatever."

When I leave, I am very careful not to slam the door.

The next afternoon, Nikos and I cut under the arch on our way to class. We don't have much to say to each other, but we both have class in the same building. We're roommates. Why not walk together? Above our head, the sky moves and a cloud of pigeons turns like a wheel.

There's a crowd under the trees. It's a pretty big crowd for Washington Square. There's music. There's a band. We can't see the band through the massive crowd, but they're singing "If I Fell in Love with You." It sounds like the Beatles. *Just* like the Beatles.

I look at Nikos.

He grins at me.

"The Beatles!" we shout.

We push into the crowd, which is the biggest crowd I have ever seen in Washington Square Park, even on Halloween. People are turning and letting us by. Those who don't, we push, slightly. Some of them are clapping. Nikos puts his hand on an older woman's shoulder. She slaps him. He stands behind her, shaking his head. We walk around. We find a park bench. I step up onto it. I turn around and pull Nikos up beside me.

It's not. It's an Asian band. But they sound *exactly* like the Beatles.

"These guys are pretty good," I say.

Nikos laughs. "They fooled me."

"Hey." Someone is shouting from behind us. Someone's pulling on my arm. It's Randy. He steps up onto my side of the park bench.

"Umm, hi," I say.

He asks me, "You listen to the radio?"

"What?"

"You hear the news on the radio?"

Something is bugging him. I lie. "Yeah," I say. "I heard about it."

"Can you believe some kids come through here beating up gays?"

I stop clapping. "What?"

"A carload of these high school kids came through the Village around four o'clock this morning, after the bars let out. They beat up every faggot they could find who was walking home from the bar alone. You didn't hear about it?"

Nikos, who is standing on the other side of me, takes a look at Randy. He shakes his head and jumps down to the ground. He pushes back through the crowd.

"Can you believe that?"

I don't know what to say. I ask him, "Why are you telling me about this?"

The music stops. Everybody around us is clapping. I clap, too, shaking my head at Randy.

He asks me, "Doesn't it bother you?"

"Of course, it bothers me." I'm looking around for Nikos, for anyone I might know. The Asian Beatles start up another tune: "Eleanor Rigby."

Randy talks directly into my ear. "They killed a guy."

"That's awful!"

"They found him on Tenth Street."

I look at him, surprised. "I take Tenth Street to class every day."

"You and all the rest of us."

I wonder how he meant that: "us."

I raise my hand to wave good-bye. I back myself out of the crowd. I wonder if I can still find Nikos.

James Russell Mayes

Randy shouts after me: "The guy that was killed, he *wasn't* gay." He lifts his hands and shrugs: the irony. "They musta thought he *looked* gay."

I slump back through the crowd, feeling everyone's eyes.

"I was fourteen," Peggy says. "My friend Lois and I spent a month in Europe."

"By yourselves?"

"Of course. I was real big on independence at that age. But it wasn't a big deal. Our parents let us go because we were with this tour thing."

She has these two harlequin faces on her wall. They look like they're ceramic or something, with ribbons sticking out of the ears.

"God, I wish I could go to Europe."

"Well," she says. "It wasn't as good as it sounds. I'd get a lot more out of it now. We were so stupid about everything, you know?"

On the end table next to her bed there is a pencil sketch of Kate Hepburn dressed up as Queen Elizabeth I. Did Hepburn ever play Elizabeth I? I know Bette Davis did.

"What do you mean?"

"We were so stupid." She sweeps her hair back off her forehead with her fingers. It is curly, a pretty color brown. But it feels brittle. She probably does something chemical to it. "We were scared to death of all the guys because, you know how the Latin men are, and we were at the Coliseum and this guy was pulling Lois into a car, and I was trying to help her, and we were both only fourteen, and it was *awful...*"

"You're kidding. You got away okay?"

Peggy has a big poster above the bed: "All That Jazz" spelled out in bright lightbulbs. "Oh, yeah," she says, staring at the poster. She is barely interested in her own conversation. "Scared to death. We didn't even see the Coliseum."

I can feel her wide legs against mine. Her skin is so soft, it could tear under my fingers like wet paper towels. But her face is her most attractive feature, really. Peggy is quite beautiful, after all.

"Why just the Latin men? Why not all men?"

"They're sexist. They're the worst, you know that. More rapes, more violence against women in those countries, the Latin ones, than anywhere else. You didn't know that? What do you think the women in Spain are marching for?"

"I didn't know they were."

She says nothing.

"I guess I should watch the news more." I feel something next to my feet under the covers, something cloth. Too big for her underpants. Or mine.

"Don't *watch* the news," Peggy says. She looks at her nails. "Read it. Television news is the worst."

I reach down and pull it, whatever it is, out from under my legs. The cloth is light and it kind of stretches when I pull it out. It's purple. "Nikos says I should watch it on TV. He says you see what's really going on that way..."

"Shit," she says. "I'm not stupid enough to think you love me. But do you have to bring him up?" She has this bored look. She's tired of me. But not *just* me: everyone. Everyone who has ever taken advantage of her, everyone who could not give her what she wants. She shows the delicate, painted gloss of her eyelids: a weariness.

I untangle the cloth.

It becomes two legs: an enormous, purple leotard.

Love and Li_2CO_3

Omar had been waiting for her. On Friday nights the editorial staff got off late. So he was already rosy with beer and a bit loud and more than ever attracted to her by the time she got to the bar. He pointed to the sign that he had pasted above their booth, but Wendy ignored him and asked, again, about the Sex Hero: "Who did you say he was sleeping with?" Something in the way that she leaned forward, aggressive with the curiosity that made her a good reporter, pawed at Omar's heart. He wished that she were asking about his own sex life. She hadn't even waited until she took off her coat.

"An art professor," he said. "Now he thinks he's got it made."

"His own teacher?"

"No." Omar pulled his coat over his knees. The booth he had chosen was near the door, and the Sweet Potato Bar had no foyer. Whenever someone came in, the winter air blew over them.

"I can't believe she's sleeping with him."

"You can't believe it when anyone sleeps with him."

"He's crazy. He'll catch a disease." She scooped her hair in a heap over one of her shoulders. Wendy had long hair, and she often played with it. Sitting across from her, Omar inhaled the smell. It smelled like blonde, he thought.

He raised his glass of beer. "He's probably spreading a disease right now." He drank from it loudly. Wendy leaned forward to read the sign above her shoulder, the sign that Omar had made and placed on the wall.

"What's a 'group poem'?"

He rubbed his hands together like a huckster. "This is big," he said. "Real big. We write a few lines, and then everyone else writes a few lines."

She said, "That sounds lame."

Omar took a breath. "Well, it sounds cool to me." Wendy sniffed and looked around the bar. He had failed, once again, to interest her.

A woman in a nurse's uniform breezed in. There were not many people in the Sweet Potato Bar, so she was easy to notice. Her eyes caught Omar's, and she beamed on him the kind of a face that reminded him of a Broadway entertainer's. The woman stopped at their booth. She smiled at him so hugely that Omar wondered where he might have seen her before.

"'Group poem,'" the woman read out loud. Actually, she was pretty. The wind had flushed her face and tangled the ends of her hair so that she had a breathless look of appealing damage. She wore a medium-long cape that she threw back over her shoulders, Florence Nightingale–style. "Can I write a few lines?"

Omar slid around the seat of their booth to make space for her. "And you didn't know what a group poem was," he scolded Wendy through the side of his mouth. He uncapped a black felt-tipped pen and handed it to his first taker.

But, "I don't know what to write," the woman said. She could make her eyes even wider at will, Omar noticed.

"Relax," he told her. "You want a beer?"

"I'd love a beer."

"Grammar Man," he called to the man with a thatch of gray hair and a dishrag. "Can we have another glass?"

"I don't know," the man said, coolly. "Can you?" His contempt resounded in the nearly empty bar.

"Gotta love that Grammar Man," Omar said. He felt suddenly desirable, at least, compared to the bartender. He pointed with his thumb. "That's the Grammar Man over there." The woman rested her chin in the palm of one of her hands and stared at the ceiling. Omar and Wendy waited while she tapped at the paper with the pen. She smiled at them absently. When the Grammar Man brought a third glass, Wendy filled it from their pitcher.

The woman complained, "I can't think of anything." She lifted her glass of beer and drained it. She pushed it across the table in front of Wendy and leaned forward on both elbows toward Omar. "Where do you get your ideas for poems?" Her eyes again: it seemed that she could not turn them off.

Omar gave Wendy a look, but she did not catch it. She was watching the Grammar Man, who wiped down the silent jukebox with a towel. So he poured the woman a second beer. "They just come to me," he said. He avoided the temptation to sound more like an expert than he was. He watched her drain the second glass as quickly as she had the first. Wendy turned around. She pulled the pitcher away from Omar and rested her hand on the handle, idly.

The woman leaned closer. It appeared that she was going to tell Omar a secret: something she did not want Wendy to hear. He turned his head and looked at Wendy, who rolled her eyes. At the same time, she placed her hand on his knee. The sensation, of the woman's hushed voice, of Wendy's hand on his leg, excited him.

She asked him something. Omar did not hear. He asked her to repeat it. She said, leaning closer, so that he could smell her uniform, and it smelled like mothballs, "Do you hear voices?"

Omar said, "Yeah, right." He laughed out loud. Obviously, she was teasing him in some girlish way. "Of course not. What do you think I am, nuts?" The woman opened her mouth. He assumed that she was yawning. She certainly could open her mouth very wide, Omar thought. She seemed to be showing him all of her teeth. There certainly were a lot of them. Omar said, "Yes. Very nice. Thank you."

He felt a pain in his leg. Wendy had pinched him there. The woman closed her mouth somewhat, and she covered her many teeth with her lips. She raised her hands in front of her lips, which formed a perfect circle. And in the air above their beer, using both of her hands, she pantomimed an obscenity with exaggerated poise.

Before Omar could think of what to say, the woman laughed at him. He must have missed something. He turned to Wendy. Wendy usually performed quite well in situations like this one. She could always think of something funny to say. And humor did seem in order. But Wendy only stared. The woman threw her head forward so that Omar had to catch her glass to keep it from spilling on him. He noticed the back of her head. Her nurse's cap had been pinned on with paperclips.

Wendy was pinching his knee, and she was not letting go. Across from them, the woman raised her head. She reached across the table and touched Omar's hand. He drew it away. "My Gawd," Wendy said. Omar stared at the woman in white. He thought of an image, a painting that the Sex Hero had done, called "Joan of Arc at the Sweet Potato Bar."

The door to the bar opened, and a napkin blew off their table. Alphonse, their good friend, stepped inside, and he grinned his Cheshire grin. The three at the table turned and watched him scraping his boots. Alphonse walked up to the table, without removing his scarf. "The Sex Hero called," he said to Omar. "He wants you to come to a party." He nodded at Wendy. "He wants you to come, too. He's hoping you'll do a story on this artist who will be there?" Omar and Wendy said nothing. "It's at Diane Knuckleman's house? The artist came all the way from New York City? He's supposed to be some famous guy?"

Then Alphonse noticed the strange woman who was sitting at their table. She stared mouth agape at him. He extended his hand for her to shake it. She brought it up to her lips and began to lick at his knuckles with her tongue. Alphonse stiffened. "You're very formal," the woman said, looking up at him. "Please don't stand on ceremony."

Alphonse, who was as tall as he was formal, nodded his head. He cleared his throat and said, "That's what I could say about you."

She asked him, "How's the penis?"

Wendy raised her left eyebrow. She glanced at Omar. They both looked a bit closer at their friend, bashful Alphonse. "I beg your pardon?" he said.

She repeated her question. With a flourish she made a gesture for him similar to the one that she had made for Omar and Wendy. Alphonse reddened. After all, he was shy. Friends of Omar's often thought that Alphonse was not bright, simply because he was so bashful. He turned around and covered his face with both hands.

"Let's go," Wendy prompted.

The woman turned to her. "Where to?"

James Russell Mayes

"To the party, of course." Wendy pulled her hand off Omar's leg. The two of them scrambled out of their booth.

"Yeah," Alphonse echoed. He clapped his hands together and held them over his heart. "That's it. The party? We're going to the party? Nice to meet you? See you around?" In less than a minute, Wendy and Omar and Alphonse had walked out of the bar and were wading through the snow. Alphonse looked at Omar sideways. "What was that about?"

Omar tried to pick up on Wendy's reaction. She was walking in front of them, and he couldn't see her face. "I'd call her your type exactly," he told Alphonse.

Wendy turned around and showed them her mittens. "You two are such fools," she said. She clapped her hands together as if she were washing them. "She's a manic-depressive," she told them. "Her lithium level is off. Last week she called from a halfway house in Traverse City. She said she was being held against her will."

"Yikes," Alphonse muttered.

"She wanted me to do a story," Wendy said. "I'm sure that was her."

Alphonse asked, "How'd she get out so quick?"

"A relative," she said.

"A relative?"

"Her husband, probably. We know she's married. Someone had to sign some kind of a release."

Omar interrupted them. "Don't you wish you had Wendy's job? All these people calling up, inviting you to parties?"

✂

Omar knew where Diane Knuckleman's house was. The Sex Hero had pointed it out to him when he first told Omar about his affair with her. It was the kind of home which might have been more beautiful if its owner had been more sure of her own creativity. There were columns in front which supported the roof above a small porch. These had been painted a lurid shade of green. Most of the rest of the house had been painted yellow, except for the window frames and shutters, which were rose. Since the porch light illuminated the color of the columns more greenly, Diane Knuckleman's house was even easier to find at night.

They stamped their feet on the porch, and the Sex Hero's face appeared through the glass of the front door. "Come in," he called through the mail chute. When they opened the door they saw that the Sex Hero had tied a bandana on top of his head. Wendy pulled at it as they walked past him into the front hall, which was dark.

"There's nobody here," said Wendy.

"Yeah, you said there was a party?" said Alphonse.

The Sex Hero told them, "There's a party. There's a party, believe me." He put his hand on the bannister and walked up the stairs. "Follow me."

Wendy turned to Omar. "Oh my Gawd," she said.

Omar assured her, "I'm sure it's just drugs." They followed the Sex Hero up the steps. Perhaps it was the darkness, but it seemed to Omar that they were quite high up in the air before they reached the landing. The Sex Hero turned, and he pounded on a closed door.

"Diane?" he called. "Diane! The woman from the paper's here."

On the other side of the door, a woman shouted, "Get out."

"They're right here," the Sex Hero said. "At least say hello." The doorknob turned, and the door opened. A woman in a long slip held onto the doorknob. Behind her, on the bed, sat a middle-aged man without his shirt on.

Diane Knuckleman ignored the Sex Hero and looked directly at Omar. What a beautiful woman, Omar thought, the Anne Bancroft type. She spoke with an edge in her voice: "I'm not sure what you're doing here, the party's over, but I sure as hell didn't invite you. I suppose you were all invited by your friend?" She raised her voice and a corner of her upper lip at the same time. "As you can see, I'm about to go to bed. I'm sorry we didn't meet under better circumstances. Good night."

The Sex Hero turned back to them, and he pointed behind Alphonse at the steps. "I'll meet you downstairs," he said in a growl. "I need to talk to Diane."

The woman lowered her voice. She spoke to the Sex Hero, but they all heard what she said: "If you want to sleep in the bedroom off the kitchen, that's fine. That's the guest room? But don't expect me to entertain your friends whenever they drop by in the middle of the night." She closed the door behind her, quietly.

James Russell Mayes

The Sex Hero smiled at Omar. "Go on," he was saying. "It's okay. Really. Help yourself to some food."

Omar and Wendy and Alphonse walked back down the stairs. They stood in front of the door. Alphonse, looking into the living room, said, "Maybe we should go?"

Above them, the Sex Hero was knocking on the door again. "Diane," he said.

She called through the door at him, "Don't you wake up Cindy."

"Let's go?" said Alphonse.

Wendy slipped out of her coat, and she threw it over the bannister. She looked around the front door until she found a light switch.

Omar said, nervously, "What are you up to, Wendy?"

"I want a glass of wine."

"Didn't you hear what she said?"

"A glass of wine. At least."

Omar and Alphonse followed her in their coats. They wandered past the stairs through a dining room and a kitchen. Wendy turned the lights on in every room. Just beyond the kitchen was the guest room. "There it is," Wendy said. She walked in and stood in the doorway. "A water bed!" She turned around to face them and dropped backward onto the bed. Pillows on the other end of it leapt off of it onto the floor.

"Wendy," Omar said. "Be careful." He replaced the throw pillows. He pulled off his own coat, and he threw it over his arm. He stood in the doorway and stared at Wendy, who lay on the bed in the dark. She jiggled. He sat down on the bed next to her hair. He was about to reach out and touch it when Alphonse stepped into the doorway.

"Omar?" he said. "Wendy?"

Wendy sat up. She held out her hand to Alphonse, who helped her up. They walked back into the kitchen. Wendy started opening up the cupboard doors, one by one. In two minutes she had found a liquor cabinet and a bottle of wine. She opened the wine with a corkscrew she found in one of the drawers. She saw that Omar and Alphonse were staring at her from the doorway. She told them to look for glasses.

Omar found them above the kitchen sink. "You know," he said, "in a strange kitchen, it's not really hard to tell where everything is. Most people put everything in the same place that everyone else does."

He tried to sound casual. The air felt suspicious. Wendy poured red wine into three glasses and held one out to Alphonse.

Alphonse stared at the two of them. He stood in his coat, aghast.

"What's wrong?" she said. "Don't you want one?"

He accepted it, silently wavering, and Omar made a toast: "To art," he said cheerily. They wandered into the dining room. They swirled their wine like brandy in their glasses, dangerously. Chairs had been pulled back from the table, and each of them held a painting, apparently by the artist who was sitting on the edge of Diane Knuckleman's bed. Wendy bent over one. "Not bad," she said. "Not bad for splash paintings."

Omar said, "I could do that."

There was a thumping that came from the front of the house. They carried their wine glasses into the living room. The Sex Hero had climbed down the stairway. He stood in the middle of the oriental rug with a broom over his head. He lifted the broom by the straw and struck the ceiling with the handle. Omar said, "What are you doing?"

Barely controlling his voice, the Sex Hero told him, "Two hours ago we were making out on the way to the 7-ll. Can you believe this woman?" He struck the ceiling again. Omar pulled the broom away.

"Swing!" Wendy shouted. She pitched something into the air at him. Instinctively, Omar swung the broom like a bat. The end of the handle struck the object neatly, and it flew up into an arc before it hit the opposite wall. Whatever the object was, it split in two and slid down the wall, and the pieces spun on the floorboards. Wendy picked them up. "You broke it," she said, holding up a piece in each hand.

She showed Omar what it was: a miniature china doll. He had knocked her head clean off her naked body. "Oh, my Gawd," Wendy gasped. She laughed out loud. She leaned the doll on the mantle above the fireplace. She put the smiling head on the doll's lap as if she were holding her handbag.

Omar turned around. He was about to apologize to his friend, but the Sex Hero climbed the stairs again. Omar and Wendy walked to the foot of the stairs. At the top, their host was bending in front of the keyhole of Diane Knuckleman's bedroom door. Wendy looked at Omar, and she raised her glass of wine. "Ask and ye shall receive," she toasted, drinking it down merrily. The Sex Hero looked down the

James Russell Mayes

length of the stairs at them. He brought his finger to his lips. He waved them away.

Wendy returned to the dining room. She looked over the food on the dining room table where a feast had taken place. Omar watched her lifting two garbanzo beans out of the salad bowl. She tossed them against a bookshelf. "Ha," she said to Alphonse when he followed them into the room.

Alphonse appeared to take this as a challenge. "That's nothing?" he said. Approaching the opposite end of the table, he lifted leaves of lettuce from under a turkey carcass. He took a book from the shelf and slid the leaves between the pages. Omar was taken by surprise.

Alphonse nudged Wendy. "Abstract expressionism, right?" They laughed. Wendy pulled two more books out. Alphonse hid deviled eggs behind them on the shelf. The two of them laughed so hard together that Omar reached under a cake safe and brought his hand out. It was covered with frosting and devil's food cake.

He flung it at the wall above their heads. "Look," he said. Wendy and Alphonse stared at his chocolate-covered hand. Omar pointed to the wall above the bookshelf. A blot of cake and frosting the size of an ashtray clung like a slug. "Now that's abstract expressionism," Omar said, admiring.

Alphonse straightened. "Damn," he said. He gave Omar a frightened look. "That's chocolate cake on the wall."

Wendy said, "I think we better leave."

They raced into the front hall. Omar and Wendy and Alphonse pulled on their coats. Omar opened the door. And then he heard something behind them. He turned around. He looked past Wendy and Alphonse, on up the stairs to see a little girl on the upper landing. "Who are you?" she asked. She wore a blue sleeper with footies. She held on to the bannister, and she stepped down toward them. They stared at her. The Sex Hero was nowhere in sight.

The little girl said in a voice that sounded, to Omar, surprisingly mature, "What are you acting like that for?" She frowned at them and played with the ends of her hair, which was long and blonde and gathered in wide curls at her shoulders.

Wendy, who stood in front of Omar and Alphonse, said, "Go back to sleep, honey. Go on."

Omar said, "Yes, go back to sleep." He stuck his chocolate-covered hand into his coat pocket.

The little girl made fists and rubbed her eyes. She asked, "Is it bedtime?"

"Yes, it is," Wendy said. "It's way past bedtime. Little Poohs like you should be in bed."

The little girl said, "I'm not a pooh-pooh."

Omar opened the door. Wendy pushed from behind him. They walked out onto the porch. Alphonse hesitated briefly. But Wendy pulled him out by the sleeve of his coat, and they ran down the steps together.

They ran down the middle of the empty street for two blocks. Alphonse tripped over his boots, and Wendy growled with laughter. By the time they reached High Street, they had all grown silent in the cold wind. Alphonse waved good night to them. And Omar walked Wendy home.

"That was great," she told him on her doorstep, turning. "That was crazy. I can't believe you." Omar bent forward to kiss her. He wrapped his arms around her narrow shoulders. She pushed him away. "What are you doing?"

This surprised him. "What do you think I'm doing?"

She ran a mitten down the edge of her door. "Omar. I'm surprised at you. Why did you do that?"

Why did she think he had done it? "Is it that big of a surprise?" He reached up with his arm. He touched her lovely chin with his fingers.

Laughing, Wendy pushed his hand away. "I think you better explain to me what this is all about."

"I like you, Wendy. I have feelings for you. Why do you think I'm always hanging around you?"

"I'm sorry."

"Can I come up for a drink?" She gave him a curious once-over. She turned in the hallway, and Omar followed her arched left eyebrow up the stairs to her apartment. He sat with Wendy on her couch, and she made a drink for him. He got her laughing about the Sex Hero's jealous life. "He was trying to keep them from going to bed together," he said. "Don't you see?"

Wendy seemed grateful for the change of subject. "What a bore," she said, relaxing. She hiccoughed. "Did you see that ugly artist guy? Did you see him without his shirt on?"

Omar's mind wandered. Actions are louder than conversation, he thought. She might feel differently about him if he tried to kiss her a second time. He leaned forward once more.

Wendy pushed him back. She stood up, and she asked him to leave.

"Why?" he said. "I'll behave myself."

She led him down the stairs. She opened the door for him, and just before she closed it, she looked at him so hard that Omar felt strange. "Omar," Wendy said. She sighed. "Aren't you gay, Omar?"

"I'm not gay."

"Well, maybe you just don't know that yet."

He stood on the porch and watched her climbing back up the stairs. "Damn it," he said to the slammed door. He lifted his hands and appealed to the curtains in the window. "I'm not gay."

✄

Omar left Wendy's apartment and walked home. He charged up the steps and nearly collided with the Sex Hero, who was standing on the porch of the apartment. He was smoking a cigarette. He hugged himself and was patting his shoulders, as if he had been standing in the cold too long. Omar asked him, "What are you doing here?"

"Diane Knuckleman threw me out." He looked at Omar keenly. "Will you tell me what happened over there?"

Omar turned his head. He stuck his key into the lock and turned the doorknob. "What are you talking about?"

"When I got back downstairs, the place was a mess. I tried to clean it up. Omar, someone threw chocolate cake on the wall."

Omar faced him. "You had an incredible amount to drink tonight. You were banging on her bedroom door. Hell, you were banging on the ceiling with a broom." He laughed. It felt good to laugh.

"If I was throwing food around, I wasn't too drunk to remember it." He grabbed ahold of Omar's elbow. "You tell me what happened."

Omar pulled his arm away. "Did you notice the place was a mess when we got there? Ask Wendy. What kind of a party did you invite us to? Exactly?"

His friend stamped his feet and wiggled his fingers inside of his gloves. "She threw me out, Omar."

Opening the door, Omar said, "What did you expect?"

"Can I come inside?"

"Finish the cigarette."

He took a long drag on his Camel. "You scare me," he said. They watched a Catholic nun, who carefully crossed a black stretch of ice under the lights on the other side of the street. "Hey," the Sex Hero called, clapping his gloves together. He whistled at her.

The nun stopped. She raised her head with a jerk. She looked up at them and waved. She crossed the street and climbed up Omar's steps. In the corner of his eye, Omar saw her make a gesture in front of herself. "Hello," she said to the Sex Hero. "Did I get that right?"

The Sex Hero cleared his throat. "Oh, yes," he said. "You got that right."

She turned and smiled at Omar. He should have remembered her. She asked him, "How you doing?" She reached out and took his hand. "How's the penis?" At once Omar recognized her. The change of clothes had thrown him off. She asked him, "Can I use your telephone?"

"Of course," he said. He remembered too late what Wendy had said about variable lithium levels. He opened the door and let them both inside of his apartment. He showed the woman his telephone. She picked up the receiver and dialed. Omar took the Sex Hero's coat and hung it in the closet. Not knowing what to say, he offered them coffee.

But no one was paying attention to him. The Sex Hero stared at the woman who had dressed as a nun. She was speaking into the telephone. "I need the number for the FBI, wherever that is. I don't know the city." Still hugging himself, the Sex Hero fell back into one of Omar's chairs.

She shouted, "What difference does it make? I notified the police. They said the van belongs to my husband. He gave it to me for Sweetest Day." Omar walked into the kitchen. He pulled three coffee cups out of the cupboard, and he set them on top of the counter. "They said they'd arrest me for disturbing the peace. What do you suggest? It's my van, God damn it." She slammed the receiver down.

Omar leaned forward to look through the kitchen doorway. The woman walked into his bathroom. Without closing the door, she lifted up her skirts and squatted over the toilet. Omar turned around and ran water into the sink. He returned one of the coffee cups to the cupboard. He opened the freezer and pulled out a bag of ground coffee. He measured it, he poured the water, he started the coffeemaker.

After he heard the toilet flush, he turned around. The woman straightened her veil in the mirror over the sink. She pulled lipstick out of a pocket and drew a gash across her face. "Drive a person crazy," she said, wide-eyed and grinning into the mirror. She walked out of the bathroom and closed the door behind her. Gliding through the living room, "Jesus Fucking Christ," she said, "I'll get that van." She turned at the door and held out her arms, appealing to the Sex Hero. "Could you make a living selling Amway products?" She walked out the front door.

Omar stood in the kitchen. Pouring the coffee, he caught a glimpse of the woman through a window. She galloped down the front steps and out into the cold, dark morning. He said, raising his voice so that it would carry into the front room: "That was impressive."

From his chair, where he sat with his hands over his eyes, the Sex Hero asked him, "What are you talking about?"

"I know you're Catholic," Omar said. "I hope she wasn't wearing that thing when you got her into bed with you." He had poured too much. He walked into the front room slowly, balancing their cups. He bent forward to give his friend coffee and his most innocent expression. "What did you think I was talking about?"

The Sex Hero changed the subject. "I want you to do a favor for me. I want you to call my wife. She'll talk to you."

Omar snapped, "Call her yourself." He stepped to the bay window and looked down the street. The woman's habit whipped in the bracing wind. She leapt from the sidewalk onto bare ice. She slid down the street like a boy.

Little Andy

My lover Paul has a crush on a nine-year-old boy.

In all fairness to him, I should start with an explanation. My lover is in his late sixties. He is a conscientious man, a retired gynecologist and a member of the local Unitarian church. He has always held an attraction to the younger set. Take me, for example. I've been his lover for almost sixteen years, come April 16. I'm thirty-five now. If you do the math, that comes out to eighteen when I met him. Some of our friends used to call that "chicken-chasing."

At first the difference in age bothered me. The first two years or so, anyway. The third year, I was more concerned about feeling old myself. After that, it seemed like both of us were old, but half of us were more advanced in our career and paid for everything: clothing, vacations, the first and second homes. After I graduated from the state university, I got a "real" job as a reporter and started paying my own way, then both of our ways. And roughly in the order that Paul had paid for me while we were dating: clothing first, then our vacations, and finally our "dream" house, with the assistance of his retirement package.

Most of Paul's ex-lovers are dead or have started to die off. Yesterday, for instance, we got the word from Bennie that his lover Rex hadn't much longer to go. The phone rang, and since I was in the bathroom, Paul picked it up. A few minutes later, I walked into the room, and he was still on the phone.

"What's the matter?" I said. He was standing there with his mouth open. I guess I was kind of sharp with him because Paul does that a lot now; he leaves his mouth open. Sometimes he does that when he's thinking about something, and other times he does that when he's not thinking about anything at all.

"Tony," he said. "It's Rex's heart." He handed me the phone.

"Bennie, what is it?"

A big sigh came through loud and clear from the other end of the line.

"I think you'll probably get the call later on this afternoon," Bennie said.

"Oh no."

"Oh, yes." He was quiet then, but air came through in rapid bursts. Bennie was weeping.

"Do you want us to fly in, Bennie?"

Paul waved his hand at me, wide-eyed "no" signals coming through loud and clear.

Bennie gathered himself. "No. I'll need your shoulders later, when I have to get away," he said.

"Call us."

"Will do. Gotta go. I have lots more calls to make."

"Love you," I said. "Bennie. We both do."

"Same to you, kid." He hung up.

The "love you" thing was something we started around the time AIDS became a popular topic among our friends. We don't use the name for the disease so much anymore, like you don't use the word "cancer" unless you have to: after it means something to you. But the "love you" thing still flies. I turned around, and I held onto Paul's forearms. His eyes were dark, as usual, but blank.

"You okay?" I said.

"Yes." He pulled his arms away. He reached up with his hand and tousled my wet hair.

"You're a mess," he said. He smiled, and then he winked.

"I know, I know." I walked back into the bathroom and combed my hair back. Bending close to the mirror, I parted it. "Old," I said. "Older. Oldest." My hair was too long, and there is nothing worse than hair that's too long on a person that's too old to have it that long. I flipped the ends back away from my face with the comb.

"Paul?" I said. When I got out of the bathroom, I couldn't find him.

"Out here," he said. He was sitting on the front porch. He never sits on the front porch.

"What are you doing out here?" I slammed the screen door behind me. Paul was sitting on the porch swing with his afghan over his knees, a gift from his mom that still held together pretty well.

"Can't a person sit on the porch and enjoy a beautiful summer morning," he said, "without someone bothering him and asking him what he's doing all the time?" I wanted to sit down beside him on the porch swing, except that we were on the front porch. And there were kids in the street. I walked past him and patted his shoulder while he looked down at his hands. I sat down on the porch railing along the side of the house.

"You sure you're okay?" I said.

He glared at me, so I knew better than to say anything else. I looked out into the street.

And there was Andy. He was clunking up the sidewalk across the street on his skateboard. "Oh ho," I said. Paul ignored me.

Andy's hair is blond, and he wears it in a style that I haven't figured out yet. His skin is still more rose than tan. He was wearing a red tank top that was too big for how skinny he was. One strap hung over his shoulder, for instance, and you could see a pale boy's nipple like a perfect birthmark on his chest. He had on what looked like his dad's boxer shorts, except that they had splashy Hawaiian colors on them. His skateboard kept hitting the evenly spaced cracks in the sidewalk and making evenly spaced "clunk" noises over each one.

Paul put his fingers up under his chin and cocked his head to one side. "Little Andy," he said, smiling dreamily. He sighed out loud.

"You're disgusting," I said.

He rode his skateboard all the way down to the end of the block, then across to our side and back up the street. Andy didn't look nine; he looked younger than nine. He rode his skateboard up to the sidewalk in front of our porch. Then he stopped and the skateboard went straight up into the air. His arm reached out and grabbed it, and he hugged it to his chest.

"Hi," he said. He brushed his blond bangs away from his head, indifferently.

"Hi," we both said at the same time.

"Do you have a calico cat that's about this big?" He showed us how big with his nine-year-old hands.

"No," Paul offered. He smiled. "We don't have a cat. We used to have a dog."

Andy scratched his armpit and explained. "Last night my mom drove over a cat when she backed out the driveway." Suddenly, he dropped his skateboard onto the sidewalk. He rolled away to the sound of the evenly spaced "clunk."

"See ya."

"Bye-bye."

We looked at each other.

Paul was dramatically enthralled, eyes wide.

"Good God," I said.

"You know," he said, holding out his arms, "I could almost smell him..."

"Paul..."

"I could almost tell what he would taste like for dinner..."

I stood up.

"Close your mouth," I said.

Then the telephone rang.

South Window

A ndy and Roger's grandfather came to live with them for a few weeks before he went into the hospital. Since company always slept in Roger's room, the older boy moved in with Andy. It was Andy's room, so Roger slept on their uncle Floyd's old army cot. If Roger was lying down when Andy came into his own room, Roger would roll off the cot and sprinkle Old Spice on Andy's head. "You smell," Roger said.

"I do not."

"P.U."

So Andy stopped spending so much time in his room, and he went there only to read or to sleep. He spent more time in the living room. Their grandfather Fred was on some new medication that kept him up all night. He wandered through the house in the dark. Then in the daytime, he would sit in the living room in his bathrobe without his teeth in. He read the sports page or watched television. He was flipping back and forth between afternoon programs when Andy read that Franklin Delano Roosevelt had died in his sleep. "What does it mean to die in your sleep?" the boy asked his grandfather.

"It means you die in your sleep," Fred said.

"But what is it like?" Andy was holding onto the *World Book Encyclopedia*. Fred eyed it skeptically.

"It means that you go to sleep, and you don't wake up."

"That sounds awful."

"I don't think so. I think that's the best way. If I had a choice, I'd rather die in my sleep."

James Russell Mayes

"Not me," said Andy.

"Why don't you read a child's book? Why don't you read *The Hobbit?*"

Andy remembered *The Hobbit*. He had found the book on one of the bookshelves in his grandfather's house in New Baltimore. He had pulled it out and read part of it, the beginning at least, while seated on a throw rug on the slate floor of the foyer, cool and dark. The light in the foyer streamed down like God's love was supposed to. Or the Holy Spirit in the pictures of the Baptism of Christ. And there were doves in the stained-glass windows on either side of his grandfather's heavy wooden door.

Andy put the book away after Fred agreed to checkers. The boy set up the TV tray and the checkerboard between them. Fred held the box of checkers in his lap, while Andy stared at his grandfather's knees. They were so white, Andy thought, they were almost blue. Fred pointed at the checkers. "These are the Indians," he said, pointing at the red ones. "And these are the niggers. Which one do you wanna be?"

"I'll take black," said Andy. The worst thing about playing checkers with Fred was that Fred was always pretending that he was stupid, a hick, a rube. He thought it was funny. He talked continuously while he played, and although he did not always win, he turned into a yokel before Andy's eyes. Since he knew that his grandfather disdained what he called "the hillbillies" in their neighborhood, Andy felt vaguely as if he were mocking him. He always kept an eye on the old guy.

"Oh?" Fred would say, as if he forgot, "When you get all the way over here, you get kinged do you?" And then, usually the next time Andy moved his king: "Oh? You mean kings can move backward now?" Andy had to interrupt the whole game to explain everything to him. And since Fred did not have his teeth in, he held his mouth so small that Andy could not look at him while he was talking.

"I wish we could get on with the game," he said, feeling a little bold.

"You're always wishing for something. You wish too much," Fred said.

"Who said I was wishing? I'm not wishing."

"You are too," Fred said. "You said so yourself." The man leaned back in his chair. "You're wishing that I'd shut up so we could finish.

But you're really wishing you could win the game." He held his finger up and pointed to the side of his head. "I can read your mind," he said and winked.

Andy moved his king backward. "What's so bad about wishing?"

"Wishing is giving up. It's dreaming, pretending. Not paying attention." Fred placed his finger on a checker. He looked up. "Them that's not paying attention, lose." Andy was glaring at him.

Later he told his mother about their conversation. She told him that his grandfather was growing older. He was not used to sitting indoors all day. "He needs to stop being depressed and go for more walks," she said, loudly enough for Fred to hear.

✄

So it happened that only a couple weeks before he was put into the hospital, Fred began to take long walks through town with his grandson, the wisher. Fred was a tall man with long legs, and, as if the neighborhood alone was not large enough for them, he stretched his legs by walking out beyond the boundaries with which he had so recently become acquainted. Past the houses of all of his grandson's friends, past bungalows with trees in the backyard much too small for Andy to climb, Fred and Andy crossed Maple Street into a northern suburb. The houses were big and the lawns stretched back from the street, and it seemed as if the single room of any one of them might contain his daughter's whole house inside of it.

Together they talked about the immense cost involved in building the "dream houses," as they called them. Instantly Andy felt sure of himself. He wanted to show his grandfather that he was really a practical boy. He had books at home about houses and solar energy, and he liked to draw out floor plans on paper. He intended to be an architect one day, he told Fred.

"You have lots of time to decide what you want to be."

"But I already know." Andy pointed to a house and said, "Dutch Colonial. And that one over there is French Provincial, but it's really not French Provincial."

"Ah," Fred said. "A purist! What is that one?" They had stopped at the curb, and he touched the boy's shoulder, lightly, to keep him from walking into the street.

James Russell Mayes

Andy rolled his eyes. "That's easy. English Tudor. Not."

"Does that mean all of our houses ought to be heaps of modern crap?"

"Of course not," Andy told him. "I believe in the log cabin. Solar energy, Gramps. Life in the country!" The boy pointed across Quarton Road. There was a field of clover and a row of pines beyond it.

Happily, Fred almost jogged across the road. Andy followed close behind him, carefully watching for cars. They explored the field together. They found an apple tree. Fred gave Andy a boost, and the boy sat on a limb. He was disappointed that Andy did not immediately climb it.

"I hear something," the boy said, turning his head to the side.

"What is it?"

"I hear birds. Baby birds." Andy saw something, and he slid down the trunk. "It's a hole," he said. "See? A nest." There was a hole in the tree. Fred put two of his fingers inside of it.

"Don't do that," Andy said. He pulled Fred's arm away. "If you smell it up the mother won't come back for the babies." The boy put his head against the side of the tree. "You can hear them," he said. "Listen."

Fred held on to the trunk of the tree with both hands. He leaned forward and placed his ear against the spot that Andy had shown him. Sure enough, there were birds, baby ones, peeping. The bark stung his ear. It felt for a moment that the tree moved, that its shadow turned in the clover field like the point of a sundial. Fred held on to the tree, and he fixed on Andy's eyes, that pleasure there.

The day that the boys caught the raccoon, Andy was the first to discover it. He ran all the way back to the house, to have his older brother Roger follow him back out to the field behind their subdivision. The raccoon reached out through the wires of his cage, and when Andy approached the trap, it spat and growled at him. The boys had brought gloves with them, and they carried the trap up behind the garage. After moving their mother's rabbits around, they made a home for the raccoon, which seemed so huge and malcontent. They poured water into the pie tin, and the raccoon drank it all. They filled it again, and the raccoon continued to drink, barely spilling any. The third time they filled it, they realized how thirsty he was, and they watched through the wire for his eyes, which they never saw.

Their grandfather pulled his pants on underneath his bathrobe. Fred had been watching them through the kitchen window. He told the boys that the raccoon was too big and his cage was too small. In front of them, he set the wild animal loose by moving all of the rabbits out of the other end of the hutch, and then opening the door and turning the hutch over on its side so that the door flew open and the raccoon got away.

As soon as the animal had dropped onto the ground, Andy ran the other direction. He watched it escape from behind the garage door. It crept across the field behind the garage. And suddenly, as if it had dropped into a hole, the raccoon disappeared. Andy hung around until after Roger and Fred had gone inside. He kicked around in the weeds. He searched for forty-five minutes, but he never found it. And there were no holes that were big enough for the animal to hide in. He avoided the field for a few days.

✄

Andy lay in bed and he dreamed of winning the Ten-Million-Dollar Publishers Clearing House Sweepstakes. The first thing Andy would do with the money, of course, would be to buy his mother a new car to replace their old clunker. His mother loved cars. He had watched her stop at street corners to admire a convertible. They played a game, in which his mother would ask him, as they drove down the street, "What do you think of that one? Do you like the Chevy as well as the Buick?"

Andy did not care for cars nearly as much as his mother did. The boy thought that any car was fine, so long as it was red, so that anyone might see it and stop in time. So the first thing that Andy would buy would be a car for his mother. He would also pay for his grandfather's operation, and a room they could add on to the house where Fred could live. And Fred's room would have his own kitchen and fireplace and a bathroom big enough for a wheelchair if he ever needed it.

Then Andy got his idea. If he won the Ten-Million-Dollar Publishers Clearing House Sweepstakes, he wouldn't need to build Fred a room: he could build Fred a house. And it wouldn't have to be a house just for Fred if it were big enough. If it were big enough, he could build a house for the whole family. It would not be a huge house. It would be practical. It would be passive solar-heated. There would be one big room where everyone could gather together, a "great room," he had read that it was called in *Better Homes & Gardens*. And in the great room, there would be a fireplace, where Fred and Roger and Andy could roast marshmallows. Sometimes they would pop popcorn, careful not to burn it as he had done in Cub Scouts.

Above the fireplace in the great room, there would be a picture, and the picture would be of the house itself, set back from a country road with half of its eaves under pine trees and the other half under the sun. Behind the house, so that nobody could see it from the road, there would be a pond, where Andy and his grandfather could swim. He pictured himself in the pond with Fred. He reached into the water and pulled a fish out with his bare hands.

"The house would not be a great house, but it would have a great room," Andy said to Fred on one of their walks. "Do you know what a great room is?"

"I think I do," said Fred. "I have an idea. But I'm not exactly sure."

"I read about it in *Better Homes & Gardens,*" Andy said. "A great room is a big room in the middle of the house where everyone comes together. It's not a dining room, and it's not a living room. It's both, all in one, and there's a fireplace and a piano and a lot of books."

"You like the books, don't you?" They had come to a corner where there was a light, and the sign did not say, "Walk." Out of habit, Fred took hold of his grandson's shoulder, and the boy immediately stopped, looking up at him, smiling and flushed from the out-of-doors.

"I love books," Andy said. "I keep having this dream where somebody gives me a hundred dollars. But they won't let me have it unless I spend it all on books. The whole dream, all I do is walk through this huge bookstore. I'm picking out all of these really cool books. They're big books, heavy books with hard covers, and they all have beautiful pictures in them. I fill a whole shopping cart."

"You can cross now," Fred said, lifting his hand off Andy's shoulder. The boy stepped back beside his grandfather, and they crossed the street together. "Tell me," he said, cleverly. "What happens when you wake up?"

Andy shoved his hands into the pockets of his jacket. "I wake up happy," he said, defensively.

"And what happens when you remember that it's all been a dream?"

"There's no hundred dollars," Andy admitted. "There's no shopping cart full of books."

"Well, if I had a hundred dollars," Fred said, feeling as if he had won and not particularly happy that he had, "I would give it to you."

"You would?" Such a small thing made the boy happy. Invisible houses, invisible books. Promises are dangerous, Fred thought to himself. Andy took his hand, which seemed to him like a gesture that was much too young for the boy. That made Fred uneasy, too. He squeezed the smaller hand inside of his own.

"Of course I would."

Andy brightened. "You're going to win the Ten-Million-Dollar Publishers Clearing House Sweepstakes. Remember? Then you can give me a million dollars, and I'll spend it all on books."

"I thought we were building a house."

"We'll do both. There'll be enough."

Less than a week later, Fred was in the hospital. The nurse, a pretty one, opened the shade in his room. "How lucky you are," she said. "A room all to yourself. And a south window." The reason that woman is pretty, Fred thought, is because she hasn't been working long enough to get ugly over things. He closed his eyes. Sometimes when Fred closed his eyes in the hospital, even with the shades drawn, he liked to imagine that he could feel the heat of the sun on his face.

Had Andy said there would be a pond? There would be a dog with them, he decided, a dog with spots. They would call the dog "Tiger." Yes, there would be a pond, and a raft out in the middle of it, close enough to swim to and far enough away so that the sound of the water, which was very quiet, would be louder than the sound of the shore. On the shore, he thought, on the shore there will be clover and the sound of bees, and Andy and Roger will be wading up to their knees.

James Russell Mayes

The house will be a wood one, he thought, because Andy likes log cabins.

A house could be a wonder, after all, he decided, whatever one wanted to make of it. Fred inhaled the memory of the citrus scent of pines, and since memories are born in a jumbled heap, he dreamed up a fire and his dead wife Martha. Together they looked out through a glass wall to the pond below them. Martha pulled on his arm. Fred loved to dive, and he dove a few times. But Andy didn't know how to swim. He knew that. He would teach his grandson to swim. Fred stood up in the water. He was coaxing the boy. "Come here," he said. "Wade deeper."

Fred felt the sun between his shoulder blades. He could almost feel the coolness of the water. He held his breath. There was something against his leg. A shiver moved up through his abdomen and caught him by the throat: the slippery blade of a fish. He tried to catch it. He had a chance to squeeze it, and then it passed through his fingers. Bloated and dry from the medication, his own lips opened and swallowed air. He touched his arm to console himself with the pressure of the I.V.

Andy and Roger were allowed to visit Fred a few weeks later. They left their mother in the enormous waiting room on the first floor, and they took the elevator up. By that time, Fred had been taken out of the intensive-care unit. His room smelled strange to Andy. The shade had been drawn. Andy stood in the doorway long after his older brother had gone inside. He adjusted his eyes. Finally he looked up at Fred, who sat on the edge of his mattress in a nightgown without his robe on.

Fred waved at him. "Come in," he said. Andy joined his brother where he stood next to the bed.

"It's nice to see you. How is school?" He was trying to be cordial. He waited for one of them to answer.

"It's summer vacation," Roger said. "Remember? I'm working at the turkey farm."

"Oh yes," Fred said. He smiled, sadly. "I've been in the hospital so long. I thought school might have started. You know how hard it is to get a window?" He pointed to the window. The sunlight made a bright line all the way around the shade, except for where it was attached to the top of the window.

"Why is it so dark in here, Grandpa?"

Fred bit his lip. He had put his teeth in to talk with them. "I'm sorry it's dark in here. The light hurt my eyes and I need a lot of rest, so the nurses, they keep the shade drawn." He lay down on the bed. His stomach, he knew, was monstrous, as if he were pregnant. He saw that the boys were staring at it, and he explained to them that it was swollen from something that had to do with his liver. "Has your mother told you?"

"Told us what?"

"Well, the doctors have told me that I am going to die. If I don't die here, I'll die after they let me go home." Fred slid over so that his legs hung over the side of the bed. He propped himself back up into a sitting position with his arm. "But I'm not afraid to die. You know why?"

The boys shook their heads.

"Because I prayed. You believe in Jesus, don't you?"

They waited to see if he was kidding them. Roger looked at Andy, and then he looked away. Andy looked at the side of his brother's face. Roger wasn't laughing or anything. Slowly Roger nodded his head. "Oh, yes," he said. "I believe in Jesus."

"Good. I'm glad to hear that. Because if you believe in Jesus, he doesn't let you die. He takes you to be with him, and you live with him forever in a place that is always light." Fred cleared his throat, and seemed to rest there for a minute, sitting up with his eyes closed on top of the covers. "In His house, there are many mansions." He breathed for a moment, and the boys listened to him breathe.

"In heaven, we'll have wings," Fred said. "Like angels. We'll fly all over the place, wherever we want to go. And the Devil could send a demon to come and get us. But they'd never come. You know why?"

"No," Roger said. "Why?"

Fred closed his eyes. He smiled to himself, cleverly. "Because Jesus sends an angel. And angels fly faster. I better lie down. I'm starting to get tired again." He lay back with his head on the pillow. Roger and

James Russell Mayes

Andy looked around the room. There was a pot of yellow mums on the table next to the window.

"You know my stomach is filled with babies," Fred said. "I'm pregnant. See?" But the boys did not laugh at his joke. They looked terrified. "Have you accepted Jesus Christ into your hearts? I mean, have you prayed for him to forgive you for everything you've done wrong?"

"Yes," Roger said.

There was an emotion in his grandfather's face that rose up into Andy's chest and held him by the voicebox. He tried to say something, but nothing came out. He listened to his grandfather breathing again. Fred made more noise breathing when he was lying down.

"That's good," Fred said. "I'm so tired." Andy looked at Roger. What should they do? "Hundreds of little babies," Fred said. "There are boys and girls." He opened his eyes. "Did you hear that noise?" Andy shook his head. "They're crying," Fred said. "Do you hear them peeping? They want their little mamas."

Roger cleared his throat. He said, "Grandpa. We better go now."

Fred closed his eyes. "Stay just a bit longer."

Roger stood next to his pillow. Fred reached up and held onto the older boy's wrist. "I'm tired now," he said, once more. He closed his eyes. He was very quiet. He said nothing more about the little boys and girls that were inside of him.

Roger looked at Andy. "I think he's dead," he said.

"What?"

"He's dead." Roger lifted the old man's hand and laid it on top of his stomach. "Don't move," Roger said. "I'll get the nurse." He walked out into the hall. Andy put his finger on his grandfather's arm. It was warm. He looked at the enormous stomach. It didn't appear as if his grandfather was breathing or anything.

Andy said, softly, "I would think heaven would be a beautiful place."

Fred said, with difficulty, "Bullshit." There was a tightness in his jaw.

"You said, 'In His house there are many mansions.'"

"That's what they say."

"I'm here, Gramps."

"I know you are." Fred was so thirsty. He dared to open his eyes. His grandson stared back at him evenly.

Andy walked out into the hall. It was a long hall, and the nurse's station was all the way down at the other end. Roger was still walking. Two white-haired ladies in their wheelchairs raised their heads. They opened their eyes widely, their mouths both gaping. A man in a gurney was sitting up. He smiled at Andy. The future was not nearly as nice as it had been.

Hearts

"I didn't know you wrote stories," she says.

"It's the first one," I say.

"What's it about?"

I haven't seen her for three months. And we used to see each other every day, every night. We started talking as soon as I came in the door. And we haven't stopped.

"It's autobiographical." I'm suddenly embarrassed.

"Well. So?"

"It's about a guy who leaves his girlfriend." She has told me that I'm really not a nice guy; I'm just apologetic and that makes it seem as if I'm a nice guy.

"So?" she says. I can tell she's bracing herself.

"It's about a guy who leaves his girlfriend for another guy."

"Oh."

I drink more of my tea. She's cleaning up food that the baby threw on the floor. She bends over and picks up a bit of mashed something with an old washcloth.

"Is the guy's name 'Clay' and the girl's name 'Sarah'?"

"No. Very funny."

"Just kidding." She's impatient, but I can't tell if she's impatient with me or with herself. She picks a pack of cigarettes off the table and tosses them into a giant ceramic ashtray on the kitchen counter. Her father smoked, her mother smokes, and her lover smokes. Even I used to smoke when I went to the bars. But Sarah never smoked.

"Why did you write it? Why didn't you write about camel hunting in Zaire?"

The man she lives with, the Sex Hero, has left his socks beside the chair in front of the television. She ties them in a knot and pitches them down the basement stairs. There's a pile of laundry down there waiting for her.

"I don't know. Do camels live in Zaire?"

"I don't know."

"Well," I say quickly, "that's why I didn't write about it. I wouldn't know." Then I realize it's me who's impatient. When I'm impatient I start to sound logical.

"Ha," she says. She picks up the toys off the living room carpet and throws them halfway across the room into the playpen.

✄

When Sarah called from the hospital, she hadn't met the Sex Hero yet. But she had been hit by a truck while she was jogging one night. A broken arm, a broken leg, and a fractured pelvis kept her at St. Luke's for a few months. She spent the whole time in a round bed with giant wheels on either side of it. The wheels would rotate so that her mattress would stand her up on her feet. This was very painful, but she had to practice standing up before she could start walking, even when she passed out from the pain. They gave her a lot of codeine.

"I'm so sorry to hear about your sisters," the telephone told me with her voice. She sounded distant; I must've been talking to the codeine.

Hearing her on the phone was like talking to Joe out in the woods: her voice was so familiar that it hurt me in the throat to hear it.

"I wish I could be there," she said.

"Don't worry about it," I mustered up. I felt that if I kept talking, I stayed alive somehow. "You've been hit by a truck..." I stopped a minute. My breath was coming so shallow that I lost it too easily. Then I offered, "I'd call that a fair excuse."

I heard her sigh loudly on the other end. I wondered if she were crying too.

"You know I feel so bad about it because I felt so close to them." She was talking about it again. "Are you doing okay?"

"Yes." I shuddered a little. She knew.

"I got your poem," she said. "It made me cry."

"Really." What a nice thing to say.

"Did you cry yet?"

"Yes," I said. "As soon as Joe got here, we went for a walk in the woods and I cried. I cried a lot. I miss them. I couldn't cry with anyone around here."

"Oh I feel so bad for you." And through the airy voice, even the pain from her own accident, I felt like she was there, right on time.

"I sat in some deer shit," I told her.

Joe was standing right next to me while I was talking on the phone. He kind of snuffled because he'd seen it happen.

"I made Joe go out in the woods with me so I could Rage against the Dying of the Light and I cried so hard that I couldn't see where I sat down. I found some nice soft moss and there was deer shit in it."

"Oh." She was quiet on the other end of the line.

"How did you know it was deer shit?"

"Because there was so much of it," I explained.

"Oh."

At first it was hard to tell if she was laughing too, because our laugh noises all came out at the same time, as evenly as if we had planned it that way.

✄

I visit Sarah at her home in Canadian Lakes. She has a baby now, fathered by the Sex Hero.

The Sex Hero thinks that he's also an artist. We think so too, but we're not sure. He paints houses for a living. Sometimes he draws on scraps of paper while he smokes his Camel cigarettes. Lately he's discouraged. He's cut off the head of his life-size Isadora, the one his last wife posed for.

Once he told me he believed that men should never be married, that men should wander from city to city and house to house, making babies and fulfilling God's commandment to multiply. He was a Don Juan of sorts in the college town where I met him. He slept with all types: an old woman, a fat woman, an insane woman who dressed as a nun and was later hospitalized, a quadriplegic. He impressed me in unusual ways.

He and I were better friends then, before I had to choose. Now he gets me high on his homegrown and I steer the conversation away from the baby and Sarah and her job as a social worker. He talks about the painkillers his doctor gave him for a Vietnam injury. He talks about the time he worked with the famous Cristo in Miami Bay. And then suddenly he gets tired of talk, walks out the front door, and drives away in his van.

Sarah and I are very pleased with this. We make a little party in their bedroom with our cups of tea, the incense, an orange we want to split between us. Even though the Sex Hero knows about me, he would get weird if he knew that we sat on their bed together. But we like to make ourselves comfortable. We want to sit on the new quilt her mother made.

Before we sit down she says, "I think I want a beer." Like she's asking. Then I remember that I was the one who paid for it.

"Go ahead. That's what I bought it for."

Instantly she disappears with her cup of tea. When she returns, she's drinking from a longneck bottle.

"It's good to have you here," she says. I agree.

She walks to the closet. Then she opens the door and starts digging around with her hands.

I sip the tea. She turns around and walks toward me holding a big book.

"What is it?" I put my cup down on the bedstand.

"It's my journal," she says. "Sort of a journal." She scoots her butt up onto the bed and sits all the way back against the wall next to me.

Then she hands it to me. When I open the first page, it is full of color pictures that she has drawn.

"I thought I should show you what I did with your present."

I look straight into her face, her wide eyes. The Sex Hero says she has eyes like Judy Collins.

"I didn't recognize it." She has decorated the cover with a collage: bright magazine photographs ripped at the edges and arranged in some kind of design.

Inside, there is a picture of a woman, the figure of a woman. All of her insides are deep blue except for a little red valentine where her left breast would be. I remember the Pledge of Allegiance in fourth grade, how they always told us that the heart was on the left side. The woman in the picture leans against a wall. In an upper corner of the page is a small, dark figure: a man.

Sarah puts down her beer and starts peeling the orange.

When I turn the page, there's a picture of an event that I remember. One day the Sex Hero took us to a sunflower field in bloom. We walked along the edge of the field until we came to some old apple trees. We climbed them. There were no apples, but we could see more of the field. It was a warm day. Sunshine made the sunflowers an even brighter yellow. The three of us sat in the trees for a long time, talking. In her picture, our heads have turned into sunflowers.

"You've been keeping this for a long time."

She hands me a piece of the orange.

"Mm-hmm. You gave it to me three years ago." She's as embarrassed as I was with my story. There's never been anything about each other that we couldn't take, couldn't finally accept in some way. But we share things so tentatively.

"You always wanted me to do something. You know, with my art."

"I'm glad that you have."

I never find the words when I need to say something important. I always envied her talent, could never figure out why she didn't want to become "an artist." And then I thought she gave it up too soon when she broke her arm in the accident. I turn back to the book, the fine lines and the colors.

There is a picture of the blue woman again, with her valentine heart. Now her belly is swollen and I know about this time too, when the two of us moved to Detroit. She was going to graduate school and I was looking for a job. The Sex Hero would visit or she'd go up north to see him on weekends. Sarah and I weren't getting along well. I was afraid for her, didn't know what was going on with this crazy friend of mine.

When she found out she was pregnant, I felt like I was the only one there and I didn't know what to do. I held her. She cried. We got through it. Or *she* got through it. I never could have.

There is a whole series of pictures for the time she moved back north, moved in with the Sex Hero. In each picture, the woman's belly grows a little, and finally another valentine appears there.

"Kayleigh." My voice is suddenly soft, as if the baby were in the room.

"That is the weirdest feeling," Sarah tells me.

"What?"

She laughs. She thinks I can read her mind.

"When she'd kick me. It was the strangest feeling, the first feeling that something alive was inside me."

"Except for yourself," I correct her. I'm trying to drink my tea carefully so I don't spill it on the pages, but we're starting to laugh again and the bed is jiggling.

※

That next time, Joe woke me up in the middle of the night.

"What is it?"

"Clay." He was still sleepy. He was still saying my name. I didn't know what time it was, but I could tell he wasn't awake either.

Then he put his hand on my arm.

"What is it?"

"Sarah's dad died," he said.

"What?"

"Sarah's dad died and I have to take her home."

"Oh." I sat up. Joe took his hand away from my arm.

"I want to go," I said. All three of us were roommates then, but Sarah had once been my girlfriend. I felt that I should go no matter how badly we'd been getting along.

"No," he said. "You have to work tomorrow."

"That's right." Joe didn't work until the next night.

In the new apartment, my bedroom had French doors that Joe must've left open when he came in. I could see Sarah in the living room. She was folding things and dropping them into a brown grocery bag.

I walked up behind her. I was wondering what I could do. And then she turned around to hug. She poured into my arms; her whole face was wet. Her breathing felt funny next to my chest. I hadn't held her for a long time. She was smaller now, as if she had lost some weight.

"I wish I could go with you." After the words came out, she turned and walked away from me. She already had her coat on. Joe was right behind her with a duffel bag.

"Call me at work tomorrow." Joe turned and nodded at me. And then he closed the door behind them.

"You have the number. I think."

We'd been there two weeks and no one had put the curtains up. I remember because the room made an echo after they left, like it does after the telephone rings in an empty room and there is nobody behind the door to answer it.

"It's true," I say. I'm being sincere again.

"You're full of shit." She's in one of those moods where she could say anything, could get mad at me or laugh in my face.

"It's true. All of my heroes are women."

"Right," she says, shaking her head. "You're just saying that because all of the sudden you want to be a feminist."

"It's because I'm gay. Gay men have more of an understanding. They have an appreciation for women that straight men don't have. Straight men need women too much to understand them."

"Ha," she says. "You're regressing. You're going back to your Gay Patriot phase. You're going back to your Gay Is Good phase."

I consider this. For a moment.

"Maybe I am. But look at all the brave women there are, women who keep going no matter what..."

"You're thinking movies. You can only think of movie stars."

"So what. Women keep going. They make do. For every one we heard of there's a hundred more who live and die that we never know about."

She walks to the table and picks up my beer. Suspiciously, she looks at the beer and then at me. Then she sets it back down and walks over to the sink.

"You're full of shit." She starts running the water for the dishes.

"Let me do that. Why don't you rest for a minute?"

But Sarah doesn't rest, she starts dinner. And by the time the Sex Hero comes home with a bottle of wine, the table is set and Kayleigh is up from her nap.

Electricity

$\mathbf{M}$ike would have stayed in the bathroom longer, except that a man came in and stood up to the urinal for a suspiciously long time. Mike wiped his hands on the dirty wet towel-thing that was supposed to wind around but never did, and when he turned to open the door, the old guy had zipped up and grabbed ahold of the door handle before he could. "Hi," the old guy said. He looked like Bert Lahr. He smelled like an awful lot of cologne.

Mike felt a chill run up his spine. "Hello," he said, coldly. He opened the door between them and walked out without turning his head. He returned to Iris, who sat at their table, wiping up spilled beer. "Are you still here?" he asked. He was hoping she would leave. That was why he'd spent so much time avoiding her in the bathroom. Iris missed the point of his question. She asked him, "Did you *see* it?"

Mike poured himself another beer. "What are you talking about?" Iris held herself still, which was a hard thing for her to do with all the red hair flying around. She raised her eyebrow at Michael until he got the joke. "Okay," he said. "It's a whopper. Is that what you want to hear? He rolls it up like a fire hose." That got her laughing, and they were still sniggering when Bert Lahr came out of the restroom. He walked slowly back up to the bar.

"He's limping! I *swear*, he's limping!"

They ran out of jokes after that. The Cowardly Lion left. Mike walked Iris out to her car, and before she could say, "Mikie, we have to talk," he told her he was going to walk home. "I could use the walk," he told her. That was true. Mike needed some air. So Iris shook her head and stood next to the open door of her car, like she used to do when he would kiss her good-bye. That felt like a very long time ago to Mike. Months. He walked away. At least the times when they were uncomfortable with one another were fewer and further between.

He walked out through the alley from the parking lot. He was thinking about how lonesome he was, doing time between the girl-friend he'd left and all the guys he wasn't brave enough to sleep with yet. So he wasn't paying attention to anything more than his own two shoes. He kicked a bud of gravel, and car lights shone between his legs. It must have been the Old Mil, he thought, but it seemed as if he could feel the light on the back of his legs. He was looking straight ahead because he was afraid of fag-bashers, even though he wasn't quite a fag yet. The car came up close alongside, and the passenger window rolled down. "You wanna ride home?"

Mike looked into the window, and he couldn't quite see who it was. But he did see an arm reaching out to him, and it was brown and muscular. He stepped backward, but before he could think, he was telling a stranger, "Sure." The door opened, and he slid into the seat and a cloud of cologne. When he turned to look, Bert Lahr was driving the car. "What's your name?" the man said. He held out a free hand, and Mike shook it. Nothing came out of his mouth. "My name's Larry," the man said. "What's your name?"

"Oh," Mike said. "Larry. My name's Larry, too."

"Really?" The man laughed an old man's laugh, low and slow and quiet. Mike asked him where he lived.

"Oh, I'm not from around here," the man said, looking straight ahead. "I got a room at the Holiday Inn. We could go there. You want to?"

"Maybe another time," Mike said. He invented a reason why he had to get home. "I have a dog named Boo-Boo. I have to let her out. She just got fixed, and she's pissing all over the furniture." It sounded a bit specific, but Larry seemed to buy it. Mike pointed him on through the next turn. When they got out onto Pine Street, the man put his hand on Mike's leg.

Mike was thinking, Okay. So what? So the guy's got his hand on my knee, so what? There's no harm in a little touchy-feely. Actually Mike enjoyed the sensation of heat against his leg. Something uncontrollable unwound inside of him. Before the man could park the car in the extra space behind Mike's building, Mike had jumped on top of him. He kissed the man deeply. "That was nice," Larry said, and it was. Larry was a good kisser. Mike didn't even mind his breath. He leaned over the gearshift on top of him. It wasn't very comfortable for either one of them. "Don't you wanna go inside?" Larry said, tenderly.

Even though Mike felt a little uneasy, he let Larry walk him up to his door. Then, as if he had lost his mind, Mike invited him in. He opened the refrigerator without turning on the lights, and he handed the man a beer. They stood in the kitchen next to the countertop and popped the tabs. They drank a little bit. They started kissing again. The man pressed Mike back against the wall phone. Mike prayed that it would ring. It didn't. He had to slow things down. He excused himself.

Mike walked into the bathroom. He closed the door and ran the water. He knew a relaxation technique that he sometimes taught the patients in the waiting room at the mental health clinic: he breathed real deep and let it out slow, breathed real deep and let it out slow. In the other room, he could hear the old man: "Boo-Boo," he called in falsetto. "Boo-Boo?" Mike looked in the mirror, and he messed up his hair. That was pretty scary, he thought, admiring his ghastliness. But he wasn't sure if it would work. "Only one way to find out," he said to himself. He walked into the living room. The lights were out, and the man wasn't in the kitchen anymore.

"Larry?" Mike said. He shivered.

"Larry?" the man said.

Mike turned around, and Bert Lahr was in the dining room. He sat naked in Mike's rocking chair on top of the dining room table. He had tied a dishtowel under his chin. He wore it like a babushka. He raised his can of beer above his head. "Charge!" he shouted. His dentures popped out and rolled down his leg.

"Jesus Christ," Mike said.

Larry felt around his toes on the table. He wore a sizable crucifix that dangled between his legs when he bent forward. "Where'd they go?" he said. "I'm sorry. Did you see where they went? Turn on the lights."

Mike picked up Larry's teeth. They were warm and moist, and he realized his own tongue had just been sliding between them. "I'm not about to turn the lights on," he said. He took hold of Larry's hand and slapped his dentures into his palm. "I'm not drunk enough," Mike realized. "I need another beer."

"Hey," the man said, gummily. He crouched on top of the dining table and set his teeth on the chair. As if he were, suddenly, much younger, he leapt onto the floor. "You wanna kiss me now? I give one hell, I'd say one hell, of a blow job."

Mike didn't say no right away, but he definitely had not said yes. He was wondering what he could say when Larry backed him into the bedroom. He didn't want to be rude. But at the same time, politeness was not a reason to fuck. Surely, there had to be someone more attractive than Bert Lahr. Obviously, Larry was desperate for whatever he could find. And someday Mike might end up as old and desperate. He'd probably be praying for someone living to come along. Besides, he told himself, as Larry undressed him, he desperately needed to lose his homo virginity before he was too old to be screwed.

When Larry tried to kiss him on the mouth again, he pushed him away. But Mike did let him kiss his neck and chest. He enjoyed the slurpy feel of Larry's rubbery lips on his skin. But when it finally got around to blow jobs, Larry wanted him to go first. Mike obliged.

The old man murmured. He said things in a moistened, intimate voice. "Laywie," he said. "Be my queen. Laywie." Mike lifted his head, but Larry pushed him down on his short fat dick. "Laywie, be my queen. I'll be yo' king."

"I'm not your queen," Mike insisted. "Jesus Christ!"

The man opened his heavy-lidded eyes and frowned at him. "How's a girl supposed to come when you use that kind of language?" Mike pushed his face back into the hairy crotch. He worked away on Larry's dick until his mouth got sore. Eventually, Larry pulled his dick out. He lay back and jerked himself off. He shot all over the pillows.

Mike forgot himself. "Jesus Christ," he said, again.

"Is it necessary to use the name of God like that?" Larry pulled Mike's dishtowel off his head. He rubbed his stomach off. He turned and dabbed at the pillows.

In the dark, Mike reached out to touch the cross and the chain. "I hope you're not a minister. Are you?"

Larry laughed. "Hell, no," he said. "I'm Catholic." He stood up and turned around. Mike saw at once that Larry had a butt that looked much younger than he was. Larry knelt down on the floor, and he licked at Mike's legs with his very long tongue. Mike thought of Iris. Sex with Iris was easily better than this. He pushed the man away. "Don't you wanna come?" Larry said, tenderly.

"Where to?" Mike laughed loudly at his own joke. He helped Larry up off of the floor. Mike guided Larry back through the dark house to the dining room table and his teeth. The man sat down at the table. He put a finger on one of the rockers, so that the chair rocked slowly above them. He drank his beer slowly. "You know any bookstores in town? You want to go for a ride?"

"No," Mike said. "I mean, no, thanks." As loudly as he dared, he yawned.

"I see," the Cowardly Lion said. He slapped his teeth back in. Mike thought he would kiss him, but Larry patted his shoulder. "It'll be all right, sweetie." He lifted Mike's rocking chair off of the table, and he started it rocking on the floor. Mike watched it rocking, slower and slower, and Larry walked out the back.

✄

Mike would not have been proud of his one-night stand if Iris had known it had been with Bert Lahr. But he felt justified in telling her that he'd had one. Iris claimed to enjoy competing over who could get laid first. So he dropped by her flat the next morning to rub her nose in it. He stood behind the screen, waiting for her to lumber to the door. But a tall guy came out of the back of her apartment and pressed his nose against the inside of her screen.

"Hello," he said. "Are you a friend of Iris's?" He opened the door before Mike could answer. He gestured with his very long arm and placed his hand on his chest. "My name's Michael," he said.

"Really," Mike said. He tried not to sound surprised, but he did wonder what such a good-looking guy was doing in Iris's apartment. He looked around the front room for signs of his old girlfriend.

"She's in the shower," Michael said. Mike stepped back into the living room, into an echo of running water and what he thought was the slow, loud singing voice of a woman who knows she's in love, who

James Russell Mayes

knows she is heard, and who knows she likes to rub it in. He sat down, as casually as he could pretend to be, across from Michael. He pretended not to be watching him while he ignored the pages of *Rolling Stone* that floated in the air under his nose. Michael had very long legs. He peered over his kneecaps at Mike, while Mike avoided the natural temptation of looking directly into his crotch.

"You said your name is Michael, too, right?"

"Yeah. Mike," Mike said. He laughed, or sort of honked, in irony. He felt for sure that Iris had told this new guy his whole story — what better way to get a good whaling fuck as soon as possible?

"I had a feeling you might be Mike, before you even told me," Michael said, sure of himself.

"Oh, really?" Mike tried to sound as bored as possible, as if he were barely listening to him. There was an article in the magazine on Rickie Lee Jones, and he really did want to read it. But when he turned the page, he felt an odd sensation of electricity travel up his neck. He was afraid of what Michael might have to say, suddenly.

"Well, you know," Michael said, "there are Mikes and then, you know, there are Michaels. You're a Mike, right?"

Mike stared at Michael, blankly. "I'm definitely a Mike," he said. "And proud of it. 'Mike' is a name for the working class, a beer-drinking kind of name." He cleared his throat, and smiled, obligingly. "If it would make things more confusing, I could be a Michael if you want me to."

"No, that won't be necessary," Michael said. "You see, I thought you were more like a Mike, anyway. Most Mikes are brown haired or dark blond, like yourself. Did you ever notice that?"

"No. Not really. I guess I never really paid attention to it."

Michael slapped his magazine down onto the coffee table and lifted his left knee over his right one. "Oh, I do. And most Mikes like, not acid rock, really, but more like the easy-listening-intellectual kind of rock, like Peter Gabriel? Genesis? The old sixties kind of folk rock stuff? Stuff like that?"

Mike smiled, out of sheer surprise. "Yeah. That's amazing. That's exactly what I like. How did you know?"

Michael shrugged his shoulders. "I told you. There's Mikes, and there's Michaels. You're a Mike. That's what Mikes like."

Mike was annoyed. "So is there something wrong with that?" He looked down at the photo spread. Rickie Lee Jones clutched a microphone up to her lips. Across from him, Michael lifted another magazine off of the coffee table and rolled it into a baton. He raised an end of it to his lips and stuck his tongue into the hole on the end of it. He Groucho-Marxed his eyebrows. The vein in the middle of his forehead bulged, and he burst into laughter.

Mike raised his voice: "What is that supposed to mean?"

"Listen," Michael said, standing up and slumping under the low light over the coffee table. "Iris told me about you, okay?" That much was obvious. Why else would he be making fun of him? Michael moved his legs around the coffee table and sat down beside Mike on the couch. Michael raised his voice as lightly as a breeze might, in order to lift a single sheet of paper off a table: "You probably have a lot of ideas about someone like me. And that's okay. We all make judgments. But listen," and he bent closer, "give me a chance, okay? I think we could get to be good friends."

Mike was surprised by the way he had said it. He laughed out loud. "You're unbelievable," he said. "Is that all you and Iris talked about? Me?"

"Oh no," Michael said. He leaned even closer, so that Mike could feel the heat rising off of his chest. Michael smelled very much like an apple. "Iris didn't want to talk about you at all. I did. I asked her everything about you, because, you know, I had seen you around. She didn't seem to mind too much. I got her drunk for it."

Mike supposed it was because they were both sitting so close together on the couch; it got very quiet all of the sudden. He looked at his hands. He was afraid to look up.

"You know," said Michael, "you don't appreciate what a good friend Iris is to you. Do you have any idea what she's going through?" Mike put his hands flat on the couch, in order to get up. Michael touched him on the hand with his hand. When Mike turned to draw it away, their faces were inches apart.

Michael put his hands under Mike's chin and raised his head gently, so that he had to look at him in the eyes. For one second, Mike thought that he was going to wet his pants. "I think I know how you feel. You think you're the only one in the world, don't you?" The taller man

James Russell Mayes

pressed his hands on either side of Mike's face, and Mike thought at once that he was going to be strangled. Instead, Michael bent down and kissed him on the lips.

Mike must have closed his eyes, because there was nothing else for what seemed a very long time except Iris's new boyfriend prying open his lips with his tongue. When he finally dared open his eyes, Michael's head was perpendicular. Mike stared at his ear. Long blond bangs draped over an eye.

At once Michael unbuttoned Mike's shirt and ran his fingers down onto his chest. He touched Mike's nipples so that they began to tickle him. Then he began to pinch them, until all of the tickles went away. Michael actually got a hard-on. "You know," Michael told him, and Mike was surprised how hoarse the other man's voice had become: "Iris takes very long showers." He pulled Mike out of his shirtsleeves, and Mike pulled him out of his.

"I know." Mike climbed him like a tree until they both fell over on the couch. He lay on top of Michael's broad chest. At once, for no reason at all, he couldn't do more. Michael lay under him and flattened his hands on his back. He rubbed Mike there until the air came back, and the room became clear again.

"Is something wrong?" Michael said. His voice was soft. Mike took so long to figure out what reason there might be for him not to want to continue, that after a few minutes he wondered if Michael hadn't asked him at all. Mike wondered what he was doing at Iris's flat, lying on top of her new boyfriend, and what Iris's new boyfriend was doing under him working his tongue around inside of his ear. The water stopped.

Mike sat up. Michael gave him his shirt. Mike stood, and he pulled it on. Michael lay back on the couch. He watched him tucking it in. He looked incredibly long to Mike, all spread out like that. When Mike looked down to check his fly, the shirttails weren't his own. In the rush, he'd put on Michael's shirt.

"Stop, in the name of love," Iris sang in the bathroom, toweling off. Mike heard her kick open the bathroom door. He ran out into the street.

Mike felt a little guilty and a lot of smug. But he didn't talk to Iris until she called him a week later. "Hey, what happened?" she said.

"What do you mean?"

"You know what I'm talking about. What did you do, Mike? Fall off the face of the planet?"

"No. Not exactly."

"Well. Michael said you came by. About a week ago? Anyway, I was in the shower. And you know what?"

"No. What?"

"He's a doll, isn't he?"

"Adorable."

"No. Seriously, what do you think, Mike?"

"He's fine, Iris. He's fine." Mike wanted Iris to gloat about this guy so bad. After all, she had scored first. Bert Lahr didn't count. Bert Lahr never counts. "So?" he said.

"What's wrong?"

"Nothing's wrong. I want you to tell me about this guy, Iris."

"I'll bet you do. And he's not just a guy, Mike, he's Michael Two."

"Michael Two?"

"Yeah, that's what I call you two: Michael One and Michael Two. How else can I keep you guys straight?"

"You're forgetting something, Iris. I'm not a Michael. I've never *been* a Michael. I'm a Mike. There's a difference."

She laughed, joyously. "Oh, that's right. He tell you that already? Damn, he's cute, isn't he? And *tall*. I hope you two get along okay."

"Fine and dandy. Really."

"Anyway, this is a business call. Michael Two has a friend in Remus who's having a party on Sunday morning."

"Oh, I don't think so, Iris."

"You're not getting away with that this time, Mike. You're *going*. Michael wanted me to invite you."

"So why didn't he ask me himself?"

"What is *wrong* with you? He's shy. He's afraid you'll say no. He doesn't know you, Mike."

"Not like you know me, right?"

"You are *so rude* sometimes." She didn't say anything for a few seconds. Mike waited, and then he realized she was going to spring something on him. "There's going to be a lot of gay people there," she said, as mildly as possible.

"How come?"

"Oh, come off it, Mike. Why do you think? I've *had* it with trying to help you out like this."

"Help me out? Help me out!"

"Yes. I'm helping you out, Michael One. You're going. I swear if I have to pull you by your dick, you're going." She cleared her throat, as if to start the conversation over. "So. Are you going willingly, or not?"

"Not," Mike said. "Not, not, not, not, not."

"Wonderful." Mike listened as her voice got smaller on the other end of the line. She was talking to someone. "No," Iris was saying. "Really. I wouldn't *do* that to you. Mike says he'll go."

"Iris," Mike interrupted. "I'm not gonna go. Okay?" Even as he said it, he didn't like the way it sounded. He *hated* it when she guilted him. And this time, she didn't even *know* she was guilting him. He sighed loudly into the receiver so that she would hear him clearly. "Okay?"

"Hurrah! Yay! Hooray! Huzzah!" Her voice got small again, and Mike couldn't hear what she said. But he did hear another voice, smaller than hers.

The voice said, "Great." Michael Two sounded candidly happy.

Mike hung up.

Iris did not have the decency to stand up to him on her own. On Sunday morning she pulled into his driveway, and she sent Michael up to the door for him. Mike sat rocking in his chair, concentrating on his fried potatoes. "Hey!" Michael said through the screen. "Mike! How come you're not ready?" Mike kept his eyes glued on the shape of Charles Kurault's head. He scraped his plate with his fork.

"Iris! He's not ready!" Something cracked in Michael's voice, and he ran back down the steps. Over the running engine, Mike heard Michael's voice rise. He hoped that Iris was telling him that he'd never intended to go. The least she could do was to tell him the truth. He expected that she would cut the engine. He expected her to come into the house and somehow force him to go. There were footsteps on the porch again, and finally Mike looked up. He expected to see Iris behind the screen, in a dress that was much too tight for her. But instead, he saw Michael, and Michael was all dressed up. He wore suspenders and a bow tie. He'd had a haircut. He looked cute. He slumped forward, looking much too tall for himself. Something unfolded in Mike's heart.

"Mike," Michael said, softly. "Mike. Can I come in?" He held his hand up to the screen, and he touched it with the tips of his fingers.

"Sure," Mike said, and panic ran through him. Michael looked disappointed. Mike rocked forward and set his plate on the floor. Michael sat down on the couch, and both of them stared at his knees.

He waited a minute before he spoke, in a voice that sounded as if he were filled with air: "Don't you want to go? I thought you wanted to go."

Mike didn't know what to say. As soon as Michael had walked in the door, he had felt dreamy and uncontrollable. He was pleased that Michael was so disappointed. Mike rocked back and forth in his chair. Iris probably had no idea how disappointed Michael really was. That was a happy thought. In spite of himself, Mike said, "I'll go." He stood and bent to pick up his potatoes, cold and covered with ketchup. "I'll go," he said, again.

"Don't go, if you don't want to." Michael brought a hand up to his face. "I thought you wanted to go."

"I said I'd go, and I'm going." Mike walked into the kitchen. He rinsed his plate and laid it in the sink. By the time he walked back through the living room, Iris had begun to honk the horn. "Come on, you guys," she called from the driveway. Michael walked up to the screen, and he called to her from the porch: "Hold on to your tits, woman!"

Mike opened his closet and smirked in the mirror on the inside of the door. He pulled Michael's unwashed shirt from a hanger. He buttoned it, and he tucked it in. "My God, he even talks like a fag. How is it that Iris can't know that her new boyfriend is gay?" He whispered it close to the glass, so that the steam covered up his mouth. He sniffed at the collar, smelled apples and sweat, and called to Michael, "I'm ready!"

James Russell Mayes

Michael insisted that Mike sit in the passenger seat in front. Iris drove so fast that the road became a roller coaster. The pavement was smooth; they rose and fell over the hollows. Iris talked about accidents. "There must've been two or three out here on this road, just last year."

Mike struggled to appear interested. "How come?"

"The hills are steep. They think they can see the traffic, and they can't. The trick is, you have to wait for the blind spot to flush out."

"Yeah," Michael said, leaning forward so that his lips were inches from Mike's ear. "Or *whammo*. There goes a nuclear family, out on a Sunday drive."

Mike said, demurely, "The countryside is beautiful in so many ways." Michael laughed. At least he had a sense of humor.

Iris pulled off on a gravel drive and drove through a leafy woods. She made a sharp right and abruptly pulled up to an open garage door. She cut the engine. Mike looked around. The house was obviously incomplete; tar paper covered the outside walls, and boards were stacked under sheets of plastic. "Where are we?" he asked. "Where's the beer?"

Iris threw open her door. "That jerk!" she said, glaring inside the garage. "I'll eat his balls *raw!*"

"You did," Michael chimed from the back. "Remember?"

Iris walked around the back of the car and climbed up steps to an unvarnished door. She turned to call back to them, "His truck's not here." She pounded on the door several times.

Mike looked over the headrest at Michael, who had caught a moth in his hands. "Could you please tell me what's going on?" Michael looked up as if he were about to tell him a secret. He rested his chin on the back of Mike's seat. "Iris had a date," he said. He followed her around the car with his eyes. "It was supposed to be a surprise." Iris walked into the garage. She stood on a cement block and knocked at another door. Once again, no one answered. She opened the door and walked inside.

"But I thought you were her date," Mike said. He felt his color rise.

"You're kidding, right?" Michael looked alarmed. "Please tell me you're kidding, Mike."

Just in time, Mike opened his mouth. "I am," he said, unconvincingly. "I'm kidding."

Michael howled with laughter. "We're both her dates," he said. He reached over the seat and touched Mike's neck, and Mike felt the hair rise on his arms. "And if Morley shows up, he'll be a third. We'll go as one big family."

"One big *happy* family," Mike corrected. He wondered what else there was that Iris had neglected to tell him.

"You guys," she called from the open doorway, "there's a note. Come on inside. Morley went into town." Her face assumed a relieved smile, and the Michaels joined her inside.

"Morley? What kind of a name is Morley?"

The two Michaels crouched in front of a fire that Morley had banked in the stove. "It's a name," Iris said, defensively. "What's in a name?" She assumed a corrected posture and lay a hand on her breast. Iris recited a jumble of Shakespeare and Ginsberg and Paul Simon. Michael laughed, but Mike shook his head. "I've heard it before," he said.

Iris stuck out her tongue and walked through a sliding glass door. It led out onto a deck. Apparently Morley was building a house that projected out over a wooded ravine. She sat down in an empty wheelbarrow, and the Michaels watched her through the glass door.

"Are you okay?" Michael asked him.

Mike wrinkled his nose. "Why wouldn't I be?"

"I just wondered," he said, shrugging. "I thought you might be jealous or something. I know you used to be in love."

"It's not like that, at all," Mike said. "At least, not for me. I don't understand why she wouldn't say that she had a date for the party."

"I don't understand why she wouldn't tell you that you had a date with me," Michael countered. Mike turned. Michael had raised an eyebrow. His expression was ironic, but sad. "I can't believe you thought I was straight," he said, looking down.

Mike laughed out loud. "I never thought you were straight. I thought Iris made a mistake." He felt his face blooming. "You know, like she did with me."

Michael opened the door to the stove. He lifted the poker and pried the wood out of the ashes. "Tell me," he said, as the sparks flew out, together with a great deal of smoke. Mike thought he was going to ask him about fires. But instead, Michael asked him, "Can we still call this a date? I mean, I know you didn't know, because Iris must not have told you. Or maybe you misunderstood. I don't know." The poker clattered inside the stove.

Mike couldn't believe how incompetent Michael was, at building fires, at asking for dates. He pulled the poker out of his hand and laid it across the top of the stove. He closed the door, and he lifted Michael's hand. He kissed it. Mike began to nibble at Michael's hand with his lips. He had only started to bite at a callus, when he sensed a certain disinterest. "What an extraordinary animal," Michael said, so that Mike looked up to see.

And it was an extraordinary animal. It stood on the deck, only feet from Iris, who drew herself up on the wheelbarrow. The animal was completely black, except for the long white teeth that stuck out at all angles from its muzzle. It looked ferocious. "My God," Iris shouted. The Michaels walked up to the glass. Iris lifted herself off the wheelbarrow. The animal began to whine. "That stupid dog!" she shouted. The animal backed away. She called to them through the glass. "He's got into a porcupine!" Morley's dog crouched forward. It made a strained gulping sound. It wheezed, and blood flew out.

"Gross," Mike said. Michael opened the door and walked out onto the deck. The dog made a move for the door. Iris blocked it with her leg.

"You guys have to help me," she said. She reached down and held on to its collar. "This stupid idiot did this before. Morley showed me." She turned to Mike. "There's pliers in the toolbox, next to the Rumford stove." Mike brought them out, and he handed them to Michael.

"This is going to be really gross," Michael said, doubtfully.

"Well, we can't sit waiting for Morley." Iris pulled the pliers out of his hand. "Just hold on to the dog," she said. Mike held its collar. Michael straddled the dog, whose name Iris seemed to forget. She rested the animal's head against her leg, and with her fingers she braced its flesh. She yanked at the quills with the pliers, and she tossed them onto the deck. Some were quite deep, and these drew blood, while others came out quite easily. The worst were around its mouth.

"How can you stand that?" Mike said, flinching. Michael had closed his eyes.

Iris cleared her throat. "I can't," she said. The dog flinched, and she seized it by the scruff of its neck. "Hold still," she shouted. She hauled it in closer. She held its mouth open and pulled out several more. Evidently, this was more painful. The dog bolted out from between Michael's legs, and Mike fell flat on the deck. "You guys have to hold on to it."

Iris straightened. She rested her hands on her hips. Blood streamed down the front of her dress, and her knees were blackened with dirt. "Look at that stupid dog," she said, pointing with the pliers. Nevertheless, it slunk back toward her. "He knows he needs us to help him. Stupid dog!" Mike caught the dog by the collar, and Michael put his leg over it. Iris wrapped an arm around its neck, and she struggled to open its mouth.

"Hello, hello," a strange voice said, and a man in a pair of overalls walked out through the sliding glass door.

"Morley!" Iris whimpered. Mike and Michael let go of the dog. Iris dragged it over to Morley. She handed him the pliers. "What is this stupid dog's name?" she shouted.

"Oscar," Morley said, shaking his head. "And he's not stupid, okay?"

"Well, he got into a porcupine, didn't he?"

Morley was more at ease with the dog, and the dog seemed to listen to him. Oscar held still while Morley pulled out the quills. Once he tried to get away, with the pliers all the way down his throat and Morley's fist in his teeth, but Morley beat him with the pliers. He roared at the dog until his face turned red. He finished the job by himself.

Iris and Michael and Mike walked inside, somewhat bloody and embarrassed. "He seems like a nice-enough guy," Mike said. "He's cute, you know?" Iris sat down on a stepladder. She didn't seem to hear him.

"Hey," Michael said. "Are you okay?"

Iris stood up and raised her arms. "Are you okay? Are you okay? Are you okay?" She walked over to the refrigerator, a dirty thing covered with paint stains. She pulled out five beers, and she handed one to each of them. "Nice shirt," she said slyly, to Mike.

James Russell Mayes

Mike concentrated on popping the top. "Hey, there's three beers," he said. "Why do you have three beers, Iris?"

Michael opened the sliding door for her. "You expecting another man?"

"Hell, no," she said, pausing in the door frame. "Three's just enough. This one's for Oscar." She brightened. She blew at a stray red hair. "He deserves it, don't you think?"

With blood all over their clothes and Oscar needing some care, the party was out of the question. Iris drove Mike and Michael back into town. Mike loaned Michael a clean shirt, and they walked to the bar. Once Mike was suitably drunk, he told Michael, over the beer he had spilled on the table, that his brother-in-law once had a dog that got into porcupines. "He finally had to shoot him," Mike said. Michael didn't believe him. He explained, "The vet told him there are two kinds of dogs. Some of them get it, and they learn their lesson. They leave them alone."

"Let's hope Oscar is one of those kind." Michael sipped at his orange juice.

"But wait a minute. There's the other kind. The other kind never leaves them alone. It's like they get it in their head to be pissed off at porcupines or something. They keep going back and keep going back. And sometimes they have to operate on them if the needles get in too far. You know they can choke to death?" He looked at his companion. Michael curled his lip. Mike cleared his throat. "Well," he said. "Enough about me." Under the table, he felt Michael's foot, shoeless, so he had to have kicked his loafers off, nudging at his ankle.

"Let's go somewhere," Michael said.

Mike thought for a minute. "Not my place," he said. "Let's please don't go to my place."

Michael said, "I know a place." He took Mike through the summer dark: thank God it was summer, and dark, Mike thought, to a place he could not have expected: the Central Michigan Community Mental Health Clinic.

"This is where I work," Mike said.

Michael grinned. "I know. Iris told me. You have a key, don't you?"

"We can't do that. What if someone sees the lights on? We have an alarm system."

"Follow me." Michael led Mike along the side of the building to the back roof, which sloped low enough for them to pull themselves up. They climbed onto the shingles.

"How did you know about this place?" Mike asked. He leaned into the slope.

In the dark he could see the teeth of Michael's smile. "Do you know what this place was ten years ago?"

"No. Wait a minute." Mike thought. "It was a church."

"Yeah, it was a church. This was the church my grandma used to take me to. Come on." They moved up far enough so they could crouch among the moon shadows of the maples without being seen. Michael started kissing him. "Praise the Lord."

"You're beautiful," Mike said. "Do you know how beautiful you are?" If Mike were that beautiful, he told himself, he wouldn't be wasting his time with anyone like himself. Michael was so beautiful, it was frightening how beautiful he was. Michael made him feel that if he turned to Mike and said, "Let's go to Acapulco," Mike would leave his job and give Michael what little money he had and go. They were naked, sitting on top of their clothes so the shingles wouldn't scratch.

"Turn around," Mike said to him. "I want to look at your butt." Michael turned around, but he stuck his butt in Mike's face. Mike poked him on the cheek and told him to look natural. He looked natural, stood up straight. Beautiful. Butt of God.

"Touch me." Michael squatted above him on the slope of the roof of the clinic. Mike worked on his butt with his tongue, right above the office of his supervisor Peggy.

"Let's do it."

"Can we?" So they did. Mike pushed himself into Michael, and Michael made a noise like he was filled with air.

"You okay?"

"What?"

"You okay?"

James Russell Mayes

"It's nice."

Mike liked it, too. He wasn't in there a minute. He jerked a couple times, awkwardly. He pulled out and spilled over Michael's bottom. He leaned into his back, breathing. Michael had a nice smell on his skin.

Michael turned around, and it was Mike's turn. At first it hurt a little. He tried to relax the muscle. He tried to open himself up as wide as he could. And then it felt okay. It took a few seconds for Mike to get used to it. Then it felt good. All of Michael was inside of him. It was like they were both inside each other. Whenever Michael moved, Mike felt like he was moving, too. Michael spilled. It felt like butterflies inside of him. Mike felt the pounding of his heart all through his hands and legs and neck.

"You feel good."

"Could you pull out?"

"What?"

"Pull out." Michael pulled out, slowly. He must have known how empty it would feel when he pulled away. The pressure made a difference; Mike carried somebody. It was the same thing when they talked about Jesus: you open up, you bloom in the heart.

Michael got around on top of him. He scared Mike because they went over backward. Mike shouted, he held on to Michael's wrists. Mike was flat on his back, and the shingles dug in. His head fell back against the angle of the roof. Michael was on top of him. He was someone who was tall and at the same time very delicate in the face. He was snorting, a laugh.

Mike looked at the leaves. A car door slammed. "It smells like rain," he said.

Michael said: "I think I'm falling for you."

"Don't say fall. I'm upside down."

Michael laughed again. Even though Mike didn't know him very well, he liked Michael's laugh. Michael could laugh at anything. "What was that?"

"I didn't hear it."

Mike closed his eyes. They listened: crickets, somebody calling out for someone.

"Come on. I'll walk you to your corner."

There were no lights along the streets in residential areas, only bright ones over each intersection, suspended from wires. Mike walked up his steps and turned around. There was Michael, standing under the light. He held onto the street sign with one arm. He leaned so his other hand could almost touch the ground. He was trying to reach his shadow.

"Go home," Mike said.

There was a moth at the porch light. Mike turned off the light and watched it flutter in the shadows. It slowed down, and when it closed its wings, it disappeared.

Mayonnaise
Sandwiches

Our father had recently raked and mowed the lawn so that when we ran out from under the mercury vapor light, we ran sure-footed, even in the early night. Olive and Betty ran ahead of me in their Easter dresses from last spring; they shimmered like ghosts near the duck pen. I turned around and saw that Dortha counted loudly against the light pole. She covered her eyes with an arm and held our dalmatian Madeline by the collar with her free hand; Dortha was the youngest and the only one allowed to use the dog in hide-and-go-seek. I heard the noise of my brother's boots near the apple trees. I ran right behind him. Above their bare branches, the sky was enormous and fragrant with the autumn.

"Ready or not."

I strained my eyes to see in the dark. Until they adjusted, I listened: there were the familiar jingles of Madeline's tags, and Dortha's voice, urging. Behind us, the frogs along the creek chorused eerily. I was pleased to be next to my big brother, although Wallace was bossy and scientific. He squatted near the trunk of an apple tree, and when I jumped onto my knees behind the same one, he punched me in the arm.

"Priss," he said. "Find your own hiding place."

His voice gave us away. Madeline bolted into the shadows that concealed us, and Dortha called out from behind the dog. Madeline was used to the game; she leapt on me in her excitement. When I stood up, a paw lay on either side of my neck, as if we were dancing partners. She licked my nose.

"Clay?"

Dortha called to me from the brightness of the yard. Although I could see her clearly, she looked straight at me and couldn't see a thing; her eyes had not adjusted. The back door slammed, and above Dortha's shoulder I saw Mama on the patio. Mama lifted her long arms and rang the dinner bell.

"Come and eat," she called.

Dortha turned for only a moment. But Wallace bolted out from under the trees. He was halfway across the lawn before I had pushed the dog away. Olive and Betty came screeching out from behind the duck pen; Dortha tried to tag them, but they split apart around her. I ran from the orchard and thought I felt the light on my skin when I gained the open yard. Betty lifted a fist and leapt a pile of leaves: "Yo," she cried. I was right behind her when Madeline jumped on me from behind. I fell forward into the grass.

"Now," Mama growled.

I pushed myself up and saw that Wallace and Betty and Olive were standing under the mercury vapor light. The dresses of my sisters glowed; their faces darkened and grew less substantial next to the vibrant material, as if their clothes contained nothing and hovered emptily above their kneesocks and Sunday shoes. Wallace pinched them, and they squealed; they ran from the light pole and became human again in the regular light off the back of the house.

Our father bought the mercury light after things had started happening in the neighborhood. Mr. Manning down the road had seen a strange man press his face against their picture window. Someone killed one of Mr. Bronson's cats and nailed it to the barn. Judy Grimewood had her pine stump set on fire. Mama begged Father to put up the light, as others on Billingsly Road had done; she reminded him that Mr. Wolff and his two sons had spent a whole night in the woods behind their house, chasing whatever it was that had riled their German shepherd. Mama had trouble sleeping.

Although Father despised the unnatural light, we loved it. The countryside gleamed at night. The mercury vapor attracted bugs, which in turn attracted bats. It lit up the backyard so brilliantly that we had begun to play outside much later than we could have without it; we felt quite safe. It was unnatural, that was true, but the very unnaturalness of the light seemed particularly suited to our favorite after-dark games: hide-and-go-seek, monster tag, war, and bloody murder. As often as we could, we continued these games much longer than we were supposed to; we would have played well beyond our bedtime if Mama didn't threaten us from the patio.

But when we had company, we knew better than to allow her to make a scene. I followed my brother and sisters up to the door, let Dortha tag me when I wiped my shoes. I had already lost anyway. Wallace punched me in the arm again. "Priss." I held my shoulder. I followed him into the house.

✄

To his credit, Father waited until we had finished with our salads and were scooping into our tuna-stuffed tomatoes before he offered Reverend Bennett a beer. Mama didn't say anything, but she took a long time drawing her spoon out from between her lips. I tried to remember if Reverend Bennett's faith were a drinking or a nondrinking one. I had attended more than a dozen different churches within the previous two years; Mother's spiritual quest had included every local parish, in fact, except the one that Wallace called "the Brothers of the Bush," who insisted that every service be held out-of-doors because of an obscure biblical reference which mistrusted "temples built by the hands of men." I could not remember what the outside of Reverend Bennett's church looked like, let alone recall their position on temperance.

"I would prefer wine, if you have it," Reverend Bennett said, and right then I fell in love with him. I thought of myself, years from that moment, in a future that would never be, floating on a boat along a narrow canal in Venice. A man as short and rotund and as unemployed as our father would call out to me from a passing bridge: "Excuse me. Would you like a beer with your tuna boat?" In my sophistication, I would call back to him, even as the Italian haze enveloped his shabbiness: "I would prefer wine, if you have it."

Unfortunately, we had no wine. Our father did not drink wine. At one time, he had taken to mixing vodka with grape juice and offering it to us as "homemade wine," but Mama had thrown out the last bottle of vodka some time before. Beer was offered a second time, in consolation, and our guest accepted it graciously. "What brand do you drink?" he asked, as Father popped off the tops.

"Miller."

"Ah, yes," Reverend Bennett said. "The champagne of beers. My mother drank Miller beer." Ah yes, I said to myself. I put down my knife and fork so that I might interlace my fingers under my chin, in the same way that our guest had. I would practice this gesture in the mirror, with great moral reserve, for the following several weeks. Reverend Bennett reminded me of my greatest hero, Roddy McDowell.

Mama walked around the island cupboard, and she returned to us with a great platter which had been warming in the oven. She stood at the head of the table, next to Father, and lifted the lid off the platter with her giant farm-girl hands before setting a great heap of sliced beef next to him.

"That looks wonderful," Reverend Bennett praised. It looked even more wonderful to us. Our family could rarely afford such a hearty meal, and the Reverend's presence with us was the excuse for such extravagance. Mama widened her gray eyes and looked around the table at each of us; at moments like these, she was most particularly beautiful. Tall and slender, she hung over the table like a tree, gracefully shy.

"Who wants roast beef?" she said happily, after serving our father and Reverend Bennett. My brother and sisters held up their plates. I could tell in advance that I would not be able to eat my meal that night, however delicious the roast beef might be. I was nervous of strangers and at the same time a victim of a very sensitive stomach. Mother had made peas and candied yams. The rice alone was exotic fare in our potato-eating home. But all I could think of, as I stared out the picture window into the blue-lit yard, was that I might choke on my meal, or spill something, or embarrass myself painfully in some other way. Temporarily I avoided detection by holding up my plate with the others; I accepted the smallest portion. I beamed over my food.

I admired our guest. Reverend Bennett did not immediately swill down his beer and ask for another, as our father would have done. Father had a weakness for good food and drink, he said about himself. After an especially good meal, he would pull our mother onto his lap, though she protested loudly. He would kiss her and tell her he loved her, all the while she complained about the smell of beer on his breath. In comparison to Father, Reverend Bennett was an understated man;

he lifted only a suitable portion of food to his mouth at a time. Mama, who would not allow us to call one another "brat" or to say "shut up" at the table, would herself sometimes hoist a potato out of the dish at the end of a meal and eat it off the end of her fork like a marshmallow.

Our guest began to discuss morality, and although the way he spoke was attractive to me, careful and deliberately passionate, I was taken more with the way he held his fork than with what he had to say. Rather than tuck his paper napkin into the front of his shirt, as Father had taught Wallace and me, Reverend Bennett unfolded it completely and lay it across his well-creased slacks. As he was our guest, he was the first offered each of the dishes passed, after Father. But once he took the plate of johnnycake or the bowl of rice, he deferred to my sisters Olive and Betty. Olive would blush and Betty might stare stonily at her plate, but he offered everything to each of them before he took for himself.

"This recent spate of small crimes," he said, "is less an issue of the growing amount of working poor in our area than an indication of the need for some type of youth program." He waved away Mama's offers for seconds with an elegant, but economical, flourish. There followed a moment of silence in which I could appreciate that he took food into his mouth, that he chewed it, even swallowed it without making hoglike noises.

"You're not eating," Mama said to me. I looked up and shook my head. I was afraid to look at our guest in case he might notice me. Nevertheless, I felt my color rising in waves. "Go make yourself a sandwich and sit up to the sideboard, if you want," she said. Mama was the best at such moments. She knew how not to call attention to me, even in large congregations.

I left the table and walked around to the other side of the island cupboard, where I could hide behind the breakfront. I opened the refrigerator door and pulled out the jar of mayonnaise. "Clay's a very sensitive boy," I heard her explain to Reverend Bennett. Wallace snorted, very much like a pig, and I heard my sisters laugh. "We took him in for tests, because his stomach acted up so many times."

I pulled the Wonder bread out of the bread box. For some reason, johnnycake seemed coarse to me. I spread mayonnaise over four slices of bread and arranged them carefully on my plate. I poured myself a glass of milk and carried it all to the sideboard, where I still might observe our company at a distance. I drank from my glass and looked out over the horizon of milk that lowered as I drank it. Everyone at the table, features distorted by a creamy film, was looking at me. Even Reverend Bennett.

One little head stuck out more than the rest. "Look," Wallace said, and I put my glass down. He narrowed his eyes. "Clay's eating a totally white meal." The others were quiet for a moment, until Father began to laugh. It was a very loud, booming laugh that we had not heard from him for some time; his was a laugh that sounded as if I could write it out like this: ha, ha, ha. The rest of my family, except Mama, joined in. I looked at my plate. I swallowed and wondered if I would be able to eat my mayonnaise sandwiches. I loved mayonnaise sandwiches.

The laughter died away. I had just begun to hope that the subject of their conversation might be changing, when Reverend Bennett said, "That looks like a pretty good meal to me." I looked up at him, because I was surprised that he would be making fun of me; it seemed such bad form. The table grew silent. Reverend Bennett smiled as if he liked me very much. He looked at me through his glasses. "I used to eat mayonnaise sandwiches. And milk toast. Have you ever had milk toast?" I managed to nod. "What about dill pickles with peanut butter on them? Have you ever had that?"

I was anxious for the end of dinner to come. When Reverend Bennett pushed his chair back, I felt great relief. I had been able to finish my sandwich only because Reverend Bennett had described them in such pleasing terms to my family. "Light and tart and still very creamy," he had said. "Honestly, they're quite delicious. You've never tried them?"

Mama asked if he might stay awhile longer. "I would like to talk with you," she said. "I need to talk with you." Father stood up and said, "That sounds great. The Reverend and I can take some beers and sit down by the creek on the log pile."

"If you don't mind," Mama said, "I'd like to talk to the Reverend alone." She looked down at the hole in our linoleum, as if embarrassed by crossing him in front of our guest. "I have some questions about the Congregationalists."

"Now, you know I don't mind at all," Father said. But it did seem as if he was disappointed. I believe my father was a lonely man. He had trouble finding people who would drink beer with him, and as much as he often had to do so, he didn't enjoy drinking beer alone.

Betty had to tuck Dortha in, so I helped Olive clean off the table. I dumped the scraps into Madeline's bowl on the patio. I watched her eat, while Mama and Reverend Bennett wandered out through the apple trees. Afterward, I went inside and walked into the living room where Wallace and Father were sitting in front of the television. Grandpa Krantz had given us the color set when he retired and moved to Florida. The color still wasn't right, and the words on the screen doubled over themselves in green and blue. I sat down next to Wallace, while Father turned the buttons. A Pepto-Bismol commercial came on; it showed a cross section of a grown man's stomach. Pain radiated outward in blue lightning bolts.

"Why is his stomach blue?" I said.

Wallace slunked over and punched me in the arm. "Because he's *sensitive.*" Father looked up and said, "You go to bed."

"It's not my bedtime," Wallace said.

"Tomorrow's a school day. You behave yourself and get on up to bed."

"Come on, Clay." Wallace pulled on my arm.

"I didn't say Clay, I said you. Get on up there."

Wallace went to punch me again, but Father told him to knock it off. I didn't get punched. I sat on the carpet next to my father's legs, and watched *The Dukes of Hazzard* with him. I didn't particularly enjoy the show. In fact, I thought it was stupid, and I would have said so if Wallace were watching it. But Father rocked the chair up and down beside me. I was proud of myself, sitting in front of the television with him while Wallace was upstairs getting ready for bed. The Sheriff's uniform was blue. I knew it was supposed to be white. I nodded off, and when I woke up the screen was fuzzy again. Father stood up at the set. He told me that I should go to bed, too. "Go on," he said, turning the dial.

I went upstairs to bed, and I was dreading it because I knew it was too early for Wallace to be asleep and too early for him not to be mad at me. He lay on top of the bed reading his *Popular Science*. Wallace was twelve, and he had a fat head; his favorite hobbies were reading *Popular Science* and trying to grow sideburns. I changed into my pajamas and crawled under the blankets beside him. Wallace pretended to yawn. He closed his magazine and put it on the bureau next to the bed. He curled up under the covers.

"You can turn the light off, now," he said.

"You were the one who was reading. You turn it off."

"The last one in bed has to turn it off."

"That's no fair," I said. "Last time you said that the one closest to the light has to turn it off."

"That's right. And you're the closest to the light. So you turn it off." He laughed.

"But I'm always the closest to the light."

"Look at it this way," Wallace said, as if he were clever, "you can turn off the light and I won't punch you. Otherwise, I will." Wallace had to explain everything.

I got out of bed and walked to the light switch by the door. I turned off the light, and then I climbed back into bed. The bed was cold, because Wallace had been lying on top of it instead of warming it up for us; our bedroom was always chilly in cool weather because there were no heating ducts upstairs. So I curled up under the covers. I was trying to breathe under the blankets in order to warm it up faster. And then I accidentally kicked my brother with one of my feet. So he hit me.

"It was an accident," I said.

"Listen, you priss. Stay on your side of the bed."

Wallace drew an invisible line down the middle of the bed. Then he reconsidered; he said that because he was older than me, he required more space. He redrew the line and gave himself more room on his side than I had on mine. This was obviously unfair, so I made a point of staying within the boundary of my half of the middle while still breaching the line he had drawn which invaded it. "I'm sick and tired of you," he said. He sat on top of my stomach to hold me down and pounded my arm several times with passion.

I knew better than to let him see me cry. Any extravagance of emotion, unless it were in some way connected to brutality, would only rile Wallace. I closed my eyes and concentrated; blue lightning bolts pounded into my shoulder. When he let me up, I rose from the bed. I walked into my sisters' room. Olive and Betty slept in one bed, while Dortha slept in a smaller bed with rails along the side. All three sat up and blinked their eyes at me. "Get out of here," Betty said. I told them that Wallace was picking on me. I asked them if I could sleep in their room with them.

"Yes," Dortha said. She looked across the room at Olive and Betty. Olive and Betty looked at one another. "He can," Dortha said.

"Okay," said Olive, "but you have to sleep on the floor."

I lay down on the rug between their beds, and it wasn't nearly large enough. I had no covers, and the floor was even colder than the air upstairs; I rolled around on the rug for a little while until I decided it was all quite impossible. I would have to tell on Wallace, no matter what punishment he might counter with, if only to get some sleep.

I walked downstairs, and the television was still on. Father had fallen asleep in his chair. I said, "Father?" but he continued to sleep. I touched his arm, and he stopped snoring. He opened his eyes. "Clay?" I tried to explain, but he closed his eyes on me. "Get to bed," he said. "Go on." I walked back up the stairs, but I sat down on the top step. I listened to *The Johnny Carson Show* until I heard Father snoring again. When I walked back down the stairs, I put my feet at the edge of each step so the boards wouldn't creak; I had read about that in a Nancy Drew mystery. I pulled my coat from the coat closet, and I put on Wallace's boots. I opened the back door, and Madeline was there, happy to see me.

The mercury vapor lit up the whole backyard as if it were daylight on a weird bluish planet. I walked unevenly across the lawn in my brother's boots, holding my stomach, which had begun to throb. Madeline followed me into the shadows of the apple trees. I would not have gone into them, feeling my way forward through the dark alleys between the rows of their trunks, if the dog had not been with me. For that matter, I would not have taken such an initiative if I were not justifiably angry with Wallace. Mama was the only person who could correct his trespasses.

I thought how frightening the sky above me appeared with the leaves off the apple trees. I wondered if the mercury light would really scare the bad people away. Its blue light shone down in patches. In places the ground appeared to be cracked by the shadows of the branches, even swollen, as if something were breaking up through earth from underneath. But I knew that Mama was sitting with Reverend Bennett on the log pile by the creek; I heard her voice rising above the noise of the frogs. I stopped when I reached the last row of apple trees, and I clung to a branch in order to see over it.

On the creek side of our orchard, the mercury light no longer held sway; the moon shone down on the water, as brightly as it often would in the autumn. Reverend Bennett and Mama were sitting on the log pile, as I had imagined they would be. But my mother sat forward with the balance of her weight on her feet. She wiped her face with her hands. "I swear if something doesn't happen soon, I'm going to go crazy," she said. From the pitch and strain in her voice, I could tell that she was weeping. I could tell that Mama had been weeping for some time. "I'll leave him, I'll leave the kids. I'll walk right out of that house and drive the car down that road, and I'll never come back."

I shrunk behind my branch. Reverend Bennett appeared at a loss; perhaps he had already used as many words as he knew. "Now, Mrs. Lester," he said. The polish of his voice had cracked. It seemed to me as I watched from my hiding place that he collected himself by looking away from her: toward the creek and the moonlight on the water. "I hate that man," my mother said. "I hate that man, and he's my own husband."

Reverend Bennett stood up. He walked to the edge of the creek, and the creek grew louder as I listened. Madeline stepped forward, but I got hold of her collar. The Reverend tossed an invisible something into the water. He turned around to look at my mother so that I could see his face. He looked very sure of himself. "You must ask God to help you," he said. "Pray, Mrs. Lester." He crossed the space between the creek and the log pile. He kneeled beside my mother's seat and rested his elbows on a log. "Love can be the only answer for any one of us. Hate," he said, extending his hand until it rested on her shoulder, "hate is nothing. Hate is what happens when you forget to love." He patted the ground. "Flora Lester, please kneel with me. I'll pray with you. We'll pray together." Reverend Bennett moved his hand from my mother's shoulder to her arm; he took it gently, and she cried out loud.

I held my breath for a moment. Mama did not immediately jump to her knees. She pulled a Kleenex from the front pocket of her sweater. She shuddered and blew her nose. Finally she turned and swung down on her knees. "Our Father," Reverend Bennett began. "I pray to you for the sake of a good Christian woman whose family has brought her down."

"Yes, Lord," Mama whimpered.

"I pray, we both pray to you, for guidance in our duty to love."

"Yes, Lord."

"And we often need you to remind us that it is a duty. To love one another. To go on when there seems as if there is no going on. And to love you too, Father."

"And to love you, too," Mama said.

I could not stay to hear the rest of their prayer, because I had to run. Madeline felt it, too, and was jumping at my legs. Something in the air had become electric and strange. I ran clumsily in my brother's boots with Madeline barking beside me. We ran through the apple trees and out into the light of our backyard. I sat down on the back step. I thought how Mama was a good Christian woman, how we all brought her down. I cried. I took off Wallace's boots, and I kneeled by the back steps. I prayed. "Our Father," I said. "Forgive us, please, forgive us. Teach me how to love like Reverend Bennett."

Madeline sat beside me until I was through. I looked up, and she licked my face. She licked my eyes. I let her lick my nose until I realized she was using her tongue for a handkerchief. I pushed her away, but I told her she was a good dog. "I love you," I said. "I hate to leave you outside like this, but you're an outside dog. That means you have to stay outside." I wiped my eyes with her ears. I realized my stomach was no longer hurting.

I went into the bathroom before I climbed the stairs. I didn't think that Wallace had fallen asleep yet. He had a tendency to punch me in the arm if he saw that I had been crying. So I washed my face, and I took a drink of water to clear my throat. I walked past the living room, where Father had awakened. He saw me, and instead of asking me where Mama was, as I thought he would do, he said, "Are you still up? Get back up to bed." I walked up the stairs and stopped at the upper landing.

Through the railing under the bannister, I looked down on my father. It was true that he drank a lot of beer. And sometimes he drank himself stupid and fell asleep in front of the television. But he never hit us. He never even scared us. Father was not a bad man. He would pull Mother out of the kitchen and waltz her out onto the porch. He would dance with her, his lips against her neck. It was clear that he loved her. How strange, I thought, that Mother does not love him back. He wriggled his toes in his sleep. His feet seemed so very small.

I stopped outside my sisters' door, until I heard Betty, breathing through her nose. I walked into our room. I climbed into bed and pulled the covers over me. "Where've you been, prissy?"

"Nowhere."

My brother punched me in the arm.

"Ow," I said.

He punched me in the arm again.

"I said, 'Where've you been, prissy?'"

"None of your business," I said, and I punched him back. But it was dark in the bedroom. The lights were out. It didn't feel as if I had punched him in the arm. It felt as if I had punched him in the side of his head or something, because what I hit was harder than an arm.

"That's it." Wallace pulled the covers off of me. He grabbed me by the wrist, so I punched him with my free hand. He punched me in the chest, and then he held both of my wrists inside of his two hands. He held them together so I couldn't get away. I pulled my fists up close to my chest, and he bent over my face so closely that I could see him in the dark. "Priss," he said.

I lifted my head. I kissed my brother on the side of his face. I did not kiss him softly, either. I made a huge smacking sound.

"Yuck." He reared back and wiped the side of his face off. I rubbed the skin on my wrists where he had held them. "What did you do that for?"

James Russell Mayes

"Because I'm a kissing monkey," I said. I laughed very loudly, on purpose. I sat up in bed and kissed the air between us, and Wallace backed away. "Get away from me, you weirdo."

"I love you, Wallace. I love you. Kiss, kiss."

He spat at me, but I rolled out of bed and onto my feet.

"You're a weirdo."

I climbed back onto the bed. I jumped up and down on my side of his line, kissing at the air. "I'm a kissing monkey," I said. "Kiss, kiss." I jumped higher and higher, until the bed fell down. Wallace rolled over against my legs. I sat on top of him. I tickled him under the arms.

"What is going on in here?" The dark side of Mama stood in the doorway. She looked like a giant until she turned on the light. "What are you boys doing?"

I sat on top of Wallace as if I were riding a horse.

"The bed fell down," Wallace said.

"Were you jumping on it?" Her voice rose up into a shriek.

"It just fell," he said.

"Get up out of there. We'll have to prop it up."

Mama walked out into the hallway and called down the stairs for Father. She came back to our doorway and leaned against the wall. Wallace and I were standing by the bed. I crouched down so that my knees touched my chest. I used my hands to bounce up off the floor. Wallace began to laugh. He hit me, but he didn't hit me hard. It was a "knock it off" hit.

"Father," Mama called.

I bounced on over to where she stood by our door. "Kiss, kiss," I said.

She stared at me. "What's wrong with you?" she said.

"I'm a kissing monkey." I bounced. I kissed the air in her direction. I could see she was trying not to laugh.

Eventually Father came up the stairs. Wallace and I held the mattress up while he pulled out the bedspring. He braced the boards within the frame. It took all four of us to pull the spring back and to line up the mattress; each of us took a corner. Then Wallace and I climbed back into bed, and Father walked into the hall. I could still smell the beer.

Mama leaned to kiss me good night.

"I'm still a kissing monkey." I kissed her long arms, her enormous hands. She laughed out loud and held me close. Her cheek was still hot from weeping. "Go to sleep," she said, and she cleared her throat. Mama turned out the light, and she followed our father into their room. I waited until I heard the door close, and I listened for one of their talks. But the light from under the crack in their door went out.

"Wallace," I said.

"What, priss."

"Do you think Mama would ever leave us?" I could feel him rolling over onto his side. I turned to look at him, and I could see the shadow of his head in the dark. He was sitting up in bed, looking back at me.

"Why are you asking that?"

"No reason," I said. "I was just wondering. I was just wondering if you thought she might ever jump into the car and drive away and never come back." I watched him stare at me in the dark. Even though I knew he couldn't see my face, because I couldn't see his, I knew he was staring at me. Then he lay back down. He rolled over and faced the other way. "I was just wondering."

"It'll never happen," Wallace said. "Go to sleep. I don't know where you come up with these things."

Saint Peter
Cut to Pieces

A rthur was seventy, and drunk, as usual. He called up a carload of whores from Detroit, who drove out to the Elms spilling all over themselves the bottle of gin and the beer nuts they had brought with them. Arthur spent a couple hours alone with the whole group in the conservatory before they escaped in twos and threes and scrambled through the guest rooms. Luckily, Bennie counted that there were seven of them before they scattered, to mess up the kitchen and needle the new caterer, to make extra cash off of various friends of Arthur's granddaughter who had come for the End of Summer party.

Arthur plunged from the conservatory, brushing dead myrtle leaves out of his hair, barely satisfied. Bennie told him to watch himself. The old man sat on top of the keyboard of the grand piano and dropped his tuxedo pants around his ankles. "You're not fucking me anymore," Bennie told him. All summer long, he had taken it up the ass. "You hired me to mow the lawn."

"But I'm your boss. How's about you fuck me?"

"It's not in my contract," he said, turning away.

Arthur cried out, "You don't have a contract!" He followed Bennie up the servants' staircase without bothering to pull up his pants. He hopped like a bunny. He collapsed in the small sitting room of Bennie's apartment while Bennie whipped off his clothes in the bedroom. "I've had it," Bennie said. "I mean it. You touch me? I call the police."

Guests had already begun to arrive for the party. Bennie ducked past the sitting room on his way to take a quick shower, and he saw that there were already two of them sitting with Arthur. Neither looked familiar. They looked at Bennie in his towel.

"Hello," one of them waved, "I'm Dennis!"

The other, who was younger and attractively feminine, was sitting on Arthur's lap. The two of them looked like a younger and an older version of Prince Charles. They plucked at the puffs of handkerchief in their breast pockets. "Don't mind us," the young one said, indifferently. "I'm Louis. We're old friends of Arthur's, which is not to say that we're as old as *she* is." Arthur covered his eyes and shook his head, as if the evening were already a disaster, even though it wasn't, not quite yet, and this kept Bennie from ordering them all out into the hall. Feeling just a bit vindictive, he walked into his bathroom, and without closing the door behind him, he dropped his towel in full view of Arthur's friends. Bennie had a nice ass, and he knew it. It's what got him his job.

"Will you look at that," Louis murmured, turning his head to Dennis, who was out of Bennie's view. "Did you see that?" Bennie leaned forward and turned on the shower. He held out his hand to test the temperature.

"My, my, my," said Dennis, but his voice was much closer. His voice was just behind Bennie's head, in fact. Louis and Dennis were in the bathroom with him. Bennie stepped into the shower, and he pulled the shower curtain closed behind him. It was a clear shower curtain with a map of the world on it. He stood approximately behind Africa and drenched his head with warm water. When he opened his eyes and peeked through the North Sea, he saw that Dennis and Louis had undressed. Behind them down the hall, Arthur sat in the wingback chair, with his hands over his eyes, shaking, shaking his head.

The shower curtain opened, and Dennis stepped inside. "You call that *hot* water?" he said. "Here." He leaned forward, and his penis brushed Bennie's bottom as he leaned forward to adjust the water tap. "There," Dennis said. He raised his voice to Louis, who had just opened the other end of the shower curtain and was himself stepping in. "You wouldn't *believe* how cool she likes her water."

"It's got to be *hot*, not warm," said Louis, moving under the spray so that Bennie had to step backward into Dennis. Louis turned around under the shower, and he drenched his head. "I *hate* cold water." From behind him, Dennis nuzzled a bit closer. "What kind of shampoo does she use, Louis?"

Louis picked up the tube which Bennie kept upside down in the brass soap holder. "Prell," he said. The two men laughed loudly.

"Prell," Dennis repeated with distaste. Louis offered some to Bennie, who nodded his thanks and dabbed some in his palms. Louis offered some to Dennis as well, but Dennis didn't want any. "I wouldn't put *that* in my hair. It'll all fall out."

"Most of it already has," Louis said, jamming the tube back into the soap holder.

Louis took Bennie's bar of Dove, and he soaped up his bottom. He rinsed and soaped it again, and he backed deftly into him. Bennie couldn't help his natural response.

"Oh," Dennis said, looking over Bennie's shoulder and calling out to Arthur, who presumably remained slumped in the sitting room, "We approve, Arthur, we approve. This boy's so much better than last year's. Such fine *hams* on this one." He lathered Bennie's backside. He wrapped his arms around the young man's shoulders, and he rubbed vigorously, rhythmically into his bottom. They were like a choo-choo train, Bennie thought vacantly, embracing Louis's back.

Louis turned around under the water and moved forward to kiss Bennie. Inches away, he stopped. He raised his finger. "Dry kiss!" he warned. "Play safe!" Their lips touched. "Can somebody else get under here? My skin's drying out," Louis complained. He pushed. As Bennie fell back like a domino, Dennis ejaculated onto his back.

"Oh," Dennis sighed. He paused one second. Then he started to shove. Apparently he wanted to get under the water.

Louis said irritably, "Can't you wait two seconds?" He stepped out through the curtain.

Dennis slid around Bennie in order to rinse off. "Ahh," he said, smiling. "Don't you want to finish up, sweetie?"

"Dennis!" Louis cautioned. He peered at them over a continent.

"Oh, I forgot. You've got a date," Dennis said.

"A date? With who?"

Dennis patted Bennie gently on his tanned stomach. "Gotta save it for the Master!" He revolved under the water, and once completely drenched with what was far too hot for Bennie, he stepped out onto the bath mat and demanded Bennie's towel from Louis. Bennie adjusted the water temperature. He soaped himself. He rinsed himself. He stood under the loud spray until Arthur's guests and his unrelieved erection had gone.

He stepped onto the bath mat. He pulled a fresh towel out of the cupboard. Through the steam in the mirror he saw the ghost of Saint Peter, above and slightly behind him. Bennie knew it was Saint Peter, because he held up his hand. He was holding the keys to Paradise, shaking them soundlessly: waving them at Bennie. The apparition also carried an enormous cross, as gingerly as luggage. Interestingly, one of his legs had been cut off. An ooze gushed around him like a ghastly halo, as dark as octopus ink. If it was a real Catholic saint having a miracle on him, Bennie thought, it was probably holy smoke. He should take a picture of it!

Still naked, Bennie rushed to his bedroom. He opened a drawer of his desk and pulled out an inexpensive camera, an Instamatic, that his aunt Vi had given him years ago for a birthday. By the time he got back to the bathroom, his ghost was nowhere that he could see. Saint Peter had disappeared. Arthur remained in the sitting room with his hands over his eyes, oblivious, as usual.

Bennie decided to ignore him until he could figure what better to do. It was, after all, a delicate situation. How does one stop having sex with the boss without getting fired? He flipped the strap of the old camera over his neck, absently. One day Arthur would kill himself fucking, Bennie knew it, and he did not want to be underneath him when it happened.

Chimp, the downstairs butler, called up to say that Arthur's wife Irene was asking for him. She wanted to know if he was going to come down to the party to greet the other guests? The party! Arthur opened his eyes and rose from his chair. He pulled up his pants and tucked himself in. He adjusted his suspenders. Bennie dressed quickly. He scrambled to the west wing to snatch the whores from out of the arms of Tina's boyfriends.

Arthur's whores were notorious for being slippery. Once a couple of them had managed to stay a whole weekend by supposedly forgetting

James Russell Mayes

to ride back with the others. Chimp found them the next Monday, brawling in the greenhouse with the dog psychologist. Orchids had been ruined. Bennie tore through the wing which Arthur's grand-daughter Tina had set up as a temporary dormitory for her friends, all of whom were men, most of them gay. But they were young, and the danger of youth, Bennie thought with resignation, is that it allows you to believe that you can make your life over. The wing was completely empty, of course, since the music had started below. The whores had probably seen him coming.

He groaned at the thought of Lucy and Yawanna at the punch bowl. The other women might pass as eccentric relatives, but Lucy and Yawanna were particularly coarse and aggressive. He walked down the stairs to the front hall, just in time to see Chimp let in some members of the Historical Society. Trevor and Phoebe Case and Gaylin the Wunderkind Hairdresser had just thrown their coats in a heap at Chimp, when a woman in a British racing green prom dress and towering, scarlet hair ran out from behind a column, and bared her bosoms for a solid thirty seconds. Everyone froze, wondering what to say. Then, halfheartedly, Phoebe screamed.

Bennie cried, "Yawanna?"

The woman turned around. No, it was not Yawanna, it was another one that Bennie had seen only briefly before, a particularly rank one with a hungry vampire look. She whipped the top of her plastic dress up over her breasts and ran into the ballroom.

"Good heavens," Chimp muttered.

Bennie ran down the steps and slid across the tile floor into the ballroom, camera flying, just in time to see the column of hair tip into the gliding crowd. He excused himself far enough into the mob to be swept up into the course of the waltz as soon as it had started, even though he did not have a proper partner. While he had been searching through the empty bedrooms of the vast west wing, an immense crowd had gathered in the ballroom. This was the mass of all of Arthur's guests, the dancers as well as the others, who tried in vain to move through them to the tables on the other side. The vaulted room revolved around the circling mob. Bennie was surrounded and unable to move any farther. All he could do was look upward. The ballroom at the Elms was the largest single room that Bennie had ever seen in his life, not including cathedrals. The mock Gothic arches had been festooned by the caterer with lavish banners and horns of plenty.

Bennie felt much more intimidated than he thought he should be. His relationship with Arthur was no secret, not even to Arthur's wife Irene, who waved to him gaily from a small group of tiny, petrified women. He wasn't sure that it was the number of the guests, or the fact that they were all dressed so fine and moved like sleek, well-trained panthers under their terribly chic clothes. He saw the fresh and well-scrubbed faces of Louis and Dennis, each with a bored-looking younger woman, each of whom wore so much makeup that their cheekbones had cheekbones. The hair was low and small, but they had a familiar starved look that Bennie recognized. This was what made him suspicious.

He swam toward them. The music stopped, and the crowd gelled, softly clapping gloved hands. A man's black shoe flew up into the air. Bennie moved slowly through the people, groped by one and another of Arthur's friends. He smiled and raised a finger to those whose faces he could remember. It was much too loud for speaking, he was grateful for that. The music, a solid-sounding chamber orchestra, started again before Bennie could reach the place he had sighted for, but suddenly he had washed up onto the steps at the feet of Louis and Dennis, who were not where he had thought they were. Each of them had on his arm what appeared to be a gargoyle in a dress.

Louis leaned forward and spoke in his ear. "You smell clean," he said.

He turned his own shining ear toward Bennie. "Thank you," Bennie said into it. "Are the girls? I mean, who are these? Are these your dates?"

Louis smiled sweetly and whispered into Dennis's ear, and then into one of the gargoyles'. The first gargoyle spoke into the second gargoyle's ear, and once everyone had been given the information which Bennie had not, they laughed. Of course, Bennie could not hear the laughter, not with all of the music starting up again and the shouting above it. The four of them opened their mouths wide and showed their teeth, which were perfect and shining and sharp. "How sweet of you to be jealous," Louis told him, touching his ear with his lips.

"What I mean to say is," Bennie said, stepping away so that he had to shout, "did they come with you or did you meet them here?"

Louis winked. "They are our wives, you lovely idiot. Let's meet later in the greenhouse."

A wave of bodies in tuxedos carried Bennie away, past Tina's skinhead boyfriend Tad, past satin and silk and lace and gowns that flowed out from women's waists as if they were waterfalls of gushing purple and red. Headdresses swam by, and a woman with a fan, and two dark-haired men passionately kissed. A man with a burgundy turban leapt up to the stage and tore rose petals out from the clusters of blossoms, tossed them onto the front of the dress of a woman below. He pulled his hand away, and it bled. Bennie watched him cover the blood with his handkerchief, as burgundy as his turban. Arthur's granddaughter Tina caught his eye, and at a table of mean-spirited laughter, the group of men that surrounded her made room for him.

Before he could sit, Tina said snidely, "Do dance with me, Bennie." She turned to the other men. "I'd introduce you, but the music's so damned loud. Wave to them, Bennie." He bowed awkwardly to her little gang. The men gave one another sly looks. One of them leaned forward and raised his voice a notch to say, "I'm pleased, very pleased to meet you," without meaning it. Tina pulled him down to the dance floor, in spite of his protests, and once she had pushed and shoved out a space for them in the dancing crowd of couples, she turned around and took his hands. "I'm afraid I can't dance," he said. "I mean, not really. Not this kind of dancing. Can we fake it?"

Tina put her nose against his ear and snorted. "It depends how good one is at faking, I suppose. At least, let me lead. That shouldn't bother you, should it?"

"By all means," Bennie said. They swept out through the couples with ferocity. Tina could kick. And it didn't seem hard to keep up with her, Bennie thought. He could be very sensitive with his hands, if necessary. But he could not tell how well he was doing. "Perhaps we should stop."

"You're doing just fine." They careened through the other dancers until Bennie felt like Anna in *The King and I*. Something clicked in his head, or perhaps he felt it in his feet. He began to lead. They glided through and around, and ever so much faster than, the others. The guests pulled back, some to admire.

His old camera beat against his chest. They stopped with a jounce. Tad cut in, somewhat reproachfully. "Quite good, my dears," he said. "It's my turn, Camera Man." Bennie was at a loss until he heard a general murmur around him, and applause. Everyone else had raised their arms above their shoulders, clapping, clapping with their gloves. Arthur appeared onstage, next to the conductor. He tried to speak, but could not. Bennie knew that Arthur had not wanted to speak anyway. He hated speaking in public. But the old man made a good show of it. He waved his hand in front of his lips and shook his head. He extended his arm toward the pale conductor, the musicians dressed shabbily in unstylish suits. The cheer died away.

Bennie felt a heat against his right ear, and he heard a woman's voice. "Arthur's completely crazy when it comes to one thing. We all know what that is, don't we? It's so much better than being half-crazy about a dozen things, don't you think?" Bennie turned and looked up and saw that Irene was standing next to him. "So many husbands are," she added. She drifted away on an island of young, darkly dressed attorneys who held her by the arms. They pulled her along like a Wells Fargo coach.

Then Arthur spotted him. He looked at Bennie, with approval. He was stepping down off the stage, bending forward to talk into the ear of the Cardinal. He turned his head and raised his eyebrows and sweetly smiled at Bennie, the old maniac. He pointed to one of the side doors to the main hall, discreetly, and Bennie pretended to make an effort to move through the crowd to meet him. But as soon as Arthur came down off the steps, Bennie headed toward the opposite door. He knew of a place where he could hide where Arthur would probably not find him.

Propelling himself through the crowd, he waved to the Cardinal, whose naked body he could remember but whose name remained a mystery, and he saw that the man in scarlet pointed upward. Bennie looked up and saw Saint Peter sitting on the railing of the balcony. His robes dangled over the railing. Behind Saint Peter, the matching white dresses of two women sparkled through his translucence. There was something different about him, Bennie noticed, he appeared more solid. Had the Cardinal seen him too? He turned, but the wheel of

James Russell Mayes

people in the ballroom had turned. The Cardinal was swept away with a woman in a cape.

Saint Peter had lost another leg. Ribbons of a sluggish darkness oozed around his robes. It rose in the air above the saint as if he were underwater. He looked very sorrowful. Bennie raised his camera to his eyes and waited for a clear shot. The women behind him, the ones in white dresses with crushed velvet sashes, waved vigorously at him. Their arms created a breeze, and the breeze turned Saint Peter himself into smoke. He wafted out over the ballroom floor, legless. He held out to Bennie his arms, which stretched into crossbeams. He faded. The women continued waving, femininely, flutteringly, until one of them visibly hiccupped. The other slugged her arm. They wrapped their hands around each other's neck and began to squeeze. Of course, Bennie realized: the whores.

✂

Arthur could deal with his own hirelings, Bennie decided. He walked back down the main hall to the stairs, and he climbed the stairs to the library. Arthur almost never used the library. When Bennie opened the two wide doors, the gardener Paris looked up from a small island of papers and books. "I'll be out of here in a minute," he called to Bennie.

"You don't have to leave," he told him, "so long as you don't tell anyone I'm here."

"That's okay," Paris said. "Arthur told me I'm only allowed in the library when nobody is using it."

"You're kidding."

Something in Bennie's tone must have prompted the young man to look up from his work.

"You mean you don't mind?"

"Of course not." Paris always wore very short shorts, even when he was not working in the sun. Bennie positioned himself so as to catch the best view. He lay back on a leather divan and made room for an elbow by shifting a pile of Forster novels onto his lap.

"You can read those, if you like," Paris said in his deep voice. He returned to the book he was reading, a red-covered copy of Proust, embossed with the manor insignia. He was very involved.

"What? You read these already?"

Paris smiled again, without looking up. "Oh, yes," he said. "Wonderful things. But Proust is poetry on every page. Even in English."

"You read French?"

"My mother was French." Bennie opened to a page of *Maurice,* and he fell into an older world of London and railroads and a romantic motorcycle ride through the country. Since, unlike Paris, he could not read and speak at the same time without losing the momentum of imagination required to read a novel, the two fell silent, although whenever he turned the page, Bennie glanced up to see if he could ever see more of the gardener's legs under his shorts. He had lovely, muscular, milk chocolate legs. Time passed, and then there was something poking out of the legs of the man's shorts that looked very much like the head of a turtle.

Paris caught Bennie by the eyes, raising his brows, amused.

In order to have an excuse to be staring at him, Bennie thought of a question. Alone in a room with someone so smart, he felt comfortable asking questions. "What makes the Elms gothic?"

Paris pointed. "The arched windows," he said. "All that castley triptrap. See the place where the ceiling meets the walls? *That's* gothic."

"Oh."

"Can I show you something?"

"Of course."

Paris led him to a bookcase with glass doors on it. He opened up the doors. He pulled out a cardboard tube from a stack of cardboard tubes. He pulled the tube apart, and inside of it, there was a scroll. "Hold this," Paris told him, handing him the two halves of the tube. Bennie held them. Paris lay the scroll flat on top of the bookcase. Inside of it, in watercolor and ink, "Perhaps a thousand years old," he said, were Chinese figures, all male, all naked, all rosily endowed with jutting phalluses that curved upward in swollen, blushed delight. "That looks painful," he said, pointing to a fellow on all fours, impaled from the rear. He rolled the scroll up, and, rather casually, Bennie thought, tapped the top of his head with it.

Bennie said, winking, "I'll file that until further notice." He handed Paris the halves of the ornate cardboard tubing.

"Are you flirting with me?"

The question embarrassed Bennie. Of course he was flirting with him. He changed the subject. "What are these?" He picked up a wooden doll out of a set of a dozen or so. It was a very old doll. Most of the paint had been worn off.

"That's a saint," Paris said. "I don't know which one. They're all saints."

Bennie looked through the whole set of them. They all seemed to have all their limbs. "How did you find this stuff?"

Paris looked at him sideways. "Arthur showed me."

"Arthur?"

"Of course, what did you think? He gave me a tour of the place when I first got here. Didn't you get one?"

"No. I found my way around."

Paris tucked away the cardboard tubes. He closed the glass doors to the bookcase. "Don't worry about it," he said. "You came late, remember? Arthur was very attached to the last guy he had who mowed the grounds here."

"What was his name?"

Paris smiled. "He was nothing like you, really. I forget his name. Honest. He was a bit too young, I think. For Arthur."

"Who isn't?"

"Irene," Paris said. "Irene is older than all of us, I think."

"What happened to him?"

"To Arthur?"

"No, to the guy who I replaced, silly."

"Silly?" Paris seemed to take Bennie's flirtation seriously. He walked past a window so that Bennie had a chance to admire his fine profile. "He mysteriously disappeared," he said. Paris raised his hands up to either side of his face, and he mimed a silent-film scream. Behind him, on the mural that someone had painted on the library wall years ago, a rolling landscape of mountains and lakes, peopled with well-dressed men and women, rose up behind the man like a backdrop.

Bennie laughed. Then he remembered his camera. He lifted it to his eye.

"What are you doing with that?"

"What do you think?" he said. "Kodak moment." The tiny blue bulb flashed.

"Don't do that," Paris said, walking toward him with alarm. "What if Arthur sees it? You'll get me fired."

"Don't worry," Bennie promised. "He'll never see it." He wondered if Paris was lying about ever being allowed in the library at all. "Are you sure you're supposed to be in here?"

Paris avoided the question. He walked toward Bennie. "You know the library isn't all that Arthur lets me use. Do you ride?"

Bennie considered. "I'm not sure what you're suggesting. Why don't you answer my question?"

"Horses," Paris said, stubbornly smiling, pressing his face inches from Bennie's. "Arthur has a beautiful white gelding. Somebody has to keep it in shape. If you ride, I'm sure he'd let you go with me sometime."

"Only if Arthur doesn't mind. It might be nice to try something new for a change." Bennie touched the man's smooth cheek. "Provided what you're telling me is true, of course."

The doors to the library swung open. It was Arthur, after all, whose nose had turned bright red. Rubbing his hands together, he approached the two young men. Breathing audibly, stupid with drink, "Let's do something in French," he said, "in honor of Paris." He raised his glass. "Ménage à trois."

"Arthur," Paris groaned, stepping backward.

Bennie had had enough. He pulled a sword off the wall. "I told you, no more fucking!" He waved it above his head.

Arthur shrieked. He dropped his drink. He bolted out of the room.

Still holding the sword in his hands, Bennie turned a bewildered face to the gardener. Paris laughed. "The last young man who had your job never tried that," he said.

"What was I supposed to do?"

"You did just fine," Paris said. He walked around the divan, and he kneeled in front of Bennie. He bowed his head. "Knight me," he said. "I am at your cervix."

Bennie could not stop his heart from pounding. He lifted the sword into its scabbard on the wall. "That's *vagina* in Latin," Paris teased him, rising. "Honest. It is. Look it up."

Bennie ignored him and counted to ten. He wanted to give Arthur enough time to find another guest or two to seduce. He stepped out through the library doors and into the last rush of a flow of merrymakers who had followed Arthur in a bunny-hopping conga line, up the staircase and through the arches into the west wing.

Bennie ran down the steps and down the hall through the kitchen, its own madness of cooks and waiters and crashing pans, and out through an open door to the kitchen garden. His legs knocked against herbs which had overgrown the path. He inhaled the lemon thyme, the basil and sage. There was a breezy place to sit down along the outer wall of the garden, secluded from the windows of the first floor, anyway. He leaned back against the ivy of the garden wall.

Saint Peter appeared again. He was cut to pieces more than ever. Both of his legs were still gone, and his ears had been sliced from either side of his head. He only had the trunk of his body to stand on. Saint Peter stood on his hands, which extended through the sleeves of his robe. It must have taken tremendous strength to do so, even for a ghost, Bennie thought. The saint lowered his trunk to the ground to keep his robes from rising in the air, like Marilyn Monroe above her subway grate.

The dark liquid pooled around him, floating in waves of the invisible hereafter. That's blood all right, Bennie decided once and for all. He thought of his own blood, too, in the toilet after Arthur had fucked him. Saint Peter got along by lifting himself off the ground with his arms and then lowering himself a good foot from where he had started. He appeared to be moving. After a great deal of time and effort, he turned a corner, so that Bennie had to stand up and walk a few paces to see where he had gone to. Saint Peter made his way along the walkway through the topiary garden, past the avenues of Lombardy poplar along the formal garden. All the while he made a slow and steady progress, palms slapping on slate.

He led Bennie straight through the rose arbor and around the back of the Elms until he reached the bathhouse. "Good Lord," Bennie thought. "I hope he isn't going to drown himself in the pool." Saint Peter turned to look at Bennie, beckoning with his hand. He shifted all of his weight onto the right one, and with the other he pointed toward the bleary light off the pool, where a familiar voice was chuckling. Bennie heard a gurgle. Perhaps there was a drowning, after all. He walked directly through what was left of the Saint, who hung in the air like a sneeze, and he looked out over Arthur's massive swimming pool.

Arthur's wife, Irene, was standing naked in the water, leaning back against the edge of the pool so that her ample breasts floated around her like three lovely cantaloupes. "How odd of her to have three breasts," Bennie said aloud, although he knew that the saint had already evaporated.

"Stop," Irene gasped, clutching the middle of her breasts, which was, after all, acting strangely. It grew ears, for instance, and she grabbed them as if she was going to screw them off.

The middle breast turned up into someone's face. Irene kissed the face long and deep on the mouth. She floated with her arms around it, out into the middle of the swimming pool. The face looked a lot like Tina's boyfriend Tad, Bennie thought. Then a whole man stood up in the shallow end of the pool. Bennie saw the scratches on his water-wilted flesh. Blood ran down his back. Yes, it was most definitely Tad. Irene shimmied up him. She wrapped her legs around his head. "Bad boy," she hooted. They fell back into the water.

Arthur appeared at the edge of the pool, naked, looking at his watch. He was about to jump into the water, when Lucy and Yawanna ran out from behind a hedge. They nabbed him by his elbows. Tall as they were, they lifted Arthur off the ground. They carried him back behind the bathhouse, very near where Bennie had hid himself behind a group of cedars. He peered at them through the flimsy boughs. Lucy said, "Put him here." They stashed Arthur up on top of an old urn of petunias.

"There," Yawanna said, holding his arms back behind him.

Lucy stood in front of Arthur. She put her hands on her hips.

"Let me go," Arthur cried. He kicked his feet.

Lucy slapped his face. "There," she said. "How'd you like that, Master Arthur? You listen to Lucy so you'll know how to act, okay?"

"That's right," Yawanna said. "You don't want Lucy to slap those big teeth out of your head." She tightened her grip on Arthur's arms. She bit his ear, hard.

James Russell Mayes

"Ouch."

"Hush up, now." Lucy raised her hand as if she might hit him again. "What the hell is your wife doing with your granddaughter's boyfriend, Tad?"

"Yeah," Yawanna said, raising a fist.

Arthur cleared his throat. He looked very old. "If it's money you want, I'd be happy to."

"Money? Money!" Lucy shouted. She tossed her head. Yawanna laughed. "We don't want your goddamned filthy money. We want morality."

"You want revenge," Arthur said.

"Morality, revenge. Shut up."

"Yeah," Yawanna said, blowing on his face. "We want morality for that innocent grandbaby of yours." Lucy walked back away from the urn. She walked a good distance of a few yards. She reached the edge of the pool, where Tad's hairy buttocks were flexing and unflexing between the legs of Arthur's wife. Arthur shook his head, sadly.

"What we gonna do with him?"

"Shut up," Lucy said. Behind her, Irene cursed in Latin. She flailed from side to side. Lucy took a running start, and she slapped Arthur's head.

"Your turn," she said to Yawanna. She took Yawanna's place holding Arthur's arms.

Yawanna walked away, several more yards. She cackled and doubled her fists and ran. As she passed by his hiding place, Bennie kicked out his foot. The whore buckled. She jackknifed and tumbled headfirst into the urn.

"Bull's-eye!" Arthur shouted. Lucy pulled him off the petunias and dragged him toward the pool. The old man fainted.

Bennie ran out from the cedars. He gave Lucy a sock in the face that knocked her into the water. Yawanna came up from behind him with the sharp end of her shoe. He dodged her. And just as he pulled Arthur up onto his feet, still unconscious, dangling, Louis and Dennis turned around the corner at the back of the Elms. Each of the them shook a pair of maracas, adjusting and readjusting their hips to the beat. They led a great crowd of people from the party behind them, including half the orchestra at play, including their own two wives and the rest of the whores, Tina and all of her boyfriends.

"Wake up, Arthur," Bennie said. He leaned him back against the shrubbery, slapping his face to revive him. The conga line moved around the pool, still bunny-hopping, unconcerned that Irene and Tad stood naked in the shallow end. The couple slipped apart.

"Mother, my God!" Tina wailed.

Irene's bosoms did a little dance.

Tad reached for a towel and bucked away through the shrubbery.

Waving a clarinet, Tina chased him. Sympathetic Lucy and Ya-wanna shuffled after her.

The Cardinal cried, "What are you doing with Arthur?" He raised an arm and the line of dancers stopped. He rushed up to Bennie and pulled at the camera. The strap tugged hard at the back of Bennie's neck.

"Hey," Bennie said, gripping the Cardinal's fingers. "Stop that."

The Cardinal slapped the side of Bennie's head. "Blackmailer," he cried. "Let go!"

Bennie did not mean to push. The old man fell backward onto the lawn, reddened, clutching the front of his garb. "This pimp," he cried, "this whore has tried to blackmail Arthur."

The crowd around him gasped.

"I did not," Bennie shouted.

"He wants money. Arthur told me so."

Louis stepped forward. "Give us the camera, Bennie."

He held on to it instinctively. "No."

"Give us the camera."

"I don't have any pictures of anyone."

"If that's true, then give us the camera."

Bennie looked all around him for a sign of Paris. The gardener was probably hiding, he decided. Arthur must have told him to keep out of sight until his precious party was over.

The Cardinal picked himself up off the ground. Chimp rushed forward. "What's going on here?" the butler asked.

Dennis piped up, "We heard this boy-whore tell Arthur that he was going to call the police."

"Get him," Irene ordered. She was still wet and naked and smelling of sex, grabbing for Bennie. He stepped back, and Arthur slid to the ground. Louis and Dennis stepped out of the crowd and grabbed Bennie by his arms.

Chimp rushed to Arthur, and he helped the old man up. "Now wait a minute," Chimp cautioned.

The angry mob carried Bennie back around the swimming pool through the back doors to the ballroom and through the ballroom to the front hall and down the front hall to the master staircase up to the second floor. From the second floor they carried him through the east wing up the servants' staircase through the servants' wing to the attic door, which they kicked down. They hauled him past all the Mexican pottery that Arthur and Irene had bought on their vacation in 1972 and out the tiny door at the far end of the attic into the height of the night air and the roof of the Elms.

"Stop!" Bennie cried, with no one to help him. He held on to a downspout. Louis and Dennis pried his fingers loose. They pushed him over the side, holding onto him by the heels. Bennie dangled from the rooftop. Above him the Cardinal shouted, "Let him go, boys! Let him go!" Out of fear, Bennie could not close his eyes. Below him Chimp waved his arms, jumping up and down. Arthur had disappeared. "No," the butler called to them, "no." Someone pushed from behind. Chimp ran out of the way. Bennie fell, headfirst, from the roof of the Elms.

A crowd gathered around the back of the house. Someone had let out the dogs, and two of the mastiffs chased a whore out over the lawn. Arthur, still naked but having recovered, climbed up onto the roof of the bathhouse. In an effort to get everyone's attention, he blew a trumpet, rather poorly. It was too late, of course. Yawanna climbed a gingko tree. The Cardinal was trying to pummel her with the handle of a rake. Lucy clung to the rails of the high fence around the greenhouse. One of the dogs got hold of her ankle. She screamed and fainted and fell in a heap.

Bennie opened his eyes. Someone dark in a helmet stood over him. The helmet had wings on the sides. It was too dark to see who it was, but it was human, at least. Bennie was pulled bodily out of the shrubs. He was carried to the edge of the swimming pool where a motorbike had made a muddy trail across the tiles. The man shouted through his visor: "Are you all right?" The voice was muffled, but sweet and low. Bennie could tell who it was. It was Paris.

"I feel like shit," Bennie said. All around them, he could hear the riot in the air: screams and splitting furniture.

Paris straddled the motorbike. "Hop on," he said.

"I'm not getting on that thing."

"They're after the whores now. Chimp wants you to get out of here. He gave me the bike to take you." Paris pulled an extra helmet off the back of the bike.

Bennie took it. He slipped on behind him. Still numb from the fall, he wrapped his arms around the fellow's waist. They rode across the grass and out onto the front drive. They pulled onto the road. The two men rode under moonlight. Paris opened up the throttle. Bennie could feel the road all through his bones and flesh. The vibration came up through his feet and knees and crotch and into his heart, which ached for what he had seen of the Merchant and Ivory life. His ears throbbed.

There was a movement along the side of the road. The head of Saint Peter, just a head, bobbed forward along the ditch. His beard fluttered under his chin where his neck should have been. Paris braked at a crossing, and a truck passed by. The head moved through the headlight of the motorbike. Saint Peter made a left. Bennie tapped Paris's arm. "Go that way," he said, pointing after the head.

"What?"

Bennie pointed. He folded his arms tightly around Paris. They followed the bouncing head up a dusty old road through a woods, past fields, up a hill. They made another left, and the moon bounced over their shoulders and hid in the trees. They were high above the countryside on a knob above the Elms. Saint Peter's head leapt a fence and disappeared into a field of pumpkins. There were hundreds. They were scattered all over the ground. "Stop," Bennie cried.

Paris cut the engine. He took off his helmet. "This is one damn loud bike," he said. He stuck his finger in his ear.

Bennie picked his way through the pumpkins. Paris lifted his leg over the fence, and followed him through the field. It was still summer, not yet fall, the season of reaping. The pumpkins were various sizes. Where had Saint Peter gone? "I have to find him," Bennie said.

"Find who? What are you looking for?"

          James Russell Mayes

He walked out past the edge of the field of pumpkins. Paris followed him. They came to a small rise. The two men looked out over the patchwork of fields. Below them the Elms looked much smaller from the hillside. The whores hightailed it through the gardens, screaming. There was a gunshot. Bennie looked down at the grass. He found Saint Peter there.

"Here he is, look. Do you see him?"

"See what?"

Bennie pointed at the face of Saint Peter, who had opened his mouth in a yawn. He had nestled himself, or what was left of him, into a small pile of pumpkins at the edge of the field. He smiled, for once. The old fellow drew in his breath. He looked very satisfied, Bennie thought, like Charlton Heston. Saint Peter grew smaller and smaller. His head shrank until he had no face. He turned into a firefly, blinking.

It flew away.

"Make a wish," Paris whispered, watching a bit of light in the sky. "There it goes."

Bennie had forgotten about wishes.

He made one. Paris wrapped an arm around him. They walked back to the motorbike, and Paris shuffled through the compartment under the seat. He handed something to Bennie. It was a thick envelope. "What's that?" Bennie said.

"Take it. It's from Chimp."

Bennie ripped it open. It was filled with cash, a lot of it, and a note from Chimp that said: "Here's a little bonus for you. Twice a day for three months is above and beyond the call of duty. You have served the Master well."

Paris handed Bennie his helmet. "What's he say?"

"Nothing. He says, they'll miss me." He started to pull his helmet on, but Paris lifted his hand to his face. He kissed Bennie, just as the sun was coming up and he could see that the field was full of fireflies. They flew in wide circles, dizzily. So intent they were on breeding that they bred themselves invisible in the early light. Paris kick-started the bike. Bennie slid on behind him. They pulled out onto the road. Some early gold leaves blew under the tires. Bennie leaned back and watched the pale moon rise, a white moon, a fingernail, the kind of moon that anyone might see in the daylight.

*Alyson Publications publishes a wide variety of books
with gay and lesbian themes. For a free catalog or
to be placed on our mailing list, please write to:*
Alyson Publications
40 Plympton Street
Boston, MA 02118
*Indicate whether you are interested in
books for gay men, lesbians, or both.*